Advance

"A captivating blend of suspense, science fiction and domestic drama. The claustrophobia and tension of Cassie's internal frustrations perfectly mirror the complexity of the phenomena gripping her insular suburban community."

— Suzanne Chazin, author of *Voice with No Echo*

ONLY THE WOMEN ARE BURNING

ONLY THE WOMEN ARE BURNING

A Novel

Nancy Burke

Apprentice
House Press
Loyola University Maryland

First Edition

Casebound ISBN: 978-1-62720-288-6
Paperback ISBN: 978-1-62720-289-3
Ebook ISBN: 978-1-62720-290-9

Printed in the United States of America

Design by Taylor Fluehr
Edited by Lauren Battista
Promotion by Angelica Casillas

Published by Apprentice House Press

Apprentice
House Press
Loyola University Maryland

Apprentice House Press
Loyola University Maryland
4501 N. Charles Street
Baltimore, MD 21210
410.617.5265 • 410.617.2198 (fax)
www.ApprenticeHouse.com
info@ApprenticeHouse.com

For
Joann Corrao Spera

In everyone's life, at some time, our inner fire goes out. It is then burst into flame by an encounter with another human being. We should all be thankful for those people
who rekindle the inner spirit.
— Albert Schweitzer

The fiery passion to know more cannot be controlled and blazes like a forest fire – cleansing out the clutter and breaking down all the possibilities of failure.
This energy and vigor is truly contagious.
— Meaww.com

PROLOGUE

DECEMBER 14, BANGALORE, INDIA

That morning of rain and mud, I searched the narrow alleys of the squatter settlement, the narrow lanes, the corrugated shacks, stepping around trash and puddles of mud, carefully counting the doorways until I reached Banhi's husband's tiny household. There she was squatting before a large stone mortar and pestle when she shouted, "Cassandra!" After she pulled away from my embrace, she reached for Lila, who was just a year old and in a carrier on my back. That's when I saw how drawn Banhi's face was, her skin not glowing as it had every day, and no broad smile on her lips as before. But she tried.

"Let me take Lila, please," she said. "Oh, she's so beautiful. My sweet thing, say hello to Banhi."

"Your father and mother send their love. And your brothers," I said.

"Let's take Lila to show Rehani. The baby will make her smile." She turned and darted inside the small dwelling and called to her mother-in-law.

I followed her into the house. There were two rooms. The kitchen was equipped sparsely with a small wooden cabinet. Three varied sizes of pots hung from hooks over a slab of stone set back against the far wall. A shrine with Ganesh, the elephant-headed boy, and multi-armed goddess, Durga, displayed itself on the slab and before the statues were bowls of brown rice, cumin seeds and a liquid which I guessed was honey. The tiny kerosene stove, unlit and cold sat next to the door leading to a small square of muddy yard. Pads and blankets were piled in two corners of the second room and a flat carpet of faded greens and gold stretched across the cement floor which looked spotless.

I heard from the other room the unmistakable slap of hand against skin, a cry of pain, and an explosive burst in Kannada I could not understand. I was there in an instant, pulling Lila from Banhi's arms.

Rehani's hands kept at her work, her eyes darted from pods to bowl as tiny green peas relinquished their shells and dropped in with the rest. Her face was set in anger.

"Rehani," I said. "If I should not have come, I am sorry. Please, it is my fault, not Banhi's."

"It is a day for working."

I said, "It is my fault for coming unannounced."

"She asked if I would like to hold the child while you two sat to visit. She is a useless bride for Harshad."

"She looks thin," I said. "Is she well?"

"She coughs to get sympathy."

"Rehani," I said. I stooped down so my eyes were level with hers. "Banhi was my aaya - I know she works very hard."

"Working for pay spoils a wife. You have ruined her."

I walked back to Banhi. A flushed red mark darkened her left cheek.

"Come outside," I whispered. "Out to the front. We need to talk."

At that, a torrent of water loud as thunder hit the tin roof.

"I will make us some tea," Banhi said.

The rain ceased after a brief cloudburst and the quiet was welcome. Rihani had joined her and noises from the kitchen reached me from the other room, two voices, subdued. I could not make out the words, but by the tone and cadence it seemed peace had returned between Rehani and Banhi. Rehani carried a cup to me and bowed. She sat cross-legged on the small rug. Banhi carried a cup for herself and sat just a bit farther off.

They settled, Rehani leaning against a support and Lila settling into the crook of my arm. Banhi sipped from her cup, silent; the red blotch had faded to pink but there was a look of a frightened cat about her. She stood suddenly. "The stove," she said. "I need to turn off the flame."

Rehani said. "You will burn down the house."

"I forget," Banhi said.

"She does," Rehani said. "A stove must be respected."

Something darkened the doorway and we all looked up to see Harshad stepping into the room dripping from the rain.

"Get your husband some dry clothes," Rehani ordered.

Harshad said, "Please, is this little Lila grown so quickly? She is a miniature of you," he said. "Isn't she, Mother?"

Rehani said, "And your son will be a miniature of you, Harshad, when it is time. You are making a puddle. Go change out of your wet things."

He vanished into the kitchen and pulled the curtain across.

I wanted to turn Banhi back into the happy, exuberant girl who translated for me, who'd introduced me to the women here. The bride in red with glowing eyes at the wedding she had insisted I attend.

My year of visiting Indian homes and feeling the warmth and love among these people of the lowest caste had taught me what happiness under struggle looked like. This was not it.

"Can Banhi take a walk with me and Lila?" I said. "The rain has stopped. The sun is coming out."

Rehani said, "She must not go out without Harshad. She is a married woman now."

"Let me walk with you then," he said, returning in dry clothes. "The mud is slippery."

He walked ahead of us. Banhi linked arms with me and whispered. "Harshad wants a child. But Rehani and Jayant sleep between us."

I said, "She hits you."

"Just make up a story that you need me in your work for a day."

I stopped walking. "Will she allow it?"

"She might be happy if I bring in some money."

I thought otherwise but only asked, "What does Jayant say?"

"He says nothing."

"What does Harshad say?"

"There is no privacy." All this in a hurried whisper, all with a hand clutching my arm, a continual checking the distance between Harshad and us, and several furtive glances back toward the row of shacks where it was hard now to distinguish which one we had just stepped away from. Harshad turned after overhearing us.

"Banhi," he said. "You can't go out of the house with Cassie."

"I live like a sister to you, Harshad. If I am to be your wife, I need to help retire the debt your father is ashamed of."

"It won't be like this forever, Banhi." He glanced back toward the row where their dwelling melted anonymously into all the other tin-walled houses. "Things will change, if your father can help us again." He turned to me. "Cassandra, can you take a message back to Kiran? The dowry money is gone. If he is prospering, he is duty bound to share that with his daughter's family."

"More dowry will help," Banhi said. "But what happens when that money is gone too?" She touched the sleeve of her sari and I saw her skin was blackened, partially healed but raw and swollen around the edges of a burn with an ooze of pus near the wrist bones. Her gaze focused on Harshad's face.

"She is awkward with the matches," he said.

"Banhi," I said. "Come on."

Harshad made a move toward her. I stepped between them. "Stop!" I said. "She is coming with me."

"Banhi is a part of my family now. I beg you not to do this."

Harshad went to touch her and she pulled away and stepped behind me.

"You can come back if you want, but right now you are coming with me to the hospital." I glared at Harshad. "If you love her, tell your mother she is going for medical care for her burn." I looked hard at Banhi. "You're going to the hospital. Tell Harshad you'll be back when your arm is healed."

Harshad said, "We have no money for a doctor."

I took firmer hold of Banhi's hand, turned and dragged her through the lane, but after a few hundred feet I let go of her hand.

"You will shame yourself. You will be shunned and left alone to die on the street," Harshad called. "Do you think your father will take you back?"

Banhi stopped and turned. She backed away from both of us. Then, she walked back in the direction we had come. She gave a cry and ran to their front door and the structure shook as the door opened, then hit against the frame. "Leave her alone, Cassie," Harshad said when I turned to follow, his hand on my arm restraining me.

"No," I said. "Let me go. You don't get her to a doctor? It isn't about not having money. It's about not letting her suffer."

He said, "Please. Even if we take her to the free clinic, they will expect us to pay." He said this, explaining it to me as though I were a child.

"Who will expect you to pay?"

"Not the doctors," he said. "Bribes so the police don't come and accuse us of…of…"

"Of what?"

"Of trying to kill her. They would ruin our family if they accuse us of a dowry murder."

I stood and stared at him. "A what?"

"Surely you know what that is." He stared at me. "You've worked with these women. Banhi and you. Have none of them shared this with you?"

I just stared at him. "Tell me," I said.

"If we went to the hospital, the police would go to Kiran and tell him their daughter was burned by her mother-in-law."

"But the truth…"

"Kiran would press charges. It would ruin us."

"But Kiran is a good man. He won't do that. He'd help."

"And Banhi would be shamed by this. She would not be able to return to her father. She would not have a home with us anymore. She would be cast out, shamed, ruined."

"This is why Rehani did not want me to visit."

"Why are you trying to take her away?"

I shifted Lila a bit. She felt so heavy, her head leaning on the back of me.

"She asked me to give her work. Was that burn an accident? Tell me. Do you know?"

Harshad looked away, then back at me. "My saying will only make Rehani punish her more."

I saw a flash of light, heard a whoosh and felt a wave of heat. I ran to their shack. Rehani's back was to me where she stood just inside the kitchen. Banhi was standing as still as a statue, her hair in disarray, flame creeping up her arm on the sleeve of her sari, up her legs to her torso and the skin I'd seen black and oozing was now under the glow of blue flame. I heard a hissing sound, blood sizzling under the flame. All of her was aflame. She collapsed and her head hit the floor. The wrinkle on Rehani's brow smoothed to silk. Her hands came together in prayer and she said, "The stove. She left it burning. She is careless." Banhi's jewel, the one she wore on her sari, the one that signified her soul, rolled away from the flame and lay there at Rehani's feet.

"I think the devil will not have me damned, lest the oil that's in me should set hell on fire." - William Shakespeare

CHAPTER 1

HILLSTON, NEW JERSEY

Friday started as an ordinary day, but that was before I failed to save Ann Neelam from burning to death. I stepped through the usual golden light filtering through the branches onto the blacktopped path through my park to the train. I greeted a squirrel poking out of a trash can with a chunk of someone's discarded bagel in its jaw. That station, with its quaint station house, its coffee window for busy commuters, its old wooden roof and neat platform will never feel tranquil again, but that Friday my girls were off to school, my coffee maker was shut off and unplugged, the front door was closed and locked into its frame, and I walked my usual eight minutes to the station. I had a vague recognition that my life was so routine that I was entering a phase of middle age where habits and patterns would repeat endlessly and I would perish from my own boredom.

My neighbors in their own routines were already aboard the midtown direct to their big jobs in New York, which stopped in Newark and would normally drop me to my twelve dollar an hour job teaching visiting school groups at the museum, but not that morning. I never got on the train. They, however, watched from the windows while I tried to save her.

That day should have been a happy acknowledgment of spring. I liked teaching the kids and I got home before the school bus dropped

Mia and Allie, my eight-year-old twins, at the corner. Before that day, it all worked.

On the platform, the whistle announced the train, commuters shifted briefcases, newspapers, and their weight from one foot to the other. A man dropped a coffee cup into the wastebasket. Headlines in the newspaper dispenser offered the only hint of dread, "Roadside bombs incinerate three U.S. Marines," along with three head-shots. I stared at the soldier's portraits, there in their young perfection, their buzz cuts, hats perched above their young scrubbed faces, reflecting their assertion of inherent toughness and pride. I thought of their mothers receiving phone calls, visits from men in uniform delivering a blow from which there is no recovery. With three daughters, I was not likely to ever face such a thing. My three daughters were not the tough female soldier archetype. More Hera or Aphrodite than Athena, although Lila was beginning to go to war with me as she entered her teen years. I knew women's struggles were very often the silent variety.

The train was visible in the distance. The weight of all that metal screamed at its approach, slowed to a crawl and stopped. On time, dependable, strong and enduring. I use my time on the train to review my notes about ancient Egyptian gods and goddesses, mythical creatures, life after death, Buddha, the wheel of law, and the Hindu goddess Durga. Whatever was on my lesson calendar for the day. I needed no notes for the god of destruction, Shiva, as I was intimately acquainted with him from my days in Bangalore.

I stepped into line among the women in low heels, their confidence obvious in their posture, their preoccupation with watches or cell phones. Next to me, a blue suited woman with a briefcase and purse, holding a cup of coffee up to her lips, tisked her tongue against her teeth and sighed. Her impatience, her gaze up the tracks, made me think she was waiting for someone or something more important and far more interesting than anything I expected. That hint, that sense that there is always something more, more than what I did every

2

day, hovered there over me and for an instant I felt envy of her. She was waiting for something so important that she was impatient. I was always patient. Often I laughed and told other mothers that God first gave me patience, then he gave me Lila.

I reached for the railing and lifted my foot. It was just then a wave of heat flowed over me like a hot flash. I turned and the heat burst into a pillar of flame the ends of which gave off dark smoke like a phantom cloud forming in the shape of a demon. Waves of hot gaseous plasma hit me, a raging tower of yellow fire, from exactly where the tisking woman had been. I can only now compare it to that feeling of time slowing when in a car you know a crash is unavoidable and you hear the metal crunching of impact. Terror knotted in my viscera. I expected the flame to roar and engulf me. Panic tasted like metal in my throat and my heart's pounding mobilized me to flee. I turned back from thirty feet away and saw the flame had now pulled into itself and towered in a vertical column and the woman was behind it, underneath it, inside it. My God, the woman in the blue suit was burning. My skin felt singed, a dry hot wind pushed my hair across my eyes and I stood, my mind saying help her, my heart saying move before it leaps and ignites you. But I could not, frozen as I was in holy terror. Stop, drop, and roll is what they teach you in first aid class, but there was nothing to roll her in and the flame was like a shield pushing back everyone. It was only me and the conductor and her and I succumbed to a helplessness I'd felt only once before. This woman in the blue suit was burning to death. The conductor was at the station's ticket booth pulling a fire extinguisher from the wall. My CPR training, as a Girl Scout leader, screamed, "first call for help" and I dug out my cell phone and dialed. The flames licked down her arms and legs while the voice of the female dispatcher came on, "911, what is your emergency."

"A fire," I said. "A woman is on fire at the Hillston train station."

"A building, you say?"

"No, a woman. She's ...was...waiting for the train. She's burning. My mind raced through what needed to happen; the calm-voiced dispatcher was too slow. "Get them here to help her. Now...hurry... before she..." My voice was deadpan, my words left me, while my heart raced and sweat pooled in my palms.

"Is there danger to anyone else?"

"What? Yes. No. I don't know."

"The station has been called. They're on their way. Please hold."

Hold? She put me on hold? Faces on the train, through the windows, stared. I could see the flame wasn't spreading to the train or the pillar holding up the roof, or the conductor and me. It was just taking her. In that fraction of a second of knowing I would be unharmed, I was mesmerized by the flame. A roaring of it filled the air, the scent of burning hair, of flesh. My throat closed, I held my breath. Banhi. Had that nightmare followed me here? The flame was colorful, flecks of blue and green mingled with the yellow and orange dancing in the oxygen it consumed. Unlike Banhi, who screamed and moaned, this woman hadn't moved under it. Hadn't run and fallen over. Hadn't waved her arms or screamed in pain. She'd simply succumbed. Like a statue. A tree. Like she was abdicating to a higher power.

The conductor aimed the extinguisher. Turn it upside down, I shouted. "You have to turn it upside down. I grabbed it from him like a child fighting over a toy. Take this,I handed him my cell phone. He relinquished the extinguisher and lifted my phone to his ear.

In a second, I had foam spraying fiercely from the nozzle, a schvwit sound starting it, a hiss continuing while the stream found her. The sizzle gave me a split second of satisfaction. The foam soaked the blue business suit with its distinct chemical scent. But then, her hair was gone. I could not see her face. I could see where the ends of her fingers had been. Her torso glowed. And despite the foam raining down upon her head, her neck, she simply melted inward toward her collar as though she were sucked into a vortex. That blue suit hung, like it was on a hanger, while all of her was no longer fuel for the flame. She was now a pile of gray ash. And there was her suit, on the ground, crumpled and blue, with no damage to it whatsoever, except that it was stained with the foam and soaking wet.

I kept the stream of foam pointed at it until I felt a hand on my arm and looked into the eyes of a firefighter, "Okay ma'am. We'll take it from here." He caught me as I groped for his arm, to stop my falling, as dizziness filled my head. He assured me I was out for less than a minute, but there I was on the ground.

"Did I pass out?"

He nodded. "Just sit there for a minute and take a deep breath." His fingers were checking my pulse. "She's gone," I said. I let him lift me and guide me to the bench. An EMT gave me an oxygen mask and massaged my icy cold hands. I never imagined I'd see this again. A human being burning alive before my eyes. I couldn't close my eyes and turn off the images. I wanted to hold my breath so I would not smell that burning human flesh or the sweet caustic extinguisher scent. The oxygen mask helped with that. I didn't dare take it off.

What struck me, in slowed time, was how I had just watched two gold rings fall to the paved platform and bounce to a stillness next to the rumpled blue clothing. The sun had glinted on a diamond as it tumbled. A sense of my own incompetence, remorse, not only from knowing I'd done nothing to save her. Banhi's jewels had also fallen to the cement slab of floor under her, bouncing, then coming to a stillness, a finality, their symbolic meaning in life now absurd immediately after death took her. It all came flooding back. My Bangalore days and my failure there to save Banhi. Dowry deaths. India. Hindu. Re-incarnation. This, I knew, was not that.

"The dispatcher is still on," said the conductor.

I took my phone from him and lifted it to my ear.

"I need your name," said the dispatcher. "Hello? Can you tell me who you are?"

"Oh, Cassandra Taylor," I said. "I am just..."

"Address?"

"578 Sycamore Place."

"Hillston?"

"Yes."

"Phone number?"

"Don't you have it?"

"Your home number please."

"Occupation?"

"What? Why?'"

I always stumbled over this one and it was no different in the middle of this crisis. "Uh, mother," I said. "And a part-time museum educator."

She repeated it. I said yes. She said thank you. Then, she hung up.

And that was it. It was over. The fire fighters had nothing to do. The police in uniform dragged saw horses around the area and put up yellow tape. I sat there as though there was something more expected of me. Faces still peered through train windows until the whistle blew and it pulled slowly away with the hollow toll of its signal bell taking my ordinary routine with it. Then, the firefighter returned to me and said, "Are you okay, ma'am?"

"Yes," I said, but I wasn't. Exhaustion and inertia now rendered me barely able to move.

He touched my arm and the signal of his touch put me into motion. A door opened before me and a chair at a table appeared and I was in the station house restaurant and a man was placing a ceramic cup with a slow stream of steam in front of me. Fire inspector Jeff Heffly, I recognized his red face and bulbous nose and short buzz cut grey hair. He'd been in the paper just last week. For what? A house fire...he'd also been on the TV news, a broadcast from town hall - a commendation to one of his men who had saved a child.

"Cream and sugar?"

"Just cream," I said.

He placed my tote bag and my purse alongside my chair. I'd forgotten about them. Then, he fetched a cup for himself and sat. He took off his glasses and wiped them with a paper napkin. I put down my cell phone. He nodded as though giving me permission to drink my coffee which tasted like smoke.

"You're not on the train," Heffly said it so deadpan, not a question, not an accusation, not anything. Just a flat observation.

"I was supposed to get on."

"So was she."

"I saw her waiting, like she was looking for the next one. This one goes to New York. The next one goes to Hoboken."

He asked, "Did you know her?"

"No," I said.

"Did you hurt her?" he asked, his tone even.

"No," I said, "I tried to save her."

"But how did it start? Did you see anything…anyone…near her?"

"No. But I wasn't really paying attention. I was just looking at the train as it came up."

"Did you see her smoking?"

"No."

"Did you see anything unusual?"

"No, just all of a sudden she was in flames."

He stared at me. "Do you think she did it to herself?"

"Is that what you think?" I asked. It was what they thought in India whenever a woman burned and women burning to death was frequent in Bangalore. But this was different.

"How old are you?" I asked.

"What?"

"Did you watch the news during the Vietnam War? Are you old enough?" I wasn't, but I knew because fixations happen when

7

you experience something like Banhi and you read a lot of archived newspapers.

"I served there. You're thinking of that Buddhist monk." He studied me.

"Yes. A self-immolation on the evening news."

He took a sip of coffee. "Yes. That's what this looked like," he said. "It has to be something else, a spark from her cell phone, a cigarette, an electrical something."

"Alice Herz did it," I told him.

"Who is she?" he asked.

"During the Vietnam War. In 1965. In Detroit."

"Never heard of her," he said.

"She was famous for her protest." I guessed not that famous. I took a sip of coffee. "It looked like it came from inside her."

He studied me. "You think she did it to herself?"

"I don't know," I said. "Her clothes didn't burn. It didn't spread. It seemed to burst out of her."

He looked squarely at me. "Do you know more about this than you're telling me?"

"There's a war on now. Not everyone supports our being there." I know more than you, I thought, but I didn't say it.

"You think she's a war protester?"

"I have no idea. I don't know her. All I am saying is that there was a time this happened in the United States and elsewhere."

He wrote down some notes.

"She didn't scream. She didn't move. She hardly seemed to feel any pain. At least, I would have expected a reaction but I didn't see any."

He wrote down some more notes. "We're inspecting the area, checking for a source of flame or spark." He looked over my shoulder and then, following his gaze, I saw one of the men in those oversized canvas coats with yellow reflective tape staring at me from the doorway. "We will figure it out, Ms. Taylor."

He brushed his hand over his buzz cut. My mind went to the hair, her hair, flaming then gone, and I drifted to the idea of a firefighter in a blazing structure with hair that could ignite like a wick on a candle. The portraits of this morning's Marines flashed and I understood buzz cuts for soldiers for the very first time.

"I just need you to give me everything you witnessed, what you did, and if you observed anything odd while you were waiting for the train - I mean before the, before she..."

I gave him what he wanted, slowly, patiently, with vivid details. He listened intently and scribbled.

"Tell me one thing, please," I asked. "Why would a fire like that burn her so completely and not burn her clothes? Even if it was self-inflicted. Even if it was something like an electric wire electrocuting her or if someone torched her or if she accidentally burned from a cigarette. Maybe a spark from her cell phone. Her clothes would still burn."

"Because you soaked them in foam from the extinguisher," he said. "You just told me how fast you reacted...you and the conductor... you both moved fast."

He didn't want me to speculate. He didn't want me to think. He only wanted facts. Observations of the surface of this thing. His words and the blanched look in his eyes signaled to me that I was dismissed and so was my question.

"Each of us is born with a box of matches inside us but we can't strike them all by ourselves."
- Laura Esquivel, *Like Water for Chocolate*

CHAPTER 2

"Is there someone we can call for you?"

"Thank you, no," I said. "My husband is out of town."

"A relative? A neighbor?" the EMT asked.

"No." I did not want my sisters, Grace and Lou, here.

I walked back through the park, remembering halfway there to call the school programs office at the museum.

"Shirley? Listen, can someone take my group? Something happened and I missed the train." I felt ashamed that this excuse sounded so lame.

"Something happened? You okay girl?" she asked in her slow drawl. "We just heard on the radio about the woman in Hillston. Thank God it isn't you."

"I'm not going to make the second class either," I said. "I'm very sorry."

"You okay?"

"I was there. I tried to help and, well, the cops are asking me questions. I don't know how long I'll be."

"Oh, I am so sorry. Don't worry. I'll tell Eric. He'll do your groups. Take care of yourself." She paused. "Girl, thank the Lord it wasn't you."

I thanked her and hung up.

By the time I crossed the park and unlocked my front door, I succumbed to fatigue. I shed my work clothes, pulled on last night's tee shirt, and wrapped myself in the quilt on my bed. I could not shut

10

down to sleep. I curled into a ball, shivered despite the sunbeam across the bed and the heaviness of the down comforter. I didn't save her, as I had not saved Banhi. The women who lived in the slums there called it a self-immolation, a choice, they said to me, to leave her current life and gamble on her reincarnation to raise her up to a new form of existence. The police only believed what they were paid to believe. Nobody paid them anything that day in the Bangalore slum. They saw no girl and, because there are six million other missing women in India, the Bangalore police added Banhi to that list and closed her case. I had let her death recede into memory, but now it roared back from the past, all the confusion surrounding that day when Banhi died, all my pleas with the Bangalore police and the pervasive indifference to her death I could not forgive.

Sleep came. I woke to the sharp ring of the telephone and an even sharper anxiety. I expected Pete, but a stranger's voice said my name with a question mark after it and I said, "Yes."

"This is Doug Bluestein from the Jersey Star," the voice said.

"Yes?"

"Are you the Cassandra Taylor who tried to save the woman this morning?"

"Yes."

"May I ask you a few questions?"

"I told everything to the fire chief," I said.

"That's where I got your name," he said. "And from the police radio."

"The police were talking about me?"

"You and the conductor. They were saying how quickly you both reacted."

"Well, I'm glad they think so. I feel differently."

"In situations like that we're always hard on ourselves," he said. "I'm sure you did the best thing under the circumstances."

"Thank you," I said, feeling my fatigue lift.

I sat up and pulled the quilt to my chin. The deep tone of his voice soothed me. It was surely not the correct response to this. He was a reporter after a story, but I was suddenly in need of someone to talk to. I said, "Why don't you come to the house to talk?"

He accepted immediately. I now had a compelling reason to get out of bed, out of my cold sweaty tee shirt, and go to the sink and press a warm washcloth to my face. I studied my eyes and tried a cold compress when the warm one did not work. I dressed and moved to my front porch to wait for this Doug person. Thirty minutes, he had said, so I went to the kitchen and filled the teakettle and turned the knob to ignite the flame under it. Tick, tick, tick, the igniter attempted to light but failed and the throat-closing scent of gas rose up. The scent from her flesh and hair burning rolled up from memory. I could almost taste the acrid smoke. Off, then a second attempt, tick, tick, tick. Still the fuel did not catch. Off. A wave of my hand to dispel the fumes. On the third try, it caught and a burst of blue flame rose on all sides of the kettle with a whoosh and a surge from the flame burned the skin on my forearm. My backing away was instinctive, my left hand moving to my right arm protectively. Heat, but only tiny hairs singed and shriveled, no damage to the skin but that, right now, was no consolation. I poured a pot of green tea, carried it to the porch, and waited for Doug Bluestein. He never came. He did not call. In the moments before I gave up, I sipped tea in the sunny oasis of calm I found on my porch and listened as sirens pierced the distance and I wondered what other awful thing could be happening.

I needed Pete. I needed to talk to him. To tell him this. I lifted the phone and dialed his mobile number. I heard his voice message. "You've reached Pete. I'm on the road in Chicago until Friday evening, but please leave a message and I'll return your call at a convenient time for both of us." Beep.

Always able to reach his phone, but never able to reach him. I slammed the phone into the base. "Now is a convenient time for me," I said to the empty house. His message was always the same. He was on an airplane. Or, he was with a client. Or driving. Or sleeping. At least that's what he always said when he walked in the door. He was returning home tonight. I could talk to him tonight.

The phone rang again. It was Grace, my sister. "Hi," I said.

I waited. Grace never called. When she did, she rarely asked questions. This time I expected them, lots of them. Shirley had said she heard about the burning. Doug had said the police gave him my name. Had the TV news gotten it too?

"Are you calling about the news?" I asked.

"My news?" she asked. "How did you know I had news?"

"I didn't know you had news. I meant the NEWS news. The radio. I thought maybe you heard my name..."

"Why in the world would I hear your name on the news?" she asked.

"The woman at the train...I was there...I was a witness."

She was silent, so I said, "Don't you listen to the local radio station?"

"Cassie," she said. "Why do you always talk so much? I can't get a word in edgewise."

"Grace, you didn't say anything. I was waiting."

"You're always talking about yourself." I heard a pause. Then, she asked, "Okay, what were you on the radio for this time?"

"Did you hear what happened this morning?" I asked.

"No."

"A woman burst into flame and burned to death at the train station this morning." I waited for a moment, then I said, "And I saw it right before my eyes. I tried to use the fire extinguisher on her, but it didn't save her."

"Cassandra, that is gruesome. Are you okay?"

13

"I'm not hurt, if that's what you mean."

"Well, thank goodness for that. When you said news, I thought you meant Catherine's news. She's going to Vassar."

"Congratulations."

"You really ought to not take the train. Driving into Newark is so much safer. I think about the crime in that city and how you take a chance."

"I'm fine," I said. "I was freaked out and the police and fire department asked me a million questions. I'm still a bit freaked out. And Pete's not here. I thought your call was Pete. It was awful."

"Well, thank God it wasn't you," she said.

"Yes, I thought that too. I was so close…"

"You're okay? What do you mean she burst into flames?"

"She was there one minute, then the next she was on fire."

"I heard a lot of sirens this morning," she said.

"I did, later."

"I'm going to turn it on when I get off the phone," she said. "Now can I take a turn and tell you why I called? Do I get a turn now?"

I gave her a long moment of empty air, just like she'd given me.

"I'm calling about Catherine's graduation." Grace stated it firmly.

I said. "Yes, great. So exciting for her."

"Charles and I decided to throw her a party at the club," Grace said. "A pool party for her and all her friends."

"Nice," I said.

"Do you think you would want to come?" she asked. "I know you won't know a lot of people there. And your girls won't know anyone either. But, well, it seems odd to not have all the family there." There was clear reluctance in her tone.

"Are you inviting us?" I said.

"Well, it isn't an invitation yet," she said. "I just need to know if you want to come. I'll send invitations out later. It's on Mothers' Day.

14

That's another thing. It's a busy family day, but the only date the club was not already booked. The graduation isn't until mid-June."

"We'd love to come," I said. "Gift ideas?"

"Gift cards are always nice. She could use it to buy stuff for college."

"Thanks, Grace," I said. "Thanks for inviting us. The girls will enjoy seeing Catherine. Especially Lila."

"Well," Grace said. "I hope she has time to give some attention to her cousins with her friends around. You know how that is."

"Yes, well, they'll enjoy swimming at any rate," I said.

"There is a dress code at the club," Grace continued. "I will send you an email about their rules. Listen, I've got some things to do and more calls to make. I will talk to you soon."

"Bye, Grace," I said. I listened to the click of her hang up and placed the phone back down. It didn't ring again. I wanted to call Pete again. Instead, I did nothing but drink tea. Why had this Doug person not come? I supposed I'd get a phone call, but I didn't. I walked to the bus but the girls weren't on the bus. I'd forgotten. Today was Girl Scout day and they'd be dropped off late by their leader. I walked home and imagined it happening to me. Imagine if I just burst into flames and disappeared from life right in the middle of a routine day full of tasks and duties? Who was she, that anonymous woman in the blue business suit? Had she been making a political statement? Or, what random mistake or malfunction or terrible path of fate had she stepped across so she was not able to step out of it. Clichés like 'There but for the grace of God', 'In the end it's a blink of an eye'. It could just as easily have been me. The difference of a few feet, maybe just a few minutes, my spot in line to board just ahead of her.

The New York news channels gave this mention, the way they would a car accident, a mugging in Central Park, a water main break, but to me, this felt too much like 9/11 when the towers fell. Innocent people dying. But it felt strangely like a dream, like it was only significant to me, not the rest of the world. My heart thudded against my ribs and I could feel a pulse in my temples. Then, the shock of what the news anchor said next. There were two other fires, two other women, two more, in Hillston, two more women stepping through their ordinary days, one at a school, one at Mills Reservation. Just like that. Dead. Burned. Gone.

I wanted to get in my car and drive to the Girl Scout meeting to bring Mia and Allie home to safety. I wondered where Lila was. My intrepid teenaged Lila could fall victim to some random accident or the evil in some stranger or even someone she knew, roaming the earth making trouble, destroying lives with fire. I wanted them all home with me. Maybe that's why that reporter hadn't come. Maybe something awful happened to him. And Pete was on planes all the time. Then, Lila was on the steps.

"Mom," she said. "We were dismissed early. Something awful is happening. Did you hear? Look, here's a notice they gave out. Everyone at school was talking about it." She shoved the door open and I followed her inside.

"I know. I saw it. A woman at the station."

"You saw it?"

"I did. I was right next to her." I closed the door firmly. I wanted the drapes drawn in the living room. I wanted the windows locked. Somehow, a dim light was preferable to the brilliant late afternoon rays slanting over the roof of the house, across the street, and through my windows. The sun's heat, usually comforting, dragged up terror. I wanted my twins home.

The crumbled notice stated that a student at the middle school had lost his mother in an unexplained fire in the reservation this morning while walking her dog. I switched on the news right away in my kitchen as I prepared dinner, waiting for my two girl scouts to arrive. As I switched from station to station, it further explained Doug's failure to appear. Edna Totten, the anchor on the NJ local news channel, who lived in Hillston, delivered the segment. "Police are investigating this incident. They are seeking any additional witnesses who might have been in the area. They're warning us to stay alert while walking in town or nearby as there may be dangerous individuals using fire to harm women."

Edna Totten, on the TV, said, "The woman appeared to spontaneously ignite. Similar incidences also occurred at various places in suburban communities around Hillston, where I am now, reporting from the elementary school where principal, Elizabeth Lindsey, burst into flame during a routine fire drill this morning, at approximately nine thirty." Edna blinked at perfect intervals and continued. "Mrs. Lindsey was standing at the curb just there," she indicated with a gesture. "The students were led back into the building through other doors while the fire department and EMT's arrived. They were too late to help. The fire, which consumed Mrs. Lindsey, is being investigated. Fire Chief Jeff Heffly indicated there was no evidence to indicate how it started." Edna said, "This fire and the death appears identical to the death of a woman at the Hillston train station this morning. We go now to the videotape of a press conference held earlier today by the New Jersey Transit spokesperson, Allen Cavallo."

The camera cut to a podium behind which stood a tall man with thick gray hair and wire rimmed glasses, tie loosened, hands gripping the edges of the podium while he read from a prepared statement. "I would like to extend my condolences to the family of Ann Neelam, a customer of New Jersey Transit, who lost her life this morning under circumstances that are still being investigated. New Jersey Transit dispatched a maintenance crew to the station in question immediately. As of right now, there doesn't seem to have been any malfunction of the equipment or the electrical system at the Hillston station. Their work continues."

I waited. Surely, they would field questions from the reporters filling this room where this Allen Cavallo delivered his speech. I wondered what Doug Bluestein looked like and if his head was one of those I could see from behind. The program switched the broadcast back to Edna. I stopped trying to cook and sat. " Another fire of unknown origin took the life of a woman who was walking her dog in Mills reservation, also near Hillston." Edna had her hand on the earpiece from which she was being fed updated information. Her gaze turned inward as she listened, then she recovered herself as she was still on camera. She said, "We're sorry. We have no visual on that report. Witnesses who were questioned by the Hillston authorities reported that the victim was discovered by a jogger along a footpath near the south end parking lot. The jogger, a local actor named Bruce Gilbert, used his cell phone to call 911 but reported that the fire was raging so fiercely he could not get near enough to try to save her. She had completely expired before the police and firefighters arrived."

One, a principal, two, Ann Neelam, three, an unknown woman at the reservation. How very strange and horrifying. The coverage continued. Here was the mayor, Bobby Moore, a close-up, with a blue background. He was plugged into a mic and an earpiece was stuck in his left ear. He kept touching it with his forefinger, tilting his head at an odd angle. His eyes stared unblinking and unrehearsed at the camera, while his face reflected the strain of listening through his left ear. Then, he came to life. I thought he was reading a teleprompter, the way his eyes didn't stay on the camera. "It seems that the women are spontaneously igniting in various locations across our suburban landscape. There doesn't seem to be a pattern associated with these burnings and there seems to be no immediate danger to anyone else in the vicinity when the fire appears." A pause while he tilted his head to listen. "No, there doesn't seem to be an indication of common circumstances." Another pause. "I have not witnessed any of these very strange occurrences." Pause again. "I am not in Hillston. I will be on a plane on my way back in a few hours." Pause. "Would you repeat that?" Comprehension passed over his eyes. "I would not say, at this time, that the Hillston citizens are in any kind of danger, but I would caution anyone to be on the alert for any suspicious looking individuals." A frown. "I have no evidence to support the idea that someone is responsible for these deaths. These are all still under investigation."

Suddenly the watching audience could hear the questions he was responding to and I was startled by the very loud voice of Edna Totten again. It went on from there. Edna attempting to pin him down to an explanation and, when that failed, she began a series of questions that required so much speculation or guess work on the mayor's part that all I could imagine as a result was panic entering the hearts and minds of anyone who lived near Hillston. It certainly had entered mine in a quiet and insidious way. Hearing the rising panic in Edna Totten's tone, asking if this was reminiscent of a Stephen King novel, the hint of suggestion that something strange and sinister was at work in this locale swelled up in me. I imagined I shared this growing fear with everyone listening to her. Mayor Moore said, after a long series of leading questions, "If I were a woman in Hillston, if I were someone who loved a woman in Hillston, and I am, actually, although my wife and kids are in Texas right now, I would discourage them from spending any time outdoors until the mystery of how and why this is happening is solved."

The news station cut to a commercial, one of those homegrown ones about a family-owned car dealership, and I turned back to my cooking. This is terror, I thought. This is how they destroy not just the one who died, but everyone who sees it. This is like the aftermath of 9/11. I still had jugs of water and canned goods, probably expired now, in the basement. We had all expected bombs and war back then. The media had encouraged us to prepare. Now all they said was to stay indoors.

I decided then and there my kids would not be out of my sight. I would drive Lila to school, no walking around town with her camera until this was over. I would be the one to drive Mia and Allie home after Girl Scouts. I would protect them from whatever this was. If it happened again, it would not be to anyone I loved. I'd rather die than let anyone or anything hurt my girls.

"I've got to get some photos done. I'm going to be downstairs, okay? You're not doing laundry down there, are you?" Lila said, suddenly behind me. I wondered how long she'd been there and what she'd seen of the news.

"Homework?" I asked.

"After dinner," she said. "Not a lot. Just some math." She retreated to the dim safety of her basement darkroom, a place where up to now I felt she'd spent far too much time. Now, I was grateful for the photo hobby and the cinderblock walls I hoped could keep her safe.

The phone rang and it was that voice, that deep soothing voice from this morning and it said, "Ms. Taylor, I owe you an apology." And the knot in my gut I hadn't acknowledged responded. I felt a letting go in the muscles in my neck. My grip on the phone loosened.

"It looks like there was more than one person you needed to talk with today," I said. "I just saw the local news."

"Tune into CNN," he said. "They're all in town. All the news stations. As a matter of fact, you should look outside. There may be news vans watching your house."

I carried the phone to my front porch as he kept talking. He explained how he was diverted to the scenes of the other fires. I looked out and watched an Eyewitness News van passed slowly, then I saw a CNN van idling down the street at the curb.

"I'd still like to talk to you," he said. "Is that still possible?"

"Yes," I said simply.

"Who was the woman in the woods?" I asked. I didn't know Ann Neelam, the woman I failed to save. My children attended a different elementary school and I did not know Elizabeth Lindsey. I knew a lot of women in town through PTA and the early moms support group

I'd started upon my return from Bangalore, from the YMCA, and my yoga studio. It was surprising that Bruce Gilbert was the jogger who saw her die. He was a bit too short and round of body to fit the stereotype of a jogger, but he was an actor. He had also been my contractor for my kitchen renovation when he was between acting jobs. I now shared an experience with him. I felt an urgent need to call him and wondered if this Doug person had already.

"Her name is Cynthia Barrow," Doug said.

"Gees," I said. "Come over." I hung up.

Cynthia. Cindy. My Cindy. Our Cindy. Cindy of the Institute for Philosophy for Children. Cindy, my partner in early motherhood. Cindy, the co-founder of our mom's group. A sister in spirit, she'd called me in a birthday card she'd once sent. I walked through my front door, dropped the phone on the carpet and there I was again in the pillows on my couch, my legs curling up to my chest, my eyes closed. Gone. Dead. Burned. I waited for this Doug Bluestein person to arrive. And, in the stillness of my living room, the faint sounds of Lila in her darkroom below came to me and I let the soft sounds of her life overpower the pounding of my own blood pulsing just under the taut muscles in my neck. I wanted my twins home. Just then, there they were and I ran through my front door to the car at the curb, pulled them quickly into the house, barely thanking Barbara Kinsley from down the street for bringing them home. She waved at me and sped off. Now if only Pete were here. We would all be safe. Instead of trying him again I tried to reach Bruce Gilbert. It rang until the message announced his unavailability. I left a hurried message and hung up. Cindy was dead. I lifted the phone. I still could dial the number from memory. But a rush of shame and a sense of self-doubt ambushed me. Cindy and I hadn't spoken in five years. What would Derrick Barrow think now if he heard my voice? What would he do? Hang up on me? He could be as righteous as Cindy. I hung up. This needed more thought than I was capable of right now. It was too soon.

21

I turned my attention to my daughters who were seating themselves at the table in the kitchen for their daily ritual of homework. Shiny brown-haired heads bent over their work as though nothing was different.

Cindy had been so often at this table, Brandon and Lila finger-painting or sharing play dough to create creatures and turn them into characters in a story. Cindy and I would drink tea in late afternoon. Sometimes it would stretch to dinner when Pete was out of town, which was often. Sometimes Derrick would join us as he stepped off the train from New York. These memories assailed me. She'd come in the house some mornings and immediately lift one of the twins from her bassinet and say, "Where's the bottle?"

Brandon would join Lila playing on the floor and we'd sit there, burp napkins over our shoulders, coffee on the table in front of us, and feed the babies and ourselves. Now, the disagreement that had severed our bond seemed so banal, so pointless, and waves of remorse and longing for those days of early motherhood washed over me. We had been sisters in spirit, until we weren't anymore. We'd even lost our mothers in the same year, hers back in Chicago, mine just about a mile from me.

Cindy had filled a huge space in my life. Pete never home. My sisters, Grace and Lou, never did what Cindy and I did for each other. Now I swallowed lumps in my throat and let my hair hide my face from my Mia and my Allie as tears rolled onto my chin and dripped onto my tee shirt.

"Fire is the test of gold; adversity, of strong men."
- Martha Graham

CHAPTER 3

There are references and mythologies in every culture about women and fire. So many stories of burning, women at the stake, witches, Joan of Arc, fairy tales with old nasty women being pushed into ovens by victimized children. And that was just European culture. I thought about Sati, an outlawed practice in India. Burning was a purification or a punishment or a path to a different world. And, as my doorbell rang and I stood to answer it, I was sure everyone in Hillston and the surrounding area was thinking about it too.

Bluestein stood at my door. The first observation I made was that he was tall and thin and slightly stooped so that his blazer hung limply and appeared a size too large. He looked up, despite his height, over the rim of his wire glasses like a character you might expect in a Dickens story. Blue eyes, sharp and clear, a slow smile, and that deep voice I found so soothing.

I stuck out my hand and he held it for a beat longer than I expected. "So sorry about that awful morning you had," he said. "Although, it was much worse for some."

"Yes. Thanks," I said. "Come in."

He hesitated even though I was holding the screen door open for him.

"We can sit on the porch," he said, then, "Maybe we're better off inside. I just heard the mayor."

Over his shoulder I saw someone emerge from the CNN van, a slim young man wearing a baseball cap. He lifted a camera to his shoulder and set his gaze on us.

"Come inside," I said. "They're watching."

He followed me inside. I shut the door firmly.

"They're going to want to speak to you," he said.

"I can see that," I said. "Let them wait."

"They haven't knocked or rang your bell?" he asked.

I shook my head.

"Expect it. Probably will right after I leave."

We sat. He on the stiff-backed upholstered chair and me on the rocking chair. I didn't offer him tea. My nerves were churning and I didn't have the energy to think even about a glass of water. "Have you been listening to the TV news? I imagined you were tearing around town after witnesses."

"I took a dinner break," he said. "At O'Bal's. They have six TV's, all of them on different news stations."

"I've been watching. They're talking a lot but saying very little. Do they know anything they're not sharing with the public?" I asked. "I mean...I know what they say they know. But causes? Three women in one day? Three separate women, all...they didn't happen at the same time, did they?"

He shook his head no. "Very close in time however."

"How close?" I asked. "The news doesn't give many details."

"I came to ask you questions," he said.

"The mayor said stay indoors. What does that mean? Do the police think there is a menace wandering our town setting women on fire?"

"Tell you what. I will ask you the questions. After I'm done, you can ask me anything you want. I will answer as best I can. But I'm a reporter, not a fire inspector or detective."

"Fine," I said. "Sorry to make you feel like I'm interrogating you. But I was so close. Why her and not me? It could have been me. She was maybe ten feet behind me, if that."

He started to jot down notes. "You really are rattled."

"Wouldn't you be?" I asked. "Cindy Barrow was a friend. You just told me a friend of mine is dead. I haven't quite taken that in yet."

His hands went still on his notepad. He pushed his glasses up his nose again. "She was? I am very sorry."

He took out a tissue and wiped his glasses clean. I watched his hands. He wore a ring with a familiar symbol over the stone. I leaned forward. "Where did you get that?"

"My ring?"

I stuck out my hand. "Me too." My college ring was gold plated and the stone was a ruby. Over the stone, where summa cum laude or magna cum laude symbols are added for those smart enough to earn those distinctions, my ring carried an unusual insignia, a lyre. Professor Fields had awarded me this honor in secret, telling me to reveal to nobody the significance of the symbol on the ring he wore, which, he said I too would receive in the mail if I accepted the honor.

"Amazing."

"Yes. I haven't met another member ever."

"You studied?"

"Geology. Archaeology. Anthropology."

"Journalism and history," he said.

"Yes," I smiled. "That makes sense."

"Where did you earn the ring?"

"At Sheffield University. England."

He stuck his thumb toward his chest. "College of New Jersey."

I laughed. "Really? I had no idea there was representation here."

"The Fraternity for Contemplative Research." He said it with reverence.

"Yes. For subjects outside the parameters of acceptable academic questioning."

He laughed. He said, "Shut out of academia for veering off in directions deviating from the path of scholarly acceptance."

"A consolation prize, of sorts." I smiled a rueful smile. "Dubious honor, huh? What did you do to piss them off?"

He leaned back in his chair. He let his pen rest on the steno pad. He took off his glasses and rubbed at them. I rocked in my chair. This was so very strange. I'd nearly forgotten my initiation into this fraternity at Sheffield. Dr. Fields, my mentor, my advisor, the man who encouraged my work, had bestowed the honor upon me on the day the university accepted my Masters' thesis but did not admit me to the doctoral program. I rocked my chair, waiting for this Doug person, whose card said, 'Investigative Reporter' to tell me what his great failure was back in his day.

"I would rather not say," he said. "It is part of membership to not reveal it."

"So you are a reporter," I said.

"Yes. And you?"

"I work part-time at the Newark Museum and I'm raising my kids."

I couldn't help seeing it, a tiny drop in the muscles around his eyes, a sign that I was more disappointing than he might have anticipated. But, of course, I was buoyed by a sense of connection and it somehow made me feel safer. I had never seen the ring on anyone, not at Sheffield or in India or here in Hillston where it seemed everyone was actively and enthusiastically employed by the mainstream. For all I knew, since Dr. Fields bestowed the ring upon me, I was in a fraternity of one, or maybe two since Fields himself was a secret member who must have redeemed himself somewhere along the way since he was a member in good standing in the academy. I would keep my secret and Doug would keep his, but the commonality of the ring and the cloud of mystery around where and what he might have explored as a student was not lost on me.

"So shall we get on with what I came for?"

I nodded. I trusted his judgment and trusted that his write-up of whatever was said here would be accurate and honest, all because he wore the ring. Doug stayed for an hour. During that one hour, he learned about what I witnessed that morning. He learned that Cindy had been my friend and how we fell apart. He also let me tell him about our mom's group and how I turned my interest in the poor women of Bangalore back in my anthropologist days into a self-help group for Hillston women. That had been the start of Cindy's and my friendship, our sisterhood in spirit, after my own real sisters seemed to hardly notice I was back in town.

I shared with him the history of my work in England, archaeology, and how, when I went to Bangalore, I diverted my attention from studying the past toward analysis of modern cultures juxtaposed onto the remnants of traditional ones. Bangalore had been the perfect place for that. Then, coming home, the museum was the only place I could find where I could use what I knew about prehistory and culture and still focus on raising my family. As I explained myself to him, I felt the desperation to gain a level of respect that I had long ago stopped experiencing and for which the old boxes of field notes up in my attic were such a catalyst for restlessness.

I knew I was talking too much, yet he was patient, polite and seemed genuinely interested. While he listened, the phone rang twice and I half listened as the muffled voices of Bruce and Pete left messages, the contents of which I could not give my attention. With Doug here, my need for Pete was receding.

Finally, Doug stood. But I said, "Uh-uh, now it's my turn to ask questions, remember?"

He sat back down. "Yes," he said.

"What are you going to write?"

He stared down at his pad. "I don't know. I still need to check in again with the Hillston police and fire department. They are sure to make another statement before today is over."

"So which witnesses did you speak to? I gather nobody was able to say anything that was helpful. I imagine they – whoever they were – were like me, mystified."

"Pretty much," he said.

"Did they say their clothes burned?"

"Actually, I didn't ask."

"Well, you should."

"Really?"

"I told you that I watched her burn and her clothes dropped to the floor, the ground, and were entirely undamaged."

"Yes, you did. I have that in my notes."

"I also said her rings dropped to the ground. Perfectly intact. And her purse...and the coffee cup in her hand. All as though untouched by the fire."

"Okay."

"I told Heffly. I asked him why her clothes didn't burn. He said it was because I used the fire extinguisher to try to save her."

"Nobody else tried what you tried," he said.

"That's why I want to know if their clothes burned. I don't believe it was because of the extinguisher."

"Really." He said it as a statement, not a question. His brow wrinkled. His tapped his pen on his pad.

"Contemplative." He smiled at me.

"Exactly," I said. "I'm asking an odd question. Heffly ignored the implication. You're ignoring it too, Mr. Bluestein."

"Please call me Doug."

"Okay, but, if you ask the other witnesses if their clothes were untouched except that they dropped to the ground, then you can prove to me that it was not what I did. Can you find this out for me?"

"Why does this matter?"

"I don't know why it matters. It may not. But if you watched what I watched, you'd know it wasn't the predictable thing. Fire captures everything usually."

"There are burn-proof fabrics," he said.

I shook my head. "PJ's for kids, not women's business suits."

I waited, staring at him, daring him to push this aside as Heffly had done, as the Bangalore police inspectors had done to me so long ago about Banhi. It was because I was a woman. They'd assumed my perception was clouded by my emotions. That, I knew, was the smug superiority they wore with their uniforms, the belief that, if they couldn't explain something to me, then it didn't need explaining. It could be dismissed. I could be dismissed.

"It's an important question," I said. "I don't know why, but isn't that part of your job? To get the answers? You can't get answers unless you ask the questions…the right ones."

I stood up and grabbed the portable phone from the side table. I hit the dial button to return the call to Bruce Gilbert. He'd seen Cindy. He could answer this. I didn't need to wait for Doug Bluestein to report back.

"Bruce?"

"Hi Cassandra," he said. "What a day, huh?"

"Bruce, I'm so sorry. We both had a tough day. But I just need to ask you one question. We can have coffee or something and talk soon, but can you tell me one thing?"

"Gees, Cassandra, slow down." I sensed a slur. He must have had a few drinks.

"Is Pam home?" I asked.

"She's on her way."

"The kids home?"

"Yes, of course they're home. It's dinner time."

"You okay?"

"I'm not sure…"

"Do you need me to come over?"

"No, of course not. Ah, here's the wife. Home at last." A rush of relief filled me. I knew Bruce. He had spent a few months renovating my kitchen and there had been a few days when he'd smelled of drink after lunch. The idea of him home with his boys and drinking set my neck muscles in a knot.

"Bruce," I tried again.

"Cassandra?" he replied.

"Did her clothes burn?"

"The woman in the reservation?"

"Yes," I said.

"I don't remember," he said. "I just remember calling 911 and watching her die."

"Bruce," I said. "Can you just think back for a second. Just try to remember."

"Cassandra, I am trying to forget. It was awful."

"I'm sorry, Bruce. Yes, it was awful. For me too."

"Can I let this wait till tomorrow?"

"Sure. Sorry. Thanks. Listen, take it easy, huh? I'll check in with you tomorrow. I'm going to call you tomorrow. Maybe you can try to remember?"

"Yeah, bye," he hung up with a firm click.

"Well, that was no help."

"I will ask the question," Doug promised me. "Heffly should be able to answer it. And I'll let you know the answer."

"Thank you."

"Thank you for bringing this to my attention." He bowed slightly and left.

I watched Doug go, feeling a strong sense of simpatico, a shared consciousness, and a confirmation that he had enough respect for me to accept my observations as sound. Still, that raging flame, from so many hours earlier, flared in memory and, like Bruce must be feeling under his apparent drinking, I felt ragged and fearful. I went to the medicine cabinet in my bathroom and dug through the top shelf. There still were a few Xanax left. I cut one in quarters, swallowed one piece, and followed it with a glass of water. India was one thing. Hindu beliefs and traditions rising out of poverty were factors I could accept as an element to help endure suffering. Self-immolation was done there. Accidents with stoves too. Burning bodies did not happen in Hillston, but it had, three times in one day. I could not imagine what the police or firefighters might say about this once further investigation was complete. My early speculation with Heffly that the blue-suited woman might have done it to herself was ending because I could not accept that Cindy would have set herself on fire. Or that a school principal would do it in front of all those school children. I also could not imagine who would kill Cindy.

In Banhi's case, I blamed Rehani, Banhi's mother-in-law. That made cultural and social sense. I had also learned there were four million missing women in India. I learned about sati, about the Hindu belief in reincarnation, and how that became distorted to encourage the destitute to end their lives in hopes of a better one next time. These fires in Hillston did not have a cultural context. The police and fire department would have to solve this puzzle. I just wanted to know my children would not be hurt or anyone else I knew, including myself. These women were in the middle years, but it had happened to Banhi when she was so young. Pete no longer discussed Banhi and Bangalore with me, not after we returned to the states. It was an agreement we made. If he learned of this morning, would he see my need to compare? Would he let me break my promise to stay away from the subject that had nearly driven me crazy and him along with me? That whole tragedy is what brought us home to Hillston, to my hometown, to the place I had fled as a young graduate student and, for the first time ever, I imagined maybe it wasn't Rehani and dowry murder that had destroyed Banhi, but perhaps there was something else at work and maybe the same was at work here in Hillston.

"Affection is a coal that must be cooled; Else, suffered, it will set the heart on fire." - William Shakespeare

CHAPTER 4

And there he is, the engine dying in the driveway, the screen door slapping, and his steps on the porch announcing the end of his week. He is home and the sun is still up and it is Friday and there is a weekend ahead for togetherness and I feel my energy create a smile and I can feel a brightness shining in me. He drops his briefcase, his hair is curly and in disarray as is his loosened tie over his Oxford shirt. He sees the girls at the table, goes to them, and drops quick pecks of kisses onto their lowered heads. They turn for kisses, real ones, and he bends to accept theirs on his shadowy cheek with the prickles and they return to their work. My hands are wet from cooking chicken and I move to the sink to wash them. He doesn't wait for me to finish and turn for a hug, but he pecks a kiss on my lips, quick, dry, prickly and moves away. I am too late for an embrace.

He says, "Have I got time for a few miles before dinner?" He doesn't wait for an answer but disappears up the hall toward the stairs.

"Did you see that I called?"

"Yes," he said.

"Do you want to know why?"

"I want to go for my run," he says.

I follow him upstairs. He is out of his business clothes. They are flat out on the bed and his running shorts are in his hand. His abdominals are lean and hard. So are his thighs and the dense hair on his chest is speckled with gray.

"Where is Lila?" he asks.

"Darkroom," I say. "I need a hug."

He lifts a tee shirt from the bed and grabs the lower hem in his teeth while his hands reach inside to the sleeves and he slides into it. He says, "I've had a tough day too."

"I need to tell you," I say.

He pauses. He sits to slip on his shoes and his eyes are on his laces.

"Cindy is dead," I say.

"Cindy? Your old friend Cindy?" He looks up. "I'm so sorry."

"And I watched a woman burn to death on the train station platform this morning," I said. "She died. Cindy died in a fire. Three women died today in Hillston in fires."

"That must have been awful. I'm sorry." He stands up. He comes to me and puts his arms around me. He kisses my cheek. He releases me before I can lift my arms to encircle him. He is out the bedroom door.

I call after him. "Pete, it was just like Banhi."

He returns. "Cassie, the Bangalore police said Banhi ran away."

"And Rehani said she set herself on fire. And the women all around that shack, we know they turned their backs. But I know better. I saw her arm with the earlier burn. I saw her in flames in that shack."

"I thought we left this in Bangalore…in the past."

"But a woman burned today right before my eyes. Two more women too. Cindy was one of them." I lifted my hands flat, palms up, then clasped them together. "I tried to extinguish the flame. This time I had a chance to save her. But it didn't work."

"What do you want me to say?" he said.

"Say you believe me. You never said that about Banhi."

"There was no body Cassie. When the police got there, there was no body. There were no burn marks in that kitchen."

"I saw her. Somehow, they moved Banhi, hid her body, cleaned up. When I got back with the police, it was as though nothing happened."

"And her husband said she must have run away," Pete said.

"And you believed him and not me, Pete. How do you think that makes me feel?"

"Did this morning really happen?" Pete asked. "Or are you having problems again?"

"Didn't you see the news vans outside?"

He went to the window. I followed. The street was now empty of vans. "They were all over the street earlier. It is on CNN. It is on the radio news. It's real, Pete. Don't you dare make insinuations about whether it's real or not. You're my husband."

"I think it flashed across the screen at the airport," he said, "now that I think about it." He sat on the floor and extended his legs to stretch. "They didn't say the women's names. I thought maybe it was a stunt, you know, like the women in China a few years ago. That was a cult, wasn't it? Falun Gong or something?"

"A stunt? That's an awful way to characterize it."

"Women trying to draw attention to something...a cause or something."

"I still don't think we should call it a stunt."

"What are you trying to say?"

"I'm trying to tell you that I was there. She was right behind me as I was stepping onto the train...and it's scary...I'm upset...I need some time to talk about it. She caught fire and died. I just need you here. I'm terrified it can happen to me...to Lila...to anybody. Can you stay please?"

He leaned back on his elbows and stared up at me. "It must have been terrifying. I can't imagine."

"I think I fainted after it was over."

"Wow."

"The EMT's gave me oxygen. There was nothing left of her to help."

"Cassie, I'm sorry. I'm sorry you were there. Maybe take some time off from that job. Maybe that would help?"

"I called out today. I spent the day at home watching the news and waiting for Doug to come."

"Doug?"

"The reporter."

"Did you call the paper?"

"No, he called me."

"What did the police say? What did the fire department say? I'm sure you called them. I'm sure they were at the scene."

"I called 911. By the time they got there, the fire was done. She was dead."

"This does sound very familiar."

"The conductor and I tried to save her. He grabbed the fire extinguisher, but he didn't know how to use it."

"And you did." He leaned forward and hugged his knees.

"Yes." My inner glow of pride that at least I'd tried faded under his scrutiny. "You can read the news tomorrow. The reporter got here later, after he…"."

"Here?"

"Yes, he called. Then, the other fires happened. And he didn't come right away, but he came later. Lila brought home a notice from school that it happened to someone's mother. Turned out it was Brandon's mother. Cindy. My Cindy. Doug told me on the phone."

"Doug? You sound like you and he know each other well."

I ignored that. "The reporter…when he called back because he was late… told me it was Cindy." I realized I was back in Bangalore in my mind. I heard myself pleading with him to believe me like I pleaded with the police back then.

"This feels like a horror movie."

"It feels very much like…"

He stood up. "We promised that, when we came here, you would not talk about that."

"I know…but…"

"Do you want our marriage to fall apart like it almost did back then?"

"No, of course not."

"Then let the police and fire department deal with this, okay? I don't want you to start butting in with their work."

"But Pete...we're in Hillston. There is no cultural context for women to set themselves on fire here, unless it's some sort of protest... not a stunt. I thought it could be that, a protest, then I heard about Cindy and I knew it was something else. She would never kill herself."

"So then it is someone murdering them?"

"Nobody knows anything. Nobody has any conclusive proof of what and how this happened."

"It's going to turn out to be some kind of serial killer. Remember that sniper in the D.C. area? He was a sharp shooter from the Special Forces, picking off people from nearly a mile away. They figured it out."

"Nobody can set somebody on fire from a mile away. That was a gun, this is burning to death."

"Watch. The police will investigate. There will be some connection between the three of them."

"Well, maybe. If they do, at least it won't feel like we're all in danger, like the mayor said."

He kissed me on the cheek. "I'm going for my run," he said. "Let's just have a peaceful family dinner with the kids."

"You can't skip your run for once?"

"What do you want me to do?"

"Help with dinner."

"You know I'm useless in the kitchen." At the door he turned back. "You see Dr. Gimpel lately? Maybe you need to talk to her about this. She helped a lot remember?" And he was gone.

Ages ago, Dr. Gimpel had showed me the newsreel I played and replayed in my life whenever I retreated emotionally, whenever I felt someone had failed me or I was on the verge of failing, and now, it whirled like an old 8 mm film in my head. I lay down again in my unmade bed and closed my eyes fighting my memory and my grief.

I had seen Dr. Gimpel weekly for that period after our return from Bangalore. She urged me toward yoga and meditation and my yoga teacher taught me to deepen my focus on the present, to look ahead, not behind, to ease the horror of the memory of watching Banhi die, to live as if each new day was my first. "The best path toward healing is to reach out and help others," said my teacher. And this started my sisterhood, first with Cindy Barrow, then a collection of new mothers, at home raising children after leaving careers. She and I had grown that group to fifty moms. NPR heard of us and featured us on "All Things Considered". Women and choices.

How much, I realized, now that she was not here, I'd always imagined Cindy and I would reconcile. I had not had the courage to attempt that reconciliation and now I would never have the chance.

I stared at the ceiling, listening as Pete stepped down the stairs, and felt a familiar hollow in my heart chakra. I flashed to Rehani's reaction to Banhi's burning. She was there in the kitchen. She watched as her daughter-in-law burned to death. And what loomed large in the present was Pete's reluctance to believe me right now which felt as dishonest as Rehani's response to Banhi's fate. That frightened me as much as the flame had and as much as the prospect of it happening to me did too.

I got up and went to the kitchen. My husband had tried to help. He had put the chicken in the sauce and stirred it, but he had neglected to light the flame under it. I turned the knob to light the stove. The gas didn't ignite. I did it again. Again, the scent of gas filled my nostrils. I shut it off. I twisted the knob one more time. This time, it lit like it had earlier, flame bursting around the sauté pan, flaring up and around with a whoosh. I pulled my hands away quickly and looked at Pete who had returned. "This needs some attention."

"That's what happened when I tried to light it."

I moved the pan to another burner. I showed him my arm with the singed hairs. No reaction.

"I want to grab a shower," he said. "Can you just finish cooking? I'll look at it later."

Lila emerged from her basement darkroom and, with a dramatic sigh as if she hadn't eaten in days, said, "Is dinner ready? I'm hungry."

She sat down with her sisters and in a moment was pointing out errors in their homework which they hurriedly attacked with their erasers. Their lack of defensiveness, their complete acceptance of her help was a pleasure to see. The way sisters should be, I told myself. I turned the chicken in the masala sauce, savoring the aroma lifting from the pan, and wished I could fix some of my own past mistakes as easily as they did their math. Pete joined us at the table. The green beans were a pallid green by then, but the chicken was ready and so was the basmati rice. I moved the sauté pan to the table and sat down to eat and found myself letting out a long sigh, "Oh, can someone please grab a ladle?" Pete didn't seem to hear me. Lila reached her long arm over to the drawer and slid the ladle out with a bit of clattering. She laid it next to the pan of chicken and said, "I hope it isn't too spicy."

"Please, let's just eat," I said. I lifted the lid and a puff of steam rose and the scent took me back to the evening when I first triumphed over this recipe with help from Banhi. I could see her hands, measuring with her fingers the spices she pinched or spooned in deliberate quantities while I furiously scrambled to write approximations in my notebook. For her, this recipe had no meat, just lentils and vegetables, and my Americanized version paled in the wake of my recollection of sitting down to her finished product with naan and chutney and basmati rice with cumin seeds and cloves. This meal was in its own condition of compromise and I felt my mood sink down and I knew I was going to sound very unpleasant if I joined in the conversation. Rarely an evening dinner at this table included Pete. I passed the plate of store-bought flatbread. I passed the green beans and I scooped into the sauté pan and served my children their portions.

I watched Pete. Here he was, the young man who stepped into my life and, well, it hadn't started with love. It started with me shouting at him from under the sarsens at Stonehenge to please step back onto the tourist's path, running toward him across the dig where my team was meticulously working in neatly drawn grids, roped off and numbered. Pete stood in the center of the blue stones with a camera, changing lenses, aiming at the largest lintel where the early morning sun was the most brilliant for it was nearly the spring equinox.

"I'm sorry, but you aren't allowed in here," I said.

"I'm a photographer," he said.

"There are professional photographers here all the time. They know to not walk in here. Their permit gives them strict instructions. Where is yours?"

"I'll only be a minute," he said. "Are you American?"

"No, you will not be a minute," I said. "Step back to the path, please."

He might have stood his ground and given me trouble, but he yielded. Then, he aimed his lens at me and took my picture. Then, he clicked another.

"Please stop," I said.

"Hold still," he said. "If you are American, what are you doing here?"

"Stop," I said, lifting my hands to my face. "I'm a graduate student. Archaeology. Please." I pulled the hood of my sweatshirt up to hide under.

"Have you found anything?" he asked.

"We're not looking for artifacts," I said. "They've all been dug up long ago."

"So what are you doing?"

"Research."

"Well I hope so."

"Please, I've got to get back to work. Stay on the path."

"Yes, Miss Keeper of the Stones."

I looked directly into his eyes. "Someone has to be."

"Would you mind if I looked at what you're doing over there?"

"There really isn't much to see and we're very busy."

"I'm sorry," he said. "I had no idea there would still be work here."

"Apology accepted." I returned to my work. I sensed his shadow moving off to where he should have been and I felt pleased and a bit relieved this had not turned contentious. This was not the end, however. We met later at the Peach and Thistle where he'd gone to wait for the local photo lab to develop his film. Phoebe, my roommate and assistant at the dig, studied him across the bar and turned to me. "He's not stopped watching you."

"Who?"

"Oh, right," she said. "Don't lie. You're watching him too. Your American."

Pete stood and Phoebe squeezed my leg. "He's making the first move."

But she was wrong. He left his empty glass and some money on the bar and walked out.

"Lost your chance," Phoebe said. "Really, Cassandra, I will have to teach you to flirt."

"I'm not looking for a man," I said. "I'm here to study."

"Right," she said. "You couldn't possibly do both, could you?"

But he returned and approached, offering me an envelope of prints. "These might just be something you'd be interested in," he said. The enlargements of those photos of the sun coming up over the largest of the stones still hang in our hallway.

Pete's laugh brought me back to the present. Yes, this was a family meal, suddenly bathing me in a glow of bonds and attachments. These are things that keep us whole. I let this well up from inside. Sometimes, life forces us to remain only in the present and lately it had been just that. But, when I was only in the present, I felt invisible. That part of me for which this life gave no opportunity for expression seethed. I knew I must fight to stop it from ruining this family dinner. Pete was always gone, always pre-occupied with business, always leaving me alone here. His photography was a hobby he indulged in England back then, back when I fell in love. He had been on sabbatical from his business development job at ISK, a high tech firm, which he still holds, now a sales vice president. He rarely has time to photograph us anymore much less be with us. Just this dinner, this simple Friday night of togetherness, even after my impatience with him and his required run, was the all-important present. But it felt off. It felt like Pete had pasted himself on the veneer of this family. I didn't feel the connecting tissue.

Pete was suggesting that Lila redo some photographs with a new roll of film. I hadn't heard all of what they'd just discussed, off as I had been on my daydream. She and Pete shared the photography hobby, not me, but I made a mental note to add film to my shopping list. She wouldn't use the digital camera. She said film was more artistic.

After dinner, while Pete and Lila cleaned up the kitchen, the idea of a walk beckoned me, but at the front door I paused. The sky was nearly dark. The park was glowing from the street lamps and commercial lighting from the stores on the other side of the train tracks. A few shadowy human shapes with dogs on leashes strolled on the path. This had been a moist day, an after the rain kind of day, and the mist had descended below the tree line so that while I watched, it thickened. Soon, the lights cast shadows of trees upon the fog and they looked to me like tree shaped cutouts in the light beams. I knew that if I turned to see shadows of trees, they would not be visible in the fog behind me, but only could be seen as silhouettes if I faced the source of light. Still, the idea of shadows of trees on a wall of fog intrigued me much like impossible things intrigue visual artists or writers of science fiction.

"Mom, you're not going out there," Lila called from the kitchen.

"Oh, please, Lila," Pete said. "If she wants to go out, I'm sure she'll be fine. I just ran five miles and I didn't burn up in flames."

"It's only the women burning, Dad," Lila said.

I listened as they launched into an argument, Lila holding her own, Pete assuming an authoritarian tone, as a man who knows best. It went on and I stood at my distance and listened. My twins had retreated to the living room and a DVD played loud enough to drown their ability to hear what was being said. I felt amazingly calm and remembered I'd taken a Xanax. I'd relied on the drug once before. Maybe I needed to do yoga again. Maybe I should pay a visit to Dr. Gimpel. Pete was partially visible in the kitchen and I felt a bit of a sinking in my viscera, remembering his earlier response to my need to talk. I shouldn't need a therapist for comfort, I thought. Then, the phone rang. Pete got to it before I did. He called to me and I lifted the cordless from its cradle in the hall and pressed the talk button.

"Hello?"

"Ms. Taylor?"

"Yes." It was Doug's calming voice. I felt a tightness leave my neck and shoulders at the sound. I turned to watch Pete hang up and that sense of a transfer of responsibility from Pete to Doug flashed as suddenly as lightning and was gone. Responsibility to soothe me. Only because Doug did it so easily while Pete did it hardly at all. It disturbed me. Stirred a mild irritation toward Pete. A sense that I must bring this to his attention.

"Your question," Doug said.

"Which one?" I asked, momentarily distracted.

"Did Cindy Barrow's clothes burn."

"Did they?"

"No."

I felt a long beat of silence pass and that beat was filled with acknowledgement for me. A small move toward knowing more about what just happened and it was because I'd paid attention and I'd asked.

"Well," I said.

"So now the police are questioning if she treated her clothes with a chemical and, if she did and if the other two women did, was this some sort of planned thing."

"You mean self-immolations," I said.

"That's right," he said.

"I think that is unlikely. Only because I can't believe Cindy would," I said.

"And why?"

"Because I don't believe Cindy would do that."

"When is the last time you spoke with her?"

I thought. "Three years maybe longer."

"A lot can change in three years."

"What about Elizabeth Lindsay, the school principal."

"Her clothes were unharmed too."

"So they're all the same." I pulled at my hair at the nape of my neck. It was an old habit when I was stressed out. I caught myself and stopped.

"When will they test the clothing?"

"It's being done."

"Okay," I said. "I wonder if the cops will close these up as suicides. I just can't imagine the Cindy I knew turning to something like this. She was smarter than that."

"I'm sorry, Cassandra. I'm sure this is upsetting."

"Does the mayor still think we should stay indoors?"

"He hasn't changed anything. He's on a plane home." Doug's next breath was deep and slow and audible through the phone. He was tired. I could tell. "Heffly and Richmond are holding a press conference in a few minutes. I've got to go."

"Okay," I said. "Thank you for calling." I hung up. That thank you felt so terribly ordinary. Now that I knew the answer to my question, I realized that the terror I'd shoved down deep into myself now rose up and through me like lava. It burned and flowed. My whole body felt hot, my hands sweating and my heart beating hard in my ribcage.

Pete could be right. It could be a cultish kind of stunt. It certainly wasn't a mass murderer trying to burn women with some kind of device like a long-range weapon. I imagined a new kind of bullet, they already had exploding bullets. Four men had died at the hands of a gunman at our local post office sixteen years earlier and he had used the exploding kind. Could there now be incendiary bullets that ignited and burned a body from inside? That's what she'd looked like this morning. Ann Neelam had seemed to burst into flame from her interior. Memory of how it tripped down her legs and out to her hands and fingers flooded me. I needed to stop thinking. I needed something else, something full of love and goodness to replace the fear and dread in my thoughts and heart. I joined Mia and Allie on the couch and immersed myself in their latest movie obsession, *The Wizard of Oz*, until the witch disappeared in a burst of flame. Once I saw that, I retreated to my bathroom, ran the faucet to fill the tub with bubbles, took off my clothes, and sank in up to my neck.

Later, Pete did his usual bedtime routine, undressing himself, brushing and flossing, and lying prone, neatly tucked under and plugged into his iPod with closed eyes, looking like a contented corpse. I arrived from Mia and Allie's room, having recited another chapter of *Peter Pan* in all its beautiful prose and imagery and after delivering kisses onto two drowsy foreheads. I kept my movements quiet. I let my own shorts and tee shirt drop to the floor. I slipped into bed. Pete rolled toward me and whispered good night.

Here was my marriage.

"Pete," my voice was soft, a whisper like the hand I was moving to him to make contact with his thigh, but he was into the music that faintly reached me in the otherwise silent night. He didn't respond. I rolled onto my side, facing him, and lay my hand on his chest. He started, gasped, and opened his eyes.

"Ah," he said. "What's wrong?"

"Take off the ear plugs," I said.

He did. He shut off the power. The small screen on the iPod went black. He didn't move otherwise. "I was asleep," he said.

"No," I said. "I could tell by your breathing."

"What?"

"Touch me," I said.

He lifted a hand and placed it over mine.

"No," I said, sliding my hand from under and rolling to my back. "Touch me, not my hand."

I took his hand and pulled him so he had to turn toward me. "Here," I said, placing his hand low on my body. He let his hand rest there. I rolled slightly and brought my lips even to his, leaned in. It was an awkward kiss, his nose bumping into mine, me turning myself to make us fit, and I felt his hand move up and around to my back at my waist. I moved my hand onto his thigh, moving toward him, then reaching back to bring his arm from around me, finding his hand, and guiding it, inviting him to my thigh, and he touched me and the jolt of it roused me to want more. I was letting the covers slide down and away from us. The room didn't feel so dark now and my skin was white and smooth and I noticed his eyes were closed. I lay my hand on top of his, to guide his fingers deeper to the spot I wanted him to find. Close, nearly there, he stiffened his fingers and pulled away.

"What are you doing?" he said. I opened my eyes and his were now staring into mine.

"I'm showing you what I want," I said, so very quiet, almost dreamily.

"Do you have to instruct me?" He pulled his hand away, rolled his whole self away, his back facing me. I sat up, I covered myself with the sheet, stripping it away from the quilt, and sat cross-legged on the bed with my elbows on my knees and my head in my hands. What swelled up in me at that moment was humiliation. I recognized it, I hated it, and at that moment I hated Pete.

"Tell me what is wrong with me showing you what I want."

"Maybe I don't want to touch you where you want to be touched," he said. "I was asleep. I had a long week on the road and I'm exhausted."

"So you don't want sex."

"No."

"Ever?"

"I didn't say ever. Just not now. You don't know, Cassie. You weren't up since five a.m. like I was."

"And this doesn't help you relax."

"I was relaxed. I was asleep, or nearly asleep."

"The kids will be up in the morning with the sun."

"We have to wait, Cass. You have to wait."

"I am always waiting, Pete. I wait all week for you. I wait, worrying about you on the road, about plane crashes, about not seeing you. I wait for hugs and this and for some love."

Pete rolled onto his back. "You don't have enough to do then."

"I am busy from 6:00 a.m. to when they shut their eyes."

He did not respond. I filled the silence with a series of ugly conclusions my mind shouted to me. I reached to the floor for my tee shirt and shorts and pulled them on. I left him there and found my way to the living room and the couch and all the words I had imagined I would say to him were no longer necessary because I knew he would not understand with or without the words. There were tears then and a heaviness under my ribcage and an anxious and sudden wave of a physical desire to be touched the way I had gently asked him to touch me. I pulled a pillow under my head, stretched out, and found the crocheted throw folded over the back of the couch and slid it over me. And, while sleep simply could not find its way through my racing heart, fear of this huge fissure cracking the ground between us did. I lay awake. My thoughts went again to that longing for the life I had let be replaced with this one and, although I had not done so in a very long time, I prayed against what my heart was trying to show me until the pale streak of sunrise shone pink through the large windows to the east.

"There may be a great fire in our soul, yet no one ever comes to warm himself at it, and the passers-by see only a wisp of smoke." - Vincent Van Gogh

CHAPTER 5

Saturday arrived with ragged edges of tension. I'd had my lions in the house dream again. The dream had visited often since childhood. In the dream I was at my childhood home in the midst of a party surrounded by extended family. But sliding quietly among the guests were lions, pawing up the stairs, lying on the floor in the living room. In my heart was panic. Nobody else seemed disturbed by their presence. I was shushed when I tried to bring anyone's attention to the danger. I urgently opened bedroom doors to lure them in and closed them off from the rest of the family. There were too many. Outside they roamed the neighborhood too. I knew they could pounce at any moment. The fear awakened me and relief flooded me with wakefulness. Returning to sleep took a long time.

I left the house and ran around the park, my shins smarting from the impact. I stopped in my tracks when a deer, silent and still, came into view in a brief stand of trees. A lone doe. Eyes on me. How unexpected. How beautiful and peaceful. Its grace was contagious. At my slowed approach, it headed up the gentle slope to a driveway on the road above the park and disappeared. I slowed to a walk for a final loop, returned to the house, and noted the twins in front of the television for the ritual of Saturday morning cartoons. Lila slept on weekend mornings, often until ten, and I did not see Pete so assumed he was showering, which is what I did in the hallway bathroom before I returned to our bedroom to dress. I called through the door and announced that I would be gone for a few hours, would he see to the girls' breakfast and clean up the kitchen. He asked, "What do they eat?" and that simple question was salt on a wound. I didn't tell him cereal and bananas and orange juice and a vitamin or that they sometimes enjoyed a warm cup of tea with milk and only a tiny bit of sugar. I simply said, "Ask them."

"Where will you be?" he asked.

"Not here," I said.

There were always homeless people at the library, a woman with a very large backpack, a man, long beard on a narrow face with a bright smile of white teeth with one gap where he stuck the tip of his tongue, as though it could fill up that empty space. He brought to mind my dreams of losing teeth I consistently had after Banhi died. In those dreams, it was always a healthy molar, white, clean but loose, and sliding out where my fingers were trying to keep it in place. Out it fell, leaving a gaping hole filling rapidly with purple blood.

He sat, gap-toothed, greeting the few early library patrons. She, the woman, was not at her usual place on the cinderblock wall. I saw her backpack, a pair of shoes, black, low, laced-up boots, piled there against the wall where she always sat. They were sometimes inside the library, at tables, with magazines or newspapers flat out in front of them, side by side, like a couple. It was odd to see him and not her. I'd never spoken to her, or him, but I did now.

"Where is she?" I asked.

"Gone, gone, gone," he said.

"Is she nearby?"

"Gone, gone, gone." His hands were up above his shoulders, straight out in front. His face turned toward the sky. "Gone."

Ten feet away, I could smell the stench of him as he moved his arms. I stepped back. His face contorted and he shouted, spit forming at the corners of his mouth. "Those shalt be for fuel to the fire; thou shalt be no longer remembered; for I the Lord have spoken it."

He fell to his knees and bowed his hands to the ground. I left him there, repeating his words, lifting his arms and eyes to the sky, and, with other library patrons, I stepped through the now unlocked door, full of self-reproach for having stirred this in him. His words rattled me. Her absence rattled me. She was always here when he was. Now only her possessions remained, like Ann's yesterday. His outburst, was it his way of saying he'd seen something? Had she been a victim also? Pressing him did not seem like a good idea.

I wanted a book. I wanted to lose myself in a story on a bench in the park, but we were not supposed to be outside. I selected a Margaret Atwood novel and checked it out at the desk.

It was peaceful at the library. It brought me back to my student days, all the hours of study, surrounded by shelves. I didn't stay. In a moment I was passing through the plaza again, the woman's things still not claimed by her. In a flash of unexplained benevolence, I returned to the circulation desk and asked if anyone had seen her.

"No. We actually let the police know she is missing. We are worried. If you do happen to see her, please call Sargent Finn at the Hillston station."

"How long?" I asked.

"How long what?"

"Since she's been seen," I said.

The circulation librarian turned to her colleague at the reserve desk. "When did you last see Helene?" she asked.

"Day before yesterday," said the brunette with very pink eyeglasses framing her brown eyes.

They exchanged a look that contained a sudden dawning. "Oh, God," said the first one.

"It fits the pattern," I said.

"Wouldn't the police put this together?" asked the reference librarian.

The first one left the desk and lifted the phone. She explained, "He can't really speak to us. Or he won't. She does all their talking. They might link her disappearance to the women who died in the fires. It may be nothing, right? But well, let's leave it to them to find out."

I decided I'd leave it to them. Heffly and his men or this Sergeant Flynn could put this together without me. I wanted to get away from this and from my own terror and my anxiety for the morning. If I didn't, I might burst into flame myself. On my way to my car I walked near her things, searching for gray ashes like I'd seen under Ann Neelam's clothes. Her gap-toothed friend intercepted me, waved in my face, and shouted as though I were a thief. I backed away without finishing my search.

"The world's flattery and hypocrisy is a sweet morsel:
eat less of it, for it is full of fire.
Its fire is hidden while its taste is manifest,
but its smoke becomes visible in the end."
- Jalaluddin Rumi

CHAPTER 6

I left the library. I worried about my re-entry to home and if Pete was doing okay with the kids and if they were doing okay with him. I told myself the cell phone in my pocket would ring if things weren't going well. And, just as my hand touched my cell phone, it vibrated. It was my sister, not Grace, but Lou.

"Hi," she said. As a ten-year-old tomboy Mary Lou had insisted we call her Lou. We still did even though she was in her late thirties. "Are you busy?"

"I'm out running errands. Is everything okay?"

"I'm having a garage sale. I wondered if you want to go through some of this stuff, see if you want anything."

"What stuff?"

"Old stuff. From childhood. Some of Mom's."

"When?"

"Now."

"Grace there too?"

"Yes. She helped me organize everything. I would have called you during the week but you work."

"I could have helped. The schools are doing standardized tests so we only had a few visitors."

"Wish I had known. Can you come?"

"You would know if you had tried earlier," I said. "I don't want you giving away stuff without me seeing it..."

"Yes, well, okay. Come over. I've got to hang up. People are arriving..." and she clicked off and I took off in the car.

Grace and Lou, that old familiar twinge of my otherness fired up as I drove. Saw horses blocked the sidewalk in front of our childhood home, the one Lou bought from the estate when Mom died. A Victorian, tall with a narrow driveway between it and the mirror image of it next door. Parking was already difficult, SUVs and Volvo station wagons at the curb all the way down past the bend in the narrow street. The bend separated two towns, Glen Brook and Hillston. Lou's house was just this side of the town line. Lou was at the sawhorses explaining the sale would not open for another twenty minutes. Grace was lugging a carton of books across the garage to a folding table covered with a plastic green tablecloth. I had been too hastily called to this. I rapidly took in the display tables, the rack full of clothing that looked familiar, and small end tables, chairs, and lamps Lou must have stored in her basement for these last five years.

Grace said, "Cassandra, can you lift this? My back is bothering me. I took an Advil but I can't do this kind of physical work."

"I can't believe you didn't cancel this," I said.

"What, the sale?"

"Yes, considering the danger. You do realize three women died yesterday. All outdoors."

"Once it's in the paper it's impossible to cancel. That's what Lou said."

"But they're telling women to stay indoors."

"I am indoors," she said, indicating the garage roof.

"But what about the customers? Isn't this putting them in danger?"

"That's their choice, Cassie," she didn't look at me when she spoke. "The mayor advised it, but it's not like an order."

"Do you have the garden hose hooked up yet?" I heard myself saying this, but I knew it might be futile if something happened again.

"Cassie," Grace said. "Stop. There won't be any self-immolating women here. There won't be any snipers with flame-throwers. We're safe."

But I noticed she would not leave the garage. Lou was doing all the work in the yard, uncovered and vulnerable.

I reached down and lifted the box for her and the flimsy table tipped and the box spilled at my feet.

"Well, at least this wasn't the tea pot collection," Grace said. "Or it would be in fragments...or what would you anthropologists call them, shards?"

"Where are the teapots?"

"Really, Cassandra, don't be so much in a hurry. Lou and I have been at this for days. Help me pick this up first."

I ignored her. I went over to Lou, "I want the teapots. They were my gifts to Mom. Where are they?"

She pointed. "On a table in there. There's a box and tissue for wrapping under the table."

I worked quickly. The crowd at the sawhorse barrier was growing. While I wrapped and gently packed up the collection, my eyes wandered to another table. Jewelry. "Everything must go," read a tent card with $5.00 each in parentheses.

Strewn on the table lay not only Mother's jewelry, but the jade, opal, and lapiz lazuli I had sent from India to my sisters for the holidays I'd missed. The gifts for Lou's wedding. The special piece of blue for her. All for sale. A heavy woman in a flowery peasant skirt was heading in my direction. With a sweep of my arm, I gathered all of it into my purse, letting the pieces tangle and fall to the bottom, into a dark pocket-like abyss, and grinned at her. "I'm one of the sisters who owns this stuff. I just changed my mind. Sorry." The crowd was now stepping quickly up the driveway, descending upon all these tables, in a mad frenzy. I went back to the tea set, finished the final cup, and slid the box under the table.

I needed to calm down. I felt hot despite the early morning cool air. Here was the collection of books Lou and I had shared, swapping mysteries in this very back yard on summer afternoons, reading in the shade before restlessness took over and we hopped on bicycles to the nearby park. Grace had just lifted the last one to the table and I saw them evenly distributed so the flimsy table would not tip again. My twins were just the age Lou and I had been when we read them.

A woman from the used bookstore on Glen Brook Avenue appeared and with a wave of her hand she told Grace, "I'll take this entire table. How much?"

And it was done. I wished for a clap of thunder, a sudden spring storm, torrents of rain, lightning, to appear, to wash this entire operation into an utter failure.

"There's another box," Grace said. "Want to see it?"

"I've already bought them," I said. I turned on my heel. There, under the old picnic table bench, was a plastic bin like the one in my attic with my dissertation notes. These were the bulk of the Nancy Drew mysteries and the Mary Stewart novels that inspired my anthropology path. *The Moon Spinners*, once a Disney movie, a novel about a woman who traveled and collected folk music from cultures around the world. There too was *The Source*, by James Michener, which fired my first choice of graduate work at the stone circles in England. The roots of it all, right here. No, these would come with me. And there, amid them, was something else. Something I had tossed in the trash decades ago. What on earth was it doing here?

I studied Grace from a safe distance, watching her charm a woman into taking a set of chairs in need of refinishing. I didn't recognize the chairs. They were veneer and could not be dipped or stripped of old finish without melting the glue holding the coating to the cheap plywood underneath. I said nothing. Just watched.

Here were the fragments of pages I had torn to shreds and tossed in the wastebasket in our kitchen years before. The cover of a black and white marble notebook, inked with pink doodles and my name and the words "do not read." There had been comments made with a thick marker in the margins and across the tops of pages, stick figures on the blank unused pages with balloons over their heads containing insults and mocking words. Ugly, pimple face, freak, and worse. Clearly Grace had read it and done this. I had torn it to shreds and dumped it in the trash basket. My journal. There it was, in with the books of my coming of age, in a plastic zip bag, bringing back painful remnants of my childhood. How had it got out of the trash and into this bag? I couldn't be there any longer. I'd been out here long enough. I lifted the box, hid the journal under the other books, and carried it to my car. I returned twice more for the teapots and a vase I had sent to Mother from England. I said, "Goodbye," and left.

I did not want to ask Grace why and how it had come to be among our books. Talking about it would give her a power I would not give. I was feeling enough throbbing of scar tissue already. I drove off, past the park where it had once been Lou and me riding bikes along those paths, Lou and me reading the books I now carried in my trunk. Lou and me, playing checkers and chess, swapping books, riding to the library together. Grace pre-occupied with her friend down the street, Lou and me collecting soda bottles for deposit pennies and saving enough to buy bottles of root beer and sipping them slowly as we read in the shade of our front porch, a contest to see who could make their root beer last the longest and finish her book fastest. Lou and me ended at age thirteen.

Lou, twelve at the time, was suddenly no longer my best friend but instead followed fourteen-year-old Grace everywhere. Grace refused to let me join their twosome. Mom had stated with firmness I couldn't challenge, "Go find friends of your own. They're different from you." I spent so much time after that in my tiny bedroom, my books, Natural History magazine, Smithsonian, National Geographic filling my mind and my time. That was perhaps when the roots of my dream of becoming an anthropologist took hold.

Sheffield was my Mecca, after that high school estrangement from my sisters that lasted through my bachelor's degree as a commuter from home. Sheffield was my landing after a turbulent flight, one of those experiences I describe as suddenly discovering that I was from another planet and here were others from my same home planet and here we all were. It was a sudden collective recognition of how we had come from elsewhere and now were reunited in a common cause. Fellow aliens as graduate students.

As I fled from Lou's house, my early flight from home was mimicked in the speed at which I drove through the streets with the bounty I had saved. My girls would love the teapots, they would adore the books and the jewelry. I felt a bit of guilt at my theft, but that was what hurt me the most. It was the thumbing of their noses at my kindness, my sharing of my world with them. These jewels had not cost $5 even in India where prices were low. There were mythologies associated with crystals and I chose for each sister with precision, for Mother also.

I wanted to be home. No matter what kind of pouting I might get from Pete, no matter if we launched into a fight, I wanted to tell him what I needed to say. This was my own home, my own safe haven, away from my sisters and their oblivious indifference, even now, so many years later. I suppose if it had been only one sister who was this way, it wouldn't be so bad, but with two, it was something so foreign to what one could expect from family. I had never really revealed the extent of this to Pete. I hadn't known how to talk about it to him. I had never told him how I needed closeness with him and what the void was that I wanted him to fill and how his always being gone left this emptiness more hollow that it should. Maybe now I could find the words to explain to him how much I needed him to be a different kind of partner for me.

The architecture of each neighborhood in Hillston reflected the town's growth through the century since the first railway station was erected to take bankers from their homes to their offices in New York City. I paid attention to all of it right now, in a way I could not when the kids were in the car. My sister's home was built in the 1890s. The gas lines for lighting were still in the walls and ceilings when my parents bought it in 1973. Small houses with front porches. The fashion had called for stained glass windows next to the main entry. The neighborhood seemed to belong to Glen Brook, not Hillston, due to Third River Park on Glen Brook Avenue. As I drove between the park's two sections of green, crossed over the river, I understood why Lou wanted to stay there. It was a secret little enclave, not yet discovered by the new people. The new people lived where the homes reflected growth in the years after the World Wars, larger properties, larger homes with center halls in the colonial style on wide avenues. More breathing room, more money and charm, each house uniquely different. I passed the park and the village where several storefronts were vacant, past one of Hillston's smaller train stations, this one with no station house, merely a platform and a few steps up to it. I came, to my surprise, to concrete barricades along the left. Backhoes and other earth moving equipment, still, like mechanized dinosaurs, were strewn about on the lawns of several homes. I hadn't passed this on my way from the library and, while I waited at a red light, I remembered the digs I had worked at Stonehenge. The roped off area seemed to be an entire block. Lawns were brown and lumpy, sidewalks looked as though they'd been lifted then replaced haphazardly. A once pretty block ruined, temporarily, I hoped. Whatever was being excavated, it surely was creating a disaster, just as May was bringing its blossoms and warmth. HPW, printed on the sides of sawhorses, told me this was not a private matter. I drove on while music filled the car. Folk rock, a good Saturday morning song. I let the song finish before I shut off the engine in my driveway. Before I turned the key and silenced the engine, a shadow moved near the back door in my peripheral vision. It was Pete. He was about to get into his car but hesitated as I pulled up. I wondered if he was waiting for me, worrying about me, hoping I was safe, considering the fires and the mayor's warnings. As I met his gaze in the side view mirror, he approached the car and I opened the door.

"Welcome back," he said. My study of his face was deliberate. My thanks were hovering there in the chasm between the real and my imagined next steps. My heart was literally holding up a yardstick and secretly, what demonstration of pleasure at my return registered on it was bound to steer us either further into conflict or back toward a sense of where we were on the continuum of our shared lives. I desperately needed him to be aware of the importance to me of what he said or did next. It was the most loaded minute I could remember and my fear was that it might be lost on him, the small fraction of responsibility he held in his hands for my happiness. I can't say now what might have been enough for me in that moment, what constituted a passing grade in the subject of marital love. I do know that after his rejection last night and the lack of regard for me by my sisters just now I needed a show of love. The newly open wound of that old diary incident had heightened my need for a gesture of contrition and conciliation. How deeply I needed this; it surely was visible to him in the smile I gave him, in the lightness of my step as I moved to the trunk.

"Can you help me with these boxes?" I asked, lifting the trunk to reveal the treasures from my past I had whisked away. I expected him to at least look at what I'd brought home. And I wanted something from him for which I could feel gratitude. From gratitude love is born and reborn in the long years of togetherness.

"Can you move the car?" he asked. "I've got to get to the bank and the cleaners before they close."

"Did you hear me?" I asked.

"Did you hear me?" he asked. "You've been gone. Lila took off. I need to get my shirts."

"I need help with this box. What did you do all morning?"

"Not much. Read the paper, breakfast."

"Where are the twins?"

"Still watching cartoons."

I lifted the box and carried it to him. "Here. Thanks. It's for them."

He took it, lowered it to the ground and straightened.

"Pete," I said. "You could have gone. You could have taken the girls with you."

"I wouldn't have to if you were home."

"That is precisely what I was hoping you would notice," I said. "That is exactly what I wanted you to say."

"Okay, well, I said it. So now, let's move the car so I can pull out."

"No."

"What is up with you Cassandra?"

"A lot."

"So are you going to tell me?"

"I did tell you," I said.

"If this is about last night..."

"Last night is only an example of what is wrong, Pete."

"I'm sorry Cassandra."

"Then why not say so?"

"I just did."

"No, you greeted me with 'move your car'."

"I didn't think you would still be mad at me since I let you go off by yourself."

"Let me?" I felt the inner tears threaten. A shiver of indignation. I turned and entered the kitchen and let the door slam.

Milk, orange juice, and three cereal bowls with a few floating Cheerios still on the table; coffee pot empty, but the red light glowing 'on'; a burnt piece of toast in the toaster. I marched past it all. Mia and Allie were still in pajamas, TV on; upstairs I dropped the novel and the remnants of my journal on my unmade bed and flopped down, fluffing a pillow under my head, rolling to my side, curling my legs so I was like a ball.

"I'm sorry, Cassandra." He was in the doorway.

"Do you know what you are sorry for?"

"No."

I waited. Surely he would ask.

"Give me your car keys," he said.

I reached into my pocket, found the cold metal, and let them fly to the wall where they made a huge sound and crashed to the floor. He took them and left.

"Among the notable things about fire is that it also requires oxygen to burn — exactly like its enemy, life. Thereby are life and flames so often compared." - Otto Weininger

CHAPTER 7

I lay there and willed him to return. If he didn't, I told myself, I would have to leave him. It wasn't the first time I felt that about Pete. The first time was Christmas Eve when my twins were not yet walking and Lila was seven and we were to spend the evening at his parents'.

"Please ask your father to not light a fire in the fireplace?" I had asked. We were hiding in the attic, wrapping presents for the girls as we did each year, the night before Christmas Eve.

"My father loves a fire on Christmas Eve."

"But we have two little ones crawling around and he doesn't have a grate. There are sparks and the twins don't understand the danger and might get too close."

"They'll be fine," he said.

"But I will be on high alert all night. I won't be able to relax for a minute."

"I'm not asking," he said.

"Then you're going to have to sit there and keep them away and make sure no sparks fly out and land on anybody."

"Not me," he said. "You're the one who's worried."

"Pete," I said.

"I'm not ruining my father's Christmas."

"No, but you just ruined mine," I said.

Here in my bed, I felt it all over again. Then, the phone rang. It was Pete. I felt a surge of hope. "I am taking a drive to the beach. I'll be home early tomorrow."

A dense black fog rose up and, like an insidious poison, began to fill up the veins leading to my heart, then, in my temples, a pulsing sharpness like an ice pick. I was alone. Mia and Allie sat downstairs, transfixed by cartoons. Lila was somewhere. I lay there, plotting my escape which I vowed would hurt him much worse than his indifference was hurting me. Mine would not be as simple as his. It would not even look like an escape. It would be something I could look back on as a triumph, an accomplishment, a reflection of how I would live the rest of my life, a role model, people would say, for those three daughters, such a strong woman, a triumphant story of a remarkable comeback. Mine would be entirely of my own making and would be a completion of all that I had interrupted. The downhill slide had been slow. My climb back would begin now.

I sat up, dried my eyes, blew my nose, and climbed the stairs to the attic. I could not lift the entire file box with all my dissertation notes, so with as much as I could carry at a time, I climbed down and up the collapsible ladder until I brought down the final stack. I re-assembled these stacks of typewritten sheets, these spiral notebooks full of my neat schoolgirl handwriting, carefully in chronological order. I rearranged the furniture in the small sun porch off my bedroom, cleared away any remnants of Pete having used it as his home office, something he pretended, a few years back, but never did. With the stacks of my old files of fading ink I claimed it as my own.

It was getting to be one o'clock, a longer morning than any other the twins had been allowed to spend in front of the television. I made a bowl of fresh tuna salad, poured two glasses of chocolate milk, then lured them to the kitchen with a promise of an outing to the park after they ate and dressed. Lila's note on the table said she was at a girlfriend's.

All the dads at the park were pushing swings, tossing footballs, catching tiny ones at the bottom of the slide, or clustered, drinking coffee and staring at cell phones on the benches in the shade. My girls ran off together and I sat with my Margaret Atwood novel on the bench in the shade where a panorama of the playground was possible. Bruce Gilbert landed next to me with 'hello'.

"Hi," I said.

"You were at the train, huh?" he said. "And I was in the woods."

"Cindy Barrows used to be my best friend. What happened? Can you tell me?"

He did. It mirrored exactly what I saw at the train, except he had no fire extinguisher or water. His face took on a furrowed look, the whites of his eyes seemed to grow while his pupils narrowed. He kept smoothing his hair back and I noticed sweat on his temples. "I couldn't do anything. The dog was there, barking and whining, look-ing at me. I never felt so fucking helpless. All I could do was call 911."

I said, "I covered that woman with foam from an extinguisher. She burned so fast I felt as useless as you say."

"You called me. I appreciated that," he said.

"Yes," I said. "But I also need you to look at my stove."

"I can stop by Monday."

"Thanks."

"Maybe you should be inside, like the mayor says."

"What about Pam? Is she hiding inside?"

"Spa visit," he said.

"You're a good husband."

"Or a fool," he said. Then, I laughed and so did he.

"Bruce, could it happen to men too? Just because it hasn't doesn't mean it can't." Or teens, I thought.

"It's only been women. Even if it can, you still shouldn't be outside."

He was right. I shouldn't be here. I shouldn't have left the house this morning. Grace and Lou shouldn't have been outside doing a garage sale. Cindy shouldn't be dead. Women shouldn't be bursting into flame and dying. Pete shouldn't be on his way to the beach. Nothing was right.

"I'd better spot Mia," I said. Mia was up the climbing wall. Allie was about to join her. Just a half a second too late and there she was, jumping to the ground, wiping dirt from her hands. Allie took off and Mia followed her to the swings.

"I'm watching your face, Cassandra," Bruce said. His boys were now trying to beat Allie's jump. "You could be a film actor. I saw about six different things flash in you in about as many seconds."

"Well, yes, that comes with this job, don't you think?"

"Yeah," he said. "But, when the fear goes away, there is something left in your eyes. And I get the feeling you're not okay."

I said, "Bruce, I'm fine."

"You might need a day at the spa for yourself."

"Don't be too nice to me. I don't think I could stand it." My eyes brimmed with tears. By now the girls were off near the duck pond. "I'm going inside. You're right. I must be crazy to be out here." I took off and my peripheral vision told me he was watching me and that gave me comfort. In the ground under my feet, as I jogged across the playground, I felt the bounce of that artificial turf and the earth underneath it felt a bit more like it was strong enough to hold me up.

When Pete returned, at noon Sunday, a hint of sunburn on his forehead and nose, when he emerged from our bedroom with his wheeled carry-on bag and briefcase to head out once again to the airport, to Chicago again, I watched Pete's automatic receiving of their kisses, barely accepted his perfunctory kiss on my cheek, and said, "Safe flight." His itinerary was held on the refrigerator door with a magnet and he was gone. After dinner, after I snuggled down on the couch with the girls for an evening movie, after tooth brushing, making of Monday lunches, and another chapter of *Peter Pan*, I slept in my bed, in the center of it, the blanket tucked under my feet, his pillow on the floor, and one under my head and another between my knees. There was my heart whispering truth to me...a question, the answer I could not pretend I couldn't hear, yes, I felt more alone when he was here than after he was gone.

"From women's eyes this doctrine I derive: They sparkle still the right Promethean fire; They are the books, the arts, the academes, That show, contain and nourish all the world." - William Shakespeare

CHAPTER 8

"Lila was just here," Ian said. I was in Holsten's storefront which had not changed since 1910. Same bright mirror, vintage ceiling, red covers on the stools. "You missed her. She was showing me some of her photos." He studied first Mia, then Allie. "Hey girls."

"How long ago did she leave?" I wanted to go to the sidewalk and check up and down the street. I could catch her and save her the walk home. I could save her from what I feared could take her from me.

"She was off to the park," he said. "Do the girls know what they want? It is going to get busy here." The bell on the door tinkled to announce the arrival of five girls, all carrying backpacks and all dressed in black jeans, white oversized tee shirts, and wearing black lipstick and heavy black mascara. Mia ordered a strawberry scoop with cherries and whipped cream, Allie, chocolate with rainbow sprinkles and just one cherry, no whipped cream.

Ian had babysat for me, Saturday night dates, Pete and me grabbing some alone time, until Lila reached babysitting age and took over. He dished up their treats making a little show of scraping large scoops, sprinkling their toppings and with a wink, presenting them. He then produced two long handled spoons and took a deep bow before winking at me and moving his attention to the group of girls in black and white.

"I forgot you," Ian said, returning. "Actually, you forgot you."

"Just a scoop of coffee ice cream and some hot fudge."

I sat on the third stool, slightly turned toward the girls.

"Here's for the invisible mom," Ian said. And he placed my small bowl before me.

"Invisible?" I asked. "Part of it was not wanting to overdo the calories."

"Indulge," he said. "Life is short."

"How's Rutgers' going?" I asked. "What year now?"

"Sophomore," he said. "Once, when we were younger, my brother Paul knocked over the refrigerator." He glanced over at the girls who were still staring at the menu sign. "Mom got so upset she walked out of the house. None of us knew where she went. So Paul and I picked up the refrigerator and all the stuff inside, well, it was all a mess so we made it right the best we could. Excuse me," he said.

I watched him make cones for the pack of girls. Allie happily shoveled whipped cream and strawberries into her tiny mouth and kept reaching for the aluminum napkin dispenser to wipe her cheeks. Mia seemed to be counting the number of sprinkles on each spoonful, careful to preserve enough so there would be some for every spoonful down to the last.

Ian returned. "So there I was. Mom stayed away for hours. Nobody knew where she went. It was getting to be dinner time."

I knew Ian's mom raised these six boys alone after a helicopter accident took her husband.

"So here we were, six of us and no mom, no dinner, no word. We got out some peanut butter and saltine crackers and a gallon of milk and sat in the kitchen and ate that for dinner."

Ian, I thought, you'd be a great bartender...one of those old-fashioned storytelling guys who serves up tales along with your drink.

"Then, around 8 o'clock, she just came back. And she said, 'I just went down to the park and read my book.' And that was that. She goes off by herself sometimes now, 'I'm going invisible for a few hours,' she says and we all just say, 'Someone make sure we have crackers and peanut butter.'"

The bell tinkled again and he positioned himself to take orders for a horde of teens. It seemed endless, the line of kids arriving now, and I waited for our check for a long time. Finally, I stood and moved to the register while Mia and Allie made fingerprints on the glass candy case along the rear wall. Ian waved me forward and I offered my credit card. Then, I dug out a five and slipped it into his hand. "Thanks, for the story especially," I said. "I will try not to be invisible."

He laughed. "My mom would like you," he said.

I was in the car before Mia reminded me about a sundae for Lila.

"We can surprise her another time," I said. "Let's get home."

There was no sign of Lila on the street or along the edge of the park separating town from Sycamore Ave. Ian had said 'the park'. If Lila had meant another park she would have said its name. But, if she'd been there, she was gone now and I expected she'd be home before us. But she wasn't home. The doors were still locked, the secret key in its place, so I settled the twins at the kitchen table, emptied their backpacks of crumbled papers and drawings, the remnants of lunchbox napkins, and one empty juice-box. Cindy was invisible now. Forever. So were Ann and Elizabeth. I called Lila's cell phone and cursed myself for not activating the location app on her phone.

I sat with the twins to get them started. The phone rang. I breathed fully when I saw Lila's cell phone number on the readout.

"Mom," she said.

"I saw Ian at Holsten's," I said. "I thought we'd see you at the park."

"Yeah. I saw him earlier. What has that got to do with anything?"

"Nothing. He just told us you were at the park. When will you be home?"

"What time is dinner?"

"In fifteen minutes. That's why I'm asking."

"Oh."

I didn't want to frighten her, but I wanted her indoors, not out in the sunshine, in the open. "Fifteen minutes," I said.

The scent of fenugreek and garam masala made me think of Banhi and her henna spotted hands at her wedding to Harshad. She'd been not much older than Lila when I met her, a young nanny to the British children across the hall from Pete and me. Banhi was frantic, that first morning, asking me for a roll of toilet paper and hurrying her little charges into my bathroom to use my toilet. She was small, with wide eyes, narrow nose, narrow face, white smiling teeth, and delicate hands.

"This family returns to England," she said. "And I need a new job."

"I've just arrived from England," I said.

"But you're not British," she said.

"No, American."

I made tea and sat at the round kitchen table while the children played in the small sitting room.

"I don't speak Kannada. But I am here to do field work. You can translate for me?" I asked.

"Field work?"

"Anthropology. Cultural studies."

"Oh." She perked up.

"I want to go into the slums and learn about the women of Bangalore and their lives."

"But your child," she said, looking at my bump that would soon become Lila. "You will need help?"

"Both," I said. "Can you help me with both?"

Her smile widened. She nodded. "Oh, yes."

In my Hillston kitchen I stood looking at the raw chicken breasts dripping in my yellow colander. The sauté pan sat there, waiting for olive oil, garlic, and onion. I turned the knob to ignite the gas. Tick, tick, tick and the scent of gas reached my nostrils. I turned it off.

Then back on. Tick, tick, tick, still no flame. On the third try, flame exploded on all sides of the pan. I drew back and so did it, shrinking back to its rightful size under the metal pan. Bruce Gilbert would have to get here soon before I set myself on fire. I set the gas to the lowest setting while I peeled two garlic cloves and chopped half an onion and tossed it all in the oil. Slowly, it reached a sizzle. The spices filled my nostrils again when I spooned them into the pan. Then, the greens, in long strips, a turning up of the heat and I turned control of this entree over to the goddess of the kitchen, remembering Banhi did this every afternoon of her life, after she spent hours grinding all the ingredients into powder first.

I washed basmati rice and boiled water. In a third pot I steamed some spinach in salted water for a single, carefully timed minute then drained it into a ceramic bowl. In India, the women of the slums taught me more than I ever imagined about food and cooking. Now, in my modern kitchen, with the flame safely under a sauté pan, I imagined myself in a squat position on a dirt floor, crouched over a kerosene stove, igniting the flame under my blackened iron skillet, my sari's flowing sleeves held just up from the elbow, while the match in my hand waited to ignite the liquid fuel. What was the singe compared to the women I'd seen with blackened scars up to the shoulder, as Banhi had the last day I saw her? The simple act of preparing the family meal might, in a single second of distraction, take their lives. In India, the domestic lives of women had fascinated me. Here, I felt tied to a ritualized schedule of everyone else's needs. Be present, said my yoga teacher, be mindful of the fullness of each moment. I was. And, while I reached for the plates and napkins to set on the table, squeezing them into positions next to Mia and Allie's papers and books, I imagined doing what Ian's mom had done. I imagined the response I would receive. If Lila were here, I just might.

Lila burst through the back door. Mia and Allie put down their pencils at the exact moment and, with their syllables just off rhythm with each other, said, "You missed ice cream."

"Mom," she said. "Can you come downstairs? I need to show you something? Something is up with my camera."

"Lila, did you see Brandon at all today?"

"No, he's still in middle school."

I'd forgotten. They weren't a full year apart in age, but they were a full school year apart. Of course, he wouldn't be in school. I went to the basement darkroom. It was cool, dim. I'd tried to pull her out of there so often to get some fresh air, to be outdoors. She switched on her light table and showed me a roll of film negatives.

"This is a fundraiser project we're doing for the camera club and these are pictures I took of some of the moms of some of our members and look! They are all blurred with this white cloudy something and the negatives are useless." She showed me and kept talking as only she could, a long, run-on sentence without pauses, with a recitation of what type of film she was using and how the developer and stop bath chemicals were brand new. She was sure she had not exposed the film to light when she loaded the camera or when she took the film out of the camera. There were five so far and she had appointments with about ten additional families and this was all supposed to be done for all of them by Mother's Day.

I put my hand on her arm. "Lila," I said. "Just be quiet for a minute. Let me think."

She kept talking. "I came up with this idea. Family portraits. We are charging the families twenty-five dollars and we develop them and enlarge them to eight by tens and the students give them to their parents, their moms, for Mother's Day or their dads for Father's Day. Everyone in the freshman class seems to be signing up for this. Even kids at the middle school."

I could see the blurred center of the photographs. "You'll have to redo all of these," I said. "But maybe Dad can figure out why it happened so it won't on the retakes." Lila's camera was the same one Pete had in his hand when he first crossed my dig at Stonehenge. She'd inherited his hobby.

"Maybe the film is defective. Maybe the camera has a crack where light can get in. You didn't drop it, did you?

"No."

"It's probably expired film. Do you check dates on the rolls?"

"Well, yeah, Mom," she said with exaggerated patience. "It's not like it's easy to redo them. I've got to go back to all these kids and make appointments again."

"You can't correct them with the printing?"

"I guess I can try," she said with a sigh. "Is dinner ready? I'm hungry."

We ate. Nobody asked where Pete was. But I noted his absence since Lila needed him right now. He knew tricks for correcting exposure errors on photographs. He was a genius at it back in the early days. That first night at the Peach and Thistle he had handed me that envelope of photographs. "Here you are, Miss Keeper of the Stones," he had said. "A gift for you."

I'd opened the envelope which was rather thick with prints.

"There are two of each," he'd said. "Take the ones you like."

He and Phoebe looked over my shoulder as I studied them. I admired the scenic shots, with rays of the sun silhouetting the lintels as though divine power descended from on high. Really, I could almost imagine angels taking up residence amid the ancient stones. Phoebe showered Pete with compliments. They were beautiful and I nodded my appreciation.

There I was, with my hands on my hips, looking indignant. Then one he'd taken of me as I had turned to resume my work. In context, it was a perfect depiction of me with my roped off grids barely visible in the background. At dinner, I suddenly put down my fork and remembered. He had seen it first and pulled the print from my hand. "Look at that," he said. "Something isn't right."

In the brighter light under the lamp at a nearby table, he drew my attention to a flaw, just like the flaw Lila had just lamented in her own negatives.

"Bad film," he'd said. "What a waste."

He pulled out his negatives and held them up to the light. He swore and blamed the photo lab. But, the next evening, while we again descended upon the Peach and Thistle, he relayed his visit back to the developing lab. The owner said this often happened at the Stonehenge site. He said the locals spoke of an ancient energy that seemed to object to photography. They likened it to a ghost story and he'd suggested Pete retake his photos after the spring equinox had faded by a few days. That had kept Pete in town long enough for he and I to find the beginnings of a friendship, a loosening of my grip on the rules about photographers requiring permits to step off the path, and for me to accept an invitation for the first dinner alone, which carried us through to dawn in deep conversation about just about everything under the sun. A few nights later, he spent the night in my bed. And, a few nights after that, he postponed his plan to train to Prague and became an unofficial member of the exploration team.

Enlargements of the prints he retook a week after those first defective ones lined the wall of the stairway in our front hall to this day. Somewhere in my box of field notes and papers were those original damaged prints.

After dinner, I dug through until I found a yellow Kodak envelope and there, tucked into a side portion of the envelope, were the negatives from those first shots.

I stepped down to Lila's basement darkroom and used her light table to study them. Yes, the same dull blotches across the film's center, every last exposure in the roll.

It wasn't the spring equinox right now in Hillston, but for a moment I wondered if what I'd told Lila wasn't true. Perhaps it wasn't defective film or expired film. I believed her when she said she hadn't dropped the camera. There was something too similar for me to dismiss this as simple coincidence.

"Lila," I said. "Check Google if you can't reach Dad to ask him."

She nodded. "I'll send Dad an email."

"You could call him," I said.

"I always get his voice mail," she said. "He reads his email. I don't know what he does with my messages."

"In order to rise from its own ashes, a Phoenix first must burn." - Unknown

CHAPTER 9

I was crossing the park, carrying my usual tote bag and nodding good morning to fellow commuters, stopping near the newspaper dispenser to read the headlines in the *New York Times*. There it was, three portraits of the dead and the words Hillston, New Jersey. There was Cindy Barrow, right there between the two others. I stared at the faces of the three dead women, but I could not make myself slip in coins and buy a copy to take with me. That would have been too much. The train arrived and I climbed aboard and took a seat. I congratulated myself for stepping through this place and not turning to flee back home. I did not look up and was grateful that nobody spoke to me. Even the conductor, my partner in my failed attempt to save Ann Neelam, simply glanced at my monthly pass, touched my shoulder, and said, "Good morning" as he moved down the aisle.

It was turning out to be a good morning. The drizzling rain was finished by the time I arrived in Newark. I walked the three blocks to the museum along University Avenue past the Halal butcher shop, shuttered and dark, and the Good Will Mission where recovering men stood smoking and talking to each other in low tones. It was a good morning for me, not for others, but I felt the gratitude appropriate to this realization.

Cindy's boy, Brandon, was the age of the kids who arrived at the South Lobby. This group was from Jersey City and they were orderly and polite, all wearing red tee shirts with Egyptian hieroglyphics across the front.

Eric, my fellow teacher, set up the Asian gallery while I pulled a cart from the closet to the Egyptian hall.

I had seen the British museum's Egyptian collection while I was in graduate school; Pete and I had spent a weekend in London before Pete was off to India. The Newark Museum's collection was miniature in comparison, but it told the story, object by object, of the pharaohs and their burial rituals, enough here to entice the kids. The sarcophagus was the focal point, painted with symbols significant with meaning for the mummified human inside. This one was empty now, of course, but its highly stylized hieroglyphics revealed it belonged to a songstress, Henet-Mer who sang at the court of a pharaoh.

Pictures on the gallery walls illustrated the rich fertile land near the Nile, the wide stretches of desert surrounding it, the rise of agriculture as the river overflowed each year allowing this culture to remain in one place, unlike nomadic peoples who roamed the desert with herds for subsistence level existence. I'd taught this program so often I made it a point to add something new to my presentation each time or to change the order in which we did the usual activities. Today, I gave them the first few minutes to wander this small room on their own, to read the descriptions, to write down questions for me.

"Eighth graders?" I asked their teacher.

"Seventh," she said.

Brandon is in eighth. Cindy is dead. Brandon is now motherless. A boy with Brandon's same thick dark blond hair stared through the glass, his back to me. For an instant, he was Brandon, then he spun around and moved across the room and became a stranger again.

I followed him, trying to get the Brandon feeling back. But this was not helpful. I would see him soon at the funeral. And I knew that my showing up there would bring him pain. Cindy and I had taken our young ones to zoos, to parks, to the museums in New York, handing them sketch pads, sitting them in the sculpture garden at the Met with crayons, pencils, watched them draw what they saw. We had betrothed them to each other so we could be in-laws.

I pulled myself back to the present. I took their questions one by one. Standard stuff. The mummified falcon first. The process of mummification. Why a falcon mummy? Hunting in the afterlife by the dead king. Why the canopic jars? Embalming involves the removal of certain organs, even today. Chills and shivers from these kids. The story of Osiris, Isis, their son Horus, begotten with Isis after Osiris' death and his assumption of the role as ruler of the afterlife, the underworld and the dead.

I explained how the pharaohs believed they too, like Osiris, would rise up from the dead and all the tombs and all the burial objects were a result of that belief that there was a life following this earthly one. To be prepared for the afterlife was the work of all of us while we were still here. I drew comfort from this. It felt like a sermon I needed to hear, about how life goes on after death, the universal thread of belief that there is perhaps something better than this life awaiting us. I was paying silent homage to Cindy, to the other women who died, even to Banhi, feeling comfort knowing all their souls had traveled somewhere without their bodies. All this, secretly, under my words for the school children.

Then, a dark-haired girl, who pushed her thick framed glasses up her nose and sniffled before she spoke, asked, "There is a big bird with its wings spread wide on the sarcophagus."

I pointed. "That is an image of the mythical firebird. You all have probably heard of it before."

Some turned their heads, eyes toward the teacher with a question. She said nothing, just looked at me with a slight nod.

"The Egyptians called the mythical bird Bennu. In other parts of the world, she is called by different names," I continued.

A hand went up. "Dumbledore called it Faulkes. It lived in a nest in his office at Hogwarts."

There was a chorus of mumbles and shouts and a few "oh yeahs."

Another myth of fire, I thought. They're everywhere.

"The myth of the phoenix is that it was the only one of its kind and it lived in a tree in an oasis in the Egyptian desert for its entire lifetime. Its life was 500 years long."

The girl with thick glasses chimed in, "It lives to be 500 years old? This can't be true. Can it? Can a bird live that long?"

"What do you think?" I asked.

"Well, tell it all to us," said a boy. "And we'll decide."

"The bird grows weak and old and, at the end of its long life, it asks the god of the sun. Who is the god of the sun?"

"Ra," they all chimed in.

"The phoenix asks the god of the sun to make it young and vibrant again. At first, the sun god says nothing. So the bird gathers up wood and sticks and builds up its nest. Then, the bird ignites in flames. All that is left is a pile of ash." I paused for effect. "But the nest and the tree do not burn. Only the bird." The teacher and I exchanged glances. Her eyebrows lifted. A sudden wave of sweat broke in my armpits and my neck felt warm. "So the bird, the only one of its species, is gone." Like Cindy, one of a kind, I thought. Just like that.

"In the movie, the phoenix does that, but a baby bird is born in the ashes," said someone.

"Yes, the phoenix rises up out of the ashes of its dead body as a new baby bird and quickly grows with purple and red feathers into its former self."

"Cool."

"Then, it gathers up all the ashes and forms an egg from all the remains of its former self. It takes up the egg and carries it to the city of Heliopolis, the city of the sun god, and offers the egg to Ra as a sacrifice to show its gratitude." I paused again, then finished. "And it lives for another 500 years and the cycle happens again."

A few kids clapped their hands. The girl with glasses said, "Well, that can't be a true story. No way can the bird burn up like that and not have the nest or the tree go up in flames with it."

"The story is a myth. It isn't true. It's just a story," the boy who looked like Brandon said. "So then it isn't important."

I said, "But myth usually tells something about the people who keep these stories alive. I want you to understand that the ancient people of Egypt knew a lot of things. They may have known some things that we don't know anymore. For example, some important science or engineering knowledge that got lost somehow or maybe was discredited by a king or a pharaoh."

"Like how to build pyramids," the Harry Potter fan said.

I nodded at him. "Myth was the first way humans explained how the world came into being. Creation myths tell the story of how the world became created. We have the big bang theory now and ways of looking into deep space the ancients didn't have. So we know more than they did. They asked the same questions back then. And the only answers they came up with weren't based on the same science we have now, but on what they could observe in their world, in nature, in the sky."

"But who observed a phoenix bird burning up and a baby coming out of the ashes?" the girl with the glasses asked.

I pointed out the pictograph of a dung beetle holding a circular disk in its hands. "The Egyptian god Khepri who brought the sun to the sky every morning was a dung beetle. It symbolized the beginning of new life and the beginning of every new day in the world of the ancient Egyptians."

They all pondered that quietly for a moment. "The ancient Egyptians thought dung beetles just came to life out of piles of dung from the animals. They didn't have microscopes, so they didn't know that the dung beetles laid their eggs in piles of dung and that's why the beetles were born and crawled out of heaps of animal dung."

We all laughed together at that. It did the job. They understood how wrong conclusions can come from partial information.

"So then there is a mystery here," said the girl with the glasses. "Where did the myth of the phoenix bird start? What mistake did they make that created that myth?"

A tiny boy, quiet until now, sitting in the back row with his platinum blond bangs covering his face, his shoulders hunched over said, "Maybe they burned birds as sacrifices to their gods. Maybe they made it up so they would feel better when the birds died."

The teacher and I again exchanged glances. The teacher said, "I think you are getting the idea. Myth makes us all feel better about a lot of things. It serves a purpose so even if it's made up, the people felt better believing it than if they didn't. Many cultures believe the soul lives on even if the body is empty and still or gone."

"Science is better," said the boy. "It can be proven. Myth is just a story."

My next stop was a statue of Shiva in the India gallery. I had a lot of history with this god of destruction. This Shiva was in his dance, his left leg raised and his right leg firmly below him, subduing a demon beneath it while the flames in his halo represented Agni, the god of fire. Shiva's four arms wave and carry objects.

"Shiva is the Hindu god of destruction," I told them. "He is part of a trinity with Brahma the creator and Vishnu the protector."

The teacher whispered to me, "We've got ten minutes until we have to be on the bus."

I nodded. "Shiva carries things in his hands. He's got a trident in one, a drum in another, a snake draped around his neck and his other hands are moving in his dance. And he has a third eye. Shiva is the god of destruction, but he also is a force that brings things to an end so that new life can begin." I paused. "So he is a perfect one to end our visit. Remember today and the lessons of the phoenix and Shiva. They both remind us that, when things end, something new always begins. I'd like to thank you all for your attention. Please come back and visit us again."

"I'd like you all to thank Ms. Cassandra for her tour today," said the teacher. They stood and applauded.

With their thundering feet behind me, synapses fired within my brain and awakened my thoughts of Shiva the god of destruction.

"The lotus flower is troubled. At the sun's resplendent light; with sunken head and sadly, she dreamily waits for the night." - Heinrich Heine

CHAPTER 10

I stepped into the tiny lunch room for museum educators and unwrapped my lunch. Shiva had become a demon for me after Banhi's death. Those statues of him planted outside tiny tin shacks in the slum, the glare of women as I passed. The refusal to look directly at me. Their hostility is what led me to the women's center at Rajendra Nagar despite Banhi's earlier caution about engaging with the woman who ran it. I went after Banhi's death, seeking assistance so that I could continue the work I had begun. Banhi had said, "When women go there, their families refuse to let them return to their homes." It was only after I had nothing left of my work that I had approached this ramshackle building on the edge of the slum and stepped through the front door.

I got the feeling at first glance that the woman there had been expecting me and that my visit was not completely okay with her. Lila was in the backpack playing with my hair, tugging at it, and I was holding my neck stiffly upright. My shoulders felt tight. Lila was growing and soon would be too heavy to carry this way. The woman who greeted me wore a bright yellow sari and peacock blue sandals. She wore her hair pulled up and back and held with a brightly jeweled clip. Her eyes, wide and brown and unsmiling, met the sight of me with a frozen frown. She pointed at an inner door and, in rapid Kannada and with fluttering hand gestures, she practically shooed me in, her glance around the room furtive, and I knew she didn't want any of the few women in the small waiting room to see me.

A worn Persian rug over the concrete floor, a ceiling fan whirling with a slight hum, a comfortable chair with two embroidered pillows casually tossed there, and a sofa, very worn brown velvet in a dark wood frame with legs shiny with polish despite the nicks and scrapes from years of use. I waited, obedient to that woman's directive because I needed her, desperately.

She closed the door softly. She took the chair, lifting the pillows and placing them on the floor and Lila went to them immediately and sat. She smiled at Lila and my sense of her severity of attitude and hostility toward me lightened. "Yes, Ms. Taylor," she said in perfect English. "Why have you come? Why now?"

"I had to," I said. "No one will speak to me or raise their eyes to even look at me. I need someone to explain why."

"Without Banhi, you are a stranger here," she said. "You must start over to regain trust. She leaned forward, "What did you do to break it?"

"I did what I thought was the right thing to do."

"And what was that?"

"It is what anyone would do. I saw my friend was in danger. And she was in danger because now she's dead."

"And why did you think she was in danger?" she asked me in a voice so soft I could feel my defensiveness dissipate in response.

"Rehani hit her in the face. And she had a burn on her arm that needed medical attention. Banhi shouldn't be subjected to a person who mistreats or neglects her like that."

"Says the American." She continued after a slight pause. "You say your work is anthropology, so you need to stick to just that."

I returned her gaze. "What is your name?" I asked. "I don't know your name."

"I am Geetha Narajaran," she said simply.

"What do you do here? What does this center do?"

"We are a refuge for women. We help educate and we offer counseling and nutritional coaching." Geetha lifted her chin and tilted her head and blinked. "And what are you doing exactly? What is your work in Rajendra Najar?"

"Studying the culture," I said. "For my doctorate in anthropology. Banhi thought I shouldn't come here. She never said why."

"She came here once. She didn't come back."

"Did she need help?"

"There is confidentiality in our work," she said.

"Yes, I respect that. Can you tell me if Rehani ever came here?"

"No, I can't tell you." She said this with a tinge of impatience. "I have people in my waiting room. I can't keep them waiting too much longer."

I felt a momentary beat of silence pass. My thoughts were not gathered.

"Did Banhi have a bad experience here?"

Geetha stood up and smoothed the skirt of her sari down across her thighs. "I like to think women do not have a bad experience in our center."

I said, "She asked me if she could work for me again, then she ran back inside. That's when the fire took her life."

"Don't you see?" Geetha said. I could feel her impatience dissipate. She stopped glancing toward the door and kept her eyes on me. "She must follow the role she accepted at the time of her marriage."

"Banhi was so eager to work when she was my assistant. Women should have some choices. They should have the freedom to make them. Don't you think? And, when they're injured, they should have medical attention, not be left to let infection kill them."

Geetha sat down next to me on the long couch. She took my hand. Her disapproving tone changed and I heard, "Ms. Taylor, should, should, should. These are your American shoulds. I'm going to tell you what you need to know about the women who live in Rajendra Najar."

I listened.

"Do you know what binds us together as a people?" Geetha asked.

"Isn't it love and family and shared beliefs?" I asked. "Hindu beliefs?"

"It's poverty that binds us," Geetha said. "And caste."

I felt my assumptions dissolve and a wish that I had come here earlier. "Why wouldn't Rehani allow Banhi to work with me and earn money for the family?" I asked. "She would still be a member of her caste. Rehani worked doing laundry."

"You encouraged Banhi to be more than she is. That is dangerous. Rehani knew that. Banhi's father knew that too. Why do you think it took him so long to allow you to find her here? If Banhi continued to work with you, she would be forever disenchanted with the role of wife," Geetha said. "Discontent breeds and disrupts the family."

"But the solution to poverty is work for pay, don't you think? And the solution to an injury is medical care. No matter what the culture dictates."

"But it is Harshad's role to take on that responsibility. Banhi's role is to support him. If Rehani allowed Banhi to work and she was to bring in more money than Harshad, Rehani would be shamed."

"But they would all gain from earning. If poverty is to be overcome, isn't that what they all should strive for?"

Geetha's brow wrinkled. "Dear Ms. Taylor, did you attend their Kalyanam?"

"The wedding ceremony? I did," I said.

"So you know the circling of the fire."

I nodded.

"And what purpose does it serve? Do you know?"

I said, "I know they circle the fire seven times."

"Fire is sacred in this tradition. The Hindu god of sacred fire is Agni. The fire at the wedding is Agni and the promises they recite to each other are witnessed by the god through the presence of the flame. The groom first says 'you will offer me food and be helpful in every way. I will cherish you and provide welfare and happiness for you and our children.'"

Geetha continued, "The bride then says, 'I am responsible for the home and all household responsibilities.' They each take seven turns to promise and seven turns around the sacred fire." Geetha said, "Ms. Taylor, do you see a pattern here?"

"They're defining their roles in their relationship."

"Yes, and it is the marriage contract. It is what each relies on the other for through the entire marriage. Do you see how Banhi leaving and going with you to the hospital would have been a breaking of her vows? Especially after Harshad had asked her not to go?"

"Harshad would consider the marriage vows broken?" I asked.

"Yes," Geetha said. "To say nothing of his shame from feeling your judgment of him. He would be free from his promises to her if she broke hers. And do you know what happens to discarded wives in India?"

"They're out on the street. They turn to prostitution. But Banhi would never have done that. She would work for me. She could get a job and support herself."

"Not if she is a runaway bride. Her father and mother could not take her back. Her leaving Harshad would have shamed them."

"She told me she came here once and that the center helps women have hope."

"She left saying the only hope she wanted was that her marriage be good and that she have children."

I pondered this, moving back over the moments of that day, so vivid in memory, of Banhi's words, whispered about how Rehani and Jayant slept between her and Harshad. No children would come; her role would stay as a servant. What she really wanted was what she married for. But as long as it was still withheld from her, she would remain in between her old life and what she had expected to be her new one, her married one. Rehani held her hostage. More mouths to feed would drain the family? Was that the reason they slept between them?

"And Rehani," I said. "Tell me why she was here."

"You are persistent, Cassandra. She came to get Banhi and bring her home," Geetha said evenly. "Usually, when young girls come here, their mother-in-laws refuse to take them back into their home. Rehani didn't refuse Banhi. She brought her back."

"But you saw nothing once Rehani brought Banhi home."

"Yes," she said. "That is true. What happened after that is between them."

"Then, I showed up."

"In Hindu it is believed that you live with acceptance of your circumstances in this life. You find peace within those circumstances. Your ability to do that earns you your next incarnation as a step up the levels of existence, to perhaps an easier life, but death must occur first."

"But Banhi was educated. Her father allowed her to work for me."

"That doesn't mean he liberated her from her life's path." Geetha stared into my eyes. "Perhaps he arranged her marriage so he would end your influence on her. Maybe he feared for her and the path of marriage would keep her in her world and not allow her to step further into yours."

"He did arrange the marriage when I was back at home."

"It is the internal conflict, the friction in her soul, between what is and what might be. That is where Shiva, the god of destruction dwells. It is he who decides what gets destroyed to make way for the new. That is why the women placed their statues after her death. Shiva took over where you were once the factor in Banhi's life. Better that Banhi marry and stay in her community. Better Banhi be in the hands of Shiva and let the sacred fire of Agni take her than see her life become even more difficult with what you were trying to do that you sincerely believed would help her."

"I still want to know who lit the match," I said. "Sacred fire or Shiva, there was a cause for her to burn, a physical cause. Ascribing a spiritual explanation to it doesn't change the fact that someone took action that led to her death. The police wouldn't go near this. Why?"

"Because nothing can bring her back," Geetha said. "Investigating can only hurt someone who is still alive." She paused to study my face, to check my comprehension of this. "You are an American. It is hard to assimilate this reasoning. If someone other than Banhi struck a match and doused her with kerosene, karma will cycle back to even out the consequences."

"So there is no punishment for dowry deaths." I stated this as a challenge.

"There is punishment enough," she said. "Grief is the punishment. For Harshad for whatever he did not do. For Rehani who must live with what she knows. And, for you, Ms. Taylor, for the unintended consequences of your best intentions."

"It is an heretic that makes the fire, Not she which burns in't." - William Shakespeare

CHAPTER 11

As the train carried me to the museum next morning, each lurch stirred up regrets and grief. I must call Derrick. Would he speak to me? Surely, he would welcome my sympathy at this awful time, release me from the silent treatment Cindy had given me for the last five years.

Cindy and my quarrel had begun after lunch, on a day I watched Brandon for her so she could go to the office of the Institute for Philosophy for Children. She pulled out the pamphlets about Spencer Krump and asked me to read them. Cindy was in such a sensitive state at that time, having just lost her mother, I didn't tell her what I thought of his ideas, not at first, not until she made a suggestion for Krump's visit to our mothers' group meeting. Krump taught and practiced Essen therapy. According to Krump, she told me with much excitement, Essen is a life-giving energy beneath all things. Essen could be accumulated in the human body by simply sitting inside an Essen accumulator – a box made of wood and lined with alternating layers of wire mesh and linen fabric.

After that day, when I'd babysit for Brandon, she stopped using that time to go to the Institute for Philosophy for Children or to the gym and instead sat in her box, alone and in the dark. It reminded me of Banhi, after her marriage, required to stay indoors, inside that corrugated tin hut in the slum, not allowed to leave unless she was accompanied by a man. I told her, "You don't sound better. Stronger maybe. But you sound so ready to anger."

"I am stronger. So you can stop all your pity."

I remembered all of this like it had just happened. It really had been five years since Cindy and I had spoken. Five years since we stopped pretending that the group was still a cohesive whole after half the group split off and followed Cindy, leaving me with a similar group of loyal followers carrying on as usual.

The train pulled in and I found myself hurrying past the platform, eyes averted from that spot where it had happened, a flashback threatening to consume me the way the flames had consumed Ann that dreadful morning. At home, in the few minutes before it was time for the school bus, I sat and Googled Lila's problem with her film. This distracted me and helped me to focus on the now. The film malfunction possibilities were intriguing and I printed several sheets of information.

I jogged across the park to the school bus knowing I still had to call Derrick Barrow. I could not skip this duty. And, in the sunlight that filtered down through the leaves overhead, I wondered if I was in danger being outside or if the mayor was wrong. The park was deserted. At the bus, the women who usually walked sat in cars waiting at the curb. I knocked on the window where I saw Dolores, the nanny for the Brennan family down the street. She smiled her wide white smile and flipped the lock on the passenger side for me to slide in.

"I will drive you home," she said. "Why didn't you drive over?"

"It's such a short distance," I said. "I didn't think."

"Well, Mama, you'd better start thinking. You don't want to leave those little girls alone on this earth." Her eyes were smiling, but her tone was reproachful. "Life is hard enough to not have their mother."

Dolores carried a set of rosary beads twined around her long slender fingers.

"It's a portal to a different world," she said. "These burning women are slipping through. You do not want to slip through. You will not find your way back."

"Dolores," I said, "is that what you believe? Really?"

"I cannot believe anything else," she said. "They are here one minute and gone the next. They leave their clothes as though they can return. Some believe they are listening to the voice of the devil and there you go. No good comes of listening to that devil's voice. You have heard the Bible passage…two will be grinding at the mill, one will be taken, the other left… The taken ones are choosing wrongly."

"You think they're choosing this?" I didn't quite believe what I was hearing.

"On a spiritual level, maybe. Think of the pain. Nobody but Satan would inflict such a thing. He turned their faces and enticed them, then, as soon as they listened, he burned them into his hell. He is collecting souls, first causing their downfall, then they enter his final eternity of punishment."

I stared at her, speechless, not accepting a word of it, but considering it seriously as part of her cultural background of which I had very little knowledge. One will be taken and the other left. Taken by whom, I wondered. I'd always thought this biblical passage spoke of God taking one and leaving the other, not the devil.

Dolores studied my face. "Ms. Cassandra," she said, "what I say may not be true. There are different ways I think about this. And I pray for protection from Satan, just in case it is the truth, but none of us knows. For every one of us, there is another explanation. That is just one of them."

I nodded.

"So there is a nanny from Haiti, she says something different. She says the only way to stop this from happening again is to burn sacrifices. She is burning sage and small birds in a circle of stone in her yard. Her family, the ones she works for, are so upset that she is doing this in their yard. But she won't stop. Every day she wrings the neck of a bird and sets it on fire and prays."

I nodded again. "Is this Santeria?"

"Oh, you know," said Dolores.

"Yes," I said. "The sacrifice is to the orishas. It comes from Yoruba culture in Africa." I was watching the corner for the school bus and hoping it would be a few minutes late so I could hear the rest of what Dolores would say.

"Yes." Dolores' fingers twirled her rosary beads. "Prayers and worship of their orishas who protect consciousness. She thinks the explanation for the fires will come from expanded consciousness – greater knowing – so we'll be protected if we know more and the burnings will then stop."

"Do you believe what she does?"

"I am Catholic. A greater consciousness of God will keep the devil away."

The yellow bus lurched to a stop at the corner and the lights flashed. Every woman emerged from her car. To my amazement, two of them carried squirt bottles and I saw their hair was soaking wet, dripping onto their shoulders. One woman emerged from a white SUV dressed in a single piece white jump suit that covered her from head to foot. She wore gloves and large clunky boots. The hood of what I realized was a HAZMAT suit hid her face so I could not see who she was. They all grabbed their kids, quickly guided them inside, and slammed their car doors shut. Dolores stepped out and little Sean Brennan jogged to her and took her hand and she quickly tucked him into the back seat.

I said goodbye to Dolores. I said, "It's okay. I'll walk."

She frowned and I could see her making the sign of the cross before she ducked back into her car.

"We didn't have recess today," Mia complained instantly upon being handed off to me. "Mrs. Anderson said it was not a good day for being outside."

"Look," Allie said. "The sun is out. It didn't rain all day."

"Maybe she wasn't feeling well," I said, feeling the dishonesty in my remark. "Go run ahead and get some exercise now."

Mia was up a tree the next moment and Allie stood below her. "I'm spotting her," she said. "That's what we do in gym class." I cringed at the thought of Allie trying to catch Mia and wondered which of them would be hurt more in that rescue effort.

"Can we go for ice cream?" Mia called from above.

"Today's a popcorn day," I said which meant we were staying home. I hurried them home, staying away from direct sunlight, not knowing why I imagined that would do anything to keep them safe or me for that matter. The only part of what Dolores told me that was the slightest bit believable was the idea that expanded consciousness, better understanding, would help us solve this strange phenomenon.

But still, I called Doug.

"Did I miss a public service announcement or something?" I asked when he answered simply, "Hi, Ms. Taylor."

"Not that I'm aware."

I explained the HAZMAT suit and the squirt bottles and the dripping hair.

"Mayor Moore hasn't released anything new."

"So they're creating their own protection." I told him about the rosary beads too.

"I've seen worse," he said. "Down on Beech Street Richmond tells me they arrested a woman carrying an AR-15 into the 711. No permit. She said if anyone tried to torch her she'd get them first."

I took that in silently.

"What are you doing to protect yourself?" he asked.

"It didn't get me," I said. "It got someone right next to me. Somehow, I feel like it isn't meant for me. Is that crazy?"

"It might be you're not thinking straight, Cassandra."

"It might be over," I said. "It's been a few days. It was just that one morning."

"Just be aware," he said. "Just don't assume anything. Nobody knows what happened, just that it did."

"Thanks," I said and hung up.

Homework, lemonade, hot kernels in the old Farberware pot with the burnt handle. Again, the gas stubbornly would not ignite until the third try, whooshing around the pot and up all sides and I jotted a note on a Post-it and tacked it on the refrigerator as a reminder to tell Pete to look at it when he returned unless Bruce got here first. Pete's itinerary, just next to it, told me he'd be home on Wednesday night, late. With the girls settled at the table with worksheets, I made the call to Derrick, an impulse and a knowing if I didn't just plunge into this without thinking I would simply not do it.

"Hi Cassandra," he said before I'd said a word, just like the old days, before our rift, when incoming call ID announced me nearly twice a day, that's how close Cindy and I'd been.

"Derrick," I said. "I'm so sorry." The simplicity of those three words hid layers and layers of ways I meant them. I hoped he could feel all of them but, even if he did, the sentiment felt frivolous and self-centered. A sentence starting with "I" was about me and I wanted this call to be about Cindy.

"Thank you," he said. Another pause.

"Can I help in any way?" Again, inadequacy of words. I expected the usual decline with polite distance, but he answered me with another thank-you.

"I have to arrange the services. Can you call some people for me? I don't have anyone here who could do this while I deal with my family."

"I can do that." A surge of gratitude washed over me. Being permitted back in to do this simple thing felt like forgiveness.

"If you want to stop in," he said. "I can give you her phone book."

"Today okay?" I asked.

"Yes."

Lila bounced in the door as I hung up so I stood and instantly took my keys and purse. "Stay with your sisters. Please don't go downstairs until I'm back."

She said, "I smell popcorn." She was in the kitchen at the table with her sisters before I was out the door.

About one and a half miles separated Cindy's from my home, four traffic lights, the timing of which, to avoid red light delays, I knew well. I'd have to be slightly over the speed limit, but not too far over, the speed trap on Grove Street had foiled me once, many years ago, and I navigated this with precise perfection.

Backhoes, earth movers, and sawhorses with the letters HPW cordoned off the block between Grove and Forest, recalling for me the neighborhood in a similar state near Lou's house after my Saturday flight from the garage sale. Cindy's house was on the corner of Forest and Prescott just next to these agents of destruction on the front lawns of her neighbors. I followed the orange signs and sat for a moment, the car facing the action, watching men move earth. They were digging, huge scoops of dirt lifted and dumped into dump trucks, two lined up at the curb to accept their cargo. The din was awful, roaring engines, gears, and a vibration I could feel in my ribs when I stepped out of the minivan.

"Radon contamination," Derrick said when he answered the door. "They've been replacing lawns with clean topsoil for two weeks."

"At least it's not your lawn," I said.

"Ours is next. They're working their way down the block."

"Oh."

"Come in," Derrick held the door back. The quiet of indoors created a void I now had to fill with something better than shallow hope for his lawn. Goldie, the golden retriever, sidled up for a pat and sat directly in front of me, begging for an ear scratch. I obliged. Cindy loved this dog.

"Poor Goldie," he said. "He looks for her."

Goldie sniffed at the accumulator booth Cindy had fit into her butler pantry just off the kitchen. "He must get a scent of her in there. He's in there all the time now. Cindy never let him in while she was here." He opened the door to the contraption and Goldie stepped in and lay on the floor.

"Is Brandon home?"

"Upstairs. Cindy's brother is here. My mother. They're both focused on him."

"And you?"

"I'm coping."

"I'm so sorry Derrick."

"Thank you." Pregnant silence. "How are your girls?"

"They're great," I said. "Practically raising themselves."

"Well, we know that's not true."

"Can I do anything more than that? I feel like…"

"You were her connection to the group," he said. "Do that. So she's not forgotten or so she's not remembered the way it was. That is something I can't ask anyone else."

"She withdrew herself," I said. "Nobody made her. It was a choice she made on her own."

"That's not how she framed it." He held up a hand. "But that's not for now. It doesn't matter now."

"No. I'm just sorry, Derrick. I've been sorry all along."

He held up his hand again. "Cassandra, it isn't time for you to do penance. Just help me, please. The memorial service is on Saturday."

"Okay," I managed a weak grimace. "Give me her phone book and I'll make the calls."

"Thanks," he said. Then, he surprised me by pulling me in for a hug and planting a kiss on my cheek. "She thanks you too." He lifted her Hallmark phone directory from the table near the stairs and handed it to me. I saw folded lists from the mom's group tucked inside and worn around the protruding edges. I had those lists somewhere at home.

"What are the investigators telling you?" I asked him, finally.

"You listening to the news?"

I nodded.

"That's about it."

"She was at the reservation."

"She was there every morning. There was nothing noteworthy about anything that day. The cops keep stopping by to ask me the same questions. They haven't answered any of mine."

Goldie went to the back door and pawed at it; in his eyes a doleful look only a dog could muster.

"Let me let him out. Come." He turned and I followed. Derrick slid the back door open and we both stepped outside. Goldie went immediately to the dogwood tree and lifted his leg. Derrick brought my attention to its lack of blossoms.

"Everything seems to be dying," he said. "That tree was healthy. Now look."

It wasn't only the tree. The grass should have been green. It was May. We'd had enough rain and I knew Derrick took great pride in his lawn, still winter brown and dormant now. The azaleas looked like petrified wood, no leaves, no buds.

"Appropriate somehow," he said. "With her gone."

My surface control caved and I couldn't hold back the tears I was trying hard to suppress. It had been five years since she'd been my friend. I had no right, but still, I broke. The hollow emptiness and the silence, as though all life, not just hers, had abandoned this place, this house, with the dog and the yard so dismal and forlorn. Was it our looking upon it that made it so? Or was the gloom welling up from some other place and capturing us in its dark aura? It had caught Cindy in its grip, my mind told me. A mood, like storm clouds descending from a gray sky, black and foreboding. It was as though this house was a magnet for it and my mind whispered to me that Cindy had not been here when she died, but had carried this magnetic gloom with her to the woods and there, somehow, something had coalesced and consumed her. Something evil. I felt it as a familiarity and I recognized it. Banhi's day of death had felt the same way. Sinister. My sense of guilt dissipated like a fog at noon in hot sunlight. It had been in that corrugated tin slum dwelling where Banhi had been a virtual prisoner and it was here too. Whatever it was.

"Was Cindy in a good place, you know, she'd been so down when you both came back from Chicago after her mother died."

"She was. She'd worked hard and she'd been running, losing weight. You know how she'd gain when she was unhappy. She was doing well."

"Was she still getting treatments from the therapist from the Institute, what was his name?"

"She was. She was doing the treatments herself. She wrote a testimonial for him. He published it in a journal of psychiatry."

"What was the therapy called? I remember when he came to our meeting. God, that was so long ago."

"Essen therapy," he said. "Essen life energy replenishment techniques."

"Yes," I said. "I remember now. Do you believe it helped her?"

"Not at first, but after about a year she was doing so well. I don't know what else to give credit for this...except maybe the woman's group, the ones who stayed with her, or maybe she just needed time to heal from the loss."

He broke eye contact then. "So you'll make those calls?"

"Yes," I said. "Do you want definite RSVP's for the memorial service?"

"No. Just call the women...all of them, even the ones she let go of. I don't need a count."

I couldn't leave yet, not without asking the inevitable. "Derrick, the police suspect a cult following of some philosophy and that Cindy and the other two women did this to themselves."

"I've heard that, Cassandra," he said.

"Do you think there is any remote possibility this is true?"

"I just told you. Cindy was doing great. Life was good. She'd never leave Brandon that way."

"I'm sorry," I said, realizing it was all I seemed capable of saying today. "I don't know why I asked."

"It's victim blaming," he said. "I told Heffly and Richmond to do their fucking jobs and figure this out."

"I'm glad you did," I said. "Okay, I'll make those calls." I stepped through the sliding door to the kitchen then made my way to the front door. Derrick followed me, thanked me again, and closed the door firmly into its frame behind me as I stepped down to the sidewalk. The front lawn was no better than the yard, as though it knew those backhoes would descend soon and it wasn't worth the energy to bloom. I turned the car around, drove close to the sawhorses and orange barrel barricades, and paused before turning right. With my window rolled down, I heard it. My first thought was of a woodpecker, but this was steady, faint at first, then its pace picked up to a repetition far too fast for a termite-hunting bird. Loud. Two men in HAZMAT suits beckoned to the backhoe operator and he leaped from the cab. One, already suited, handed him something and, as I turned the corner, I saw the HAZMAT trailer parked along the curb, the backhoe operator opened the door, and disappeared inside. Then, while I watched this mini drama unfold, one HAZMAT suited man used the backhoe to dump its shovel of soil back into the hole and the other aimed a garden hose at the pile and wet it down. With his other hand, he waved me on, a hurried urgent gesture accompanied by a shout, "Roll up your window, ma'am." I did and fled.

"The inward fire eats the soft marrow away,
And the internal wound bleeds on in silence."
- (Aeneid 4.93-94)

CHAPTER 12

"It was a Geiger counter," I told Pete on the telephone after my visit to Derrick. "It was getting a very high reading."

He'd called to announce his trip would extend to Thursday and he'd be home after midnight Friday morning. Nothing unusual there. More disappointment. The girls were planted in front of *The Wizard of Oz* again, homework done, and Pete's call interrupted my night of making calls. I had made about ten phone calls already and there were another twenty to get through. The big question was where to make a donation in her memory. I had to endure the same conversation with everyone about what and how and how awful it all was. As I waited for Pete to fill in the silence, my gaze wandered down the various lists. Names, some familiar, some not. Then a jolt when my finger swept across the name Ann Neelam on a sheet of names. I paused there. The woman I did not save. Then, further down, Elizabeth Lindsey, right there after my old friend Alice Bryant's name, scribbled in as a fairly new addition. I missed what Pete was saying. Why had nobody I'd spoken to all evening mentioned these other dead women? These other women were members. Then I realized I really had called the women I knew first, the ones who had stayed with my half of the group. This sheet listed the women who joined Cindy's side after the divide.

"Cindy's house is next to be excavated," I said to Pete. "Poor Derrick. Having to deal with that disruption in the middle of this."

"I guess it is the least of his worries," Pete said. "And maybe they'll postpone the work on his place out of respect for his situation."

"We used Geiger counters at the stone circle," I said to Pete. "Do you remember?"

"Yes," he said. "Now I do. Now that you remind me."

"We found high readings."

"Yes, I remember," he said. I wanted to remind him of more. I wanted to ask him if he remembered how, for three months when he kept postponing his departure from England, when he stayed with me instead of using his Eurail pass to see Rome and Munich and Prague, he became so fascinated with my project and with me and the "way my mind worked." I wanted to tell him that my mind was still here, inside me and that, if he would just give us some moments together, he might remember what it felt like to be close, to share more. Instead, I speculated out loud about all the questions everyone must have, the ones the investigators were not answering. Then, I said, "I wonder if the radon levels are more dangerous than they are letting on."

"Cassandra," Pete said. "This is starting to sound familiar."

"What?"

"This is what you did after Banhi. You're grasping at straws. The radon and the deaths are not related. Radon causes lung cancer, not self-immolating women."

"They're not self-immolating and I'm not obsessing, Pete. I just spent two hours helping Derrick let people know about Cindy's memorial service…"

"Yeah, that's what I mean. She isn't even your friend anymore. Why are you doing this?"

"Pete, she's dead."

"Yes, and your friendship with her ended a long time ago."

"But if I can help him somehow…"

"You might be making it worse."

"How could that be?"

"Painful memories for him."

"So I shouldn't have called him?"

"I don't know. If I were him I'd just want people to leave me alone."

"He asked me to call the moms' group members. That means he doesn't really want to be alone, otherwise he would have a small private service."

"He might just be doing it because it's expected."

"Maybe he is doing it because he loves his wife and he is finding a way to honor her life. That's what a funeral is for."

"You're the anthropologist. You know it's just ritual."

"Is that what you would do if it happened to me? Just do the ritual as though it had no meaning?"

"That's not what I meant."

"Then what did you mean?"

"It just seems a bit showy."

"I can't believe you're saying this. I feel like you're acting like what I am doing to help is meaningless. What Derrick is doing is meaningless."

"Well, it won't bring her back."

"No, but it will comfort the people who loved her who are still here."

"When is the service?"

"It's Saturday."

"So I have to go?" I heard annoyance in his voice. "On my only day off I have to go honor a woman my wife isn't friends with anymore?"

"Pete," I said. "I'm hanging up." And I did. It wasn't for Cindy that I wanted him there. It was for me.

Where had the man gone? The man who had won me over that day in the Peach and Thistle, whom I'd invited to the dig the following day, who had allowed my enthusiasm to be contagious. Pete's assistance, his knowledge of electromagnetic current and how to measure it, from his undergraduate studies in electrical engineering, helped me so much, supplementing evidence I'd collected - samples of magnetic rock deep in the earth excavated by my team. How much I owed to him! That simple instrument he'd obtained for me. By semester's end, I had gathered and recorded enough physical evidence to confirm my hypothesis. There was energy in that place on the Salisbury Plain where they'd built the circle. I turned my research to the cultural behavior of the people of ancient times in that locale that might reveal that they had some primitive way to detect it and perhaps that had fueled their decision to choose that precise place on the Salisbury Plain to build their stone circle. How they detected it was the unanswered question in my research.

Now, I sat on my couch again, the place I habitually sought when my own emotional gravity weighed me down. He had done this before. He had left me feeling selfish and shallow. I had sat in this same place before. The twins age four, Lila ten, before my part-time job. He'd called mid-afternoon. I'd picked up the phone when I saw it was him, feeling the worry of a trying year in which his mother was in a slow slide toward death like mine. Strokes, a series of them, had left her without speech. This was the final mid-afternoon call.

"She's gone," he'd said. "This morning. My Dad was there."

"Oh," I said, "I'm so sorry Pete. It's been such a struggle."

"Well, yes," he said. "But it's over."

"I'll get the girls," I said. "We'll go out there." Out there was eastern Long Island, a three-hour drive.

"I'm on the George Washington bridge," he said.

"Oh," I said again, thinking of Cindy and Derrick and how they'd packed their minivan and trekked to Chicago when her brother's call came in. They'd all gone together, Brandon in pajamas in the back, Derrick driving through the night, Cindy navigating from the passenger seat.

114

"Well, one of my sisters will take the kids," I said. "I'll come. You shouldn't be alone."

"Don't," he said again. "It's over Cassandra. She's gone. I'll deal with Dad and the funeral home."

"I would like to help," I said.

"Can you bring her back to life?"

I didn't answer.

"This isn't about you," he said. "I'll call you later." And he hung up.

Now, I knew. Pete needed fixing. I needed fixing. Our marriage needed fixing.

But that ticking sound of the Geiger counter sent me to the computer and Google. Derrick had said it was radon. We had learned about radon when we bought this house. We tested. The results were negative. But, at Cindy's house and the neighborhood near Lou, they were excavating and replacing topsoil. Why? A new Google search told me.

The sheets I'd printed earlier were still in the printer tray and I lifted them along with the sheets about radon. Perhaps Lila's was not a film malfunction at all, but quite possibly the film was functioning exactly as it was supposed to function. I'd printed an abstract from an article about NASA. The International Space Station carried risk of exposure to radioactive energy from the sun, unfiltered by the earth's atmosphere and its ozone layer, that protective blanket high in the upper layers. Excessive radiation-- if it struck strips of photographic film placed around the space station-- would leave cloud shaped patterns in the emulsion indicating radioactive energy levels were accumulating in the space station.

I should have gone to bed. I was due at work for an early tour in the morning, but I kept clicking on URL's that led me to more and more articles about radon, but nothing about Hillston and radon until I plugged both words into the search field. There was the Superfund project, photos and all, where residents discovered dozens of half empty cans of phosphorescent paint under their lawns. Diagnoses of leukemia for several young children in a cluster of homes built on the site later became known. A movement, Clean Soil for Hillston was still active.

Radioactivity, I read, in soil is a natural occurrence. Radioactive particles disintegrate, create radon gas, which rises through topsoil, and is only dangerous when confined inside the walls of a home. We had tested when we bought the house at the advice of our realtor and I had retested for radon when Lila started spending so much time down in her photo lab in the laundry room. We were clean. But now two neighborhoods undergoing backhoe excavations of lawns seemed to have escaped the local news reports.

I lay in bed later, recalling the sound of that Geiger counter, click, click, clicking away. It felt like a warning. Quite different from the elation I felt upon hearing it at my dig sites at Stonehenge. There, it had created such excitement and cause for a small celebration, me, Pete, Phoebe, and the undergraduates. There was something under the earth and we'd found it. The ancients had perhaps found it too and built above it. We were drunk on our own adrenaline back then. We speculated for weeks, Phoebe and I formed a hypothesis that would have room for a cultural element, a tie of geology and earth-based energy to religious ritual. How could the ancients detect radioactivity? How had they detected magnetism? Both were under and around those ancient stones.

We conceived Lila in a drunk and careless mood brought about by such excitement and discovery. Stupid, I thought now, lying there waiting for sleep. Foolish and in love, and now, here we were, Pete and me, on the brink of marital self-destruction and failure after fifteen years together, Lila the only glowing remnant of that early chapter.

I sat up in bed, ambushed by a sudden memory. I flipped on the lamp and slid into a sweatshirt and went to the porch where my fading files were all lined up in neat little rows.

There somewhere were the drawings of the soil discoveries that contained evidence of fires, soil that was darker and full of chemical evidence of high carbon materials. We had mapped every discovery on grid paper, in pencil, overwritten later with India ink when it was time to turn in our results. Phoebe was very good with architectural style drawing, penciling everything to scale, and being so very careful to not move anything that might turn out to be important until she had drawn a separate sketch for each two-inch layer of soil. Testing, then sketching again. I could run it like a film in my head. And as it played out, I considered which file these notes might be found in. It was so late. I was excited but had to wait until the light of the morning to attack my stacks of data. I was tired. Yet, I did not sleep. I lay awake, staring at the ceiling, my heart thumping hard against my ribs. Unformed shards of ideas floated near enough to each other to form a whole thought, then faded, then another detail I recalled sent me off in a different direction until, knowing dawn would come and I would have to function on zero sleep, I got up, went to the bathroom, and took a Tylenol PM, something I had not done since just after our escape from Bangalore. I knew something then just as I knew something now. But it eluded me.

"Keep a little fire burning; however small, however hidden." - Cormac McCarthy, *The Road*

CHAPTER 13

I'd slept, but my mind had kept working. Just as wakefulness arrived, I stayed in that in-between state for long enough to recognize the idea my brain had offered to my subconscious state. It was about Lila's film. Lila's film malfunction might not have been a malfunction at all. That NASA article. I needed to read it again. The women in her undeveloped pictures, with the clouds of white - Lila had blamed on defective film - could they have been exposed to some kind of radioactive energy? The radon, of course. They were exposed to radioactivity because of the radon problem. Then I remembered that snapshot, Pete's first of me that first Stonehenge morning. An obliterating cloud of white nearly eliminating me from that shot. We had discovered radioactive energy on that site. And if these women in her photos had been exposed to radon? That would explain the blurred images on her contact prints and negatives. I stepped quietly down the hall and peeked in at my sleeping daughter. She stirred and rolled to watch me. "What are you doing in here?" she asked. She sat up.

"I want to see those defective negatives."

"Why?" she asked.

I said, "Where are they?"

She got up and shuffled a bit in her backpack and handed me an envelope. She collapsed back into bed and pulled her quilt to her chin.

"Never mind," I said. "Just tell me, where did you take the defective pictures?"

"I didn't take them anywhere. The prints are in the basement."

"I mean, where were you when you shot the photo shoots?" I said. "Were you at school? At their homes?"

"Different places," she said. "Around town. Some at the park. Some at their homes. Why? Really Mom. Dad's right. You do get obsessive. It's MY project, not yours. I retook all the photos anyway."

"Sleep for a few more minutes," I said. "Sorry I woke you." I carried off the negatives and returned to my room to shower and dress, all the while, my mind running over all I knew. Cindy lived in a neighborhood that was contaminated with radon and she had died in this mysterious phenomenon. Two other women had also died the same way. Did they live near a radon contamination site too?

"Lila," I asked when she passed me on her way to the shower, "did you by any chance take Cindy Barrow's picture for the project?"

"Yes," she said. "Just because you and Cindy weren't friends anymore…"

"Yes, it's not why I'm asking."

"She died, Mom," Lila said.

I nodded.

"I read about it in the paper. Does Dad know?" Lila watched me closely. I didn't know what she was looking for.

"He's out of town." I knew I was evading her purpose.

"Yes, but does he know?" Lila asked.

"Yes," I said. "Can I see the negative or the print of Cindy?"

"Sure," she said with a softening of her expression and her voice.

The twins were soon up and sliding into jeans and tee shirts and Lila was in the hall bathroom with the door locked against an invasion by her sisters. I poured Cheerios, milk, and orange juice.

While the kids ate, I went to Google and typed Ann Neelam and Elizabeth Lindsay in the white pages online directory. There they were. I jotted down their addresses on a notepad and stuffed it in my purse.

If the film proved to be contaminated by radon, I should tell the families in the photographs they should test for it.

And the town should know, unless these women lived in one of those neighborhoods, near Lou, near Cindy, or near the earlier site of the watch factory where efforts were already underway, and they knew already.

Could the existence of radioactive decaying substances under the ground in Hillston have anything to do with the fires? They all died outdoors. I needed to be careful to not share this farfetched idea with anyone just yet; it was the question that nobody would take seriously if I actually asked it, at least right now. This was the guiding principle of the Fraternity of Contemplative ; never reveal the contemplation before the evidence is gathered. Never feed rumors. Never discredit yourself with premature discussion of a line of inquiry. Get your empirical data first.

Dr. Gimpel said I had not had the opportunity to reap the rewards of my earlier discoveries in England. I had been eager to make my in Bangalore a success too. I was shorted again by not being able to complete my work in the slums and by my grief over Banhi's death.

I showered, letting soap and shampoo suds run down my naked skin, my face in the stream of hot spray. I dried myself, looked in the mirror through the steam, and thought maybe, just maybe, I hit on something nobody will think of. I knew I needed to prove it first, then I could share it. As I dressed, I thought of Doug Bluestein and his membership in the secret fraternity. I might tell him. I could trust him. I wanted to talk to him. But I also wanted to snoop a bit first. While the girls ate breakfast, once again I opened my computer to Google. This time, I typed in Doug Bluestein.

With only a few minutes for this, I scanned quickly through countless links and listings for the Jersey Star with his byline. I scrolled and scrolled. Then, I did an advanced search with his name and College of New Jersey and there I opened a world. Doug did a stint in the

Army, stationed in Germany and spent some months in Colombia as a special ensign to the embassy. He attended college on the GI Bill after his honorable discharge in the late 1980's. I clicked on images and there was a younger version of him, eighties style, in a press conference of some sort, deep in conversation with an older gentleman. Clicking on that image took me to an obituary, a memorial page at a funeral home where the photo was posted along with quite a few others for this older man, a beloved professor of journalism apparently for more than Doug. His name was Micky Dolan. This Micky might just be the mentor who granted Doug membership in the Fraternity of Contemplative , so I opened a new Google search page and entered his name. As I did, I remembered Doug when I asked about his field of study. "I'd rather not say."

Money laundering was his field. Or it was the field of Micky Dolan whose life ended suddenly when a bus hit him in downtown Manhattan in 1991. Scrolling further, I scanned a long list of newspaper articles "by Micky Dolan" and "by Micky Dolan and Doug Bluestein."

"Mom," I heard. "Our lunches." That brought me back to my girls patiently waiting for me with lunch bags in their hands, juice boxes and packs of pretzel snacks, but no sandwiches. I closed the laptop, but didn't close the browser. I'd be back to this later. The clock. I made the fastest peanut butter sandwiches of my life, tucked them into sandwich bags, and into their lunch bags. We flew across the park and the bus driver waved to me and gave me a thumbs up. They were off to their routine day, safe, happy, and not late. Thank goodness.

CHAPTER 14

I dashed home from dropping the kids to finish my morning cleanup and to grab my tote bag. I tucked the laptop into it. No wireless on the train, but I would have a break between groups today. Back across the park, with just fifteen minutes on the train to peruse the printed NASA piece again, I arrived in Newark at Broad Street Station, my mind full of facts about safety in the face of radiation for the astronauts during space walks. But money laundering and Doug and a dead journalism professor distracted me.

The Goodwill Mission was shut up tight, no loitering men with cigarettes leaning against the plate glass where the morning sun slanted and reflected. Today's schedule included a planetarium show and a tour of the new environmental science floor. I would do this alone, Eric was busy with a high school group at the Gordon Parks photography exhibit, which we would only have for a few weeks. Eric would do a full morning starting with our standard Civil War program and end with Gordon Parks' work. Photography, I thought. I should really let Lila skip school and come to work with me while this exhibit is here.

I would run the projector in the planetarium, no lecture needed there, easy duty for me. I called this type of day "museum light" and focused on fun.

The planetarium show was about our sun. I hadn't seen this one yet, but assumed I could sleepwalk through this morning after the lack of sleep and the residual effects of that sleeping pill. A cup of coffee had helped to awaken me, but as I ushered the students to their seats, I felt the early morning caffeine wear off.

The planetarium is nothing more than a theater with the screen on the ceiling. It had been retrofitted with a new sound system and, as the film began, I felt more than heard a rumbling of vibration as the sun burst forth in a fiery orange ball the size of the domed screen. I heard gasps from the children, smooth voices saying "cool" and the teacher shushing them all. Then, the narrator's voice, a famous movie actor's, said, "The Egyptians worshipped it and called it Ra and built the city of Heliopolis as its home." And I was suddenly paying much closer attention than I ever had in all the times I had taught this lesson and run this show. I was now seeing it with a new mind. "What is the difference between what they knew and what we now know about our sun?" he asked. And for my little class of fifth graders, he answered.

According to the narrator, the last twenty years has revealed more information about our sun than any other time in mankind's quest to know his world. The ceiling beamed gorgeous views of the aurora borealis, a diagram of the magnetic poles of the earth, and an animation of the flows of electromagnetic energy bombarding the earth. Our own planet's magnetic shield shifts shape when the sun's bursts hit it and, as I watched this, I marveled at how well it protected earth. The lesson cut to a segment on the power grid, our electrical system, and how the explosions from the sun, solar flares, and CMEs (coronal mass ejections), at intervals of eleven years, rained down excessive electromagnetic radiation which disrupted our power grids and caused massive power outages. A major hit to the power grid in Montreal/Quebec in the mid-nineties created a power outage affecting seven million households and shut down commerce for a week. It went on, teaching these young fifth graders about how our distance from the sun was ideal for the creation of life. Too close and we would burn up, too far away and we'd freeze. It fascinates, the long list of reasons life on earth thrives, the presence of oxygen, the size of our sphere. If much smaller, gravity would hold nothing close to the surface, including our atmosphere, too large and we would not be able to resist the pull of gravity to stand upright. The program went on, in a logical sequence, through the importance of our sun and the dangers we face from the wearing off of the ozone layer - skin cancer, climate change, the melting of the polar ice caps, the deserts dry and inhospitable.

Contamination from radon gas seemed small compared to the powerful possibilities in our sun. Light travels ninety-three million miles from sun to earth and it only takes eight seconds to do so. But that is only after the energy deep within the sun finds its way to the sun's surface and launches into its journey to us. The corona, the plasma layer surrounding the molten sphere, the narrator explained, sends massive ejections and, with such little time, we earthlings can do absolutely nothing if one were to burst forth and head toward us. So, he said, we are trying to study the inner core of the sun, not only the visible part so we can predict when the ejection might start. The kids in their reclining chairs stared up at this lesson unfurling in all its beautiful cinematography. Then, he said it. The visible light is the smallest and least powerful element of all the energy that originates and emanates from our local star. "But it is the only form detectable by humans without instrumentation and science. And what you can't see, CAN hurt you."

Back through footage of forest fires raging during times of drought, sunburned skin on children at the beach, wrinkle-skinned aboriginal peoples in Australia, squinting through eyes shielded only with oversized leaves worn as as wide as umbrellas as they crossed arid landscapes. Then, a darkened screen and a pause, then fields of grain, lush green plants, endless spans of farms and fields full of food crops, and a segment on how photosynthesis creates our food supply. The good stuff. The film's final note was a happy one. Right away, a hand shot up.

"Yes?" I asked, my hand on the dimmer switch to raise the lights.

"So our sun could send big bursts and kill us all," said a kid with glasses and purple hair.

"Well," I said. "It hasn't happened yet and we do have protection from our magnetic field."

"What's a magnetic field?" he asked.

"We just saw it," I said. "There is a field around the earth. It bends when the sun's ejections try to penetrate it. Electromagnetic energy hits it and creates the aurora borealis, the northern lights."

"But why do scientists want to know? What could they do if they knew a big burst was heading our way?"

"Well, they could shut down the power grid to protect it from damage," I said. "Or they could make sure the international space station was on the other side of the earth, away from the sun, on the dark side, so it wouldn't be hit."

"But those of us here on earth," said the boy. "We would be sitting ducks."

"There would probably be some warnings to stay indoors," I said.

"What about those women who burst into flame," said another boy, this one with long straight hippy hair that hung limply across his shoulders. "Maybe that's what's happening. Some kind of light energy is hitting them from way out in space and bam, they're toast."

"That is quite impossible," said their teacher, a tall middle-aged woman, maybe in her fifties, with a tight French braid pulling at her eyes and giving her an intense intelligent severity.

"Why?" said the longhaired boy. "Why is it impossible?"

"Because it is," said the teacher who then looked at me expectantly.

"Don't you think something like that would take out everyone, not just them?" I asked.

"I can just see it," said the boy, "a single neutrino, invisible and deadly, traveling from the center of the sun, a microscopic particle to incinerate a random person who happened to be in exactly the right place for impact." He was enjoying this. "Pow!"

He sat down. He had accomplished his mission which, by the self-congratulatory look in his eye, was to scare the girls and get attention.

"This would have to happen three times in a single day," I said. "The chances of this really happening are zilch." I knew nothing about neutrinos. Apparently, the teacher didn't either. "What is a neutrino?" she asked.

"It's a tiny nuclear bomb!" he said. "I saw it on the Sci Fi channel in a cartoon. It was heading toward earth like the comet that killed the dinosaurs except it was microscopic, so the government couldn't hit it with their missiles. The earth was destroyed. Boom!" He sat down again.

"Ah, science fiction, not real," I said. I gave him a long quizzical look. "Good imagination."

"Thank you, ma'am," he said with a grin. And we all stood up to go to the science floor. But I knew I was going to look up neutrinos when I got home.

I led them to the lunchroom and hurried to the break room to open my laptop. Back to Doug and money laundering and his dead professor. I read quickly, taking it in and marveling at the reach of the Fraternity. Doug was an intern, trailing Micky Dolan through his work as an investigative reporter on Wall Street, covering the business and financial beats. That was the era of Oliver North when North was responsible for selling arms to Iran to raise money to fund the rebels in El Salvador. Doug apparently had assisted Micky Dolan in his investigation of other money sources during that era. Micky had been raising questions in the *New York Times*. Richard Grasso had traveled to the jungles of Colombia to meet with the FARC leaders and, according to a piece Micky wrote, his purpose was to educate the leaders on the financial markets and to invite them to participate in them. But Micky sensed a different purpose and, although he was not explicit, even I, right now, could sense the trail Micky had decided to explore. He had taken Doug along on this ride.

I had time for one more article. I found one, also by Micky, which exposed the level of compensation Richard Grasso received as chairman of the NYSE and reviewed his career from a mailroom clerk as a young man culminating in his ascension to chairman. This article was dated – I checked – only a few weeks before Micky stepped in front of a NYC public bus and was killed. I bookmarked the sites I knew I would return to later and fled the break room to the lunchroom to retrieve my class.

My head was spinning. I wanted to know more about Doug. I knew I was focusing on him instead of my own scientific trail. Why, I asked myself, although I knew why. I had not shaken that feeling of gratitude for his instant respect for me and my past work. I was also excited to meet someone else who was part of the fraternity. And I was mad at Pete and very much aware of how it felt to have Doug's attention, an unattached man near my age who peered at me over those glasses with such intensity. I needed to get back to learning more about radon and radiation from the sun. Doug's past was not nearly as important. At the same time, I wondered why he was working for a small local newspaper after some of the investigations he'd done with Micky, especially after Micky's death. I would think he would pick up the baton and run with it if only to honor his friend and mentor. I also hadn't looked up neutrinos. I was off my game a bit in the afternoon visit to the science floor.

The class disbanded across the environmental science gallery, walking in pairs through the various habitats. In New Jersey, there are four geologic regions: Coastal Plain, Piedmont, Valley and Ridge, and Highlands. The display reflected them. Not that these kids paid attention, they just pushed buttons to watch how the continents drifted apart to form Europe, Africa, North and South America. They ran through the cave where fake bats perched upside down on crevices and stopped to stare at a stuffed coyote. They also stuck their hands in wooden boxes to sample various kinds of rocks.

"Education or entertainment?" I said to the teacher with a wry smile.

She nodded. "It's spring. Can't teach them anything. They'll remember this. They won't remember anything I make them do in the classroom."

"Hey cool," I heard a girl say. "Magnetic rocks." She had her hands in one of the sample boxes and was holding two apart in mid-air, releasing them, and watching them pull toward each other and smack. The sound was sharp.

"Teaching moment," I said to the teacher and went to the girl who was surrounded by three others. They opened their little circle and let me in. "Look," I said. I pointed to the map of the state on the wall. I used my red laser pointer and indicated the Highland region in the north and west. "This region is very rich in iron."

"The film said we have a magnetic field around the earth? Is that caused by rocks?" asked the girl holding the magnets.

"That is a complicated question," I said."There is solid iron at the core of the earth. There is molten iron in the outer core. Look." I used the red laser dot again. This time it was on the layers of earth, the crust, the upper and lower mantle, the outer and inner core. "When there is movement in the outer core, there is energy created and that energy is the magnetic energy that forms the magnetic poles - north and south." I smiled. "I think that is enough to answer your question."

She nodded and handed the magnets to a friend. "Here, your turn," she said. And she ran off to another hands-on display. Her friends followed her. I watched through my very heavy eyes and glanced at my watch.

Soon, the kids were back on their bus and I was on the train reading the morning paper. That's when I saw this:

Hillston's Collapsing Iron Mines

At 23 Upper Road, a section of front lawn caved in, leaving a sink-hole. According to reports, the family discovered the sinkhole after storms dropped six inches of rain in a matter of five hours. The area has been roped off with safety tape and the Larksap family has hired surveyors and a geologic testing firm to determine if mines below the ground pose hazards to the structures on the property. The Larksap family purchased the property in 2008 for $1.1 M. according to tax records.

Hillston served as a source of iron for musket balls during the American Revolution. Long before that, the mines supplied early blacksmiths with ore for farming implements and shoes for plow horses. Now, it seems, these old iron mines are posing a hazard as they collapse from centuries of neglect. They were abandoned in the early 1800's. Residents with concerns can view historic maps at the Hillston Public library if they have concerns about their properties.

Now as the train rattled toward Hillston, I found I was contemplating my discoveries at Stonehenge long before Bangalore and Banhi. Not only did Hillston have radioactive materials under the ground, we also had iron, which meant surface magnetism. The train pulled into my station and I tucked the newspaper into my bag. Hillston has two elements under the ground that were similar to the Stonehenge site...radioactivity and, because of the iron, magnetism.

By the time I'd arrived, there hadn't been much left to excavate near the stone circles, especially Stonehenge, the largest and most studied of all of England's ancient stone monuments. Still, I wanted to focus on that and no other in my graduate work. I remember when I asked Dr. Field the question, "Why here? Why did they choose this site to build? Why did they carry these huge stones from Wales to the Salisbury Plain to build this circle?"

Dr. Fields had paused before he'd answered me. "You've brought up a question that nobody has been able to satisfactorily answer. Many have offered theories, but none have been proven."

He went on to discuss the position of stones found on the site and how they aligned with the winter and summer solstices. But he said, "The Maya did the same at Chitzen Itza. Ancients often chose to build on sites peoples before them also chose, but nobody has been able to go back far enough to answer why that particular spot for the very first people who erected there." Later he said, "You might pursue this, but you may find yourself at a dead end when it comes to evidence."

That is what I chose for my masters' thesis question. Coming up with an answer to the question proved as difficult as Dr. Fields predicted. Enter Pete, with his electro-magnetometer, a result of a weekend visit he and I had taken to a haunted old inn and an old man who insisted there were electricity fluctuations in his rooms through which he could detect ghosts. We still had that electro-magnetometer somewhere.

I crossed the park toward home, the sky blue and the shade of the trees cooling between bands of direct sunlight. Someone's discarded ice cream cup had melted into a puddle on the blacktopped path and I imagined what child left the park screaming in indignation at the loss of his treat. With light, comes heat, I mused. Basic science. With light, comes other energies we do not detect unless we have instruments. The sky show, the electrical grid, the bending of the magnetic field I'd just watched, these images seeped in and mingled with these recollections of my early, nearly forgotten work. I paused under my favorite red oak and surveyed the lush green of spring all around me. I had asked this in my thesis…I discovered high electromagnetic energy at Stonehenge and I discovered my possible explanation for the "why here" question. But how did the ancients detect this energy? That was the still unanswered piece of my puzzle. That was my unfinished work. This was the dead-end Dr. Fields warned me about.

Then, from the remote compartments of memory, came the explanation Pete had received from the photo lab owner at Salisbury that long-ago evening just before our first date. Pete had told us the man's explanation for his first blurred photographs, the myth that the ghosts of Stonehenge don't want pictures taken and sometimes interfere with picture taking. Mainly, he had said, they unleash their mischief around the time of the spring and autumn equinoxes. The photo shop proprietor had advised Pete to wait a while and he'd turned out to be correct. Pete's later photos were perfect. We had laughed and thanked the ghosts for leaving him alone.

Back at home, I imagined that now that I was safely inside, the threat of whatever had taken our Hillston women was not going to get me, I spent the next half hour rummaging through my boxes of field notes from my Sheffield days and my dig at Stonehenge. I would fetch the twins from the bus before I found what I needed. But later, after dinner and after they were in bed, I read a piece that was more a diary entry than an official field note.

It made me dig into another plastic storage bin and pull out that old electro-magnetometer. Hillston had iron mines. That meant magnetism. That old thing looked like a relic. It was made sometime in the 1980s and was analog with a needle that gyrated across a graph. It took 6 C batteries to run and I remembered they didn't last long. No wonder whomever sold it to Pete at that flea market got rid of it. I wanted to play around with it, see if I could detect any geomagnetic energy. Contemplative? Yes. I deserved this membership.

"Success isn't a result of spontaneous combustion. You must set yourself on fire." - Arnold Glascow

CHAPTER 15

I returned to my notes. They were faded and dusty and made me sneeze, but I didn't bother with the notion that perhaps I should wipe everything down with a dust cloth before I dug into their depths. And sitting on the floor in the sun porch wouldn't do. My back was stiff from the curve I'd locked into over those plastic storage bins. I could feel the hard floor under my pelvic bones too. I moved all of it to the dining room table, all with minutes to spare for meeting the bus.

I sat Mia and Allie at that table, the mahogany one with a table pad to protect it from their pencil scribble as they bent to their homework, and I sat down the other end and read.

"What are you doing, Mommy?"

"Reading some old schoolwork of my own," I said.

"There are a lot of papers there," Mia said.

"Yes," I said.

"What grade?" asked Allie.

I looked up. "Seventeenth grade," I said. They laughed.

Then, I remembered myself at their age and remembered something else I'd let slip. It seemed I'd boxed up so much of my past, so much of myself. It all had to be set free. For now I unearthed what I had rescued from Grace and Lou's garage sale. One by one I lifted stacks of books from a corner of our garage and brought them to the dining room.

First Allie looked up. Then Mia. And they put down their pencils and closed their notebooks where they were meticulously writing each of their spelling words six times. I said nothing, curious to see how long it would take them to give the pile of books their attention. It didn't take long, but long enough for me to dig through my own stuff until I found the notes I was looking for. Funny, that. I knew some of the sentences I'd written back then in Sheffield and could recall them verbatim. I just didn't know which notebook contained them. Or the dates. I only knew the truth that was in them, so, when I found what I was looking for, it felt odd, as though I'd remembered a lot more than what was actually there. The sense of disappointment was acute. My recollection seemed so much more complete than what I was able to find in these notes. I feared too much time had passed and with it so much had faded into nothing. I hadn't gone as far as I thought I had. I went to the shelf where my bound thesis sat among my old books from my university days. This might be quicker and better. Why had I not thought to look in here first?

I read. I jotted down notes. I forgot about cooking dinner. A sideways glance told me which of my childhood books captured the twin's attention. They divided them into two piles. "This will be my pile," said Mia. "And you can choose for yours. When we're done, we can swap." I not only enjoyed seeing which books they chose, I loved the way they so eagerly shared with each other. Mia stockpiled the yellow-spined Nancy Drew mysteries, Allie selected anything with an animal on the cover, including *The Rats of Nimh*. She also chose Madeline L'Engle's *A Wrinkle in Time*. It brought back Lou and me, ages eleven and ten, in our summers, swimming in our backyard pool, then riding our bikes to the library and coming home to sit in the shade of our front porch or sometimes we just lay on our beds indoors to read. Lou and I were not twins, but no more different from each other than Mia and Allie. We were separated in age just by a year. My mother's words from long ago still puzzled me. "You're different from them, go find friends of your own." Mia and Allie abandoned their homework and took seats side by side on the couch in the living room, each buried in a book. I ordered pizza and salad for delivery. Then I went back, burying myself in my young adult past while Mia and Allie discovered my childhood inside those books. I just let them read, freed them from the drill of homework for an evening. I would make excuses to their teachers.

The doorbell rang. I was in such a daze that I don't remember paying the delivery boy or tipping him. And the girls helped themselves to pizza and salad and eventually I ate a slice myself.

"Baths?" I asked. They took them without me.

"Teeth?" They nodded.

"Story?" They asked for *Peter Pan*, then looked at each other. "Why don't we read ourselves? Mom has homework," Mia said and laughed. I let them go, with a pang in my heart, thinking how I told Derrick my twins were raising themselves. Later, I found them in their room, Allie taking a turn with the book, reading in a soft voice. I paused in the hall and listened, hiding so as not to disturb them. It might have been the text, the rhythm of the language of J.M. Barrie's prose, but Allie sounded like a British child as she recited the words. I waited until they turned off their light, kissed them goodnight, and returned to my work. The arguments as presented in my thesis and the evidence to support them lined up in logical sequences. This brought me back in more than an academic sense. It brought back the other discovery that altered my path in ways I had never anticipated.

"It was a pleasure to burn." - Ray Bradbury

CHAPTER 16

I submitted and defended my master's thesis in mid-June. It drew on all my physical work and what was known about religious practices in recorded history that had taken place at the circles. By then, my period was late. By early July, Pete was gone to Bangalore and I still had not menstruated. Phoebe found the packages in the trash bin one night after class when I had gone to the library. Maybe I wanted her to find them. I could have taken out the trash receptacle myself. She found me at my usual hiding place, high and away on the second-floor balcony next to the reserved books room at the library.

"How late are you?" She wore a navy windbreaker with the hood up over her usually sleek blond hair. Her hands were deep in her pockets, her chin tucked in. At my stare, she said, "Don't lie." And she put the cardboard scraps of the boxes on the library table.

"A month or so," I said.

"I know a place to take you to do it," she said. "Do you have student medical coverage? No, never mind. The state covers abortions. The clinic on campus will refer you."

"Phoebe..."

"Does he know?"

I shook my head no.

"Do you want him to know?"

I wiped the heels of my hands across my eyes and blinked at her. "How could we be so stupid?"

"Did you use protection?" she asked.

"Not enough, apparently."

"Well, a mistake, a malfunction of a device, not enough stupidity to punish yourself for."

"You're jumping way ahead, Phoebe."

"I am?" she raised her eyebrows.

"I'm Catholic," I said.

"Well, let's jump way back, Cassandra…to the dark ages. It's not necessary for you to accept this. You haven't told him. He's gone. He's back to his life. Now that he's ruined yours, for God's sake, but that is only if you let this, ruin everything, that is."

"He hasn't ruined my life. He helped me. He helped us. Look what we've got that we might not have gotten to if he hadn't bought that ridiculous electro-magnetometer…"

"Oh, we'd have gotten to it soon enough. He just collapsed the time in between our meager beginnings and our end game."

"I'm well aware of that Phoebe. I just can't help thinking of this as a life, not just a problem."

"And your life? Your purpose? Your mind and your ideas and the contribution you talk about making?"

"Are they mutually exclusive?"

"Not if you can afford a nanny or if you had a mum to raise her for you or a man who would support you. Good idea to bring a little bundle home to your mum or maybe your sister will raise it so you can keep on with your work. From what I hear, they're dying to be a support network for you. And for God's sake, Cassandra, he was on sabbatical. This was all a lark for him. I thought you were enjoying a little springtime fling. Nothing more than that. Getting preggers isn't going to change that outcome."

"What if I'm in love with him?"

"So what? You can still be in love with him. It doesn't mean you have to have this baby."

"I couldn't just do it. Just abort and never tell him. It would be so dishonest and it would put a wedge between him and me forever."

"He's gone, Cassandra. He's in Bangalore. You are here. Let go. Go back to the Cassandra you were before he waltzed in here with his camera and flattered you."

"You just said I was going backwards. Now you're telling me to go back. I'm changed because of him."

"Yes, you are now in the most vulnerable place a woman can be. Alone and pregnant."

"What if I'm not alone?"

"What on earth do you mean?"

"What if I told him and he came back?"

"What if you tell him and he doesn't? It will just hurt you more."

"At least I will know."

"Know what?"

"Know if he feels about me the way I feel about him."

"Oh, gees. Now you sound like one of those women who gets pregnant to trap her man. You won't want him to come back because of duty or obligation or guilt. That's the kind of leash I've seen women put on men."

"Oh God, Phoebe. It's all so awful."

"And it doesn't have to be so. Just go to the clinic and this will all go away. If he loves you, you don't need this baby to prove it."

"I've got to think some more."

"Think about this," she said. "Where does he go and what does he do when he goes off on his little side trips?"

"He's exploring," I said. "That was his original plan for his sabbatical. He changed all of it for me."

"Are you sure?" she asked.

"Yes," I said. "Why would I not believe him?"

"Do you ever imagine what he might not be telling you?"

"I can't imagine what you're suggesting," I said.

"He's gone a lot for someone who is so in love," she said.

"He is on sabbatical from his job. He should be exploring and seeing London and Paris and ..."

"I can't help you if you won't help you." She got up and walked out. I went to the phone booth where I put the call in to India. I sat in that booth waiting for the miles of switching stations and satellite's beaming signals, all another technology Pete had taught me, realized the time difference too late, and then he answered.

"It's Cassandra," I said.

"Hi! This is nice," Pete said. "Except for the time."

"Sorry," I said. "I've got news."

"Good news?" Then he said, "You don't sound like it's good news."

"Pregnancy test. Positive four times. I did four tests. They're all positive. I'm sure, I'm positive, I missed my period. I was late when you left. Now I know. Now you know."

It was so silent in that booth. Of course, the library was always quiet, even this tiny alcove near the rest rooms where the booth hid away in the corner. It was dead silent and I could hear my heart's rhythm and a tiny internal fluid draining somewhere below my ribs. And he breathed. It came across the wire like a sigh. I was breathing too. And it was soft, emphasized in my consciousness to remind me that I was here inside this moment and so was Pete and I knew there was a togetherness and this was going to be okay, somehow, it would be okay. The fear that masqueraded as pretending walked like a phantom out the door and there we were.

Then Pete said, "Well, abortion is out of the question."

My own ambivalence rose up right there, a contrariness I recalled my mother always telling me I had. "Why can't you just go along to get along?" she often said to me in my youth. That had always loaded me with shame, as though I was flawed for wanting something different, and I recognized it now, that resistance to someone else's will. This was as deep a part of me as was my very soul. Pete was triggering that now and I felt my heels digging in. Phoebe's stare. Phoebe's

141

incredulity when I had said, "I'm Catholic." Which would I choose? There was no middle ground or compromise between what Pete had said so simply and Phoebe had assumed so unthinkingly.

Then Pete said, "India's got lots to study. Come here. We're good collaborators, Cassandra. This is a bit quick and unexpected, but we would have gotten here eventually."

And I said, "Gotten where?"

"To marriage," he said.

"Oh," I said. "Really?"

"Well, yes," he said. "I was planning to ask."

"When?"

"I don't know. Christmas time. I want to come back to spend it with you."

A kaleidoscope of confusion.

"So I can plan on marrying you." I stated it like a fact awaiting confirmation.

"Yes," he said. "Will you?"

"Is this because of my news?" I asked. "Or because we want to spend our lives together."

"Yes," he said. "To both."

"Ah," I said. "So only the timing is different?"

"Yes, that's a good way to say it," he said. He paused, then, "So?"

"Yes," I said. "I will decide. I need to hang up and take this all in."

"But it isn't just your decision." He said it so evenly. I took that to mean we were together on this, that this meant this was the continuation of a collaboration we had already begun, that his love was in this and he was waiting for me to put mine in too.

I said, "It is mine. Both are my decisions. One, whether to marry you, since you asked. And two, whether to have this baby."

"I have plenty of fire myself. What I need is the dandelion in the spring. The bright yellow that means rebirth instead of destruction." - Suzanne Collins

CHAPTER 17

If I had known in England that Pete would be gone as much now as he was on his sabbatical, I might have chosen differently. But I reminded myself, I wouldn't have Lila or Mia or Allie.

Now it seemed the chaos and the huge interruptions to my academic work had all led me to today. I could not know what I now knew had all that fateful crossing of the stone circle by Pete and the divergence from my planned path not happened. Even the birth of Lila and her adolescent obsession with photography played a role. I had to find the missing pieces of why and how Cindy and the other women had burned to death. They were not ritualized sacrifices on the altars of an ancient stone circle, like the animal carcasses we found at my dig.

I kept digging into my thesis and my notes. There was something else we discovered at the circle. Something to do with sacrifices, burned offerings. I gave up after a half hour, saw the lateness of the hour and climbed the stairs to my empty bed. This would have to wait.

I woke up the next morning and glanced at my mound of notebooks and journals and diagrams from the past. On my way to the kitchen for morning coffee, I could see all the twists and turns, detours and obstacles to my getting where I wanted to and I could see how they all served a purpose. This charged me up, gave me a sense that new brain synapses were firing, triggered by my re-activating some from the past that had been latent for so long. All my recent feelings of having been trapped into a life as a role instead of as a person began to ebb. All my frustration with Pete and his always being gone, all my feeling that I had been careless, stupid, getting pregnant so young, right in the middle of a huge surge of discovery. All my worries that I was flawed, that I had deliberately, on some subconscious level, sabotaged my own success, used Pete as my excuse for leaving Sheffield with my work unfinished. It all evaporated. Had I used Banhi's death as an excuse to run too? Go home. Retreat? This is where it had all lead me, back, full circle, and all of this accumulated collecting of data, all of the failed attempts to bring what I had learned to the attention of the Bangalore police department, all the calls I made to that *New York Times* reporter in Bangalore, who wrote the Pulitzer winning feature about the burning and scarring of brides, dowry deaths, the false claims that women had self-immolated, the ones the mother-in-laws swore were due to carelessness with kerosene stoves by young inexperienced brides. And before that, the dissertation disappointment when only Dr. Fields believed in me and my theories at Stonehenge. All those obstacles I had encountered in my pursuit of the truth, my search for something, somewhere to help me prove what I knew. Here, now, instead, I just might prove it myself, to myself, what I knew to be true about this strange and mysterious phenomenon. I'd figure it out and, if I did, they might believe me and they might not, I didn't care. I would do it for me, for those millions of missing women in India and for the memory of the women in Hillston who succumbed to it.

"You got your small fire all right."
- William Golding, *Lord of the Flies*

CHAPTER 18

I fished quarters from the coin jar, grabbed my yoga mat, and pulled the backdoor shut behind me. It was 8:30 and the buses were still slowing traffic, flashing their red lights, and stopping dead in the middle of the streets to pick up school kids. It was one of those days I remembered my patience. The driver behind me leaned on her horn each time the yellow bus shut off its red warning lights and pulled in its stop sign, as though I could now pass the bus, as though I had enough time to pass before it stopped again. Chill, I thought. I saw her slapping her steering wheel and talking to herself back there and I wanted to get out of my car next stop and give her a Namaste or a talking to. She could use both. I heard tires squeal behind me and saw in the rearview mirror how she turned right at the next corner and fled the line of traffic. I bet she doesn't have kids, I thought. Then I remembered. She was probably anxious because she was outside and just wanted to get safely to wherever she was going. I could feel it, a few minutes later, as others crossed the parking lot to the Y, walking fast, heads down, or furtively searching nearby for anything or anyone who could hurt them. Fear and more fear.

It was my first time doing something for myself since my library visit Saturday. Watching the hurrying, the ducking in to shadows, the strain in the eyes of others, I sensed I might be out of step with the fearful ones and while I waited for the traffic to pass so I could jaywalk toward the tall steps to the Y's lobby, I second guessed myself. Why was I not soaking my clothes and hair and darting from closed place to closed place? Why was I not feeling the terror manifesting itself everywhere? Was it because I was so close to Ann Neelam and didn't burn and die? Me, Goldie the dog, all those school children outside for the fire drill surrounding Elizabeth Lindsey? We'd not been hurt. We'd been spared. If God or the universe wanted me, he surely would have taken me right then and there last Friday right along with Ann. But here I was. I imagined someone saying I was spared for a reason. But that leads to the question of what reason? Why them and not me? I imagined everyone else asking, am I next? Is there any reason it would not be me? I should be frightened, I told myself. Why wasn't I? Was I pretending I wasn't?

I held my card under the scanner to clock in and found my way to the cycling room. I changed shoes, clicked my bike shoes into the pedals, and adjusted the handlebars, waiting for Jan, the instructor, to begin. The sun lit up the room, a window was open and light spring air, fragrant with lilac scent, wafted in. We had a full class and Jan started with a good James Taylor song. I pedaled, took a sip of water, and adjusted the band holding my hair off my neck and shoulders. The music distracted me from my preoccupations and I let my thoughts dissipate as the lyrics replaced them. I would get back to my investigating after I finished. I just pedaled, checked my heart rate on my wristwatch, tightened the tension on the bike to challenge myself, and felt sweat break from my temples. The intensity of Jan's instructions, the music switching to something loud, rock and roll with a beat, upped the exertion she demanded of us. Fatigue is weakness leaving the body, she reminded us. We pounded away and I tried to imagine I was on an open road, cycling into a beautiful landscape with blue sky, pine trees, and only the sound of birdsong and wind in my ears. The hour flew by. Then, finally, the longed for cool down, the slowing of our spins, the return to gentle music. Ah, nearly done. I used my hand towel to dry my forehead, my neck, my temples. I gulped water. So did all the others. I hadn't been here in a while and none of these women looked familiar. That's what happens when you take a job for your mornings, I thought. The familiar ones for me are the night crowd now, although with Pete gone so much even the evening yoga classes were hard for me to do on a regular basis. I stopped pedaling and clicked out of my pedal clips. Jan led us through a short stretch. Just as I crossed my right leg over my left thigh and leaned over, I heard it and lost my balance, landing awkwardly on both feet.

Then I felt it again, that whoosh of combustion and a wave of heat. Before I looked, I knew it was that again, somebody else, and disbelief and denial swept through me. We're inside. It can't happen indoors. But it was happening. Jan was shouting. The spinning class members, all of them, shrieked and made for the door. The first woman pulled at the door, but the others crowded too near and she couldn't get the door open. She yanked hard and knocked a blond in electric green spandex to the ground. The others stepped across her, but she fought to her feet and fled, leaving Jan and me and the burning woman to it. To what? What was there for us to do? Jan pulled an emergency alarm near her bike at the front of the room. The overhead sprinkle system kicked on and water poured from the pipes above us. She screamed at me. "Go! Get out! Save yourself!"

But I didn't flee. I couldn't. Hers had been the bike near the open window. I remembered now. She is the one who opened it before class started. She was aflame. She was blue flame, orange tipped, black smoke spiraling up toward the ceiling tiles. The sprinkler system activated but the pressure was not very strong. Déjà vu. Same response. I went for the extinguisher. It was just outside, on the stairway. It was a very large one. Heavy, but I lugged it into the spinning room and flipped it, turned the knob, opened the stream of dry chemical again, just like I did at the train, and watched the pointlessness of my effort. Still, I had to keep trying. What else was there? Jan meanwhile, ran down the stairs shouting at the top of her lungs. "It's happening. Evacuate. Everyone, there's a fire. Get out. Protect yourself. Go home.

Oh my God, one of my students is dying. Someone help. Call 911."
I kept doing what I had to do and Jan's shouts faded as she must
have run through the entire building sounding her alarm. Footsteps
pounded up the stairs and bodies rushed through the door, which was
glass, and the Y director, a handsome athletic guy with curly brown
hair whose flat abs class I'd taken a few times, stepped in. "I'll take
over," he said. "Get yourself out of here."

Sirens interrupted the formerly silent spring day and I saw red
swirling lights through the window. Men in black canvas coats and
yellow helmets streamed up the outside stairs, up the indoor stairs,
and arrived. That's when I suddenly felt trapped in that room. There
were so many swarming in. But they were too late. Whoever she had
been, she no longer was. And her gym bag, a bright pink, lay beside
her athletic wear and her aluminum water bottle and a tiny pile of
gray ash that had once been her. The lights went out, the air conditioner shut off. The exit lights, powered by the emergency generator,
came on and I thought to myself, the mayor is wrong. Staying inside
doesn't keep you safe. Then, I sat on the floor and put my head in my
hands and closed my eyes. It was a nightmare. It had been over, or
so we thought, but now it certainly was not and it was going to take
this town some time to grasp. At a tap on my shoulder, I looked into
Heffly's eyes, under his helmet, and saw something I did not like.

"Anywhere else?" I asked.

"Yes," he said. "Three others this morning. Can you walk?"

"I don't know," I said.

"Are you hurt?"

"No."

"Who else?" I asked. "Where?"

"Come with me." He reached out a hand, which I did not accept.
I got to my feet and went to the corner where I'd stored my mat
and my gym bag with my street shoes. He jumped ahead of me and
grabbed it.

"I can't walk in these," I said.

"You're going to have to," he said, "let's go."

Bike shoes are not made for walking down steps. Already I could feel blisters and I'd nearly lost my balance twice. Heffly's hand on my forearm had steadied me. Now I took them off and sat in my socks in the hot back seat of a patrol car, sweat still coming out of my pores and soaking my light tee shirt.

I waited. My watch told me it was fifty-three minutes. Then, Richmond sat next to me and said, "Heffly tells me you might know something about this. You better tell me what's going on."

"I don't know," I said. "I'm sorry."

"You were at two of these."

"What was her name?"

"I am not at liberty to disclose…"

"And who were the others? Heffly said there were others today."

"No answers until you answer some of our questions first Ms. Taylor."

"I can't."

"You can't or you won't."

"I can't."

"Why is that?"

"Because I don't know the answers. Cindy Barrow was my best friend…until a few years ago."

"So was there hostility between you?"

"Oh, please. You think there's a mom war on?"

"Tell me there isn't."

I stared at him hoping my incredulity was obvious. "Seriously?" He stared back, so I said, "There isn't."

"What were you doing here this morning?"

"It was a cycling class."

"Why didn't you run like the others?"

151

"Because I saw this already, remember? And I survived. It didn't get me. It only gets one at a time."

"It?"

"I think it's a phenomenon."

"What kind of phenomenon?"

"Some kind of energy convergence."

"Where in the world did you get that idea?" Richmond had leaned back against the seat. He was staring straight ahead, not at me. I sensed he was lightening up on his accusatory tone. I expected he was coming to his senses. I hoped Heffly was doing the same thing, but I didn't know if he was finding something upstairs that would contribute to his investigation, whatever the heck he and his team were up to. It had been long enough and the news was reporting nothing over and over hundred times a day.

"What's your name again?" he asked.

"Cassandra Taylor."

"You used to coach."

"Yes."

"Why'd you stop?"

"I got a job."

"Doing?"

"At the museum in Newark."

"Really? Doing what?"

I looked at him square. I had to lean forward and turn to face him. "I was on my way to a PhD when my work was interrupted and I came back here." I watched him for a response. " I studied stone circles as a geo-archaeologist."

"I thought you were just an at-home mom with kids."

"I thought so." I leaned back and stared out the window at the fire truck. "Listen, I did some work a while back that I'd like you and Heffly to know about. I might have some information for you and Mr. Heffly that could help you with this investigation. But it's not

152

about the moms' group or any nonsense about a moms' war or even about a cult doing self-immolation."

"You sure?"

"Mr. Richmond…you're victim blaming."

"That's not true."

"Yes. I've heard the speculation. Women in a cult. Women in a moms' group making some kind of statement. Self-immolation…I think if you both widen the investigation just a bit you will discard all this erroneous thinking."

"What makes you so sure? How do I know you're not deflecting blame? How do you prove to me and to Heffly, after we find you at two of these incidences, that you have nothing to do with them?"

"If you recall, I tried to save both."

"You could be faking that." He frowned. "Look at how calm you are. You're like a cold fish. You should be more upset like the other witnesses, like the other women in town. There is hysteria and now, after this morning, it's going to get worse. And you hardly bat an eye. That's a sign."

"Of what?"

"A sign of guilt or complicity in something."

"Did you ever consider that I am not the kind of woman who gets hysterical? That I can think instead of going crazy? There are women like that, you know. Just because I didn't run doesn't mean I'm a cold fish."

He sat in silence for a few seconds.

I said, "Why her? There were at least eight women in that cycling class."

"We're detaining everyone who was in the building." He frowned again. "Listen, we know who you are." He opened the car door and stepped out. He leaned in and said, "If you've got anything you want to tell me, call the station. I've got two other scenes to get to. Now get yourself home and inside and away from the windows. This one was

153

inside. How the building didn't burn is a miracle. I have to go find out about the others."

"Did you notice the power went off?"

"That's part of the emergency system. It happens automatically when the emergency alarm gets pulled and the sprinklers turn on."

My parting comment to him was a reminder. "Her clothes didn't burn. Why would you expect the building to burn if her clothes didn't?

"You might have had something to do with that," he said.

I moved myself out of that patrol car and through the gathering of YMCA members and other spectators gathered on the sidewalk. Blue uniformed policemen had created a divide between those who had fled and the more casual observers. If Richmond's instructions to go home and stay away from the windows were sound, why were the police holding people outdoors on the sidewalk in the bright sun? I was filled with a sense of disconnection and felt the banality of these decisions by the authorities. This was not protection against this. These people were more vulnerable following the orders of the police than if they all just went home. Gees, the cycling room had emptied so fast. Even the woman who fell, the one with the green leggings, had vanished down those stairs so fast. Through these observations I felt stares from the gathered crowd.

"Richmond told me to go home, to pull the blinds, and stay away from windows," I announced to them all. "If I were you, I'd do the same."

An officer pulled me roughly aside. "Do you want me to arrest you? Don't make trouble."

"You're first job is safety," I told him. "Let these people go home. Or bring them indoors. It's on you if it happens again."

Melissa, the Pilates instructor, whose class I would have been in on a normal day, echoed my sentiments. "Go home!" she shouted. "Get to safety."

The cluster of Y members behind the barrier of sawhorses erupted. I watched the barriers fall, the cross bars and the supports collapse, the indignant people stepping across and spreading out along the street, crossing the street, forcing passing traffic to screech to a halt. They fanned out in all directions, some running at a full tilt, others at the fastest a pace they could muster. Some of the women carried young children who had been in the day care room while they exercised. Two men showed some chivalry and gave assistance to a woman trying to manage twins, a huge gym bag, a diaper bag, and a stubborn stroller that would not open. To add to the chaos, the traffic lights were not working. The power was still out and it wasn't only in the Y building. Patrolmen were divided between the need to step out and manage the passing cars and buses and the need to stop the fleeing crowd. I jogged to my own car, slid in and waited while SUVs backed up, turned and lined up at the parking lot exit where some drivers defied the one-way signs and took off up the street. Richmond was going to be very angry. Heffly too. And those officers would remember it had been me, stepping out of the car, who had incited this rebellion.

I followed the line of cars and got out of there. But I didn't go home. By now, my heart rate had returned to normal, I was no longer sweating, and the air conditioner was drying my tee shirt nicely. I glanced at my reflection in the mirror. I'm still here, I told myself. Do something. I wanted to know where and to whom this horror had occurred. Heffly had said two others. I played the local radio news and waited. It didn't take long. They said Hillston. They said the YMCA, then they said a private home, a woman gardening, the third in the park, our park, my park, the park where Lila always took photos of the ancient oak and other trees. She was at school, so I didn't worry. Just then, my cell phone rang and I heard, "It's me, Doug."

"Where else?" I asked. "I was at the Y. Gees, this is growing. Three more."

He interrupted my urge to babble on and brought me back to calm. "I'm at the house on Missouri Avenue."

I knew someone on Missouri Avenue. "Who?" I asked. "Who is it?"

"Kathy Emling. Know her?"

"No." Relief was hardly a comfort. "Who was it at the park?"

"Danusha Petrovski."

"She's an artist."

"Yes."

"I don't know her personally, but I know her work."

"Are you somewhere safe?" he asked.

"In my car."

"Go home. They're letting schools out early."

"Oh, gees. Thanks. The radio didn't say..."

"They just released a robo call to all the district parents."

Lila would be walking. The twins would be on the bus. I thanked Doug and turned toward the high school. I knew her route home. But she was not on Park Street or Hadley Place. I passed the park, but there were so many police cars, a fire truck, an ambulance, it was impossible to see. But then there she was, my intrepid girl, standing in the middle of the grassy lacrosse field, camera in hand, and I could see she had mounted her zoom lens. She was oblivious, giving rapt attention to whatever vision she was trying to capture and rendering my effort to get her attention pointless. I got out of the car and ran across the field. "Lila!" I shouted. She didn't notice until my shadow crossed her field of vision and ruined the light she was apparently trying to capture.

"Mom!"

"Honey, please, you shouldn't be out here."

"No, you shouldn't be out here, Mom!" But she snapped the lens cap on and followed me. "I'm only coming because you're going to stand there in danger and it will be my fault if it happens to you." Clearly, she was annoyed. But so was I.

"It is only happening to women, not teenagers."

"So far," I said. "Let's keep it that way, please."

She took the passenger seat and I pulled to the corner where the bus would drop Mia and Allie. We sat and waited.

Lila said, "Where were you Mom?"

"At the YMCA. I was in my cycling class. It was right there in the room, the woman, she was in the class, right near the window. Keep your window up."

"Wow, inside?"

I nodded.

"So inside or outside, it doesn't matter. So why can't I go take my pictures?"

"I just want you near me. I just want to know you're safe. Until they figure this out, please just listen to me."

She opened her mouth to speak. I could sense the resistance she was about to unleash. "Listen," I interrupted before she could say anything, "don't try to use logic with me. There is no known logic that applies to this. Just please don't fight with me."

She closed her mouth and sank back into her seat. When the bus pulled up, she put her hand on the door handle. "I'm getting them," she said. "The odds are more likely against you than me." Before I could object she was out, gathered up her sisters, slid the van door open, and shut it behind them. She was back in the car in less than two minutes. We drove home and I wondered what reason they had given the young ones, Mia and Allie, for the early dismissal and how much I would need to explain to them.

"We each have a special something we can get only at a special time of our life. like a small flame. A careful, fortunate few cherish that flame, nurture it, hold it as a torch to light their way. But once that flame goes out, it's gone forever."
- Haruki Murakami, *Sputnik Sweetheart*

CHAPTER 19

The press was all over town. The national news was hovering over Hillston waiting for the next burning. Vans with logos of NBC, CBS, ABC, CNN, MSNBC lined the main streets or circled outdoor gathering places, like the plaza outside the library, the parking lot of the Safeway, the schools at recess when teachers brought the kids outside for fresh air. Places women crossed through on their daily duties. Lunch places where friends gathered. I noticed there were new canopies over the usual outdoor dining cafes on Church Street just spilling onto the sidewalk. I didn't see any vans near the basketball courts at Brookside Park or the little league fields where little boys and their father/coaches held practice or games. They were parked in front of the day spa, the meditation garden at the Unitarian Church. When I saw Fox News at the pre-school at the Methodist church, where the Mother's Morning Out program allowed women to drop their toddlers one morning a week for a nursery school experience, next to the library where I stopped in to renew my Atwood novel, I couldn't help myself; I found this terribly offensive. I knocked on the window of the passenger side of the Fox News van. When the cameraman rolled it down, I said, "Do you have a fire extinguisher in there too or just your camera?" He moved his cell phone away from his ear and squinted at me, "I beg your pardon?"

I repeated myself.

"No, ma'am," he said.

"Why not? If it happens, you could save her."

"We're a news reporting crew," he said. "We can't MAKE news."

In the back seat, the reporter scribbling on a notepad looked up and grabbed her microphone. She slid the rear door open and stepped out. "You're Cassandra Taylor," she said. "You're that witness."

I ducked my head and marched away. She followed me. After about fifty paces, I turned.

"I find this terribly offensive," I said. "Women's lives are being tossed out and you all act like some freak show is going on here."

The reporter who had jet black hair and striking blue eyes and too much make-up said, "So why do you think this is only happening to women?"

I said, in a deliberately even tone, "Because there have been no burnings of men." I thought I ought to follow that with "duh," but I kept that urge inside and simply stared at her.

"Well, yes," she said, trying to recover from the obvious, "but do you think it can happen to men?"

"Why are you asking me that?" I said. "Your fellow news folks seem to be watching women's places only, so you must think so too."

"Are you Cassandra Taylor?"

"Yes."

"Well, we did some background on the witnesses. You seem to have experience with burnings of women...in India I believe."

"When men burn in India, they are usually dead and on a funeral pyre. Or they self-immolate."

"And women?" she asked. I had no idea where she thought her questions were leading me.

I blinked. "There are 4.6 million missing women in India. Did you know that?"

"Ms. Taylor, can you comment on what's happening here in Hillston? You witnessed the first woman who died. I understand you acted heroically to try to save her." She tossed her hair over her left shoulder and stared into my eyes. "Then you were there at the Y."

"I could, but you'd be better off asking Fire Chief Heffly or our chief of police."

"There are some in town who speculate that these are not accidents but might be foul play."

"Again, I wouldn't know. The police are not saying much publicly. I hope they know more than they seem to feel like sharing with the public," I said.

"Were you part of that mothers' group?" she asked.

I said, "I have to go." And I turned to walk away.

"Was it a cult?" she called after me.

"No," I tossed back over my shoulder. "It was a support group for career woman who left their jobs to be stay at home moms."

"Were these women vulnerable? Why did they need support?"

"Do you have children?" I stopped and turned. "Are you married?"

"No," she said.

"You planning to do that some day?"

"Maybe," she said.

"It isn't something I can explain to you. You either know the answer to that question or you don't. An explanation will only sound banal."

"Try me," she said.

"Turn the mike off," I said.

She did.

"Tell your cameraman to stop rolling."

She glanced at him and nodded. He retreated.

"I was on my way to a PhD when I got pregnant. I gave up a lot to be a mom. There comes a time when you feel regret and you can't climb back onto the horse you were once riding because it's left the barn."

"You need support for that?" she asked, a slight smirk crossing her eyes.

"No," I said. "There are different expectations of you after that. They come from the people around you and from inside yourself." I paused to observe her, but she was an unreadable blank. "It's a polarity and you swing in between both expectations for the rest of your life. Motherhood done well, a mind with so much unused bandwidth while you dole out all your energy for your children and family. The cognitive machine in your intellect doesn't become subsumed by all that. It lays there in a latent state. It needs somewhere to go." I paused. "The group gave that part of us somewhere to go."

"If it doesn't have anywhere to go?"

I laughed. "Well, maybe you go up in flames. Or maybe that part of you does and, when that happens, the rest of you goes with it."

"So is this what you think?"

"What do you mean, think?"

"These women couldn't resolve internal conflict, so they died?"

A knot of irritation rose up and my antenna for bullshit went on high alert. "You think a psychic phenomenon can burn women?"

"Well, at this point," she said. "I speculate on anything."

"But it's your job to report the news, not offer your speculation on it. My point is it was a support group for like-minded women who understood this. Not a cult of self-harming fanatics."

"So what's happening then?"

"Like I said, the police and fire department should be your sources for that question."

"So you'll listen to my speculation but not offer yours. I thought you were going to do that." I heard the challenge and something in me wanted to divulge, but I remembered as a member of the Fraternity for Contemplative Research you don't reveal your speculation until you have evidence to back it up. I didn't trust her like I did Doug despite her seeming willingness to listen. The mike was off, but still.

"I have my own way of understanding this, but I'm not going to share it with you on or off the record unless evidence supports it. I think everyone in town has their own idea too."

She nodded. "I might want to interview you on the record, maybe now isn't the time."

"Why?"

"I Googled you. You're a scientist. I saw more than your stint in India."

I nodded. "Maybe later. I'm in the phone directory. Sycamore in Hillston."

"Thanks," she said. She offered her hand to shake and I did, then turned toward the library doors. The old homeless man stood up from his bench. I didn't pause, but I felt his eyes on me as I passed. I renewed my book and hurried to the car. The school bus would be arriving. I had just five minutes left to meet it.

"You are not required to set yourself on fire to keep other people warm." - Anonymous

CHAPTER 20

The days no longer felt ordinary. There was a current running through everything, a tension, a new fear, and I was not immune. And there were my three images of women succumbing to fire burned into memory. It seemed all I observed now, every sound, every scent, every color and shape, every moment of movement was tinged with an expectation, an anticipation of something sinister repeating itself. Lila was close in age to Banhi. In Hillston, she was still a child. In Bangalore she would be considered an adult. Even though this had only happened to middle aged women, were my daughters in danger? Was I? No matter how much I pondered the idea of radon as a factor in this, I couldn't ignore the reality that far more people were dealing with radon gas than were dying in mysterious fires.

PBS aired Arthur Miller's "The Crucible" the Friday night before Cindy's memorial service. Evil witches were burned at the stake in European superstitions. St. Joan of Arc was burned at the stake. Every culture had its own variety of mythology about fire and the burning of women. And my own discontent, raising its ugly head, a sense of seething frustration, the choices my life drove me to make, my lack of a channel for the passions that burned inside me, terrified me. I imagined I too could just burst into flame, disappearing from this life, entering the dimension of death where my soul would inhabit a new person, a new set of circumstances, and what I knew now might just help this new version of me to stop making mistakes. My only non-mistakes were my children. My fear of this actually happening to me was wrapped in the fear for them for the wound they'd carry in a life with their mother gone, like Brandon would have to do now.

Lila moved through her days as though nothing was amiss except that her camera was perhaps in need of replacement. It was that self-confidence that grows in teenagers, that they are invincible, that death is far away, that they can step through life nearly untouchable by danger. Invisible and bulletproof was a phrase Phoebe used once in England. Now I just worried about my young daughter, intrepidly stepping through life unmindful of all this terror.

"Dad's not here," she said. "I need to ask him something about those articles you printed for me."

"Well, call him," I said. "Or ask me."

She left him a voicemail and hung up, sighing. This was on a sunny afternoon midweek. Then she just said, "I've got more appointments with families. For photos. I'll be back after dinner." And she headed toward the front door.

"Lila," I said. "Let me drive you."

"Mom," she said. "I can walk. That's why we live in a town with sidewalks. That's what you always said."

"That was before," I said.

"Stop," she said. "I am not letting your fear change the way I live." And I let her go, but not without needing a few moments to calm myself, talk to myself, tell myself she was right, and resist the urge to follow her in the car, as though my very presence could protect her, which, considering Banhi, and my failed rescues at the train station and Y was self-deception.

I had laundry to do. I took a pile to the basement and spent a few minutes re-arranging some of Lila's mess down there where she had draped the windows with black fabric and run a string for a drying line for prints. Her pans of chemicals had to be carefully lifted and moved to the folding table I usually used for clean dry laundry so I could open the washing machine. As the basin filled with water and the detergent bubbled and the clean scent reached my nostrils, I dropped clothes in, then gently shut the lid. I turned and paused to study the latest prints she'd hung on that string. They were just at eye level.

This was one of those slow reveal moments that comes along and heightens what one might call the inner anxiety of living. Accompanying that was the excitement of discovery. There, right there in my laundry room, was a line of photographs of families, with the mother dead center, some sitting, surrounded by their children, some standing with arms draped across the shoulders of their young brood. In every photograph, the same cloudy blur, the same obliteration of just the woman, and some were familiar faces, members of the mother's support group Cindy and I had started and divided so long ago. I stood and studied these prints in the dim light of my laundry room. Included in this lineup was Cindy Barrow and her boy Brandon, posing with slight smiles and soft eyes. This was the picture I'd asked Lila to show me. Now, I studied her closely. Derrick's description of her, the contentment she seemed to have found, the evidence that she was in a good place in her mind and her heart, was there. I felt a sense of ironic gratitude for her having found this level of happiness, mingled with the grief that came with knowing she was no longer here to savor that hard-won contentment. My friend was gone forever but for such things as photographs. Of course, it was a natural eventuality that these women have children who might know of Lila's project. I studied these. Some were people I'd never laid eyes on before. I would have to ask Lila who they were. The washing machine, now full of water, lurched into its agitation cycle with a sharp mechanical sound. I jumped. I listened as the water sloshed back and forth inside the tub. I returned to my kitchen and called Lila's cell phone.

"What?" she said, her impatience clear.

"I want to do a picture of us," I said. "From your project. But I want you in it."

165

"We can do that," she said. "I have my tripod."

"When?"

"Whenever," she said. "I'm with people. Can this wait?"

"One more question," I said.

"Mom."

"Can you give me a list of all the families you photographed? I want to know whose pictures had to be redone and who's turned out right the first time."

"What on earth do you want this for?"

"I'm not sure. But will you show me when you get home?"

"Why do you want this?" This was new, Lila showing me a defiant side I'd not seen before, ever.

"I just have an idea."

"Well, you're going to have to tell me your idea before I agree."

"Fair enough," I said.

"I'll be home later." She hung up. I waited for her. Actively waited, pacing, fussing, even going to her bedroom and searching through the mess of school notebooks, papers, binders and folders on her desk. It felt better than doing nothing, better than the worry gnawing at me.

When she did get home, she was furious to find me in her room. Something new, which I attributed to her age and teenage rebellion was emerging and we had quite a shouting match. At my insistence, she shared the list and a contact print of each of the women she photographed. Then, the phone rang. It was Pete calling Lila back. The quiet that settled over her with this interruption, the softness that returned to her voice and expression when she spoke to him, was quite obvious. I found myself jealous of him and angry at her. And I felt that sense of invisibility that comes from being the ever-present parent.

She handed me the phone and Pete informed me he was not coming home for the weekend. The client he'd been to see needed him on Monday so rather than fly home, he was going to stay in Chicago and visit an old friend. With Lila right there, listening to my side of this while she shuffled through to find me the things I'd asked for, I didn't have an opportunity to say what I wanted to say. I took the phone into the bathroom. "Pete," I said, "This is a weekend when I really need you. We talked about this. The funeral for Cindy is Saturday."

"Yes, we did talk about it," he said.

"But don't you understand how I feel?"

"I'm sorry Cass."

"You've never been away over a weekend for business before Pete. Why now? Why can't you come home?"

"The company is tightening budgets for travel. This will save them at least a thousand on airfare."

"Who is the old friend?"

"You don't know him."

"Still, I want to know who it is."

"He's from Long Island. A high school buddy I connected with on Facebook. He lives in Chicago. We're going to play golf."

"You're going to spend the weekend playing golf while I go to a memorial service for someone who used to be my best friend." I stated it in a flat tone.

"Do you have to say it like that? You're the one who is always telling me to set some time aside for some fun."

"That's when I want you to be with me and the girls for some fun, not this."

"That's very selfish of you Cassie."

I went cold. My fingers numbed and I shivered. "Pete, what's selfish about this? Who is being the selfish one here?"

"I think maybe you should answer that one."

"You know, I'm feeling very unnerved by all this. Six women died, one of my best friends. I watched. Right before my eyes. And my effort to save two failed. I need my husband here so I have someone to lean on. Can you please come home? Pay for the return plane yourself."

Silence crossed that phone connection for an endless few seconds.

"Cassie…"

"What?"

"I can't cancel the weekend plan now. It's too late."

"No," I said. "It isn't. You never should have made this plan. You knew this was happening."

"I have to go," he said.

I said, "You may never recover from this." I hung up on his goodbye.

I hid in the bathroom until the lump in my throat melted away. I couldn't stop the sense that I was recognizing a pattern, perhaps one I had been ignoring for a long time. It loomed before me, surprised me, awoke something so resentful that it filled me with a dread and a fear I'd not experienced. A string of similar chapters between me and Pete lined up from memory and indignation swelled up like a mushroom cloud.

In Bangalore, when I was seven months pregnant, Pete had said, "And you should go stateside for the birth. Maybe fly a week before the due date."

And we did, together. A three-week plan for which he stayed for six days and left me and Lila in the hands of my mother and Lou and the stewardesses who hovered over us on the flight back. Pete met me at the airport with a warm hug. In the cab, on the way home, he said, "Banhi's father found her a husband. The wedding is in three weeks. I'm not sure she is going to be able to continue working for you."

I remember trying to describe that incident to Dr. Gimpel, trying to set it in a context of a husband who was only out for my welfare, who wanted a safe delivery for the baby, and good care for me.

Dr. Gimpel had asked what had I felt at the time. Had there been something urgent waiting for him in Bangalore? Were my needs being met? Were my first post-partum weeks physically challenging? Most importantly, she said, a couple should make decisions together. I had

168

insisted he was a responsible man who did the right thing, leaving me in the care of my family, my sister, at my childhood home while he went back to his job to earn the money we needed. "My sister was a godsend," I had told Dr. Gimpel. And Lou had been. She soothed Lila, rocked her so I could get some rest, brought me tall glasses of water when I sat down to breastfeed.

Now, the sense of something very wrong about Pete having left Hillston early rose up and wouldn't leave me, something I hadn't the confidence to reveal to him back when I really wanted him with me. Now that I did tell him I needed him, it felt like a wake-up call I hadn't asked for.

I would not take my twins to the memorial service. They were too young. I paged through a mental list of women friends I could ask to babysit. All my Hillston friends would be at the service. Ian, the college sophomore would be working at the ice cream parlor. There were nanny's, Dolores, from the bus stop, but I hesitated to burden her, knowing Saturday was her only day off to visit her sister.

Lou had been the one to fill in for Pete back then. I'd never asked her for this in all the years I'd been back in Hillston. She'd be more likely than Grace to say yes. But she wasn't home, so I left a voice message and hoped she'd call soon.

In the middle of dinner, the phone rang. Lou's number appeared on the incoming call id and I lifted the phone to my ear wondering how I could word this so she'd find it hard to refuse.

"Lou," I said. "Hi, thanks for calling back."

"Hi," she said. "What's up?"

"I have a memorial service on Saturday and Pete is going to be out of town. Lila needs to go too."

"You need me to watch the twins?"

"Could you?" I felt a surge of hope that this would be easier than anticipated.

"What time?"

"It starts at one."

"Can you bring them here?"

"Sure. They'd love to come there."

"I have dinner plans at 5:30. Will I be done by then?"

"I'll make sure you are." I felt a rush of gratitude. "Thanks, Lou."

"Is it for that friend of yours who died in the fire? I heard about this."

"Yes. Cindy. You met her at the twins' christening."

"Grace is afraid to leave the house," Lou said. "This thing is scary. Aren't you nervous about being outside?"

"Yes," I said. "But…"

"Everybody thinks it's someone like a sniper, like that sharp shooter in Washington DC a few years ago. Remember he was picking off victims from a mile away?"

"But that was a rifle, not fire," I said. "I doubt it's…"

"What about a laser or something? Some new kind of weapon that throws flame or a special kind of bullet with chemicals that erupts into flames?" Lou asked.

"Everyone has a theory," I said. "None of them make sense."

"I read about the mother's group…how the first three women were all part of that group you started. Like it's a cult and they're doing it to themselves. I heard rumors about that too."

"You saw the paper?" I said. "I don't think so."

"Well, what then?" she asked. "I hope they find out before Grace ends up canceling Catherine's party. It's next weekend. She is having it outside…unless she changes it."

"She probably will change it," I said. "If she's that worried. I would. Just to have peace of mind."

"Charles wants to cancel it," Lou said. "He said we shouldn't make people come out for a non-essential reason."

"But there's only one high school graduation for Catherine. I see why she won't cancel it. It's important. Maybe we'll know something before then," I said. "Listen, I'm feeding the kids. Okay if I bring them over at noon?"

"Yup, that's fine. And I promise they won't be playing outside."

"Thank you, Lou," I said.

"No problem," she said and hung up. The old Lou, from our childhood, was still in her, I thought with a warm sense of our old closeness.

"What matters most is how well you walk through the fire." -
Charles Bukowski

CHAPTER 21

Derrick's gratitude was evident when he bent to plant a light kiss on my cheek at the memorial service. Lila and I entered the ballroom at the Hilton together, then she saw some friends of Brandon's and I let her go sit with them. There were at least fifty of us, the results of my long string of phone calls, some to women I had never met, and, when I took my seat next to Mary Howe, the memory of that division, the petty disagreement so long ago, gave me a moment's pause. We were all here and we must have all been remembering.

Then, in walked that man, Spencer Krump from the Institute for Philosophy for Children. He carried the same arrogance that had first put me off back when he first came to speak to our group. Now I felt a reprise of my distaste as he stepped up the center aisle wearing a poppy in the breast pocket of his steel gray suit. I experienced more than a tinge of revulsion at the perfection in the way he put himself together. He was like a smug evangelical, entitled to happiness because his choices in life were the correct ones. I watched him take a small stack of index cards from his inner pocket and I realized he would speak to us about Cindy. A dead coldness crept into me. This was the ballroom at the Hilton Garden Hotel on the highway that bypassed Hillston. The air conditioning cranked and the air was dry and near as cold as my refrigerator's interior. Everyone seemed disturbed by this excessive cold. Derrick and Brandon and Cindy's extended family walked up the center aisle. It was time to begin.

A priest led us in prayer. I knew these prayers, I recited them now verbatim. There was an emptiness these words did not fill. I needed someone, someone to be here for me while I was alive the way Derrick was up there for Cindy who was dead or Mary's husband there on the other side of her, holding her hand. I dared not let myself feel this. I was here for Cindy, mourning for her and the friendship I had let slip away, a failure that she too was complicit in. I wanted Pete to put us above his own stubborn pre-occupations and love me. I wanted that he would have come as soon as he heard me. I wanted to call Pete and say, "The world stops for us when someone loses a friend. The world respects that families, couples, husbands and wives need each other. Why can't you?" Of course, I didn't, not in the middle of all this. I stood there and mumbled prayers and responses to the psalms. I sang the songs, Amazing Grace, Eagle's Wings, and then a woman stepped up from the crowd and sang "Both Sides Now" by Joni Mitchell and I couldn't sing along for the lump in my throat.

Krump rose and stepped to the podium. Derrick just sat there, his back to us all, his head held still, eyes straight ahead.

He began, in one of those deep voices that sounds like he is imitating someone he would rather sound like than himself. Phony, the same word had come to me so long ago when he spoke at our meeting, when the rumbling and grumbling about Cindy among members started.

Back then, he said, "The world is made of energy and energy never dies, it only changes form and we all have the ability to harness it." He'd gone on to say he wanted to teach us a method for doing it. I remembered he said it was simple and had been known since the 1950s when a man who had studied with Sigmund Freud identified and perfected it.

I remembered the incredulity at the idea that you could sit quietly inside his phone booth-like device and energy would accumulate in your body, enough energy to combat depression, anxiety and sexual dysfunction. I sat now, stiffening in my shoulders and neck, resistance growing with each word. This man had divided us, had duped the weak among our members. I knew of Cindy's struggle after her mother died so suddenly, I knew of a few other members who struggled with finances, with developmental issues with their children, with what seemed to be normal obstacles to serenity. He had exploited it. For this, my anger at Pete for not being here with me, for my having to go it alone, grew. Pete was my dysfunction right now and it brought on a fear that this chasm between us would weaken me. I could succumb as easily to this man's bullshit or to something else. My mind raced on. All this flashed across my inner vision with a new knowing and, with it, a new question. What, underneath our engagement with each other, with our forming of community, had been left vulnerable to this man's ideas? Then, I asked myself why some of us had not bought into his ideas. Some of us had resisted, had seen through the illogic, the falsity of his claims and, while not able to open the eyes of our friends to his empty promises, we refused to embrace or incorporate his ideas into our lives.

He was speaking. But I knew this man was not offering universal truth, only his own version of it. Oh, how I wished I could see Derrick's face.

His story was about a flock of birds that had not migrated before the cold of winter had come. This flock of birds was shivering on the branches of a tree on the property of a farmer. It was near dusk. The farmer and his helper knew a blizzard was on the way and these tiny swallows would most likely perish. So they opened the barn door wide. But the birds seemed to have lost their natural self-protective instincts. The farmer and his partner took turns and climbed the tree and swished their arms to flush the birds out of the tree. They flew into the air at the urging of the farmer and his helper, but they only returned to the branches again. Then, the helper turned to the farmer and said, "If I could become a bird like them, I could fly up and fly into the barn and be warm and safe. They would see me and do the same."

Spencer Krump paused. "Cindy was that kind of person. She led by example. When she believed in something, she lived it. And for that, I am grateful to have known her. Without her, the work I am doing through the Institute at the college might have stayed theoretical. For her, for her example, like the helper in the story who tried in a simple way, to help those little birds, I will hold her in my memory for the rest of my life." And, with that, he sat down.

I glanced across the center aisle toward the cluster of women who had followed Cindy. Alice Bryant was nodding her head, her eyes brimming with tears. Gina Jones had her arm draped across Alice's shoulders and her eyes averted, a tissue crumpled in her other hand. Those on my side of the aisle sat in collective recognition of the dissonance of his words and the reality of the day. Cindy became the bird to lead the others to safety? She's dead.

Derrick stood. It was his turn.

I heard the door at the back of the room gently close. Pete came, I thought. He's here after all. I turned. Doug Bluestein stood with his back to the rear wall. He caught my eye and nodded slightly. I pointed to an empty chair just behind me on the aisle and he moved to it.

"Cindy is not the only woman to die this way this week," Derrick said. "I think it right that we give a moment of silence for the others."

We all obeyed, the only disturbance of the utter silence was a weak dry cough from directly behind me and I knew it was Doug. Then Derrick said, "Above all things, Cindy was a loving wife and mother. All of her life, especially her education as an early childhood teacher, then with her masters from the Institute for Philosophy for Children, was preparation for raising her own children."

His gaze moved slowly around the room. He took a deep breath and slowly let it out. The room was warming up a bit. I was no longer sporting goose bumps on my naked arms.

"Cindy took in everything and she remembered it all. And for this I am so grateful. She taught me to pay attention and I did. And she taught Brandon the same thing. Pay attention, she would tell him." He looked over at Brandon and smiled, "Right? Brandon? That was her, all the time." I saw Brandon nod. "So it is almost like she was preparing me and Brandon." Then he said, "If any of you would like a chance to share a memory, I invite you up here to speak. Thank you all so much for being here, for being in her life, and for giving her the memories she takes with her." He sat down and I saw his hands move to his face and his shoulders bend forward.

I didn't need the stories the rest of the speakers told and I didn't trust myself to hold it together long enough to speak. I had nothing to add, really. I listened and applauded and waited for it to be over. Then, suddenly, it was and we were filing into an adjoining room with buffet tables and a bar and small round tables arranged for sitting. The balcony was open, a wide veranda, also with tables.

Doug was behind me as we entered. Lila was not in sight, but I knew she'd be with the young crowd, so I let Doug accompany me to the buffet table, then we sat together outdoors. He glanced at me as though to question the choice of the veranda, but I nodded and he held the door while I balanced my plate and a glass of wine. I felt a connection when I saw his ring with the insignia and this helped me to be here without Pete.

In his easy company, I gave him the story of my and Cindy's friendship and its demise. I shared with him the story of the afternoon when I stopped by her house and saw the Essen accumulator tucked into the corner of her butler pantry, the final episode of our falling out, the day I let my angry words fly, the results of my research about this fraud which had been perpetrated upon her by Spencer Krump, the injunction against the man who had originated this theory of Essen energy, a life giving force that could be concentrated in a box with metal wire and cotton? I had said, "Seriously, Cindy, with all

176

your education and all your intellect, I can't believe you are invested in this." Doug listened while I spoke in low tones so nobody passing us would overhear me.

"Who was this guy who had the injunction?" Doug asked.

"His name was Bruno Brandt. He ended up in jail when one of his protégées sold one of his accumulators across state lines. He sold it to a woman who believed it would cure her cancer."

"When was this?" Doug asked.

"The 1950s," I said. "The FDA was watching this man. They had him in their sights as a fraud. He died in jail. I read all this back when we were still friends."

"Did you ever try it?"

"Her accumulator? No, please, no."

"So why do you know so much about it?" he asked.

"I was so disappointed with her for falling prey to this man. I read up on it, hoping to learn enough to convince her to give it up." I looked around to see Krump was still in the room. I held up my hand with my ring. "Contemplative Research? That's me. I am a member in full."

"Yes," he said and laughed. "So what did you find out about Brandt?"

"I'll give you a book I found. But I wanted to tell you…I found out how you earned your membership in the fraternity."

"Oh?" He lifted his eyebrows.

"Micky Dolan."

"Gees, you are quite the sleuth. No wonder you're in the Fraternity."

"Doug, it's all on the web. I just Googled you."

"Yes, I wondered how long it would take you to do that." It was his turn to smile. "I did the same on you."

"You were cut short by a death too."

"Yes."

"And you have an unfinished investigation."

"Cassandra," he said. "Are you making statements or asking me questions?"

"Both," I said. "What was Richard Grasso doing in the jungles of Colombia with FARC rebels who funded their arms with illegal drug money?"

He looked at me long and hard. He fingered his ring and held it for me to see. "My membership in the Fraternity is more about silence on my unfinished work than anything else."

"So you won't answer me?"

"Can you stay silent if I tell you? You're a member. You've sworn to secrecy and silence."

"Only until my knowledge of something can save a life or improve humankind."

"Yes, well, if you divulge this you might just cause my death."

"Doug, I'm sworn to secrecy." I held up my hand like a Girl Scout.

"Micky had instincts. He saw that picture of Grasso in the jungle and knew immediately this was a bigger story than Grasso's PR men made it out to be."

"Money laundering for drug cartels." I said it, plain, simple, quietly.

"It's so obvious, isn't it?" Doug said. "It was a secret hiding in plain sight. Most won't put two and two together because they're not paying attention. High stakes investors don't care as long as they're getting rich. But Micky wasn't a slouch. He wasn't a high stakes investor, he was just a regular guy. He remembered the informant on Watergate said 'follow the money' and he tried to do that with Grasso's incredibly high salary at the Exchange. He wanted to know who was behind decisions on executive compensation. When he started to ask questions about the jungle visit and went to Spitzer with something he knew but didn't tell me– well, Micky died for asking too many questions. And later, Eliot Spitzer lost his lawsuit with Grasso over his exorbitant salary, of course he did. That effort was all for show. So, yes, what might have been another Oliver North and the Iran Contra affair, illegal gun trade funding rebels – this one was illegal drug trade funding rebels with money being laundered in the stock market – well it turned into nothing because they got Micky." Doug stared into my eyes. "I don't want the same fate as Micky. I'd rather be alive than be a hero. This one was too big for anybody to win."

I leaned back in my chair. "So you're walking around with a big piece of knowledge and you can't share it with anyone."

"I can't write about it," he said. "It actually feels good to tell you."

"I'm glad you did."

"Well, I'm kind of glad you asked."

"I wanted to know why you're working for a small-time newspaper when you could be doing more."

"And you're working for chump change at the museum sitting on a whole encyclopedia of knowledge."

"I guess we're both underachievers?"

"No, but I think we've been drawn together for some kind of collaboration on this." He indicated the room and I knew he meant more than the memorial service.

I nodded in agreement. "Who initiated you into the Fraternity? It was after Micky's death?" I asked.

"I can't tell you. That would reveal that person's membership."

"Oh, of course," I said. "Sorry."

"So now that you know all this about me and I know all about your background and now that we have to trust each other and keep secrets, we can be friends."

"Yes," I said, feeling a bit of that glow that comes from knowing someone appreciates you and you appreciate them and it's all full of possibilities. It hit me too that if Pete were with me, Doug and I would not be having this conversation. If Pete were around, Doug would not have sat with me or, if he had at my invitation, Pete would dominate the conversation, asking Doug superfluous questions that would float on the surface and likely leave me out of it entirely. I liked that Doug and I had secrets. I also realized the glow I was feeling had a bit more to do with my finding him handsome in his dark colored suit and the way his eyes stayed on mine while we spoke instead of wandering around the veranda aimlessly taking in nothing important. I had worn a simple sleeveless dark blue dress and jacket. I felt pretty with my hair swept up in a bun and earrings glittering. I wanted to know he noticed. I believed he did.

I glanced around. "Do you want me to introduce you to some people?"

Doug said, "Sure. Thanks. I'd like to write a story about Cindy for the paper. You know, kind of like they did in the NY Times for the victims of the towers. Derrick told me I would be welcome and I thought he might introduce me to some family, but I didn't want to get in the way."

I had imagined he'd come only because he knew I would be here, but even I knew I was being ridiculous. "I will introduce you to Alice Bryant. She was close to Cindy after she and I were on the outs. The last one who spoke earlier. Come on," I said. We stood up. I lifted my glass of wine and stood for a moment wondering if I needed to clear away my empty plate and silverware. Doug did too. There were staff standing by to do that. We turned toward the wide-open doors to the inner room where I had last seen Alice. I was squinting, the bright sunlight made it difficult to peer inside to the darker interior. But she was smoking in the far corner of the veranda with a cluster that included Stephanie Oakley, Jennifer Douglas and Luz Bullock, all old friends from the early days of our group. Alice was in their midst, puffing on a cigarette that wafted acrid smoke upward. I'd never seen any of our group members smoking and that Alice, a self-described health nut who insisted on organic everything when meetings were held at her house, smoked, suggested how little we can know of each other, no matter how close a friendship may grow. I touched Doug's elbow and stepped toward them, readying words with which to greet them, knowing how impossibly inadequate anything said in solace was at a time like this. I silently prayed they would not carry our past hostility into such a day. Doug followed me toward them. I turned and said, "These are people who knew Cindy well in the years since she and I, well, divided."

Then it was three times happening again, all at the same time, there on the veranda, overlooking the hotel pool, under the sun-drenched blue sky with puffs of glorious white. Three pillars of flame where Stephanie, Jennifer, and Luz had been watching me approach. I felt the screams from the people behind me and stood frozen. Alice backed away, pitching her cigarette over the railing as she did. She slammed into me and, had Doug not been behind me, we might both have fallen to the ground. This time, I was looking directly at them when it started. I saw their faces. I saw incredulity as they all saw what was happening to their bodies, a panic, then, as the flames engulfed them, peaceful expressions as though they were already beyond any pain such burning should be causing.

"Get inside," Doug said. I felt fleeing bodies pressing past me toward safety. I got out of the way. Doug did too. We knew, the way the uninitiated did not, that the flame would not spread to anyone else and we were in no danger. If it hadn't taken Alice, it wouldn't take me. I stared, trying to see under the flame. On a nearby table was a glass of water with a few nearly melted ice cubes. I flung water in their direction. Useless. On the wall was a red metal enclosure with a glass panel and a fire hose folded in neat concentric circles. I moved toward it, opened it, pulled the nozzle out, and Doug worked in tandem with me to do the unfolding, then turned the nozzle to make water flow. I knew the force of the hose would be strong and the water would knock them hard. I let the stream hit first one, then the second, then the third. The strength of the water was too much for me and I couldn't hold the hose steady and Doug took it from me. They were clustered in one place, a corner of the veranda. Doug blew the water at the flame. I watched. They had no chance. They were gone. Same thing. Clothing dropped to the floor, rings last. A dissipation of the smoke. No charred black on the ground, only ash. Gone. A white-jacketed waiter arrived through the door and stared. Alice Bryant pulled me, but I resisted. Doug dropped the hose. He backed up, turned as the waiter reached him. I shook Alice off.

"You can't stay out there. Cassie, please..." Alice tugged at my arm. I turned to her. "Alice, get inside. I'll be right there, please."

Heffly, the fire chief, appeared and held my gaze with what I knew was recognition. He told everyone to go inside and sit down. More chairs were brought in so more could sit. No one was allowed to leave. Then, the power went out. That sent many from their chairs to the double doors to the hall with desperate pleas to be allowed out. The police refused and lined up with their arms linked to block any exits from that room. They were taking no chances this time, I thought, remembering how the train slowly pulled away that awful morning taking anyone and everyone away from the scene in the chaos that ensued. And the Y when the crowd fled. They weren't letting that happen here. Here, women dumped pitchers of water over their hair and poured whatever they could grab that was wet on their extremities and their torsos, not caring about their expensive black dresses. I shivered as I watched. We sat there as the afternoon light from the tall windows and French doors slanted over us like an unwelcome blanket. The police did their work checking identification, jotting notes on pads, acting tough toward anyone who whined or shouted about getting the hell out of there before someone or something struck again. I heard the pleas. I read their faces. I listened to their cell phone calls to home.

The firefighters were useless now, but they hung around. Lila was sitting along the innermost wall with Brandon and two other boys. I caught her gaze, she widened her eyes, a familiar signal to not approach I'd grown accustomed to since her transformation from little kid to teen. She soundlessly mouthed words, "Mom, I'm okay." Then, she turned to Brandon and put her arm around his shoulders. I could see his blanched face, darkened eyes and a faint tremble in his shoulders. The house manager arrived, a short mustachioed man in a maroon blazer and gray slacks, slick black hair. He gave orders to the service staff in the room.

I watched Heffly take the drivers' licenses from their purses. Stephanie Oakley. Jennifer Douglas. Luz Bullock.

Alice and I sat at a tiny round table close to the bar. The line for drinks grew as time passed. Doug returned from the veranda, unwillingly by the look on the face of the officer who escorted him through the door. He took the empty seat across from me.

"This is awful. Why don't they let us leave? Don't they think it's dangerous here?" Alice must have repeated this one hundred times and it was getting on my nerves.

I counted the number of children who were now motherless. God. I also took note that Stephanie, Jennifer, and Luz were here without their spouses.

"It's not dangerous anymore," I said.

"It must be an electrical short," Alice said. "The power is out now. I need a cigarette."

"I never saw you smoke Alice," I said. "This something new?"

"No," she said. "I quit when I was pregnant. I tried to not go back. I was good for a while, then I lapsed." Alice continued, "I have an anxiety disorder. This is something you don't know, Cassandra. You didn't follow the self-help program Cindy turned the group into once we split."

I said, "I thought we always were a self-help group."

She said, "I went off my meds because Cindy and that man, Krump, said the accumulator was a more natural way to deal with anxiety. I only got worse. So here I am smoking again." She lifted a pack of Marlboro Lights and a Bic lighter from her lap.

"So you quit the therapy?" I asked. "How long did you do it?"

"I tried once. I was claustrophobic. I couldn't sit inside that box."

"So you didn't really agree with Cindy?"

She shrugged.

"Why didn't you go back on your med?"

Alice shrugged again.

Did she really think the therapy was genuine and not just a huge hoax? If she hadn't been claustrophobic, might she have actually practiced? It didn't matter. The idea that the cure for anxiety made someone anxious just at the thought of trying it wasn't lost on me.

Alice always loved to talk about herself to the exclusion of just about everything. She did now, about her post-natal depression after Cara's birth. About her mother coming from California to help her. She went on a bit and I imagined saying, finally, "Three women just died. Three women you knew just lost their lives. And all you can think of to talk about is yourself?" I didn't. Instead I tried to be sympathetic. It could just as easily have been her, or me for that matter. Why it hadn't been us, that question crept into my mind too. Why them? Of all the people here at this memorial service, all these women, why Stephanie, Jennifer, and Luz? Why not Alice? Or me? Doug was reading my mind. I could feel it, his gaze resting on my face, his quizzical expression. Why not Alice? She'd been standing there among them smoking a cigarette.

Doug leaned over and touched Alice's arm. "Alice, think for a minute. Did you notice anything at all unusual when you were right there with them before it happened?"

Her eyes enlarged slightly and I could see she warmed to his sudden attention. "Like what?" she asked.

"Well, if I knew, I wouldn't be asking you," he said with a faint smile.

"I can't remember anything," Alice said.

"What were you all talking about?" he tried.

Alice glanced at me. "Our kids," she said. "And when we last saw Cindy."

"And when was that for you?"

"Well, we don't really meet any more like we used to. I ran into her at the supermarket a few months ago."

"When did you stop meeting?"

Alice glanced at me again. "It happened slowly. People just either moved on or went back to work or moved away. The group dwindled then it changed into a bit too much with the Krump followers. Then, I think Cindy told me it grew again, but with a different set of people. It wasn't stay at home moms focused. It was less of a social outlet and more of a..." She hesitated. "It became too much about following Krump's ideas. Cindy was giving out homework...reading of some fringe literature. I left after about two or three assignments of reading for discussion. It just wasn't my thing anymore."

"So the group didn't stop meeting. You dropped out?"

Alice nodded. "Others did too."

"What about the three?"

Alice turned her head toward the door as though looking for them. "Yes, they still met. They were pretty loyal to Cindy."

Doug jotted down notes. "And they all practiced this therapy?"

"I really don't know. You'd have to ask, um, I guess ask their families."

"Doug," I said. "Were there any power failures on the day the first women burned?"

He pushed his glasses up to the bridge of his nose. He scratched the back of his head. "I don't know." He flipped back through the pages of the small notebook in his hand. "What does that have to do with anything?"

"It might have nothing to do with it," I said.

"Were they smokers?" asked Doug. "Alice, is that why they were outside?"

"I was the only one smoking," she said.

"Smoking a cigarette doesn't burn a person this way," I said. "Or Alice would be dead too."

"Three women setting themselves on fire at their leader's memorial service? Some kind of cult statement?" Doug said. "Three women did that in China. They were in a cult. Falun Gong. Remember?"

Alice's eyes swelled open, round and fearful. "That's China. This couldn't happen here."

But I never thought it would happen here either. And, suddenly, I was spinning thoughts about Spencer Krump's speech about Cindy. Cindy living her ideas. Cindy as a role model for other struggling women. Then Cindy as cult leader. Cindy bursting into flame while off in the woods for a walk. Cindy one of the first. The other women-- that first day-- could it be intentional? What for? Why die? Why by fire? Then, I reined myself in. Couldn't possibly be this. Alice would have seen something. Maybe she did and isn't saying. Or maybe she's right. Not here. Not unless there is something to be known about these women the surface veneer is hiding. I looked over at Doug. He said he would write up a piece about each of the dead women for the paper. I wondered how deeply he could dig and what he would discover.

"You were there at the train station," Alice said. "You are the only one to be close to two of these. You were out here when it happened. What did you see?"

I said, "Do you know I witnessed a burning death when I was in India?"

Doug studied me closely. Alice did too.

I stared at each of them in turn. "Well, not exactly like this. It was a dowry death." I changed the subject. "Doug, was there a power failure that Friday? Do you have any notes?"

Alice leaned in close. "Really Cassandra? What would a power failure have to do with this? What are you talking about?"

"I need my field notes from my work in England. I need to get home and pull together my notes and the test results from the stone circles."

"I'm confused. Cassie, what are you talking about?" Alice said it again. "You're not making sense."

"I know. I'm not. I am trying to piece some things together."

"Such as?" Doug looked blankly at me.

"I'll tell you if I find something," I said. I lifted my elbow to the table, my forearm straight up, twirled my school ring so he could not miss my signal, my eyes begging for his deference to our common membership in the Fraternity for Contemplative Research. He gave a quick nearly imperceptible nod.

We sat for hours. Heffly and Richmond questioned everyone in that room. Quite a few were getting drunk. That made some more vitriolic, others sank into their nursing of a whiskey, a glass of wine or a beer. While they did, Doug and I took advantage of Alice's presence to ask her about Cindy's group, how had it intensified as a self-help group. Alice was only happy to be the center of our attention. Doug did a lot of scribbling. I did a lot of the questioning, slowly, gently, bringing Alice around from her self-indulgent "I" sentences to talk about meetings and Cindy.

"Cindy renamed the group 'Essen-tials of Support for Women' and started a blog," Alice said. "She reached a lot of women who weren't local to Hillston. She started to sell advertising on the blog site and started to make money. Most of it she plowed into the treasury for the group. Some, after she put it to a vote with the members, she kept for herself as a kind of salary."

Spencer Krump was still in the room. I left Doug there with Alice and pretended to need a drink. There he stood, leaning on one elbow, tie still perfectly in place, his hair slickly clinging to his scalp, and I

noticed as he lifted his drink that his fingernails had been profession-
ally manicured. His eyes, however, showed red veins around his irises,
puffy bags underneath. He looked like a weary traveler trying to put
his best veneer over his fatigue. That made him more human, less the
snake-charmer I'd suspected him to be all along.

"Mr. Krump," I said. "I appreciated your memories of Cindy.
Thank you."

He brightened slightly and nodded. "I only told it as I saw it."

"Is it unusual," I asked, "to have such a group of practitioners all
in one place? Essen energy therapy isn't exactly in the mainstream of
American psychology or healing."

"It is growing," he said. "The more we know about pharmaceuti-
cals, the more people turn to natural healing."

"May I ask you how you came to be such an advocate of Brandt's?"
I asked. "I'm just curious how you found this. How you became such
a disciple of his?"

Doug's eyes were on me. Heffly was also watching us. I continued, looking at Krump expectantly. He was obviously flattered by my
attention and seized this opportunity to evangelize his message. If we
weren't interrupted, I might learn something, such as the existence
of a cult of self-immolating women. My suspicions of his maniacal
quest for aggrandizement of himself by followers, the way cult leaders
preyed upon the vulnerable, drove me. Cindy had been vulnerable
when she met this man. How vulnerable I likely would never know.

Krump was looking at my hands. I'd been holding the edge of
the bar, waiting for the barkeep to bring me a glass of wine. His gaze
rested on my ring with the insignia. He looked away quickly. I noted
that, but assumed he was sizing me up. University educated, obviously
some sort of academic honor. I was no pushover and I hoped he saw
that. I waited in silence for his answer.

"You know Brandt was jailed for violating an injunction by the
FDA," he began.

"Yes," I said. I didn't reveal I knew more. I just let him talk.

"They were afraid of him."

"Why?" I asked.

"He fled the Germans. They feared he was Communist. They used his work to silence his politics." Krump said this so matter-of-factly, almost deadpan. "He sealed his papers for fifty years. Then, he died in jail. The fifty years was up in 2005. Nobody else in the science world believed his work was worth a second look. I did."

"So you were sympathetic to a political victim of the Red Scare? So you picked up his work."

"Yes. And I replicated all his experiments. Nobody else was interested. Well, maybe there were some, but I didn't learn of anyone else."

"And you got the same results?" I asked. "You believe he was on to something with this energy accumulation when nobody else was?"

"As I said, others probably looked too, but I didn't connect with them."

"Was it a competitive effort?" I asked. "To be the first to rediscover?"

"You might say that," he said. "Why are you so interested?"

"Cindy was my friend. I never understood why she was so taken by the Essen philosophy."

"You're one of the skeptics," he said. "If you really want to know about this, not only to criticize, I'd be happy to meet and take you through some of it." He reached into his pocket and produced a business card.

"I read one of your books," I said. I had, but I only read enough to reach a point of incredulity.

"Then you'll be a good student," he said. "Will you excuse me? I have a few people to speak to." He bowed ever so slightly and left me. I lifted my glass of wine and returned to the table with Doug and Alice.

Doug was paging through his notebook. He finally squinted at a page, looked up at me and said, "Cassandra, there was a power failure. There were a few that day."

"Why is that important?" Alice asked.

"It may not be," I said. "But I saw a film at the museum about power failures and CMEs."

Doug just looked at me. So did Alice. "Coronal Mass Ejections… bursts of energy from the sun. They cause power failures. They come in eleven-year cycles."

"You're fishing," Doug said. "Sunbursts causing humans to burst into flame? Then why aren't we all dead? There were quite a few of us out on that veranda."

"Yes, why aren't we all dead?" Alice asked.

"I don't know," I said. "But if they don't let us out of here soon, we're all going to make up theories just to keep our sanity."

Doug began to search with his phone. "Okay," he said. "Here's outlandish theory number three…He held up the phone. "Spontaneous Human Combustion."

"Three?"

"One, self-immolation by women members of a cult. Two, they were hit by sunbursts of energy that came just at the right time and place to hit three women. Three, Spontaneous Human Combustion. It's a cause of death the FBI attaches to cases of unexplained death by fire." He read, "A case of a woman in England was blamed on SHC after fire investigators could find no external source of flame and after witnesses stated that it seemed that she was fine one minute then, in the next instance, she was burning and it looked like it was coming out of the center of her body."

Alice said, "I never heard that term before, but it makes sense. That's what this was like. They were there, then it started in all of them at once." Her hand was trembling when she lifted her glass.

Doug touched the screen on his phone. "Here's another one...a man's apartment was untouched by flame including his clothing. His body was gone, entirely consumed. When police arrived, they found his clothes and a book on a chair in his living room and a small stump of a charred foot and ankle had fallen to the floor next to the chair. Look, there's a picture." He passed the phone around to us.

"Where in England?" I asked.

He studied the article. "Brent Borough of London."

I sat up. "Brent? What is the town name?"

"Killburn," Doug said. "Why?"

"Look up what Brent means in old English," I said.

That took less than a minute. "Burn," he said. "Isn't that something."

"And Killburn," I said. "Isn't it obvious? Kill and burn in the town name?"

"Surely you..."

"When did that man burn?" I asked. At Doug's frown, I said, "Please. Indulge me?"

Doug read again. "Well, Cassandra, it was about eleven years ago."

I could feel Doug acquiesce. Alice gulped her drink.

"Doug, "I said. "Look up CME."

"CME?"

"Or sunspots," I said.

He did. "Just read it," I said. And he did, silently, while I watched as the police made their way through questioning and recording the name of every person in the room until they arrived at our table. The young officer asked us a few standard questions, recorded our names, addresses, and contact information, and we were free to go.

"So there is an eleven year cycle," Doug said when we stood to go. "But what does it have to do with our burning women?"

"Maybe nothing," I said. "Because of what you said...we'd all be burning if it was that."

Heffly came to the table and sat down. "Would you mind a few questions?" he asked. He stared at Doug. "You need to leave. This is not for the press."

"Can I go?" Alice asked.

Heffly nodded.

"Your daughter is here," he said.

"Yes," I said.

"You were a good friend of Cynthia Barrow."

"Yes."

"What was her mental state?"

"Why?"

"Was she distraught?"

"We hadn't been close for a few years. Did you speak to Derrick?"

"Yes," he said.

"Did you speak to Spencer Krump?"

"I plan to."

"He might know better. He might know, but he may consider himself her professional therapist and maintain her privacy."

I explained the Essen therapy. He stared at me. "You've got to be kidding."

"That is why our mom's group splintered. That nonsense."

I found Lila waiting in the hotel hallway and, while we hurried to Lou's house to retrieve Mia and Allie, Lila said very little which was unlike her. She just closed her eyes and leaned her head back while I drove. She stayed that way when I retrieved her sisters and apologized to Lou for being late.

"We all live in a house on fire, no fire department to call; no way out, just the upstairs window to look out of while the fire burns the house down with us trapped, locked in it."
- Tennessee Williams, *The Milk Train Doesn't Stop Here Anymore*

CHAPTER 22

Poor Lou. She was dressed up for her dinner, in high heels, which I knew she absolutely despised, and a cocktail dress. She looked fabulous but for the scowl that made her eyes dark and threatening. Jack looked handsome in his sports jacket and khakis. My girls had heard stories of Lou changing her name from MaryLou when she was a tomboy and how she refused to wear dresses for the duration of middle school and high school. They complimented her, having never seen her dressed up before. Lou seemed frazzled and rushed the four of us out the door, grabbed Jack's arm and pulled him toward their car as we climbed into mine. I had no time for more than a simple "I'm sorry I'm so late" before she said, "It's okay, I'll see you at Grace's party."

"Be careful," I said. "Did you hear?"

That stopped her. "Hear what?"

I closed the car door so the girls would not hear. "More fire deaths."

"Where?"

"Right there at Cindy's service, three women. They were friends of Cindy's, members of the group I started with her. Right there on the veranda at the hotel."

Lou studied my face. "Gees, no wonder you look ashen. I thought it was just the grief." She bent down to peer into her car at Jack. "I think we shouldn't go."

"Lila saw it too."

"Good lord, no wonder she looks ashen." Lou reached into the car and smoothed Lila's hair, then pulled her close for a hug. "Let's go inside. Jack and I can go out for dinner another night." Jack was all dressed up. Clearly, he was not pleased, but he shut off the car, loosened his tie and followed us inside. "It's following you around Cassie," Jack said. "Where's Pete? He ought to be with you."

Lou set her gaze on me and I knew she knew something was up. Something other than expected. "Jack," she said. "Why don't you take the girls for pizza. Bring us back a few slices. Cassie and I need to talk."

Lila wanted to stay with me. I saw exhaustion and sadness in her face. A hug, a smoothing down of her sleek hair, and a suggestion that she go up and take a nap came next, from Lou, which surprised me. Lila said, "Can I just get lost in a movie or something?"

I sat at Lou's kitchen table. She found me with my arms crossed, ankles crossed, my head thrown back against the chair back, staring at the ceiling. I was waiting. I felt it well up like a wave at high tide inside and I fought to keep it down, but, when she sat across from me, after placing the kettle on a burner for tea, I felt like I could breathe at least.

"I knew at the garage sale that something is up," she said. "You ran off with those books and didn't say anything."

"How could you and Grace just get ready to dump all that stuff and not give me any time at all to help or to decide what to keep and what to sell?"

"Cass," she said. "I've been holding onto that stuff for so long. I got a burst of energy and couldn't stand it anymore, all that clutter in my basement. And I've got a radon problem. We have to vent. I had to make room."

"You're in the zone?"

"Yes," she said. "I'm in the zone."

"Well, still, Lou," I said. "I don't know why you didn't call me to help. I only work part-time. It's not that I'm not available. And it hurt, seeing all our childhood things and some of Mom's, all laid out for sale."

"I'm sorry," she said. "I didn't think any of that mattered to you."

"How could you think that?"

"Grace and I hardly ever see you. We don't hear from you. You run in your own orbit. She didn't think…"

"Grace never thinks," I said. "She just does. And she doesn't consider me. Don't you see that, Lou? Has she got you so duped that you don't see?"

"She doesn't have me duped, Cassie. I don't know what you're talking about."

I stood up and leaned on the counter near the sink. "This goes way back, Lou. Now that we're on this topic, let's do the whole thing, okay?"

"I thought we were going to talk about Pete and why he's not here," she said. "I'm a bit surprised we're doing this."

I stared at her. She was right. I should be talking about him. I didn't. I said, "I've been back in Hillston for what, eleven years? In all that time, how often do either you or Grace call me or make plans or see my kids?"

"Cassie," she said. "I just watched your kids for you. This is how you say thanks?"

"I did say thanks."

"So where is all this coming from?" Her tone was hard. She kicked off her shoes and reached up to take off her earrings like she was preparing for a fight.

"You and Grace were selling all those gifts I sent you from India."

I kept going. I couldn't stop. "And all our books from when you and I were best buds when we were little. All just thrown out like a bunch of trash. That's our past, Lou. That's what I remember about us, our family, before Dad died, before Grace kicked me out of your lives and took over our sisterhood."

She just sat and stared at me. "This is fucked up," she said.

"Who took my journal out of the trash? It was in with our books. I had thrown it away after Grace invaded it. Do you know?"

She stared. "It was me."

"Did Grace know you did that?"

"I have no idea."

"Why didn't you tell me?"

"You had thrown it away. I didn't want you to lose everything you wrote. I thought some day you'd find it at home…a long time ago…but you never came back and never looked at that stuff after Mom died. And, that day, you were so mad. I was pretty surprised actually."

"I do care. I always cared," I said. "I got kicked out of our sisterhood. I didn't just leave. You don't remember Grace acted like I didn't exist? She was trying to erase me when she mocked that journal. Did you even notice?"

"Wow," she said. "No wonder Grace didn't want you to help with all that stuff. You really hate her."

"I don't hate anyone," I said. "I just need my sisters."

"Big surprise here," she said. "You came home and started up that group. You had so many friends. I didn't have a clue you felt this way."

"I came back and you and Grace acted like I was still away. Birthdays for Catherine I never got invited to. Confirmation for Catherine. Not invited. Vacations at the beach…you and Grace always went, but never once asked me if I'd like to do that too. Rent a house for a week with the whole family together. It was always just the two of you and the guys and Catherine. My kids never had that experience with their aunts and uncles and cousin. Now, Catherine is going off to college and it's over. The chance for that has passed. It hurts me. I don't understand why it is this way."

"You don't do that," she said. "You travel on your vacations."

"Well, just because I never did it, doesn't mean I wouldn't if I were invited."

"Did you ever ask?"

"Invite myself, you mean?"

"Yes."

"I don't think that's the way it's supposed to work," I said.

She said. "Yes, you're probably right on that."

I felt a tingle of satisfaction. Maybe she got it, at least a bit of it.

"Are you afraid?" she asked. "Are you afraid it's going to happen to you?"

"Yes," I said. "Aren't you?"

"I am," she said. "I wonder if all of this is coming out of you because you're afraid."

"That may be," I said. "But it doesn't make what I'm saying less true. Maybe I am having all this come up because I'm afraid I'll die and this won't ever change."

The kettle whistled. She reached for teabags and two mugs and poured steaming water into them and placed one before me on the table. She took two spoons from a drawer, a jar of honey, and sat.

I sat too. I dunked my teabag up and down watching the black swirl into the hot water.

"This goes way back," she said.

"I think it is the reason I left," I said. "Now that I reflect back. Why do you think I came back to Hillston? Why, if I didn't care about my family, did I choose here for raising my girls?"

"Mom was here then," she said. "Mom always said you were different from Grace and me." She dunked her teabag too.

"I never knew what she meant by that," I said. "I thought that was just to excuse the way Grace and you walked off to high school and left me to walk by myself. It was like I didn't have permission to go with you. Her permission."

"Hmm," Lou said. "That's fucked up too."

"Yes," I said. "It was."

197

"I always thought it meant you were smarter than either of us," Lou said. "I thought Mom didn't want to hold you back."

"How would being with my sisters hold me back from anything?"

"You probably wouldn't have studied as much." She stirred honey into her mug. "I always thought that's why she gave you the baby room for a bedroom. So you could study."

"I thought it was because Grace didn't want me there."

"She wanted a room of her own. She always did."

"Now that's a revelation," I said. "She made me feel like I was some sort of reject."

"Well," Lou said. "That was Mom's fault, I guess. I imagine you getting that room made her jealous. Like you were the favored daughter. But you'll have to ask Grace," Lou said. "Although I doubt you'll be able to have this kind of conversation with her."

I hesitated before I said, "Do you think I should try?"

"No." Lou drummed her fingers on the table.

"Then I have to accept that I will never have the kind of sisterhood I always thought we should have."

"Not with Grace," Lou said. "But now that we're talking, you and I can."

"That would be good," I said.

"So okay, yes, let's try," Lou smiled and lifted her hand for a high five. I did too.

"Why not with Grace?" I asked.

"Stop worrying about what Grace wants or what she thinks," Lou said. "Do what you want. She's just competitive. Don't play her game. I don't. That's why she and I are okay."

Lila entered the kitchen and asked for a cup of tea, which Lou quickly poured for her. She sat with us, twiddled with her camera, which was always in her bag. I watched her. Lou had just told me she was in the radon zone. With a bit of an anxious buzz in my viscera, I said with a deliberately casual tone, "Lila, take a picture of Aunt Lou in her pretty dress." Lou scowled, but she put her earrings back on. Lila said, "Smile, you two," and clicked a photo.

"Lila," Lou said. "You okay, hon?"

Lila nodded. "Freaked out. But I kind of wish I'd been outside."

I was glad she wasn't, but kept quiet.

"I could have taken pictures. It might have helped to have pictures. The police came when it was all over."

"I hope you didn't take any at the service," I said. "It's not really a place for photographs."

"Mom," she said. "Please, I think I know better than that."

I nodded. "Brandon say anything?"

"Not a lot. He was very quiet. He kept talking about Goldie seeing Cindy die."

"Maybe it keeps him from worrying about himself."

Lila looked at me. "Is that what you're doing?"

"Me?"

"Worrying about me too much so you don't worry about it happening to you? It's kind of obvious, Mom." She turned to Lou. "Mom wants to drive me everywhere, but she walks across the park to the bus, to the train. But she wants to keep me locked up at home." And she turned to me, "Why did you sit outside today? It could have been you today, Mom. I was so scared it was you!"

"Cassie," Lou said. "Are you nuts?

Lila said. "There's other ways to deal with the problem. You don't have to explode in flame and exit."

I stared at my daughter. "What problem? What are you talking about?"

"You and Dad," she said.

Jack returned just then. I packed the twins in the car while Lila hugged her aunt and, as I drove home, a wave washed over me. The tight little compartment of pain was cracking open and I was feeling it. More than the underlying terror I felt earlier, that Lou felt, that our lives might be snuffed out at random unless these burnings stopped, Lila's words were like a billboard with flashing lights. We were getting to the truth. We rode home in silence.

Decades of misunderstanding just got laid on the table. I needed to do the same with Pete. I would. And I'd go see Dr. Gimpel to prepare myself to do that. Meanwhile, I said to Lila, "Develop those photos for me right away, would you?"

"She's mad but she's magic. There's no lie in her fire."
- Charles Bukowski

CHAPTER 23

The news channels were all over these women's deaths, yet they reported nothing new as the days passed. The anchorwoman said the phrase publicly first, just before a break for a commercial. Spontaneous human combustion. She said it referencing Charles Dickens' novel, *Bleak House*. Her partner responded with a quizzical bend in his brow, to which she replied, "Dickens said in his introduction to the novel that nobody has ever proven it can't happen, so he put an incident of it in his book."

He said, "Did anyone prove that it can?"

I watched this with curiosity. Doug had said that same phrase at the memorial service. It was, I thought, exactly what is happening.

With Pete still out of town, a gulf was widening between us with each day he was gone. Each time I reached for my ringing telephone I hoped to discover it was him calling.

The next time it rang, we were watching *The Wizard of Oz* again, the twins' latest movie obsession, and the call interrupted the scene in the apple orchard when the Wicked Witch disappears in a burst of flame and smoke on the roof. Another use of fire in a fairy tale, a woman and fire. This just might have been him, calling to wish his children goodnight. But it was a different familiar voice, deep and male, with a Midwestern flatness.

"Cassandra?"

"Speaking."

"It's Bruce Gilbert," said the voice.

"Oh," I said. "Are you working right now or do you have some time to meet?"

"I can tomorrow," he said.

"Afternoon," I said.

"How about the playground?" he asked.

"It should be indoors," I said. "Want to come here? You can look at my stove."

"Oh, yes, of course," he said. "Oh, but I'll have the boys with me."

"Holsten's after school?" I said. "Get two booths. One for the kids…"

"Okay," he said. "See you then. What is this about Cassandra?"

"I'll tell you tomorrow."

"Okay," he said.

I pressed the "off" button and, while the phone was still there in my hand, I dialed Pete's cell phone and sat down. There, in the quiet of my house, the kids watching the movie, the windows open and a low hum coming in through the windows from distant traffic, the vibration in my ear was thunderous. I held the phone slightly away as it repeated its signal. The advantage of surprise was not available. Of course, he would look first to see who was calling. He could opt to send me to voicemail.

"Pete speaking," he said.

"Cassandra Taylor," I said in response, irritated by the tone of business formality. Already I wanted to show him that, when he did that, answered a call from me as though I was an unknown, instead of greeting me with warmth, with a welcoming something, even just a "Hi," to differentiate me from the rest of his world, it manufactured a tiny hurt to my heart.

"It's late there," he said. "I didn't think you would still be up."

"It's not that late," I said.

"What's up?" he asked.

"Us," I said.

"Us?" he asked.

"Yes," I said. "We're both up, so let's talk."

"What would you like to talk about?"

"Us," I said.

"I've only got a few minutes before my dinner," he said. "I'm not sure this is a good time for that."

"There has to be time made for this or we're not going to make it, Pete," I said.

"Well, this may not be the time," he said.

"When are you coming home?" I asked. "Will you be home this week?"

"I think so," he said. "We can talk all we want when I'm in town."

"I'm going to make an appointment with a couples therapist," I said.

There was dead silence following. Then he said, "I never agreed to that."

"Well, here's the thing, Pete," I said. "If you don't come to a session with me, I think a lawyer might be your next appointment, or a realtor to help you find an apartment."

Another dead silence.

"Cassie," he said. "I don't need counseling. You do. Again. I don't know why I need to go. There's nothing wrong with me."

"So you're happy."

"I   am   pretty   content,   yes."
"With the way things are."

"Yes," he said, "except how you're always mad at me. I don't know why you are always so angry with me." I heard an impatient huff. "Did you ever think that's why I stay away?"

"Pete, even when you're home, you aren't engaged in what's going on in our life. The kids don't even ask where you are. They're so accustomed to you not being there, even when you're in town. And I miss you, Pete."

"Then why did you get up and leave our bed last week and why did you go off for the whole morning?" Before I could form thoughts, he said, "My friend is here. I have to go."

"Pete," I started.

"Can we do this when I get home?" he asked. "Please, Cassandra."

I hung up.

If he refused to come with me, my next appointment for him would be with a realtor and I would see a lawyer for myself. And, again, as the hours following this phone call moved on, I found myself hoping against hope I would not have to take those steps.

What kept me awake was a war in my mind. Was this all on me as he suggested? Was I driving him away? No. I didn't really believe that. But how could I make him see? I felt the heaviness of my ring on my hand, touched the insignia of the fraternity, and wished contemplative research could be applied to matters of the heart.

"Have I missed the mark, or, like true archer, do I strike my quarry? Or am I prophet of lies, a babbler from door to door?" - (Cassandra. Aeschylus, Agamemnon 1194)

CHAPTER 24

Bruce Gilbert met me in a booth at Holsten's. He had ordered coffee. His kids were already into ice cream sundaes, so I helped him move them into what he called the "fun booth" with Mia and Allie. His boys looked dubious, but obeyed him. "Girls," he said. "They're getting to that allergic stage about girls." He hesitated, then said, "Why are you so brave? My wife is working from home. She won't leave the house. Your Pete should be as worried for you as I am for Pam. He ought to keep you inside. Or YOU should keep you inside."

"I've been spared three times," I said, although I wasn't sure I believed my own words. "I was right there again on Saturday."

"And you're not taking any precautions? Are you taking meds or something to keep you calm? Really, Cass, the town is panicked. You're the only one functioning like business as usual."

I read the menu and signaled Ian, who was working the counter again. He flagged the waitress who arrived and snapped her gum. I ordered a dish of coffee ice cream.

Bruce sipped his coffee and glanced past me at his kids, who were watching Mia and Allie make flowers out of napkins. "I feel like the cops suspect me of something. They keep asking me to tell them over and over. Now, after the three new victims they're doubling up on me. The news folks are hounding me too. They want commentary for their broadcasts. Why isn't this happening to men? Or kids? Or animals?"

"They just burn witches," I said, smiling at my own foolishness.

"Seriously," he said.

"There is something real here. I think I might know what is happening. I just don't know the final piece."

I reached into my purse and took out a hand scribbled list. It was Lila's photo project customers. "Look at the names," I said. "The women who burned are all on this list. There are others too." I took out a stack of contact prints, Lila's failed project. "If you look at the photos and at the list, you can see that the women who burst into flame and burned to death had photographs taken and the photographs were showing this dull cloudy result on the film."

"See here?" My very meticulous daughter had cross-referenced her list. She had numbered the women in order and had used a felt tipped pen to number the contact print to match the photograph to the name of the woman on her list.

Bruce studied it. "I recognize a lot of these people," he said. "They're moms of kids at my kids' school. I know some of them."

"I'm not surprised," I said. "I know some of them too." I told him of our mom's support group and how it had started and said, "That's how Cindy and I became friends."

"What does this mean? What does this have to do with anything?"

I pulled out the printed piece about NASA and the use of film emulsion for radioactivity detection on the space shuttle and the international space station. "Film reacts to radioactivity."

"These women are radioactive? Is this what you're saying?"

"That is what I want to find out."

Bruce dropped the print sheet. He sipped his cold coffee. The waitress arrived with my ice cream and he asked for a refill. "How?"

"I'm going to find out where radon excavations are going on and where the next excavations are scheduled and when."

"But if they're already ventilated, they wouldn't be exposed any longer to radiation."

"Yes," I said. "I need to know if any of these people who are all clouded up don't have radon contamination."

"So," he said. "You think that radon contamination and radioactivity is creating this bursting into flame thing?"

"Partly," I said.

"It is very farfetched." He pushed his cup toward the waitress who was standing there with a coffee pot. "You sound like you're reaching, Cassandra."

"That's why I need to gather more information." I paused for a moment. "I want you to find out something for me."

"Find out what?"

"Find out if these women's houses are vented for radon – look at the town work permits. You know the people who issue them."

"Cassandra, I'm not sure this is lucid. How did you come up with this idea?"

"Have you got time to listen to the whole idea behind this?"

"First, I just want you to answer one thing. If the radon contamination is the cause, why aren't more people, why aren't all the people in those radon contaminated zones bursting into flame and dying?"

"It's not the only variable." I stared at him. "I'm glad you asked that. There is further investigating that I am going to do, that Doug Bluestein is going to help me with."

"The Jersey Star guy?" he asked.

"Yes," I said.

"And what is that? Are you going to try to recreate the conditions?"

I watched his face. "You've got a volunteer to die?" I didn't tell him about the Fraternity for Contemplative Research although I did twirl my ring to remind myself I wasn't crazy. "Hillston used to have iron mines, we've got magnetic energy down underneath us."

"Yes, I know," he said. "What has that got to do with anything?"

I looked at him. I didn't have time to sit in Holsten's with him for as long as it would take to step him through my Stonehenge discoveries.

"Maybe radon is the answer. Maybe something else," I said. "Magnetism."

"Really." His eyebrows went up.

"Just humor me. This may be nothing. But it might be a puzzle with some missing parts. I'm trying to piece it together."

"Cassandra, why did you pick me to help you?"

"Isn't it obvious?"

"Because I watched it happen?"

"Yes, and because you know the contractors and the permit people at town hall," I said.

He was silent. The noise from the kids' booth was now increasing. Laughs and shouts. I turned around and they were all blowing bubbles in their water with straws. The table was slick with spills from glasses and bowls. Bruce's boys were apparently no longer allergic to girls and Bruce and I exchanged looks. "Maybe we can do play dates," he said.

I said, "Sure, you first."

"Deal," he said. "I've got summer ahead. Maybe we can co-op babysit."

"I don't work in the summer," I said. "I'm home."

"I've got Shakespeare in the Park in July," he said. "That's about it."

I swallowed a spoonful of ice cream and felt a cold numbness in my right temple. "What part? What play?"

"Henry VI," he said. "The one with Joan of Arc. Seems burning women is a theme of this year."

"Yes," I said. "Seems also that only the women are burning."

"Like you said," Bruce said, tapping his hand on the table to emphasize his words, "They only burn witches. Or those they think are witches."

Then I said, "Do you know the character from Greek mythology whose name is Cassandra?"

"She was a daughter of Priam, sister of Hector."

"Yes, she was a seer. Apollo gave her the gift of sight, of prophecy."

"Is that what you are, Cassandra?"

"No, well, yes, actually I kind of feel like her right now. The story is that Apollo loved her and gave her that gift. But, when she rejected his advances, he cursed her by casting a spell so that, even though she could see the future, nobody would listen or believe her."

"So that's you right now? You're cursed?"

"Something like that. Only I think if I can have someone else on my side the police and the fire department will believe them even if they won't believe me."

"So you want them to believe me?"

"And the Jersey Star, if Doug writes this up." I ate my ice cream. "Cassandra had a twin brother named Helenus. He had the gift of prophecy too, but the people listened and believed him."

He lifted his spoon. He poured sugar into his cup and stirred. "There is this distrust of women, isn't there?"

"Heffly wants to think these are self-induced deaths."

"What does Pete say about your radon idea?" he asked.

"He doesn't," I said.

"Does Pete really exist? I've known you for three years," he said. "I've done work in your house and I never once met Pete."

"Will you help me?" I asked. My ice cream was melting.

"Yes," he said. "This better not be a wild goose chase. But, if it is, hey, I'm between acting gigs right now. I've got time on my hands."

"Great," I said. "Let me know when you can come fix my stove."

While I drove the girls home, my phone rang and I broke all my own rules about phones and driving to answer it. Doug Bluestein was on. "I've been to see Derrick Barrow," he said.

"Oh," I said. There must be something or why would he call me?

"Their dog is missing."

"Oh, poor Brandon."

"Yes, first his mom, now his dog. He's got signs up all over the neighborhood." He paused. "Can I stop in?"

"I'll be home in ten minutes," I said and hung up.

Lila was already there, downstairs in the basement. I heard her. And her school bag was on the floor next to the kitchen door and I had to shove it out of the way to get inside. I shouted down the stairs. "We're back."

"Don't open the door," she said. "I'm working."

"Throw the laundry into the dryer please."

"Mom!" she shouted. "Don't interrupt me!"

I shut the basement door and the funny idea of locking her down there came to me and I giggled. That would show her how she could not talk to me with disrespect. That disdain in her voice was familiar and I didn't like it. It rang a note from my own adolescence when Grace started up with her disrespect and her dismissal of me. While I settled Mia and Allie for homework, I felt a rising dark mood. A flashback to just this time of day, after school, returning home, and Grace and Lou walking far ahead of me, the two of them together, two of them waiting for each other on the corner by Hillston High School and my wave from the big steps where I emerged after my last stop at my locker for the day. Them turning toward home, walking swiftly, not turning at my shout to them. Grace, at one point, running and laughing, Lou slowing but urged on by Grace to keep up. It started that way, that fall, and it continued. And Mom, after Dad died, how could I bother her with this? I tried once, her response was not helpful. It seemed small compared to what she was coping with at that time. I never tried again. But I still needed to tell Lila she needed to change her tone with me. I would not have her becoming a Grace. So far she'd been wonderful to her two sisters and, if I had anything to do with it, it would stay that way.

I settled the twins and went down to Lila. "You need to understand something," I said. "Open the door."

She did. "What?"

"There is a way to speak to me and a way to never speak to me," I said. "I expect politeness. I expect respect. I expect a level of obedience when it comes to things I ask of you. I ask. I don't give orders. If you want me to be one of those mothers who barks orders to get cooperation, I can become that. But I would rather not."

"Okay," she said. "I get it."

"I'll be watching to make sure you do," I said. "And, when you don't, I'll have to create some consequences you may not like."

"Oh, please," she said. "You're not going to ground me."

"That might be the place to start," I said. "Or I could take your camera away."

She stiffened.

"Do we understand each other?" I asked.

"I think so, Mom," she said. "Can I keep working please?"

I smiled. "I like the please. Yes, but please put the wet clothes in the dryer for me." I hesitated. "Actually, they aren't my clothes. It isn't for me, it's for you and your sisters so you'll have clean stuff tomorrow."

She nodded. "Enough of you being the house servant?"

"Something like that," I said.

"Okay. Got it. As long as I can keep my camera."

"So far, so good. I think we understand each other."

I heard the doorbell and climbed the stairs. Doug had arrived. He and I sat on the front porch and he took out his steno pad and said, "This might be nothing."

"What?"

"This friend of yours, Cindy, might actually have been a cult leader. Well, not officially, but maybe by accident."

I waited.

"She had a lot of followers on her blog," he said.

"Really."

"She and that guy Krump."

"No kidding."

"Can I borrow that book you read about Brandt and his Essen energy?"

"Yes. Stay here. I'll get it."

It was somewhere on my shelf in the side porch. I tried to think back to when I last looked at it. That was five years ago. This could take a while. No, there it was. I pulled it down.

"Bruno Brandt," I said. "I can give you the quick version of his science…so called."

"The women who died," he said. "They posted comments on her blog."

"I'm sure a lot of other people did too. What did they write?"

"They asked her a lot of questions. She helped a lot of people. And you know she had an accumulator in her pantry."

"Yes." I watched him closely. "I told you when she got it she and I had our final falling out. Her half of the group believed in this non-science science too. I knew that."

"Yes," he said. "I read through the entire blog. Five years of it."

"She must have started it right after the split."

"So there is a common denominator here Cassandra."

"They all believed in bogus science," I said. "Okay. Some also had their pictures taken by my daughter for her photography club fundraiser and each of them appears to have been exposed to some kind of radioactive energy. I think it could be the radon." I told him quickly about my visit to Derrick and the Geiger counter and the HAZMAT suited men. "You must have seen the cleanup."

He nodded.

"I'm finding out if they have radon ventilators in their houses. Bruce Gilbert is a contractor. He knows the people who give out contractor permits. Adding a radon ventilator requires a building permit. So he'll find that out for me. I am going to town hall to see if any are on the excavation list for contaminated soil. The ones who don't have ventilators yet."

"You're doing my job," he said with a wry smile.

"You could say that," I said. "But you wouldn't do it this way, would you?"

"You mean follow this idea of yours about radon?"

I nodded.

"I would never have linked the radon to the fires. I don't know anyone who would. I liked the connection to the power outages and the CMEs."

"What do you believe in your gut, Doug?"

After a brief pause, he said, "I'm really starting to lean toward the cult idea. Self-immolation."

"Nine women in one town set themselves on fire to kill themselves. Not one of them leaves behind a statement or letter or suicide note," I said. "Three of whom do it all at the same time at their friend's memorial service? All these women had children."

"They also had history of depression," he said in his own defense.

"So do I," I said. "I'm still here."

"For now," he said. "We should be indoors."

"I don't have radon here. Women don't die for a cult and leave their children motherless." I said it with certainty.

"You wouldn't," he said. "That doesn't mean they wouldn't."

"Have you done your pieces on them yet?" I asked. "The ones you mentioned at the service?"

"Still working on them," he said.

"When will they be published?"

"This week," he said. "I hope."

"And what is going to happen to these kids whose mothers are dead if they read in the paper their mothers were part of a cult, suffered from depression, and committed essentially a mass suicide?"

Doug stood up and paced back and forth on my porch in the late afternoon slant of rays. He sat back on the railing. "I just told you what I believe. It doesn't mean I'm going to insert what I believe into what is essentially an obituary. I report facts. I'm not going to speculate until something is proved."

"But isn't that going to creep in anyway? It might not be in there explicitly, but you know, in your subtext."

"I'm planning to write about their lives, not how they died. That's already been sensationalized everywhere."

I stood up. "Then are you going to write about their depression? Are you going to write about their treatment? Their therapy with that Krump guy? They're going to look like they're mentally ill and their deaths will carry that stigma."

He studied me. "It's part of how they lived."

"What about Krump? Have you spoken with him?"

"Yes."

"What did that tell you?" I fully expected him to respond with a disdain to mirror my own.

"He sincerely believes he is helping his patients."

"He's too slick for me. And he tried to suggest I make an appointment to see him. He gave me his card."

"Well?"

"Not for me. Not as a patient or, I should say, a follower."

"Hmmm. Neutral, Cassandra. I think you're hurting still from your split with Cindy and her group. And you know what PTSD is, don't you? You watched five women..."

"Six women," I said.

"Yes, okay, that's true."

"That doesn't compromise my integrity, does it?" I asked.

214

"Not yet," he said. "I still trust a fellow member of the fraternity." He held up his ring. "I'm not sure anything would compromise my opinion of you."

"I appreciate that. Same here." I smiled. "Did their families talk to you? Did you speak to their kids? Their husbands? Other people not in the women's group?"

"I basically spoke to their husbands."

"So all you know about them is from the husbands. Is that how you know they all had a history of depression?"

He nodded.

"Their husbands revealed that to you?"

"The blog did too. Confirmed it."

"How did the husbands feel about their Essen belief?"

"Pretty much how you feel about it. But most said they put up with it because their wives believed it helped. Mentioned placebo effect."

"Did their husbands understand their depression? Can you say they were supportive emotionally?"

"They are…were…the closest person to them. I would imagine so."

"Doug, have you even been married?"

"What does that have to do with anything?"

I swallowed hard. "A lot. I'm not sure my husband is the person who knows the most about me."

He watched me closely. "Who is?"

I wanted to say you, you know me in a few short days better than my husband does and you're more interested in me than he has been in a really long time. Instead, I said, "Good question. It's like a person is a conglomerate of what pieces of themselves others have grown to know. Lila knows me one way. The twins know me another way. You know me too, Doug. Right?"

"Yes," he said. "I do feel like we know each other pretty well."

I wanted to say more. I wanted to say we felt for each other too, but I didn't. I shouldn't. I just couldn't. It wasn't just me. It was because I was married and married people shouldn't, no matter what.

"Cindy did know me the best, I think."

"You were close."

I nodded. "What about their parents? Siblings? People who knew them all their lives, not just since, well, since they were adults."

"Not easy. Most of them moved here for jobs or their husband's job."

"But they're in town for funerals."

"Yes, but there's a limit to how much time they'll give me and I have to respect their grief."

I nodded. "Can I see your notes?" I asked.

"I'd rather you didn't ask that," he said. "There's personal stuff in there. The flip side of grief is that once the relatives start talking to me, they sometimes say too much."

"You need to talk to their women friends who are still alive."

When he didn't reply, I said, "Women reveal things to their friends they may never say to anyone else. Women confide in complete strangers sometimes. I'll share with you what I learn tomorrow, if you share what you know with me. I have no classes at the museum, so I was going down to town hall right after I drop off the girls."

"You still have to tell me why radon contamination is killing just a handful of women and sparing the rest of us." Doug's voice had a patronizing patience in it and I found it distinctly irritating.

"I don't know yet," I said.

Doug stood up. "Better get on it, Cassandra. If you have anything to support this, I am very interested in seeing it." He looked uncertain.

"You'll let me see your notes?"

He blinked his abdication to my request.

"Have you seen Heffly since the memorial service?" I asked.

"As a matter of fact, I have," he said.

"He isn't returning my phone calls," I said. "I've tried him a few times."

"He's a busy man these days," Doug said.

"I want to tell him my theory about the radon."

"Cassandra, if you want people to listen to you, don't give them your suspicions. Get your ducks in a row first. You can't give them half a story. That isn't the way to get their respect."

I felt a flush rise in my cheeks. "I wanted their support to investigate the rest."

Doug shook his head. "Maybe in academia that's what you do. You ask a question that is intriguing. They give you a fellowship to help fund research so you find an answer. Police don't run investigations that way."

"Is that what they told you?"

"They didn't need to tell me that. I know."

"Well, I guess I would ruin my chances if I did get him to call me back?"

"Cassandra, Heffly and Richmond aren't scientists. They're cops. They need hard evidence." His expression softened. "But I would defend you if you found something compelling."

"Thank you," I said. "I need someone on my side."

"I am on your side. If you weren't married, I'd ask you out on a date," he said. "That's how much on your side I am."

"And I'd probably say yes," I said. "As a matter of fact, I'd definitely say yes. But that's probably a topic we should stay away from."

"At least for now," he said.

"Why do you say that?"

Lila came up and Doug and I shifted to silence. She hadn't heard. She couldn't feel or see the internal glow that had just ignited in my heart. Its warmth spread through me and I found myself avoiding Doug's gaze until he looked away and I could study him for a quick undetected second.

My phone rang. I stood up to answer and left Lila and Doug in the kitchen. And, when I answered it, I pulled back to the present and the glow left me. It was Grace's cell phone number on the display.

"The graduation party," she said. "For Catherine."

"Yes," I said. "It's next weekend."

"Yes," she said. "It is still going to be at the country club."

I waited.

"But I'm not having it outdoors."

"That is probably a wise decision," I said.

"It will be in the ballroom," she said. "Everyone is getting dressed up. No pool party dress. The guys are going to have to wear jackets and ties."

"That's fine," I said. "Pete's got suits."

"Not suits," she said. "More casual than suits. Sports jackets and khakis are good enough."

"Okay," I said. I listened but under this conversation, my mind was questioning why I should even go to this party. I suspected she was inviting me so as to not raise questions from her guests about why I was not there. "And the girls all have pretty dresses."

"One o'clock," she said. "That's a change too. We decided to do a lunch menu instead of a dinner. And it will be a sit down."

"It sounds lovely," I said. "How is Catherine? Is she still a vegetarian?" Grace had once called me, years back, asking how to adapt to Catherine's sudden sympathy with animals, telling me how she was refusing to eat meat. I had explained some of the cooking I'd learned in India.

"She's still not eating meat," she said. "I've got a meeting on Wednesday with the caterer to go over the menu."

"Need some help?" I offered.

"Lou and I are doing this," she said. "Thanks, but I think I know by now what she'll eat."

"Is she excited?"

"It's a surprise party," Grace said. "She doesn't know."

"Oh gees," I said. "But her friends do?"

"I hope they all keep quiet about it," she said. "You never know with teenagers."

"Well, good luck with the secrecy and the menu," I said. "I will see you there. I'm looking forward to it."

"Yes," she hesitated for just a fraction of a second, "me too." And that was that.

I turned to see how the twins were doing with their reading. They were curled up on the couch, each with a book in hand. That's when I noticed Doug had left without the Bruno Brandt book. There it was on the table.

I joined the girls on the couch and opened it to where I had tucked a Post-it in long ago as a bookmark. I had read just enough to give me some ammunition to challenge Cindy on her belief in his theories. As I read, I saw there was so much more. I let supper go, ordered Chinese takeout this time, and, when Lila emerged once again from her basement darkroom, I roused Mia and Allie from their books, left mine on the couch face down on my last page, and went to the kitchen where Lila stopped me in my tracks.

"Brandon's dog is missing, Mom."

"I heard. That's so sad. How's Brandon doing?"

"He lost his mom and his dog," Lila said. "And their yard is full of dead trees and flowers."

"I wonder if it can happen to animals."

"What, igniting into flame and dying?"

"Yes, Goldie was with Cindy but he didn't burn with her. Think about it, he disappeared a few days later." My thoughts churned. "Was Goldie in that picture? The one with Cindy all blurred?"

Lila ran to her basement room and returned with the negatives and a thumbnail print. "Look, no Goldie."

Lila handed me a print of the shot she took of Lou. She'd enlarged it to a five by seven. "Here Mom," she said. "You and your sister."

I took that as a peace offering after our little confrontation. The first was a gorgeous shot of Lou, looking less like her boyish self than I remembered for a long time. The second print was a nice domestic scene, the two of us sipping tea in her kitchen. "I like them. Thank you." Then I said, "Can I see the negatives?"

"Mom," she said, "can't you just say thank you?"

"I did," I said. "I just want to see if there were any of those cloudy markings on the film."

"They would have shown up on the print," she said.

"You didn't doctor them to eliminate anything?"

She just stared. "Uh, I might have. Hang on, I'll go get them."

I said with a small smile. "I'm your mom. I get to be a pain once in a while."

She sighed and, in a moment, returned with the strip of negatives. "There," she said.

Lou was in the excavation zone. There she was engulfed in a cloud of milky fog on the film emulsion like I expected. But I was there, clear as could be. "Lila," I said. "Let's take that picture of us I asked for. Get your sisters. Get the tripod. I want a photo of all of us for Dad for Fathers' Day."

I called Lou. She answered on the fourth ring just as I was expecting her message to come on. "Cassie?"

"Lou," I said. "I want to show you the photos Lila took the other day."

"Oh, well, sure, why don't you just bring them to the party?"

"I could, but there's a reason you should see them before then," I said.

"What, Cassie?"

I picked up a vibe, an old one. "Is Grace there?"

"As a matter of fact, she is," Lou said. "How'd you guess?"

I ignored her question. "Listen," I said. "The negatives for the photographs are blurry with a white foggy something."

"So they're not good," she said. "So why do I need to see them?"

"Lila repaired the color in the printing process."

"Cassie," she interrupted. "Why do I need to know all this? Lila's good at photography and in the lab. We all know that."

"It means something and I need to warn you," I said. "As a matter of fact, if Grace is there, she should hear this too. Can you put me on speakerphone?"

Her voice became echoed and I heard Grace say, "What is this about, Cassie?"

"I've been doing some research," I said.

"Go on," Grace said. I could feel myself shrinking into myself. I was seeing the eye roll I knew would be Grace's response. That was always her response. I admonished myself to ignore my assumption, stay in the present, and keep going.

"You are both in radon excavation zones. You know that, right?"

I heard "yes" in unison.

"There is a chance that radon contamination is a factor in the burnings."

"Grabbing at straws, huh, Cass," I heard Grace say. "Does the fire chief think so? He's the one who should know."

"Heffly still thinks there is foul play or a suicide cult."

"You always think you know more than anyone," she said. "Even the experts."

"Do you have time to hear all the details of this?" I asked. "I'm trying to give you the short version."

"Why? So we think you're smart?" Grace asked.

"No," I said. "Because your lives may be in danger. All the women who died in the fires are also in radon zones. And the ones Lila took pictures of for her school project all had the same blurry problem on the film...just like Lou."

"So you think we're next?" Grace asked.

"Well, I don't live in a radon zone and I'm not obliterated in the photo of Lou and me."

"Well, aren't you lucky," Grace said. "So we're in danger and you're not?"

"I don't know for sure, but I had to tell you just in case this means anything."

"Okay," Grace said. "Thanks for sharing your expertise with us. Are you finished?"

"I think we should take a picture of you Grace, with a film camera, not digital," I said, "so we know if you've been contaminated with radon."

"Lila can do one on Saturday at the party."

"I wouldn't wait that long, Grace. And maybe you both should stay away from your houses until they install the radon ventilators."

The response was complete silence for a few seconds. I waited out the pause. Then Lou spoke, "Cass, we're in the middle of the party plans. Can I call you back later?"

"Okay, I'll go stay at the hotel where those three women died." That was Grace.

I waited for Lou to say something, to counter the scorn in Grace's response. I hoped she'd do it, just this once, object to Grace's hostility and take my side. "Cassie," Lou said. "Thanks for telling us. We'll see you on Saturday."

There was an abrupt click as she hung up. Lou, I told myself, was a different sister whenever Grace was around and always would be. My fear that they could be victims, that I could lose both of them, lay there in the silence along with my sense of powerlessness to do anything about it.

"God will bring you through the fire." - Psalms 66-12

CHAPTER 25

Here we were, a sunny morning and it had been just over a week since my encounter with Ann Neelam at the station. It seemed like a month. With no need to catch the train, I felt buoyant, relieved that I would not have to revisit that dreadful spot at the station. I had a sense of purpose and anticipation that I would learn something today. I didn't walk the girls to the bus, I drove them to school and let them off at the curb. Lila's negative and print of the four of us had developed clear and crisp, no blurring clouds obscuring any of us. That buoyed my spirits too. They each clutched one of my old books in their arms, having read a few pages in silence on the ride over. They waved and blew me kisses and disappeared through the wide front door of school.

Back home, I dug through my boxes to find the Geiger counter Pete had given me in England. I drove to the hotel and entered through the main lobby and took the stairs to the mezzanine level where Derrick held Cindy's service. Luckily the ballroom and balcony were empty, but a yellow tape across the door sealed the entrance. I made a quick decision and broke the tape and found the door unlocked.

"Careless security," I said.

I turned on the Geiger counter.

I knew this wouldn't be the same as outdoors.

I scribbled on the back of my copy of Lila's list. The clicking of the counter increased on the veranda but returned to a low reading as I moved away. "This is why," I said to myself. "Someone right nearby can be spared while someone at exactly the perfect spot gets it."

Next I drove to the train station and repeated the test. The results were the same. Where I had been standing, the reading was low. Where Ann had stood, so close to the rails, but about ten feet from me, the reading was high. I drove to the reservation and the spot where Bruce came upon Cindy. With no buildings or infrastructure to mask nature, I discovered the entire reservation had significant fluctuations in the readings.

And, sure enough, despite the sidewalk and the road and the proximity of the school building, I got an equally high reading just where principal Elizabeth Lindsey had met her demise. The three other locations proved the same.

"You know the cops and the fire department are not going to believe you," Doug said when I called him. "You've still got an uphill battle. Heffly's going to paint you as an unqualified stay at home mother who doesn't know anything."

"That's where you are going to help," I said.

"I am?"

"Yes, publish a news article in the Jersey Star."

"I'll talk to my editor. I left without the book," he said. "The one about Essen."

"I know. Want to stop by again?"

"I'll get a copy at the bookstore," he said.

Town hall was my next stop. I parked and checked the time and dropped coins into the meter. The public works office was down in the basement, around the back of the red brick municipal plaza with its newly planted cherry trees, behind a line of pickup trucks with HPW painted on the doors. An older man I'd seen often around town smoked a cigarette and leaned against the tree shading the door. He was wearing a tee shirt with the same HPW. He nodded as I passed. I smiled and tugged at the door where again the letters HPW greeted me on the smoky glass window. Inside was cool. At the end of the marble hall was an old wooden door. I stepped through to find myself in front of a huge metal desk and a pink-haired woman with leathery skin, too much tan, and too much lipstick. She was friendly enough. And I launched into my request for the records of the addresses where the soil excavations were taking place, past, present, and future.

She said, "The list won't be complete."

"Why's that?" I asked.

"Radon canister tests in basements," she said. "We're going neighborhood by neighborhood to install them. They have to be in place for two weeks. Then, they go to the lab for results." She squinted at me through her blue-framed bifocals. "What do you want this for?"

"I'm a homeowner," I said. "I live on Sycamore. We're clean. We tested when we bought. But I want to check some addresses."

"You a realtor?"

"No. Just checking some friend's homes."

She smiled. "Look," she indicated a wall map of town with tiny pins with colored heads, orange, yellow, and red. "These are the areas identified, finished, scheduled, and still in testing phase. This might be all you need to see."

"Great," I said.

I pulled out Lila's list. I would have to find all the addresses myself at the library before studying this map in detail. It didn't open for another hour so I grabbed a cup of coffee at the Starbucks across the street. I sat and pulled my laptop from my bag and whiled away the time surfing the web about the burnings, checking CNN and USA Today to see what the larger world was learning about our burning women. Nothing new here. While I did that, I couldn't help remembering 9/11 and how so many in other locales were so removed from the experience and how we had lived through funerals and memorial services for neighbors. Still, the entire world poured out sympathy and solidarity with New York and places like Hillston where so many of the dead had lived and commuted each day into the World Trade Center. Here we were with a smaller disaster, but the trauma was still so fresh and there were so many people out there who would just never know what this felt like. They could read the newspaper. They could watch the national news. They could hear the short updates on news radio, but they didn't feel the immediate terror I saw all around me like the two women at a nearby table, dousing themselves with water from Poland Springs bottles while sipping their lattes. I didn't feel so lucky, that word Pete and I had shared and used to describe ourselves when things were going well. Cindy certainly had not been lucky. She had struggled against her depression and anxiety and seemed to have risen above it, strong and happy, at least according to Derrick. But it hadn't been enough. I mused. Surely, it was just her large role in helping others that raised her up and out of her own trouble. I felt the loss of her deeply now. And with the sadness came a resentment of the catalyst that ended our friendship. Remembering Doug's comments about Cindy and Spencer Krump's blog, I Googled both their names and up came the link.

Cindy's blog was entitled *The Essen-tial Healing Source* and the entries had started just about five years ago. They were dated, one a week, with some skips. And in the series of pieces each had a unique title. I worked backwards from her last posting. This one was a reflection on the cycles of spring, written in April, just weeks ago, accompanied by photographs of early blooms she'd noticed around Hillston. It was a lovely piece and a popular one by the list of comments from her readers. I didn't have enough time to read every post, so, for the next few minutes, clicked only on the posts I thought might pertain to Krump and Brandt's Essen philosophy. Every piece mentioned the life altering power of Essen energy and most held anecdotal stories of success, contributions she had received from readers, success stories, accolades, nearly all women who had embraced the idea of this life-giving energy. She was making money with this blog. Advertisements for crystals, for jewelry with Essen accumulating stones lined up in the margins of her posts. Yoga studios also ran ads here. I noticed they were not all local. Cindy had reached beyond Hillston. Yoga and meditation practitioners in the Chicago suburbs also bought ad space targeted at her readers. In the corner, I read 7,857 subscribers. I saw the share button where readers could share her writing on social media. Someone should post about her death on her blog, I thought. I'd speak to Krump, no matter how unpleasant I imagined that would be. First, I'd check with Derrick.

There was an early piece and in it I found reference to the use of anti-depressants and anti-anxiety medications and how these all were unnatural, dependency creating, and should be avoided at all costs. Examples too, of women who became suicidal on Zoloft or Prozac and testimonials about their discovery of Essen as a replacement therapy. "It helped me," stated one woman. "Beyond the help yoga and meditation give. Beyond the soothing falsity of sleeping aids or Valium or Xanax."

Here too I found myself reflecting on my own flight from Bangalore, from the nightmare I'd witnessed, the self-incriminating thoughts that haunted me as much as the image of Banhi burning to death in that kitchen. I owed a lot to all the therapies Cindy and her Krump followers had rejected in favor of Essen. I saw in this blog the same instincts that saved me back in the day, the urge to help others and, by doing so, healing myself, which I did through the mother's group and all that came with it, the friendships especially. I sat there now recalling Grace's phone call of yesterday. I needed those friendships.

I read Cindy's blog and clicked on the comments from readers. Some had questions about building the accumulators. This was all familiar. Bruno Brandt had discovered this energy back in the 1930s. When he escaped from Europe before the Nazi invasions, he brought his experiments to the United States. But, although later on he was discredited by the FDA and forbidden to sell accumulators, some continued to practice his methods. An early post explained that his papers, sealed by Brandt's directive in his will for fifty years after his death, were unsealed in 2005 and shared with scientists, psychologists, and philosophers who applied to Brandt's Essen Institute for access. Krump's experiments were referred to often. I made a mental note to read the pieces on those.

I skimmed through much of Cindy's writing on this subject. I was looking for something, but I didn't know what I was looking for. Something to indicate that someone who'd visited this blog had disagreed or found the energy to be non-existent. There was an early post by Alice Bryant. She simply said she was discontinuing her Essen therapy in favor of "other methods." That was the extent of any dissent I could find. Alice, I remembered, went back to smoking. Not exactly a therapy, I thought.

Then, I saw my sister Grace's email address in the comments. No name, just her email address. The thread of comments was long, an exchange between Grace and Cindy. I downed my last gulp of cold coffee, glanced at the clock and saw it was time for the library to open. But the very idea that Grace and Cindy had corresponded held me in my chair. Grace had never accepted my invitations to join the mom's group. But yet, here she was, engaged in an active plea for advice from my former best friend.

This piece was dated ten months ago, July of last year, and while I sat and read this, I marveled at how much Grace had revealed to Cindy and to any stranger who could access this and read it. Here was a saga of a woman trying to float above attacks of anxiety, depression, fear of losing her daughter, worries about health, about her marriage. She told Cindy that Zoloft had brought on suicidal thoughts, how she no longer had her mother as her safe harbor, how she lived with feelings of guilt that gave her nightmares, and how she believed her problems were punishment. Should I keep reading? I was so mixed up. The past reared its ugly head and with it the torn up diary pieces I had resurrected from the garage sale, the adolescent writings she had invaded, and defaced with her nasty remarks, insults, and mocking. The idea crossed my mind, that I could copy and paste all of these blog comments into an email and simply forward them to Grace with a huge question mark. The taste of revenge. Or an offer of forgiveness? I wondered if Grace even knew that Cindy was my Cindy or if she thought she was corresponding with someone far, far away, safe, and anonymous on a blog. Here was evidence of Grace's own personal searching. She had scorned my need to form a community. Cindy had given her compassion in responses so kind, so supportive, so very gentle in their intent to soothe. I felt grateful to Cindy. I counted the number of exchanges they had shared. The span of time was months long, six months at least, from July through December, stopping just after Christmas. Cindy instructed her on building an accumulator, the materials she needed, the step-by-step instructions conveyed through a link she posted in a response. A listing of books to read, a therapist who practiced Brandtian therapy in a nearby town. Grace's early experiences with the therapy, sitting inside a small phone booth sized box lined with steel wool and linen were here in questions and notes of thanks. I hadn't been to Grace's house in all that time.

I felt the ambush of regret. Grace was my sister. I would never be able to help her and it wasn't my fault. She had built a barrier between us early. That barrier had hurt not only me but had lived long enough to ambush her. Karma, I thought, was a bitch. Grace might have used this Brandtian Essen to help herself, but like Lou had said to me, she would never be anyone other than herself.

I was out of time. I needed to get to the library and back to HPW. I closed the site but not before bookmarking Grace's comment thread. I wanted to keep reading. I would get back to this. But now, to the library and the town listings to find the addresses of the women in Lila's photographs. At the library plaza, I saw the homeless man. And, to my great surprise, there was his female counterpart, the shabby woman whose clothes and shoes and personal belongings seemed abandoned last Saturday. She sat there next to the bearded man and quietly the two of them read from a Bible they held together between them in the sunlight.

"Two women will be grinding at the mill...one will be taken and the other left." Their voices were just enough above a whisper that I could hear as I passed. I stopped. "Where is that quote from?" I asked.

"Matthew," they said in unison.

The circulation librarian smiled at my next question, "She returned on Wednesday. Apparently she went to the hospital. She's fine."

I went to work, using the town database and, in short minutes, I had identified the addresses of the women on Lila's list. Then, I returned to the HPW door and my friend with the pink hair and together we plotted the addresses on the map. While we identified them, I thought about all the other women who were not customers of Lila's photography project. I studied the map. My eyes rested on Grace's street, her being foremost in my mind. Lou's house was on the periphery of the zone I had passed on my way home from her house after the garage sale. Grace's was dead center in an identified zone that was marked with a tiny flag with a date, August, this summer excavation would begin.

Now what? I needed to check in with Bruce. At home, I gave him a call. He answered.

I said, "You're slated for a radon canister test in October."

"Great. Gees, Cassandra. I hope you're wrong. I did find out a few things," he said. "The dead women do not have radon ventilators. It was much easier than I expected."

"I was at town hall today," I said. "Those who died are either being excavated now or are on a future excavation list."

"So what does this all mean?" he asked. "They're glowing with radon contamination?"

"The ones in the damaged pictures Lila took are," I said. I didn't say anything about Lou.

"Cassandra," he asked. "Are all of Lila's pictures damaged?"

"No. Only some. She's got another dozen that showed none of the blurring on the film."

"Did you check their addresses?"

"I should, shouldn't I?"

"Yes, of course."

That took another hour and a second trip to HPW. The undamaged photos were of families who were in the radon-free zones. I started to feel excitement that I might just be on the right track. I couldn't wait to tell Doug.

My lunch was a peanut butter and jelly sandwich. I chewed as I stood in the dining room and gazed at the boxes of field notes I'd left there in a bit of a mess. The books I'd taken from Lou's garage sale had been neatly stacked and now had tumbled like dominoes across one end of the table. I remembered the pieces of my diary and that led me to remember why my purse had been so heavy this last week. The jewelry I'd hurriedly collected from Lou's five-dollar table was still deep down in a tangle of chains and stones. In the kitchen, I dumped everything out of my purse. It took some effort and patience to separate all of them. I recalled which piece had been given to each sister and to Mom. Silver chains with jasper beads, lapis lazuli set also in silver. A tiger's eye pin for Grace. A blue aquamarine set in gold had been for Lou's wedding.

I'd discussed my sisters with Dr. Gimpel during our sessions after my arrival home from Bangalore. Her advice to me had been to direct my energies to the mother's group, to stop giving my sisters any kind of effort because their deflection of it hurt me too much. I had to stop giving them chances to behave differently toward me and accept that they would not. I now became angry at myself for having run to the garage sale at first call. I thought long and hard now about whether

I should attend Grace's graduation party for Catherine. At least Lou would be different now, or I hoped so.

I chose a bracelet from the collection. One, on a silver chain, was a series of pieces of amber, golden brown. Inside each, if you looked closely, you could see a tiny prehistoric insect fossilized and perfectly preserved. This one I would wrap and present to Catherine for a graduation gift. The rest I would save for my girls for the time when they might appreciate them for their beauty and for the story I'd learned from each woman who had made it. Those stories were somewhere in my notebooks. I'd have to dig those out too, after I found and organized my notes about the earth beneath the stone circle. My Durga lesson came to mind. The one the kids at the museum loved. Durga was an eight-armed goddess who used each of her eight hands to hold a weapon of self-protection. At her chest, where we'd expect her heart to be, her one hand cupped a jewel prominently visible in her open chest. These weapons protected her jewel. The short version of this tale of this brave goddess was that each of us holds a jewel inside of us. The lesson reminds the students to honor the jewel that is theirs alone and to honor the jewel that is in each and every person we encounter. "Namaste," I told them, "means 'I salute the jewel that is you.'"

I called Doug again. "How are the up close and personal stories coming along?"

"I'm still working on Elizabeth Lindsey's. I met her husband today. You know something," he said. "Elizabeth Lindsey had one of those accumulators in her house."

"I'm not surprised. She was in the group."

"So did Ann Neelam."

"Oh, please," I said. "We'd be better off in a yoga class if we want to tap into positive energy. And it doesn't seem like that positive Essen energy did anything to save them. Stop by the house," I said. "I'll be home in a few minutes."

I drove back home. Doug was already on my front porch. He stood as I approached and met me on the lawn as I crossed from the driveway. "Walk with me to the school bus," I said. "I've got about three minutes until the kids are here."

He fell into step with me and we passed through the park where a few senior citizens wearing Hillston Clean Up Committee tee shirts wandered carrying long pointed tools for lifting trash into large black trash bags. They stood and watched us pass, smiling, and I could feel their sense of usefulness. I also noticed that only men were working today. The park would look lovely for a day or two, then these folks would be needed again after the middle school kids converged here on Friday afternoon. The kids always left ice cream cups and water bottles on the ground right next to the trashcans. It occurred to me that I should carry the Geiger counter with me and keep the batteries charged.

"I read Cindy Barrow's blog this morning," I said.

"Really?"

"Yes, and I saw she reached a lot of people."

"She was quite a believer," he said.

"Yes," I said.

"Did you read the whole thing?"

"No. I bookmarked it so I can see the rest later."

The girls were coming. Mia stepping down first and Allie next, always together. They looked up and saw me and then hugs all around and kisses on cheeks. Then, they noticed Doug.

"This is a friend of mine," I said. "Mr. Bluestein."

They said hello and handed me their backpacks as usual and headed into the park. We turned to follow and he took one of the backpacks from me and slung it over his shoulder.

I stepped along, my eyes on the girls who were already halfway across the grassy field in the bright sun, but my awareness of Doug in this private part of my life was on high. He seemed so natural with the

233

backpack slung over his shoulder, his elbow touching mine intermittently as we moved toward home.

We reached my house and I settled the girls for homework.

Doug picked up the book where I had left it on the couch and handed it to me. "Looks like you're reading it."

I showed him the Geiger counter and the readings I'd recorded on the back of Lila's list. He nodded and said, "Cassandra, if radioactivity is the culprit, why, if the dog was with Cindy, didn't the poor dog go with her? Surely Goldie was exposed as much as her family was."

I knew right there I'd lost his confidence, or that maybe I never had it.

"Doug, you know this is all speculative. I'm not absolutely certain. I don't have the whole picture, not yet. I'm looking for patterns."

He held up his ring. "That's the problem with contemplative. It can go on forever without ever finding the answers."

"You don't think I'm on a feasible track?"

"I don't know. I'm a reporter. It's not my job to know. It's to report what is happening and what the public needs to know."

"I don't give up. Not like you did."

"That doesn't have anything to do with any of this and you gave up on your friend in India."

That stung.

"We're having our first quarrel," he said.

"The cult and self-immolation theory could be just as wrong as this one," I said.

"True," he said.

"I'd like some respect for pressing on, at least from you, even if I turn out to be wrong."

"It would be very hard for anything to change how I feel about you." I felt the blood rise in my own cheeks. His face had brightened to a rosy pink. I studied him. He was noticing the notebooks and my thesis on the dining room table. He picked up the thesis. "I'd love to read this," he said. "Can I make a copy?"

"I have another," I said. I dug out an unbound Xerox from deep in the plastic bin and handed it to him. He looked straight at me, his gaze holding mine. "Too bad you gave it up."

"Well, I'll never be sorry I have my girls."

"And Pete?" he asked very deliberately.

I just stared.

"I can see why," he said. "Thanks for the copy. I think I'll enjoy the read."

He gave me a little nod of goodbye and turned to leave.

"Words are only painted fire; a look is the fire itself."
- Mark Twain

CHAPTER 26

The girls were asleep, all three-- Lila having stayed up late with homework. The light was beaming from under the closed door of her bedroom spreading across the hallway like a carpet, then, at eleven, going suddenly dark. I was in bed, just a table lamp lit so I could wait up until Pete arrived. I'd already watched the late news and some of *The Tonight Show*. Then, I turned the volume down low and picked up the book Doug had left with me, its spine now broken from lying on its face and some pages separated and loose from its binding. Brandt had strayed away from medicinal and psychological applications for Essen and experimented with the possibilities of restoring deserts to life with the introduction of Essen to dry barren landscapes. He did this by concocting an accumulator attached to large fans to send the accumulated energy into the atmosphere to create clouds and rain. The Arizona desert was his chosen place for these experiments. He claimed success. He failed to gain attention with the report of his results and no scientist ever attempted to duplicate them. I wondered if Krump had repeated these experiments. I found a profound sense of empathy for Brandt. Yes, his ideas were on the edge of soundness. I fingered my ring and the insignia. He just might have been some-one to be admitted to the Fraternity for Contemplative Research. The questions he raised were perhaps beyond the ability of man to answer. His intentions were noble, his ambition a bit grandiose, but perhaps his genius lay just outside the field of consciousness shared by the learned scientists of his day. In honor of Cindy, I softened my disdain just a bit.

A car door slammed outside announcing Pete's return. I closed the book and waited, listening. I was usually fast asleep when he arrived in the middle of the night. But the unfinished conversation about couples therapy needed to be finished and his re-entry to home might just be the right time to drive home my ultimatum. Couples therapy or the couch for him.

This midnight arrival was his ritual and I didn't know how quickly he moved from cab to bed at this hour after a long day. I sank down on my pillows and closed my eyes. I turned off the light and waited. My heart was pumping hard and I realized my adrenaline was flowing. When he didn't come upstairs, I got up and slowly stepped down in the dark. If I wanted him to be more in my world, I needed to show him my willingness to be in his. I would join him in the kitchen or wherever he was right now. I imagined he would need a few minutes of unwinding time. Trying to drop off to sleep after a stimulating day would be foolish and I thought, if he was pent up, he would most likely toss and turn and wake me which he never did. So much of his life was on the road. A warm and inviting welcome and a step into his transitional moment between the road and home might just turn the dynamic between us. It was at least a place to start.

I took the steps carefully while my eyes adjusted to the lack of light. The steps did not squeak under my weight and my bare feet made no sound. He wasn't in the kitchen where I imagined he'd grab a snack or drink. A low glow emanated from the dining room and, when I reached the first floor, I saw him there, the light from his laptop reflecting on his face and throwing a shadow on the wall behind him. Pete was intent on something, so intent he didn't look up because he was not aware of me.

I came right behind him and still he didn't waver his attention.

"Work email?" I asked. I peered over his shoulder to see that I was wrong. Before he turned to me, the screen went dark.

"Gees, you scared me!" he said.

"What were you doing?" I asked.

"Checking emails," he said.

"That screen wasn't your email account."

"Yes, it was," he said. "Look."

He touched a key and the screen lit up and yes, the open window was his email account for ISK. "I was clearing out SPAM." He stood up and planted a stale dry kiss on my lips. "I'm exhausted. That's enough for now."

"I waited up for you," I said.

"You shouldn't have." He closed the laptop. "Let's go up."

"What were you doing? What was that website?"

"I get emails from the oddest places," he said. "I was just following some links on one, trying to find a way to unsubscribe."

"Did it work?"

"I'll know in a day or so if the SPAM stops."

He reached for a hug, pulled me in close and held me. He planted a kiss on my hair. I could feel his heart pumping in his chest as I made contact, or was it my own? I pulled back.

"You go on up," I said. "I need a water bottle. Do you want one?"

"Sure," he said. "Thanks."

"I'll put this away for you," I said. I lifted his laptop from the table and hugged it to my chest as I turned toward the kitchen. I could feel his eyes on my back.

"I need to plug it in."

"Oh," I said. "Go ahead up. I'll do it for you."

He didn't move at first. I was in the kitchen when I heard his footsteps on the stairs. I opened the computer and light flooded as the screen lit up. His password had not timed out so his account was still open. I clicked on "old mail" and there it was, the reason he shut down so fast. It was an email from a dating site and he was not deleting this, he was reading it. It was not spam. I clicked on his deleted folder. It was empty. The invitation to visit the website said, 'see your daily matches'. I clicked on it. It was password protected. I tried his birthday. I tried my birthday. No. Lila's. Mia and Allie's. Then, I typed the word running and it worked.

This was his life away from me, from us, from home. I clicked on his My Account. He'd been active since we arrived home from Bangalore. I read the one final devastating piece of information...on his profile...his preferences...listed...male seeking male...age twenty-one to forty.

The profiles of the men he'd contacted with flirts and messages came next and, after that, a single page of faces of anonymous men and the contents of one message. That old friend from high school was a man and he wasn't from high school and he was not a golfer. I slammed the laptop shut and stood in the dark with weak knees, a trembling in my hands and a heart that thudded so hard I swore if someone came in the room they'd hear it like the soundtrack of a horror movie.

I took two bottles of water from the refrigerator and turned to climb the stairs. The light from our shared bedroom went dark when I was halfway up. I sat down. If I waited long enough, he'd be asleep before I returned, before I had to lie in the dark and be awake with him. I was afraid of what I would say, what I would do, what this meant to my life, my daughters, my home, my base, my family. This meant it was all built on a lie. It answered all the unasked questions though. Why he was never home. Why when he was, he was off in his own little world, why he lay in bed hiding himself under his professed exhaustion from his work, his lack of interest in me, sexually and otherwise. Period. The person I was supposed to be closest to in life...all a lie. I couldn't bring myself to go to our bedroom. I spent the night on the couch, not sleeping, my mind and heart racing, fear filling me, numbing me and rendering me completely unable to form a thought that could stay in my head for longer than a second, except one...that I must be the biggest fool in the world. Dreaded dawn finally arrived. I would have to look at him. It was the last thing in the world I wanted.

"Stars, hide your fires; Let not light see my black and deep desires." - William Shakespeare

CHAPTER 27

When I woke up, he was gone, his running shoes missing. By the time he returned, I was shepherding the twins out the front door to catch the bus and Lila was halfway to school as usual.

"You never came up," he said. In his eyes, a faint shining, as though he were teasing me. In that instant, I saw that shine like a veneer daring me to smash through it with what I now knew. He sneered under his even tone, "I was waiting for you."

"Insomnia," I lied. "I finally fell asleep with the TV on."

I was operating on autopilot, but rage rose against the impassivity in his half smile. It frightened me. The surface of things looked the same. If I fractured it, I knew it could tumble everything. I needed to see Dr. Gimpel before I said anything. I would not be able to be in the same room with him until I saw her. So instead of returning home and cleaning up the kitchen after the bus arrived and before my train, I sat at the same table I had that morning of Ann Neelam's death, at the station restaurant where Jeff Heffly questioned me, and sipped a cup of comforting coffee until I heard the whistle of the train.

"You look like you've seen a ghost," said Eric later while we waited for the buses from a charter school in East Orange to arrive.

"I'm not feeling well," I said. "If I leave early, can you handle the second group?"

"Sure," he said.

"Thanks," I said, mustering a weak smile.

Dr. Gimpel had an hour free at one o'clock and I made it with minutes to spare. In the waiting room, where I sat until she opened the door to her inner sanctum, I didn't have time to read the National Geographic with the picture of a solar eclipse, but I doubted I'd remember any of it considering the frazzled state of my mind. I moved to the chair across from her and waited as she closed the door and sat.

"My husband is cheating," I said.

After I relayed last night's discovery, she sat back in her chair. "Did you ask him?"

"No."

"There may be another reason he was looking."

"He wasn't just looking. He was active."

"Did you say anything?"

"No. I'm so shocked. I didn't know what to say or how or if it would do anything except destroy everything I have."

"Bring him in for a couples session," she said.

"I gave him a warning on the phone this week. That was before I saw this. I told him we go to couples counseling or he goes to a realtor to find an apartment and I go to a lawyer."

"Now tell me what precipitated that warning. I'm assuming things haven't been good?"

"It's because he's just gone all the time and when he's home he's like a cipher. He is so uninvolved with the kids, with me." I told her about the night when he turned me down for sex.

"And he said?"

"He said he was too tired to give me what I wanted."

"Okay, but what did he say about couples counseling?"

"He said it was not a good time to talk about it. He had a dinner appointment."

"And now, the first few minutes he is home, he somehow creates a situation where you see this." She stated it so simply.

"So he wants me to know?" I asked.

"He let you take his computer. He didn't try to take it from you."

"True," I said. "This is almost like he wanted me to know. I thought if we just communicated better we'd go back to how we were in the beginning."

"He did just communicate. He just did it in a very passive aggressive way. He doesn't want to talk. He wants you to know what it would mean if he did move out."

"If he's gay, he's gay." My eyes teared up. My throat muscles stiffened. I swallowed hard. "I am so mad. Whenever I try to talk, he makes like I'm the one who has something wrong with me." I told her how he said on the phone that things were fine with him the way things currently were and suggested I come back to therapy if I was unhappy.

"A good defense," she said. "Make you the bad guy."

"It's been going on since we got home," I said. "It might have been going on before too." A rush of knowing flooded through me. Phoebe's words so long ago in England. "Where does he go when he's not with you?" she'd asked. Then the flip side. Pete's wanting to get married and have the baby. I thought it meant we loved each other. This poured out of me with sobs and much nose blowing and a stack of used tissues accumulated in Dr. Gimpel's wastebasket.

"He most likely wanted you and a baby and family, Cassandra."

"But this is not a marriage," I said.

"Maybe to him it is," she said.

I felt like a worse mess.

"This weekend in Chicago," I said. "I only know of this one. If this is what he thinks a marriage is, open to sex with others, I never would choose this. I feel like I'm being punished for telling him I'm unhappy. I feel like a fool."

"If you're unhappy it means he's failed, Cassandra. He's failed to make a marriage and family work. I'm sure he probably wanted that very much." She let that sit with me.

"You mean to hide it."

She nodded.

"Or it means he doesn't care if I'm happy or not." I reflected for a moment on that thought. "He says I chose my path when I decided to have the baby and marry him and move to India."

"It is what you chose, isn't it?"

I paused. "And he thought coming home to Hillston would let the whole debacle in India fade away."

She studied me. "And you came home to the same dynamic that was here when you left."

"Yes," I said. "And it still is with me...so is the Banhi thing. And now the whole thing with Cindy dying and this burning thing. And now my marriage is just a veneer pasted on the truth."

She said, "I saw your name as a witness, how you were there at the train station. I thought I'd see you before this, Cassandra. That had to be pretty traumatic."

"It was," I said. "And Pete was out of town all last week. And I went to Cindy's service alone because he said he had to stay away for the weekend and he didn't understand why I'd go to Cindy's service since we were no longer friends. You know what happened there, right?"

She nodded and said, "If he stayed away because he was seeing someone on the road, Cassie, whatever he said was covering up his own...he was giving a good offense to defend his not being there for you."

"Oh."

"He's got you second guessing yourself so he can keep his own secrets and keep you from seeing what he's doing."

"Then why do you think he let me see what he was doing on the computer?"

"Maybe he wasn't. There is another way to look at this. Maybe he didn't know how to take the laptop away from you. Maybe he just took his chances. Maybe he's not really gay, maybe bi? Maybe he's just experimenting."

"I was planning to tell him something about doing marriage counseling. I was going to tell him to sleep on the couch if he didn't agree to go with me." I blew my nose. "Then who ends up on the couch?"

"You didn't confront him right there. He might take that as consent."

"I'll never really know, will I?"

"Not unless you ask him. And chances are he'll lie if you do."

"I feel like my whole life is built on a lie."

"Not your lie, Cassie," she said.

"Isn't it my fault for being blind?"

"You did all the right things for all the right reasons, Cassie."

"I knew he had to travel for his job. I respected his work."

"Yes."

"In a way, I wanted him to have his work just like I would have liked to have my own work. Maybe I was even a bit jealous that he had so much success in his work."

"Yes, and you reaped the benefits of his success. Your lifestyle is pretty good."

"But that never mattered to me that much. It started to feel so empty with him gone all the time." I felt another wave of tears well up. "Now I know he was using it all as a cover so he could hide his life on the road and pretend to be such a dedicated family man. Oh God…"

"He was dedicated to keeping up the appearance of a family. You decided to have the baby and marry him." There was a frown in her brow, a furrow that made her look almost mean. "There's a difference in what it meant to you and what it meant to him, obviously."

"It all works until I really need him."

"Yes, and there have been difficult times," she said.

I felt so grateful that she remembered so much of what I'd told her in the past. It came back to me…how I'd told her I was grateful to Pete, for his acceptance each step of the way starting with his help at the dig, then our hurried wedding, my move to India, our having Lila, then the work in India, then the return to Hillston, my devotion to the mom's group, our surprise at having twins. I realized when I said this to her that all those things made me need him less because I relied on my other relationships to carry me through. All until now. So much of the world of my making was no longer here. So he was a larger percentage of my world, but he just wasn't there, ever. I now understood why.

"I respected him for doing so well in his work, I admired that about him. I did. I wanted my work too though. I gave that up for us, for the dream of a family. Now I'm not going to have either." Tears leaked and a sob filled my chest. There was a box of tissues on the table. I wiped my cheeks and blew my nose. "You know, this is the first time he stayed away for the weekend."

"I'm so sorry, Cassie. This has got to be very difficult. More difficult than some of what you dealt with in the past. We haven't been meeting much. You're going to need to come back regularly for a while."

I nodded. "How do I talk to him? What do I say? I just don't know how to approach this with him."

"You'll have to find a way. Do it gently. Try not to make it a confrontation. No anger. Do you think you can do that? Ask him straight and keep a poker face no matter what he says."

I laughed. "You're kidding, right? I'm so angry right now, I could hit him. I could run him over with the car." I blew my nose again. "Of course, I would never. But what if he denies it? What if he says I'm crazy? What if he says he really was just playing a game and he never really meant any of it?"

"Then you're going to have to decide whether you believe him or believe what you saw. Have you two been intimate?"

"Not lately."

"If he is active, you need to get checked."

I stared at her. "Oh God. I didn't even think of that."

"Make an appointment right away. Come back next week? Same time? And call before then if you need me."

I nodded. I left. I went home, hoping he would not be there, that he was at his office and I could take some more time to prepare myself to see him.

"Five and forty steps the sky will burn. Fire approaching the large new city." - Nostradamus

CHAPTER 28

Pete wasn't home. Nobody was home. It was still early afternoon. I searched my face in the bathroom mirror and pressed a cold cloth to my eyes, red from my crying. Then I forced myself away from my urge to collapse on the couch and circled the living room and dining room where my notes were piled up, feeling a restless energy that needed to be channeled into something.

There was my ancient electro-magnetometer, the one from my days in England. I turned it on. Nothing happened. I replaced the batteries and jumped into my car. I returned to the sites of all of the burnings. One by one, I measured the level of electromagnetic energy at each spot. After the reservation, the train station, and the school, I felt a bit foolish. There was no elevated reading at any of these places. I knew the hotel veranda might be so distorted by the electricity humming through the hotel that it would be inconclusive. I sat in my car and tried to think. What did I know about electro-magnetic energy? What had I learned in England when I discovered it there? At Stonehenge, the huge stones had been placed in between the highly magnetic spots. Maybe the precise placement of the stones was a protective move on the part of the Neolithic builders of the ceremonial site. The stones were placed in the areas where the magnetism was low to stop the energy, lightning or CMEs from striking those places.

I returned to each site and this time I took my time. I drew an imaginary circle around the exact place at the train station where Ann had died. I walked around the circle, starting with a twenty-foot circumference and moving closer to the center with every rotation. Each walk around gave me the same result. The northernmost point on my imaginary circle set the meter off to an intense vibration, same with the southernmost point. I moved up and down the platform moving east to west, north to south. There were lines of magnetism and lines of low readings where no magnetism registered at all. Veins, I thought. Veins of iron underneath. There are strong areas interspersed with weak areas of energy. Then I knew. If there was a strong electromagnetic field and there was a break in that field, or a drop in intensity, a void is created, a void that the universe, which is made up completely of energy, will strive to fill. These empty spots became hot spots when the electromagnetic bursts from the sun traveled to them. The collision of the CME with the radioactive energy in the women, standing in an empty spot, well, it might just be the perfect storm for a burst of destructive flame.

"...it is then burst into flame by an encounter with another human being..." - Albert Schweitzer

CHAPTER 29

Between the time I got home and the time to meet the school bus I wandered aimlessly around the house, puttering, putting away shoes and toys and books. I picked up the book with the disintegrating pages that Doug didn't take, the one about Brandt and his Essen therapy. I lifted it from where I'd placed it on the floor next to my bed and muttered "Shit" to myself when the pages scattered. Sitting down on the rug, I gathered them and shuffled them into the right order before I tucked them back inside the hard cover. One page floated again to the floor and the words Deadly Essen Radiation caught my eye. I'd not read this chapter and the word deadly seemed incongruous to the whole concept I had read about, the healing properties of this alleged discovery. How could he call his Essen deadly? I read the page. Then, I dug through the tattered book for the following page, then the next and read about Brandt's notion that Essen, a life giving energy, might combat radioactive contamination. Of course he'd be interested in that. He lived through the age of the discovery of the nuclear bomb and the powerful exposure sickness the citizens of Japan suffered when we dropped on Hiroshima and Nagasaki. The pages explained how Brandt placed a bar of uranium inside his accumulator in his lab in Freeport, Maine. Brandt's lab assistants became ill, plants in the area surrounding the building withered and died. A gray pallor and a low dismal cover of clouds hovered in the area for weeks. I remembered Cindy's property and the dead flowers and bushes, the brown dry grass. Brandt reported that the experiment revealed that the power of radioactive energy, a negative life destroying energy, was far more powerful than the life giving one he'd discovered. Brandt buried the uranium in a lead container on the grounds of his laboratory and abandoned this line of experimentation. The final footnote about this stated that Brandt's assistant, who had monitored the experiment disappeared the following day. A pile of his clothing was discovered on the steps of the dormitory room he shared with another lab assistant. He left no note. Brandt assumed he had lost faith with him and his work and left the project.

I called Doug. "Did you read the Brandt book?" I asked.

"I picked up a copy. I haven't started reading."

"Turn to page 179."

"Hold on. I've got it with me at the office." After a pause, he said, "Okay. Hold it. Give me a minute." I waited while he read.

"DER is Deadly Essen Radiation, something Brandt says gets formed when his Essen energy, the good stuff, the life-giving stuff, collides or mingles with radioactive energy."

"Good. Now turn to page 190 and read the footnote."

"Shit," was all he said. "I'll be right over." He hung up and in ten minutes he was at my door.

Suddenly, I felt a fear I had never known before. "Doug, I know this sounds nuts, but I need you to stay here. I need you to meet the school bus and watch the girls. I've got somewhere I've got to go."

His eyes widened. "Cassandra," he said. "I've never babysat in my life."

"There's a first time for everything," I said. "Only until Lila gets home."

And I was gone. I dialed Grace's number as I drove. She didn't answer. I called Lou. She didn't answer. I arrived at Grace's house in less than ten minutes. There were no cars in her long curving driveway. I knew she had an alarm system on the house. I didn't know if knocking would trigger it or if ringing the bell would. I ran up the front walk. I saw that her usual border garden, where she planted impatiens every spring, was dry and brown and barren. The holly bush below the windows looked petrified into dead wood just like Cindy's property. I rang the bell. I rang it again. A third time. Then I remembered the party. She was probably meeting the caterer at the country club. Lou was helping her. I had been there only once before, for the repast following my mother's funeral. I remembered the way and in another ten minutes I was there. No, I was not in dress code. I wore jeans which were not allowed. My running shoes and YMCA tee shirt would definitely not earn me entry. I said to the receptionist, "I'm here for a meeting with catering. Grace Byrne and Lou Catalano are here to choose a menu for next weekend. I need to be there."

"Well, you weren't on the list for the meeting," said the young college-age girl with beautiful Asian features and a pair of rimless glasses that magnified her eyes.

"Just point me to where they are, please."

"They are out by the pool," she said, her gaze sliding down my body, a frown wrinkling her brow. "I'll page the manager."

I waited. My phone rang. It was Doug. "Lila is here and I'm leaving," he said. "You okay? Where and what are you doing?"

"My sister," I said. "She is an Essen practitioner. I have to warn her."

"Water," he said. "If someone has accumulated Essen in their body, water dissipates it."

"Really?" I said. "It's that simple?"

"When you get home, read page 201. Odd," he said. "Water was too late to save them while they burned. Fire extinguisher didn't either but if they are submerged in water the Essen energy dissipates."

"Okay," I said. "I've got to hang up."

I didn't wait for the receptionist. I found my way through the lobby and there they were under a canopy near the pool with a large pedestal fan blowing the afternoon heat away from them. Lou and

253

Grace sat with the red-haired very pale catering manager in a white jacket and black slacks. They sipped iced tea in tall glasses.

"Grace," I said.

She turned. Lou did too.

"Why are you outside?" I asked. "It isn't safe out here."

"We're under a heavy roof," Lou said.

Grace said, "We're safe here. There's no way a serial killer can get in here."

"This is not a serial killer," I said.

"That's what the police think," Grace said. "I know it isn't what YOU think."

"Grace, please. Let's not have a confrontation. I have to talk to you," I said. "I'm interrupting. Sorry, but this can't wait."

"It is really not very polite to just barge in here, Cassandra." Grace turned toward the door I'd just come through.

"This is more important than politeness," I said. I looked at the red-haired guy. "I'm sorry. I've got to talk to my sister. It's urgent."

He stood up with a haughty look and said, "I'll give you a few minutes." He turned a strained smile on me. "Would you like some refreshment?"

"I'm good, thanks," I said.

Grace turned to me and scowled. As she did, the power went out. I heard the hum of the air conditioner cease. I saw the whirling fan come to a slow turning so I could make out the individual blades inside its cage. This I knew meant a CME might have just hit the power grid. Grace froze like a statue. I ran full tilt at her, dragged her to the edge, and shoved her into the pool. Then, I went in. I held her down in the water. I dunked her head under so all of her was wet. I let her come up for air and did it again, over and over. She struggled. She swung her arms at me, tried to get free of my grasp, but I was always stronger than her. I didn't know how long the water would take to dissipate whatever she had accumulated in her body. I had, in the last

254

twenty minutes, become a believer in Bruno Brandt and his Essen energy theory. I also knew this was going to take some explaining. But right now, the relief of knowing I had quite possibly saved her life made me giddy as I dunked her one last time and released her. First she went to shove me but I backstroked just far enough away. Lou was leaning over the side, holding out an arm to help Grace up and out. Grace ignored her and found the ladder and hoisted her fully clothed, dripping self up.

I just waited in the water, watching Grace who I knew would not shout, not here, not at the country club. "If you want me to explain," I said, "I will, but you have to really listen to me."

Grace glanced around and saw nobody else nearby. She turned to Lou, "Let's get out of here."

Lou said, "Sit down, Grace. I'll get you a towel." Lou went to the shelf behind the counter near the entrance to the showers and carried three over. Grace wrapped herself in one. Lou left one on their table and reached over to offer one to me. I took it, holding it high until I could also climb out.

"What, Cassandra?" Lou said. "What was that?"

"She needed it," I said.

I wrapped the towel around me and stood off a few feet. I wasn't sure Grace wouldn't shove me back in the water. "You are such a bitch," Grace said. "What do you think you're doing?"

"Get dry," I said. "Then we'll talk." I turned to Lou. "You never sat in that accumulator, did you?"

She shook her head and rolled her eyes.

"Did Catherine?"

Grace said, "What does that have to do with this?"

"Did she?"

"No," Grace said. "She thought I was nuts."

"I did too. I thought the whole Essen energy thing was a big fraud. But I think I just figured out that it's real. I didn't know you used it. I found out earlier this week."

"How did you?" Grace asked.

"Cindy's blog about Essen-tials," I said. "I saw your comments... and hers...I didn't know you even knew her."

"I don't," Grace said. "I just found her online."

"So you didn't know she was my Cindy?"

Grace looked stricken. "That blogging woman is your friend Cindy?"

"She stopped being my friend," I said.

"I thought she was from Chicago. I never thought she was local to Hillston."

Grace blinked a few times, deliberately, and gave a quick shake to her head as though to clear it. Then she noticed the red-haired man standing there with a tray and a glass for me. "Why did you come here, Cassie?"

"I've been trying to answer a question about the women burning up," I said. "And, all of a sudden, I knew that if you practiced that Essen therapy, you might be the next to go."

"Well, Cassandra," said Grace, "who do you think you are, a detective? A fire inspector?"

Her disdainful judgment didn't bother me in the least right now.

"So you think that you just saved my life by throwing me in the pool?"

I nodded.

"You weren't just being a bitch?"

I said nothing. I just stood there and stared back at her.

Grace exchanged a glance with Lou. "Notice she didn't try to save you?"

"Lou wasn't in danger. Just you, Grace."

"How do you figure that?" She rubbed at the ends of her hair with the towel.

"Lou and you are both in the radon zone. But Lou doesn't sit in an accumulator. That Essen thing is the only variable that's different."

We all sat there in the sun at the pool's edge. The manager refilled their ice tea glasses from a pitcher, left a plate of lemon slices on the table, and left us.

"Grace," I said. "Do you know why the power just went out?"

"Oh," she said. "Here we go. Miss Know-It-All is about to teach me something."

"There is energy from the sun."

"No kidding," she said.

"No, I mean bursts of it. You've heard of sun spots?"

Silence.

"NASA knows that the sun has a cycle of eleven years when sun spot activity is at its highest. This is one of those years. When the activity is high, energy in coronal mass ejections breaks through the outer layer of the sun's corona and heads toward earth. It's high electromagnetic energy and, when it reaches us, it can impact the power grid. Hillston has been having power outages lately. Have you noticed?"

Lou responded, "Yes. I have."

"It just so happens that the women who died from burning, each time it happened there was a power failure that coincided with the fire."

"Who told you that?"

"Nobody told me. I figured it out myself."

"So then why isn't everyone burning?"

"The Essen energy factor," I said.

"Of course," said Grace. "And you figured that out too, I'm sure."

"You have radon contamination in your neighborhood," I said.

"We're taking care of it," she said. "We're having the basement vented."

"The radon raises the level of radioactivity. You've been exposed to it even before the CME hits."

Grace was silent. Lou was riveted, but Grace feigned boredom and sipped her tea.

She looked pathetic sitting there in her towel, a drip from her clothes making a tiny river of water under her chair. Eye makeup made black smudges on her cheeks.

"How do you know you haven't been exposed too?"

"My house was tested. My neighborhood was tested and passed."

"I'm on the list for radon," Lou said. "So that's why you didn't throw me in the pool too. The Essen is not in me."

"It's only in Grace and all the other followers of Cindy in town."

"Cassie," Grace said, "radon causes lung cancer. It doesn't cause people to burn to death."

"Did you notice your flowers are all brown?" I asked Grace. "Your holly bushes are dry and dying?"

"The gardener doesn't know why everything is dying. Is it the radon?"

"No, it's deadly Essen radiation."

Grace looked at Lou. Lou raised her eyebrows. Grace rolled her eyes.

"If you don't want to hear the rest that's fine," I said. "I'll tell someone who gives a shit."

"No, no," she said. "I'm listening."

"It's a three way combination," I said. "I didn't bring the book, but I'll show it to you. The man who discovered Essen energy did an experiment with radioactive uranium and an Essen accumulator." I paused. "When he did, all the vegetation nearby shriveled up and died. It made people sick. His assistant who was monitoring the experiment disappeared. They found his clothes on a step near the laboratory. They never found him...just like what was left after the women burst into flame and died. Everything they wore was intact, only the women's bodies burned."

"So you think it is the combination of radioactivity from radon, using an Essen accumulator to create Essen life giving energy in our bodies, and energy traveling from the sun increasing the radioactivity temporarily and the women who sat in their accumulators attracted energy, causing them to die by fire."

"That's why I tossed you in the pool. I think you were in danger because of the Essen energy therapy." How many times would I need to repeat this?

Grace took this in. I watched the adjustments in her facial muscles as she struggled to maintain an aloof demeanor.

"Is this happening anywhere except our town?"

"Not that I know of."

"There are Essen practitioners all over the country."

"They don't have radon contamination possibly. There's another missing piece of this puzzle," I said.

"What is that?" she asked, her tone even and emotionless.

I twirled my ring around my finger underneath my own towel as a way to remind myself to keep still about the ideas until they are proven correct. Doug would be proud of me for not answering her. I thought of Dr. Fields too. Never speak too soon, he used to say. You lose credibility if you offer your theory too soon before you have supporting evidence.

"You know about the iron mines under Hillston?"

She just waited.

"Hillston is a magnet for the CME energy because of the high iron content underground. It's strong enough in some parts to create a vacuum in between the veins of ore. Those voids attract the CMEs more than elsewhere."

Lou said, "Grace, promise you will get rid of that accumulator and never sit it in again?"

Grace frowned. "I'm not promising. If it turns out to be true, everything she is saying here, I'll promise." She reddened suddenly. "What else did you read on that blog? Did you read everything Cindy and I discussed?"

"Not everything," I said. "Enough though."

"I hope you can keep quiet and not divulge any of the personal stuff I shared with her. I had no idea Cindy was your Cindy. I wondered why there was no new blog post this week."

I held up my hand like a Girl Scout. "Promise," I said with a quick smile. I stood up. "Party still on schedule?"

"Yes," Grace said. "Sunday."

"Not Saturday?"

"No."

"Grace, you told me the wrong date."

"Sorry."

"Okay. I'll see you then," I said, "I'm leaving. I'll call you later."

On my way across the pool area, toward the door where I saw the young Asian girl watching us, the catering guy passed carrying another pitcher of iced tea. He froze at the sight of me. Then he saw Grace. His polite smile struggled to control itself. And he laughed. "Thank you," he said. "Whatever that was about, she probably deserved it." He continued toward Grace's table, pulling his facial muscles back into his polite and aloof expression.

"Purpose is the reason you journey. Passion is what lights your way." -
Julia Gardien

CHAPTER 30

I drove home soaking wet, but proud of myself. Doug was sitting in his car, writing on his steno pad. He looked up when I slowed down. I paused, rolled down my window, and said, "Give me a minute. I've got to talk to you."

"You're all wet," he said. "What in the world? Where did you go?"

I just held up my hand, parked and went through the kitchen. Lila and Mia were at the table, Mia writing and Lila watching over her shoulder, speaking in a low voice, teaching her sister something. "Where's Allie?" I asked.

"On the couch," they said in unison.

"TV?"

Lila nodded. "And Dad's home," she said.

"Where's his car?" I asked. Did I see it in the driveway? I'd been in such a hurry. I passed back through the door to the yard. There it was, parked in the garage, door down.

"Where is he?"

"He's running again," she said, a steady gaze at me. "You're wet, what's up with that?"

I smiled. "I just tossed Aunt Grace into the pool at her country club and I went in with her."

"Clothes and all? Mom, are you losing it?"

"Yes," I said, leaning over to take off my soaked running shoes. "I've got to change and talk to Doug."

"He was babysitting when I got home." Lila considered me. "What's up with him here all the time?"

"He's a friend."

Upstairs, I stripped off my clothes, stood for a moment in front of the full-length mirror, and looked at my skin. I looked so white and raw, goose bumps on my arms and legs. I rubbed myself with a towel and some color returned at least to my face and neck. I dressed again in jeans and a tee shirt and found a pair of old running shoes. By the time I returned downstairs, Doug had taken a seat and was sitting quietly watching Allie watch television, smiling a private smile that indicated his enjoyment of her absorption in her afterschool entertainment.

"Well, Cassandra," he said. "You're looking a bit more normal."

"I am feeling a bit more normal," I said.

"And dry," he said. "Your girls are charming. I had a bit of explaining to do to your husband though."

"Were you here when he got home?"

"Yes," he said. "I went outside to sit in my car, but he knocked on my window and asked me some questions."

"Oh."

"I told him I was the reporter." He gave me a steady gaze. "That's what you wanted me to say, I hope."

I nodded. There was a beat of awkward silence. "There was just a power failure," I said.

"Yes," Doug said. "I'm wondering if it happened again."

"I just prevented one, I think," I said. I told him what I had just done. "DER. Deadly Essen Radiation."

"How are we going to prove this true?" he asked. "Nobody will believe it."

"We should present it all to Heffly and Richmond."

"First," Doug said, "I should publish this in the paper. It should go viral on the Internet and any woman, or man for that matter, who ever tried Essen therapy, should take a long bath or a swim. Then we will see if it stops."

"So you believe me now?" I asked. "Then Heffly and Richmond will have to take this seriously too?"

"You just created news. I'm just reporting it," he said with a smile.

"I wasn't quite as thorough as I ought to have been with that book or I might have figured this out long ago."

"We all skip pages," he said. His cell phone rang. He stood up. "It happened again. I'm off."

"Call me once you learn who and where?" I asked.

"Of course," he said. And he was gone.

I called Derrick Barrow. "Did Goldie ever sit inside Cindy's accumulator?"

"I don't know," he said. "He might have. He followed her everywhere. You know he's missing?"

I took a few long minutes to explain to him what could have happened. He listened in silence.

"Brandon never sat in it, did he?"

"Not that I am aware."

"Do yourself a favor and destroy it."

"I will," he said and I could hear his throat tighten around the words.

"I may have to take down those signs too, huh?"

"Take a walk and see if you find his collar anywhere."

"Goodbye, Cassie."

"Take care of yourself, Derrick. I'm so very sorry."

I thought about all of it as I sat there in the late afternoon pool of sun shining through my western facing window. It was the time of day I usually devoted to the kids and getting dinner ready. Lila was here. Pete was here, a few hundred yards away doing laps in the park. I remembered Ian at the ice cream parlor and his mother who said, "I'm going invisible for a while." It was time for me to do it.

"Tell Dad to get dinner ready," I said. "I don't care if it's pizza." I took my keys and purse and the stack of notebooks from my student days at Sheffield and drove off.

Where? I asked myself. The library would close shortly. Too many known faces at Starbucks. I parked in the back of the McDonald's on the highway, found a table as far away as possible from the ball court where I sometimes took the twins on rainy days. I ordered a Coke and faced away from the windows, staring at an odd colored wall, not quite yellow, not quite orange. I felt invisible. For the first time in so many years, I was completely alone. Even my cell phone was home on the kitchen counter drying from its dip in the pool.

I had to review and remember. How had I constructed my arguments in my thesis? What had I strung together as evidence? It had been so long. I wanted to be sure. I wanted to leave no unanswered 'what if' questions. Doug said he would publish a story in the paper. I had to be sure it had everything covered. It was then, even before I started to dig through that stack of notebooks, that I realized I would have to visit Spencer Krump. I had to find out if his followers and accumulator-sitting patients included other locales. Locales that also had radon problems and magnetism and those that did not. But now, I focused and read.

Under Stonehenge's huge stones my team had discovered the burned remains of what were later identified as humans. I could use it to defend my theory about Hillston's women. I could also use Hillston's women to defend my old theory of "why here" at the stone circle. Why there were burned human remains under the ceremonial circle of stones. Why did the ancients build at that particular spot? Protection, of course.

I had discovered two characteristics of the rock and soil under the monuments and in the surrounding Salisbury Plain. One, we had discovered high radioactivity readings all around the stones. Under the stones. Above them. And the Geiger counter indicated to us clearly that it was not the huge stones themselves that created the high readings. It was the ground upon which they were built. It was seeping out of the soil and dissipating above the stones into the atmosphere. That meant uranium had been there and, according to the science I knew, decayed to form radium. Radium, as it continues to decay over many, many years, creates radon gas and some metallic elements. Fully decayed uranium, after 4.5 billion years, becomes the element we know as lead, which still emits radioactive energy.

It was as though the stones had walled in radon-contaminated air just like a basement of cinderblock would trap air here in a home in Hillston. Yes, the stones were not so close together, but there was some speculation in scientific circles that Stonehenge had once been a fully closed circle and some vertical stones had been removed long ago. Aerial infrared photography had yielded some evidence of this. Something, a closed circle or something else, trapped the energy and that was what I now searched for in my notes. There was something I'd forgotten: radon gas itself decays with a very short half-life. In a matter of hours, radon gas disintegrates, but, when it does, the heavy metal elements it creates is the source of the poison that causes lung cancer. So it isn't the gas itself that is dangerous, it is the byproduct of its disintegration. So gas in a home must be vented before the radon half-life runs its course. It was very possible that at the stone circle, when the gas disintegrated, it left radioactive metals in the vicinity. That would explain the high Geiger counter readings I collected there.

Two, I discovered the presence of iron through the discovery of magnetic energy fields in, under, and around the stone circle. I knew that radon gas was a non-magnetic element. The by-products of its disintegration, however, included magnetic metals. If the disintegration of radon had gone on for thousands of years, that would explain the presence of magnetism in the soil and underground. Those characteristics were shared with Hillston.

From its very beginning, Stonehenge bade the society surrounding it to look skyward. The path of the sun was predictable and the length of the year could be known by observing the position of the rising sun over the stones. Yes, maybe Neolithic man had just built a very large calendar, a means to track time and seasons. Or maybe there was more. Maybe the circle was built to attempt to manage or manipulate the heavens. Maybe they believed it protected them from lightning. Or maybe they believed it protected them from those sunbursts that in modern times interrupted our power grid. Sunbursts that burned humans on the ground. But the ancients didn't build Essen accumulators so here I was at a dead end.

"So how could I prove this to be correct?" I silently asked the odd colored wall at McDonald's. "They didn't have photography and film or Geiger counters, so they could not detect radioactive energy. All they knew was their fear. Those bodies under the stones... they might have been victims of this same thing." I stood and muttered all this quietly to myself as I went to pour another Coke. It didn't really matter if I was right about the Neolithic people. I would never recover the complete record of the distant past. What mattered was that I was right about what was happening today. What mattered was making this all go away. I returned to my booth and opened notebooks from the adventure Pete and I had taken around England visiting towns with other stone circles nearby. I found notes about electromagnetic readings at the places known for fires in towns with the root "Brent" in the names. How do you tie the present to the past? Pete's scribbled numbers and notes and Phoebe's neat calligraphy filled some of these pages. That earlier time when he and I were so new and when he was so much my ally, so much in support of what I was trying to do, came back like a rogue wave knocking me off balance. I lost my focus and a surge of nerves swept over me. My concentration dissipated. I wished my recall of details was not so complete, that Phoebe's warnings about leaving my work did not feel so prescient right now. Yes, I'd needed to consult these notes to recall my work, but I needed nothing to recall the last scene between us when I'd told her my plan to leave England for India, to marry Pete, and have my baby. She'd unleashed a tirade at me finally after trying to gently warn me of the long view I'd have of that decision later. Now, I only could berate myself and admit she was absolutely correct. She'd looked long at me and said, with very sad eyes, "You are changing your path from what you'd set out for since the time you were in high school. You're letting yourself digress." Her eyes narrowed. "Or are you?"

Maybe she'd been right. Here I was in Hillston with no career and at risk of no longer having an intact family, a home and a partner for life. I had an irresistible urge to speak to Phoebe. I closed the notebooks. None of the Neolithic past mattered. I needed to go home and confront Pete.

Lila and Mia were still busy with Mia's homework at the table. Pete walked in with a pizza box and a bag from Antonio's.

"Hi," he said. He landed a kiss on the top of my head. "I'm home."

"Great," I said. "So am I. I've eaten."

I'd speak to Pete after the kids were in bed. In the dark. Just us. I walked out and took a turn around the park. I wasn't ready for what I knew was necessary.

The park was empty. Everyone indoors. I knew at least one house would be full of sadness tonight. But, as I circled the park, slowly, staring at the pin oaks, wondering where the deer was since she was nowhere in sight, I knew there would be sadness in other houses for other reasons and that much of it wouldn't be caused by the kind of convergence I'd discovered here in Hillston, but by other things not converging, but failing to come together, inflicted by people making things difficult for the people they love despite their best intentions.

I thought about the scraps of my diary in my garage. Who salvaged it from the trash so long ago? By admission, it had been Lou. I thought about Pete and how he had said so long ago that he and I were good collaborators, that he didn't want someone in the far future to look into our dustbins or middens and find the residue of misguided ideas about what was important to us after we were long gone. I was going to have to remind him of that. Bringing up the subject of his secret life of dating sites and strange men would probably destroy us. Choose, I told myself. You have to choose. I could feel the burning inside. It might be easier to just burst into flame and disappear. Easier to escape this and find another plane of existence or a rebirth to a life without what I must now face. I turned the last bend toward home and there he was, trotting to meet me. He turned as I approached, matched steps with me, and we took a lap together.

I said, "You missed a lot being away this week."

"I heard on the news about Cindy's service."

"And you didn't call?"

He heard his own words. "I was busy with my client."

I heard the lie in his even tone. "So do you want to listen?"

"Sure," he said.

"It started with the photographs," I said. I was playing an avoidance game. I needed to work my way indirectly toward the necessary topic. While he listened, or at least seemed to be listening, I told him every last detail about my week, about all that just happened. He nodded as we walked. I waited for a question or two. He had none. He had nothing to say about any of it. That, in itself, widened the void between us. Then I asked him about himself, about his week away, his work, his flights. Who was the old friend in Chicago? Where did they have dinner? Who was the client? I listened to his omissions more than what he did say. I gave him the same silence to his responses he had given to mine. Then, I stopped dead in my tracks. "I know," I said.

"What do you know?" he asked.

"That we can't do this anymore."

He pretended to not understand, but I knew it was a surface veneer across his truth.

"You are cruising dating sites," I said. "You're meeting gay men."

"What?"

"I saw your screen over your shoulder before you closed the window."

"I wasn't doing anything but checking email."

"No, I saw the window before you closed it."

"That was spam and I made the mistake of clicking on it."

"I think that isn't true."

"Cassie, I can't believe what you're saying." His face was red, his fists clenched.

"Well," I said. "I don't think I can believe anything you say, ever again, unless you tell me the truth right now."

"You're leaping, Cassie. You're thinking about when I wasn't in the mood for sex that night and you're building an explanation."

"No." I kicked a stone and it spun forward and landed in the grass.

"Yes," he said. "That's what you do. You look for ways to blame me for being away from you. This is really a fiction you are building so you don't have to take responsibility for anything. You did the same thing with Banhi. You give things meaning they don't have. I thought your therapy with Dr. Gimpel and the meds broke that pattern in you. I see now it didn't. Maybe you need to go back to her."

"I saw her today," I said.

"Well, that's good. So you recognize the pattern is back?"

"No, Pete," I said. "She recommended we do couples counseling."

He was silent for a long minute. "You know how I feel about that."

"If you won't do counseling we're separating and you're getting an apartment."

"If you want to separate, then you leave," he said with a coldness that surprised me even with the new knowledge I had of him.

"I saw what I saw," I said. "I looked later too. I took your laptop. I opened your history and saw more than you think I saw."

"Spying on your husband Cassie? Really not healthy."

"So were you flirting and doing nothing or were you meeting them?"

He said, "I'm not honoring that with an answer. That has nothing to do with us."

"Are you having sex with men?" I asked. "I deserve an answer."

"Well, that's what you think. You just saw a website. You don't really know if I did anything."

"So tell me. Did you?"

"Who is that guy Doug?" he asked. "He seems to be quite at home around here."

"He's a reporter. He and I worked on this whole mystery of the women burning. He's connected to the local paper and to a fraternity I was in." I held up my ring.

"Well, how do I know you're not doing more than you say?"

"Because I'm telling you the truth."

"So am I," he said.

"Then explain the messages on that site. Explain the arrangements for meetings I read."

"If I did anything you are accusing me of, it was meaningless because I love you."

"Did you?"

"I don't want to leave you," he said. "I don't want this to destroy us, what we have together, our family."

"You know, Pete. Here's the thing that's wrong here. I am attracted to Doug. He's around. He's interested. He thinks a lot of me. I could probably have an affair. He'd likely be willing, but I know and he knows I am a married woman. I don't take that promise lightly. And here I discover you have an entirely different attitude. You're on the road being an opportunist. I'm home being a loyal wife and mother and you're trying to find fault with MY behavior?" I said, "This is what's destroying me."

"Only because you let it," he said. "I think maybe you're right and the couples therapy is the place to start," he said. "If you stop this accusation, I'll go."

"Oh, now you agree? It's a place to start what?"

"I don't know," he said. "A new beginning?"

"It's probably starting our ending," I said. "I can't live with a lie. And I can't tell the difference in you from what's real and a lie. If you want to have sex with men why are you married to me?"

He said, "You've been with me for fifteen years. If you keep accusing me I won't go to therapy."

"Pete, if you keep sidestepping I can't trust what you say. I can't unknow something once I know it, no matter what you say."

"Don't pretend this is a big deal. It isn't."

"I thought you were gone because you loved your work. I was even jealous of you for having work, a career, where mine never got off the ground."

"You wanted a family. I gave you all you wanted," he said. "So you're going to break us up now?"

"I am breaking up our family?"

"Yes, you're the one this will hurt the most, and the kids. You care that little about your kids?"

I stood and stared at him. Then, I realized that, no matter what, he was not going to see what this was doing to me unless he wanted to see.

"Did you think about the kids when you were hooking up? Did you think about me? You could be HIV infected. I could..." Tears overflowed and the hard wall of muscles in my neck tightened. I swallowed hard.

"I assumed we understood each other."

"What are you talking about? We understand what about each other?"

"Grace told me she always suspected your preferences." His tone was so even and I almost swore I saw a twinkle of amusement in his eye as he said this.

"What?"

"That was why I thought she and Lou didn't want you around. They were uncomfortable." Now his tone was insinuating that I ought to feel something else, as though their indifference to me was somehow earned, a mocking of my perennial disappointment. My palms were so sweaty. I wiped them on my tee shirt.

"And you never asked me about it? This is bullshit, Pete."

"Nobody knows you like your own family," he said. "Sometimes they know you better than you know yourself."

"When did you and she have this conversation?"

"When we came home for the baby." There it was again. A hint of glee in his eye. He was getting some sort of perverse enjoyment from this. Right then, a coldness swept me and I shivered. To him, this was a contest to win. He was not interested in the truth. He simply wanted to win this by flipping my accusation, making it into a mere game of name calling so he could escape any sort of admission.

I stopped walking. I sat down on a bench and averted my eyes. I could not look at him. "So you married me because I was pregnant."

"I loved you. I still do. I did the right thing. I didn't want to abort the baby." He stopped walking and said, "We wouldn't have Lila."

"You've been pretending we're a loyal couple when you – you're on the road all the time…now I see this lifestyle suits you. Even when I tell you I miss you and want you home with me, you don't respond or change or accept that what I want is what any married woman would want with her husband."

"No, Cassie."

"I don't get it, Pete."

"Cass, you were so involved with Banhi. You were so wrapped up in the lives of the women. Then, you were so close to Cindy…"

I couldn't believe the choice of words he was using. "It was a friendship that fell apart." I felt weak. "Is this why you didn't want to go to the memorial service?" I didn't wait for an answer. "Pete, you've convinced yourself of all of this because you needed to give yourself permission to lead a double life. I can't believe what I'm hearing."

"So you don't love me?" he asked. "You want this to be it? The end of us? It could be an open marriage for both of us."

"What?" I asked. "You were hoping I'd say yes about Doug, weren't you?"

"Kind of," he said. "Although no man wants to think his wife is with someone else."

"But you don't want me that way."

He didn't say anything.

I looked off into the distance again. The sun was floating down behind the ridge to the west of the park. The sky was streaked with pinks and purples. I saw the doe stepping from the underbrush along the railroad tracks. She froze as though a statue and I felt her eyes on us. Then she retreated back to the cover of the brush and high grass. Animals are much better than humans at avoiding danger.

I felt the surging energy from the sky. I felt the solid ground under my feet, a swoosh of wind, blowing away the illusion that I mistook for love and what I thought married love meant. That illusion had made me stay in this place, to hold fast to all I had made of it because a wife and husband have a promise to keep to each other. Pete had made me believe something existed between us that would hold us together forever. Now I knew his words, the ones I had hoped to hear on that long ago day I dialed him in India to tell him of the pregnancy did not contain the promises I had believed they held. All the small incidents from the past fifteen years all lined up like a row of dominoes and fell, crashing the next one down and the next, all now flat and dead. Then, my sense of guilt for taking him away from Bangalore, his insistence that coming here was for my sake, for my failure, because of my weakness in Bangalore, went away too.

Until now, I had believed Pete's mind and heart contained all of the same desires, beliefs, hopes and dreams I held in mine, that he was in this life as much for me and my happiness as he was for his own. What I knew now was how that premise upon which I had built our life together was false and that he had constructed our life together not for us, but as a blind where he could hide a part of himself and suit himself without my ever knowing. And to suggest my sexuality was somehow in question as an excuse for him to go find sex partners? Or suggest I join in with my own infidelity? It cut to the core of my confidence. How I wished I could talk to Phoebe back in England. Had she seen something I had not? I remembered her insinuation about why he was on the road traveling when he was supposedly in love with me. I had dismissed her subtle hints.

Older, ancient beliefs about myself from Grace's early scorn I had suspected had been because of some flaw in me fell away now too. The obsequious going along to get along with her I'd done since we were young for the sake of family, so I would have a family, was done. I realized I had done the exact same pattern of acquiescence with Pete. It was in my subconscious self, a pattern fixed in stone that only now was I able to see.

I was done with the mythical word "us." It was a word they borrowed for their own agendas. At one time, my role in their "us," my family's distortion of it, had sent me fleeing to England and grad school for escape. Banhi believed in that word "us" with Harshad and Rehani, her role as wife and daughter-in-law and because she could not have a world without that role, she was dead. I had fallen into a tailspin from which I had slowly recovered, because I could not grasp how she could allow the cultural "us" to supersede choosing a life without such suffering.

Now I saw I had been doing the same thing, believing in the Pete and me I expected would prevail over anything if we were both dedicated to that idea. I was released from that. I knew with this revelation about Pete that I was exhausted from the effort of holding onto "us" alone. I was not required to set myself on fire to keep Pete and his idea of "us" intact. I would define it from here on out.

With Cindy and the mother's group, our friendship, our shared sense of that same word, "us" had been real. I saw how close I might have come to sharing her fate except that something kept me from embracing the healing she had chosen. Had I gone along to get along with her, I too might be sitting in a box or dead. Two women will be grinding at the mill. One will be taken, the other spared.

I felt a hollow feeling, recognizing the wide divide between what I believed for so long and what was real. It was possible to pull back out of this life with Pete and resuscitate all the parts of me that I'd let go. I was exhausted, had suffered anxiety, had suffered depression and self doubt from the effort of carrying illusion alone and it had burned part of me to ash.

I would give myself permission to take care of myself and, of course, my girls with whom there was no falsehood. I would teach them that for women there is always a choice. If he loved them as much as he loved himself, maybe there was a slim sliver of hope for us to stay a family and if he loved me as he said he did. I certainly didn't feel love for him at this point. Maybe I could hold out at least until the girls were grown. Maybe an ultimatum would work. "What I wanted was for this to start being a real marriage. If you're not in this the way I expect a husband and father to be in it, this is the end of us," I said. "You think about this. And you don't have much time."

"Not any women, perhaps not all women, but Burning Women. Women who have stepped out of silence and into the fullness of their power." - Lucy H. Pearce, *Burning Woman*

CHAPTER 31

The next afternoon, I drove to the university where Cindy had worked in the office for the Institute for Philosophy for Children and found Krump in his office. He listened at first. Polite. Attentive. Interested. When I reached the part about Essen accumulating and creating a danger to the women who followed his methods, I asked him if he had any reason to believe this could not be true.

Krump pulled out a binder stuffed with papers. "Take a look," he said. "These are my notes and case histories of every person I ever suggested treatment for."

"Are you allowed to share this?" I asked. "Aren't patient records confidential?"

"This is not recognized as medicine," he said. "I am not a licensed practitioner of medicine or psychology or social work. I am simply a scientist."

The binder was four inches thick. There must have been thousands of pages. I would need months to digest all of it. "Can you give me your brief take on this?" I asked.

"If one believes in something as a cure, then they are cured," he said. "If one has doubt, well, then they are not cured."

"So it's a placebo," I stated.

"Do you believe that?" he asked.

"I did for a long time. I believed the whole thing was bogus. That's why Cindy and I were no longer friends."

"And now?"

"I think there might be something to this."

"And what changed your mind?"

"It's the only variable that differentiates the women who died from the rest of the women in Hillston."

"That you know of," he said.

"Do you know something about them I don't?" I asked. "Would you tell me?"

"There is always more to know," he said. "They may be the only ones who could know."

"This is not helpful," I said.

He said, "I haven't any idea if you're correct or not."

"If I am correct, would you stop promoting Essen as a therapy?"

"Of course," he said. "But first you must prove yourself correct."

"Did you experiment with uranium like Brandt did?" I asked.

"It isn't possible to obtain uranium," he said.

"Did you invite men to participate in your ?"

"No," he said.

"Why not?"

"They are too difficult."

"Too difficult for what?"

He stood. "I prefer not to continue this line of questioning, Ms. Taylor. You may read my notes, but I won't answer any more of your questions."

"I wish some ravenous wolf had eaten thee!
Dost thou deny thy father, cursed drab?
O, burn her, burn her! hanging is too good."
- (Henry IV Part I, Act V Scene IV)

CHAPTER 32

Pete slept in the guest room. I didn't have to ask him. He just did. It was like an afterquake of an earthquake and I watched as more of the foundation of my life crumbled. In my heart I had felt alone but now, in the house, with him still home my aloneness was unmistakable. It hurt. I vowed it would only hurt myself. It would not touch my kids any more than I could help. I decided he hadn't chosen yet, but that he'd gone to his corner like a boxer in the ring. There would be another round.

While I drank coffee at the train station, I read the first of Doug's up close and personal pieces, this one Ann's, the very first woman to succumb. He kept these to only a few paragraphs and that surprised me. I'd expected feature length tributes to their whole lives. This however, was brilliantly insightful and I nearly missed the train while I read and re-read the piece. Her husband was quoted. So were her young children. Doug had written it like a love letter from them to her. How much we are loved, I thought, is more important than anything else we use as a measurement of our lives. In this, I found my own heart tearing into bits. I had to run to the restroom to vomit. It wasn't what was said about Ann, so beautifully expressed here. It was my own sudden empathy, my self-absorbed self, imagining, if it had been me who had burst into flame and was gone, what might be said in such a piece about me? My mother was gone. I imagined

Grace's words for me or Lou's. I tried to conjure what my Lila might give to someone like Doug or Mia or Allie. What did they know of their mother other than what I did for them everyday? And Pete. So checked out. So focused on whatever his truth is that I might never really know. In his indifference, his response to such an attempt by Doug or another reporter wouldn't contain one kernel of truth about who I am. It would likely be best if he said nothing at all because whatever he did say would reveal how very lacking of content our relationship had become.

My retching left me weak and hollow, but I climbed onto the train and breathed deeply to calm myself. I slowly stopped sweating and let the air-conditioned air soothe me. I needed a mint or a tooth-brush. I needed a Xanax. I was jealous of a dead woman for having been deeply loved and so fully known while she was alive. I didn't like myself for this. A wave of self-reproach washed over me, then anger replaced it. Then, as I breathed, I found forgiveness and let it all go. You're alive, I repeated silently. It's going to be okay.

I stopped at the stationary store next to the Goodwill Mission for a bottle of water and Tic Tacs. My reflection in the plate glass was wavering and shadowy. I needed a comb and some makeup before I scared the kids with how I looked. So, in the ladies room, I fixed my appearance and remembered the line "Act enthusiastic and you'll be enthusiastic" from a speech class in my distant past. Today's tour would include American folk art.

By the time I had my class of fourth graders lined up in front of the family portrait of the Baker family, I looked better and, inside, the flutters and churning in my viscera had subsided. It was an oversized family portrait where the characters are life-sized. The sister of the matriarch of this family had been widowed and taken in by her sis-ter's husband. The women's status was indicated in their dress. Those who were unmarried were painted with their neck and shoulders naked. The young daughter was dressed accordingly. Those married or widowed wore tight lace collars up to their necks. Once a woman was owned by her husband, her physical gifts of beauty were his alone to enjoy. Married women wore brooches, the gift at marriage much like a wedding ring of today. These were proudly displayed on their jet-black dresses. No one smiled in this portrait. I told the children that sitting for a long period of time while the painter did his work was not conducive to smiles. But there was something else. I asked them to look for a clue as to why they all looked so somber, all, that is, but the young boy whose hand held a red ball and whose other hand was petting a dog.

"The clue is in the painting," I said. "Look for something in the painting to prove your idea before you raise your hand."

"Is it because the man who died isn't in the picture?" asked a boy.

"Very good," I said. "The husband who passed away isn't there, of course. Notice there is a blank space behind his widow? That is where he would have stood to be part of this. That's a very good observation, but there is something else too."

I waited and watched fifteen pairs of eyes scan the painting. The children consulted one another, pointing out different details to each other, testing ideas before raising their hands.

"One other thing too," said a girl. "There are no grandmothers or grandfathers in the picture."

"Yes," I said, "look for something that is there, not something that isn't."

They all grew silent. They studied. The teacher watched from her place at the back of the cluster of kids. Finally, someone raised his hand.

"Yes?" I said.

"The little girl looks like she is floating," he said. "Look at her feet."

"Oh yeah," I heard a few of them say.

"Good eyes," I said. "Now here's a question...do you think she looks that way because the painter was not good at painting feet? Or could there be a different reason?"

The child wore a white lace dress. She was likely five years old or so. Her feet were bare and although casual observers might not notice, they were in an odd position in relation to the detailed parquetted floor she stood upon.

"Oh!" A bunch of hands went up and waved excitedly. I called on a red haired girl in the back row.

"Maybe they're not smiling because she is on her way to heaven?" she said.

"Ah," I said. "Yes. Now I want you to notice how each and every other family member in the picture is touching another person or with the boy, he's touching the dog. This indicates they are alive and together. She's the only one no longer connected to the living."

"How did she die?" someone asked.

"The story says she died of a fever at the age of five." I brought them back to studying the painting again. "The story that came with the painting also included the elder daughter," I said, pointing to the young girl in a sapphire blue dress with an off the shoulder cut. She stood between her widowed aunt and her mother, shoulders touching her aunt, hand on her mother's shoulders too. Connected. "She married a doctor and they had ten children. At her home in Pennsylvania, she hid slaves escaping north to freedom. She gave them food and water and kept the sick ones until they were well. Her husband had no idea until he realized she was taking supplies from his medical bag. He exposed her little hospital and she was so enraged she left him. Her family wouldn't take her back home after that. They were shamed by her leaving her husband. She lived in New Orleans after that. Raised her own children by herself and worked as a nurse in a hospital there."

"If their stories were flames, you'd have to keep your distance, otherwise you'd get scorched." - Father Gregory Boyle

CHAPTER 33

The binder from Krump and I spent the evening, the midnight hours, and the early dawn together upstairs in my bedroom where I spread out pages and piles of notes all around me on the king-sized bed. Krump certainly was a scientist with a methodical record keeping habit. He used tabs to separate his records on each experiment. Each practitioner of Essen had been assigned a number. That initially disturbed me. It brought to mind victims of death or labor camps and survivors with their numbers tattooed on their wrists. He, according to Doug, was truly intent on helping people. While I read, the notes on each practitioner of Essen therapy confirmed to me that Doug's characterization of Krump was correct.

I couldn't search this binder for the burning victims by name unless I knew which number they'd been assigned. So I began with the low numbers and assumed, which I later learned to have been correct, that low numbered followers had been the longest users of accumulators. I tried to recognize them through the notes from what I knew of each of them. I knew Cindy. I knew three others. I didn't know Ann or Elizabeth or Lucy or the others at all, except for Doug's newspaper profiles.

What I learned was that Krump asked each user to get a medical examination and to share the results with him. These were in the files. Some also saw specialists for particular symptoms like skin problems, back pain, allergy symptoms, breathing difficulties, joint aches, stomach distress, weight gain, rapid heart rates, and menstrual pain.

Krump apparently wanted to see what medical specialists diagnosed and recommended as treatment for these ailments. Many more went for psychological evaluations and the files contained diagnoses of depression, post-partum particularly, anxiety, some with more intense disorders for which symptoms were meticulously listed in the record. Often, the most unwell patients chose conventional treatments and didn't return to Krump. I'm sure he had a cross-referenced list. I realized I would not get specific background information about specific persons. I had wanted that more than anything. I hadn't asked Grace if she had consulted with Krump. All I knew was that she had built and used an Essen accumulator per Cindy's blog instructions. That was another disappointment with the contents of this binder. It was possible many of the women in Cindy's group didn't consult with Krump but simply followed her lead. Krump would know nothing about those cases.

Each file contained a statement of treatment. Krump had obtained an agreement from his followers to consult with him monthly to review their symptoms and to allow him to review their use of their Essen accumulator. Records included logs of numbers of hours, frequency of what he called visits, dates, and times of use of the therapy. I read through some of these logs. Some showed followers who used their accumulators for several hours a day, some sequential hours, some with visits of short duration but high frequency throughout the day. Comment sections of these logs noted any changes in mood or in the level of discomfort for whatever ailment they were treating. Most of these were for mental or emotional distress, anxiety, depression, low libido, and fear. Krump recorded anecdotal comments on elevations of mood, levels of sadness, energy levels. Some logged the frequency of sexual contact with their partners.

After hours of flipping through these notes I grew tired of the repetition. It all seemed to reflect a genuinely dismal level of existence. So many people were unable to find joy in their lives. So many were burdened by grief, disappointment, unmet expectations, desires for elements of life they'd lost or never attained. Many blamed their choices in partners. Many cited parent relationships, anger, and frustration at failures in communication. Some admitted their lack of love for their roles in life, their disconnection from their former selves, loss of childhood enthusiasm for exploration, and a general malaise. For some, there were real life tragedies, a miscarriage, death of a child, illness and caregiving for loved ones, parents particularly. I felt the burdens they each carried. I cried when I read the case of a woman coping with a traumatic brain injury and the long process of recovery. It wasn't her own injury; it was her twenty-six year old son. Essen therapy? She also prayed while she was sitting in the accumulator. I wondered when I read the entries indicating that she seemed to have gained strength and energy if it was the prayers that were to be given credit and not the Essen energy at all.

Essen therapy infused them with resolve. That was my final conclusion at the end of each file. They fixated their hope for change on the practice of sitting alone in a phone booth-like box and breathing. The notes reported improvements in their mood, a reduction of thoughts of suicide, an abandonment of fantasies about starting over elsewhere with something new on which to build, improved relationships, better sex with their partner. Krump reported an upturn in the energy, more smiles, more positivity, and an increased glow in their complexions. Essen therapy, I concluded, was a self-care technique. It was no different from taking a yoga class, taking a walk, practicing meditation, or prayer.

Being with yourself alone in the dark by choice led to an inability to hide from oneself, Krump's endnotes said. Confrontation with one's own foibles and not being able to ignore them helped these people to defeat their own demons or at least to recognize what was threatening them was not out there in the real world, but instead a part of themselves they would take with them wherever they went. Maybe this did more than all those other self-care techniques, I thought. So much resides within us and so often it is obscured by what is around us. The outer world shouts all the time. In the dark, in the box, the whispers of the self are not drowned out. They climb out of the recesses of consciousness and speak and, while no distractions are allowed, the practitioner cannot ignore them. Of course, I briefly compared this practice to the culturally imposed containment of women in India where Banhi was not allowed out of that tiny house unless she was with a man. I wondered if the ancient Druids did the same to their women at Stonehenge. We would never know.

Krump's results and his footnotes for each of his experiments suggested a redefinition of what Brandt had originally entitled Essen energy. It is simply the purification of the self, a ridding of the clutter, a quieting of the noise, he wrote. It is turning the self toward the demon that threatens from within and staring it down. If one can extinguish those, he wrote, the outer world becomes trivial, the difficulties one faces no longer loom insurmountable.

I found what I believed were Cindy's notes. An early case, but not the first. I knew from the dates on the note pages. I knew from the notes about her outer world, the death of her mother, her grief at the unresolved conflicts they'd had before Cindy left Chicago for New Jersey. These pages included some hand written notes by Cindy after her first early Essen therapy sessions. All that she had faced in the dark. I read, not really knowing what I was looking for, just wanting to see where Cindy's turning point had been. How long had she been trying the therapy before she introduced Essen and Krump to the group? I did memory association starting with my own mother's death, then counting the months in between that and Cindy's middle of the night flight to Chicago. I remembered the lunch when she left the pamphlet. It had been spring, early April. What year? Then, I knew something else. In September of that year, the towers fell in New York. That December was the culmination of our argument over

Krump's guest speaker appearance. How many Essen therapy practitioners had begun then? I arranged the experiment cases chrono-
logically and separated them by year, then month of the first entry.
The number of Krump's experiments swelled after 9/11. Of course,
I thought. That had hit our town hard. So many commuters to New
York in Hillston. We'd lost seven in the towers that day. I recall how
we talked about it in our group, how close we all had come to being
one of the widows of 9/11. Not one of our members had lost a spouse
or family member that day. We'd felt so fortunate. We'd also felt survi-
vor's guilt when we learned the names of those from our community
who did lose their spouses. I recalled my fear after that whenever Pete
had to fly. His response had always been to remind me that more
people die in car accidents than from plane crashes or terrorist attacks.
"Not in this town," I had said.

I wondered how many Essen experiments were women whose
husbands died. The notes during that time period revealed none. But
here was a woman who lost her twin. I slowed my reading to take in
all that she'd told Krump, all that she'd written in her journal notes.
After a lifetime, they had been fifty-four in 2001, she struggled to
continue to live with what she believed was a half of herself. In her
Essen therapy, she wrote that her sister, whose name was Charlotte,
spoke to her. Krump concluded her healing took place in the dark.
She could say goodbye, visit, be reassured that her sister's spirit existed
and was still a part of her life and she found courage to go on because
of this.

One could have been Ann. I read. She was exhausted from her
battle with infertility, her longing for another child. She was in battle
with her own body, with her revulsion at the site of the hypodermic
needle piercing her flesh each morning. She wrote of her shame in
front of her mother, who suggested to Ann that she had brought this
upon herself. All her career successes, the travel, the promotions, the
weight of it growing with each new triumph. "Ann, you're not getting

any younger." And, "Ann, your Sarah needs a little brother like you had." And, "Ann, John, like every man, needs a son." The tangles this formed with those other desires, Ann's own, her brilliance as a financial analyst, her drive to create in her own way, silencing, even for a short while, the dissonance. This had built the fire that consumed her.

I knew, between Cindy's blog and this record of Krump's experiments, the struggles that led these women to embrace Essen therapy as their cure. I also concluded that Krump had wanted to find something to confirm Brandt's discovery of Essen energy, that it really was a counterbalance to the destructive forces in our contaminated world. That it gave life-affirming energy where pain and suffering depleted it.

Elizabeth? Her secret was her drinking. School principals do not carry flasks, most of them, at least. And lipstick tubes do not carry white powder. Over a summer, Krump noted, she had transformed from a round figured woman into runway model thinness. Had Essen therapy worked or not? Aside from the accumulated force of it in her muscles, in her organs, it had done nothing. It was her daily substances that had kept her functioning. It was the lie of her brilliance with the children, an inspirational energy the teachers emulated at her school.

After reading this entry, I had to close the binder.

Lucy's section revealed nothing more than her discovery of her husband Larry's second family. The tattooed daughter from Larry's first wife had turned up at the memorial service for Larry's father ten years into their marriage. The girl, snapped her chew, spit on the cemetery path, took pictures with her smart phone and called Larry "Daddy" in a deep tobacco tarnished voice. Lucy watched her sons turn to him, whispering to each other. And Larry, pale already from the strain of his loss, lifting a hand to the shoulders of each son, pretending she was not there. His refusal to discuss it with Lucy later, or ever, had driven her to utter despair. But she stayed in her marriage for the sake of her sons. This had kept her practicing Essen.

Grace. Somehow, I still clung to the belief that I had saved her life. I lay there surrounded by a chaos of pages full of stories of pain and relief. Slowly, meticulously, I put all of them back in order and returned them to the white plastic binder and snapped the rings. I closed the cover, closed my eyes. I thought about the insight that came through these experiments of Krump's and switched off the lamp so that I lay there in the dark. I pulled the blinds to make it as dark as possible. My demons didn't show themselves. I fell asleep. When I awoke with the dawn, I reflected what these burnings had left in their aftermath. These women, pillars of marble who no one imagined would ever weaken, taken by a strange and thorough flame. It was as though they had escaped, that they were spared the reveal, the pain of the curtain pulling back to reveal the pain of truth. I thought for the first time that they might be in a safer place now.

This binder had to go to the police. They had to ask Krump for the list to cross reference these notes to the women's names to be sure they'd found all of the Essen therapy users in Hillston or elsewhere. And I wanted Doug to see this. His profiles of the victims, however beautifully rendered, did not reveal any of what I found in these notes. Just goes to show, I thought, how much you can love someone and not know that deeper part of them.

"Remember, the firemen are rarely necessary."
- Ray Bradbury

CHAPTER 34

I could see the gleam in Heffly's eye. He spoke into the radio he held in his hand. Soon, Richmond was at his side. Richmond knew me.

"Coach Cassie," he said. "That's what they called you, right?"

"Yes," I answered, my pasted-on smile feeling like an utter failure to convey my false friendliness.

"You wanted to speak to us?" Richmond's manner was so polite I could feel the disdain immediately.

"I do. It's about the causes of these deaths."

Richmond actually said that anything I said could and would be used against me in a court of law and I had a right to a lawyer. I couldn't believe this man actually thought I was going to confess something or incriminate myself. "I'll take my chances," I said.

They exchanged glances with each other. "Listen, Ms. Taylor, if you're going to waste our time..."

"I have a Master's degree in geo-archaeology and cultural anthropology. I studied the energy in the earth and the stones and the bedrock underneath the stone circles, you know what Stonehenge is, don't you?"

"Of course," said Richmond. He said it as though I'd insulted his intelligence.

"Well, I'm going to give you the very short version of what I know."

Richmond couldn't hide his confusion. Doug glanced at me. When I had asked him to come with me to public safety headquarters, he agreed, but warned me to lower my expectations. He looked back at Richmond. Heffly had been silent from the moment Richmond had entered his office. Now he said, "About ancient stones?"

"No," I said. "About Hillston. The town, this whole geographic area. There are conditions that may help explain some things."

Heffly and Richmond looked at each other, glanced at Doug as though he could interpret my words. When Doug said nothing, they gave me their attention.

I opened my laptop and the browser and searched for NASA's website. Then, with a sigh of satisfaction, I turned it so Heffly, Richmond, and Doug could see what I wanted them to see. "The power failures we've been experiencing? Look…they were due to hits to the power grid. It's not totally the utility's fault. We're in a high CME time period. And look, the same kind of power grid hit happened on Friday when the first three died and when the second three died and at Cindy Barrow's memorial service and again when Lucy Jones died."

I had to explain to them what a CME was. I had to explain how the eruptions from our sun intensify every eleven years and that this year was a peak year in the cycle. "There is radioactive energy coming in those bursts from the sun," I said. "When these bursts hit the earth, they bend the magnetic protection shield and, when the bursts penetrate, they cause damage to the electric grid. They are also raining radioactive energy down on our town and everywhere."

It was my turn to glance around and I exchanged looks with Doug and fingered my ring. Doug nodded slightly to let me know he was with me.

They all just stared at me, a long silent pregnant pause.

"Yes," I said. "Charles Dickens called it Spontaneous Human Combustion."

"Charles Dickens?"

"Yes, in his novel Bleak House," Doug said.

"And that was in the 1860s," Heffly said.

"Right," Richmond said. "And I've heard about SHC as a cause of death. The FBI doesn't recognize it as a cause."

"They recognize it in England." I handed both men a copy of a front-page piece from the Daily Mail in London, the same piece Doug had shown me on his smart phone at the memorial service. "There are towns in England with the root word for burnt in the town's name. There is local history among villagers of unexplained fires that seem to have no explanation…barns, homes, and people."

"This is mythology," Heffly said. "Ms. Taylor, I appreciate you coming to us, but this isn't helpful."

"Just hear her out," Doug said.

"People make up myths when they don't understand natural phenomena. They call things magic or miracles or curses from the supernatural." I paused. "Or they call it something inaccurate like Spontaneous Human Combustion. If you look at this NASA website and their data and check with the weather watchers at the National Weather Service, you will find out the earth was hit with a CME strong enough to impact the power grid each day the fires occurred."

"What is a CME?" Richmond asked. "Tell me again?"

"A coronal mass ejection," I said. "It's a surge of energy that bursts forth from the inner layers of the sun, breaks through the surface, and is released in a big wave, almost like a volcano, but it isn't lava, it's electromagnetic radiation – light."

"I don't know anything about this," said Heffly.

"But I do," I said.

"Sounds like a stretch," Richmond said.

"Thing is, I checked the conditions in Hillston under the surface. The iron in the old mines creates magnetism."

"So we attract more of the sun's CME discharge to our locale?" asked Heffly.

"That's exactly right," I said.

"Then why don't we have…"

"We also have a radon problem in Hillston," I said.

"Oh, that's right," said Heffly. He looked at Richmond. Suddenly he was paying very close attention. "I'm in the neighborhood where they're digging up. I know all about this. It's costing my neighborhood thousands."

"So we've got geological sources of magnetic energy. We've got a baseline of radioactivity from the radon we're excavating. We've got year eleven in the sun spot cycle," Richmond repeated this in summary. I nodded.

"I have something else I need to show you," I said.

"And what is that?" asked Richmond.

"Some photographs," I said. I pulled Lila's photographs and negatives from my tote bag. I pulled out the article on how NASA uses film on the space shuttle and International Space Station to monitor radioactive bursts for the safety of the astronauts. "If the film negatives and the clouds on the film are an indication of radioactive energy, these women have higher concentrations in them than the rest of us. So we may just be able to identify who else might be in danger."

When I was done talking, Heffly and Richmond looked at each other. Then they looked at me. I could see the reservation in their demeanor. I could see the struggle to be polite, to not laugh, and I felt a sinking sense in my gut.

Doug just sat there with an amazed expression and jotted down notes. I could not get a read on his response. Poker faces and the heat rose in my head while a small throbbing in my left temple started giving me pain.

"So I would be in danger because I'm in a radon excavation zone," Heffly stated simply.

"You're forgetting the big question," I continued, "why these women and not everyone."

"Well, I'm glad you said that because that is what I was thinking." Richmond scratched his buzz cut and waited for me to continue.

"This is the big answer to that," I said. I had to go into a rather long explanation of Essen energy therapy, Bruno Brandt, his claims, his experiments, his public disgrace. When I ended with the list of women who died and the list of other women in the still active self-help support group who practiced the therapy, I said, "I left this group because I thought this was a hoax, but this is the only variable in the lives of these victims that is not shared by anyone else in this town."

Doug knew how to allow a pregnant pause to follow my last statement. He said, "I am publishing a front-page story about this in tomorrow's paper."

"So you believe it?" Heffly asked.

"It makes more sense than a cult and self-immolation," Doug said. "It makes more sense than that rumor floating around that someone is torching them from far away with some new sort of weapon."

Heffly stood up. "She might just be right," he said, looking at Richmond. "You got any better explanations?"

"We'll have to round up these Essen practicing women for pro-tection. We'll have to ban these accumulator boxes. Don't you agree? Just to be safe until we can eliminate this as a possibility?" Richmond scratched the back of his neck. He stared off into the distance. He made no eye contact with any of us. "Let's get on this."

"I'm sorry I didn't return your calls, Miss uh, Ms. Cassandra, uh, Dr. Taylor." Heffly reached across the desk to shake my hand.

"It's Ms," I said. "Ms. Cassandra Taylor. Just call me Cassie."

I turned toward Richmond. He shook my hand too, but he seemed unable to stand up. Then, suddenly looking into my eyes, he said, as though it was important, "You were a good coach too."

"Love, like fire, goes out without fuel."
- Mikhail Lermontov

CHAPTER 35

Doug sent me his draft of the piece for the morning paper. I did some major edits and corrections and sent it back.

When Mayor Bobby Moore's aide called me and asked if I were available to speak to him, I was ready for a conversation. I imagined him giving me abrupt thanks and dismissing this as too politically risky for him to get behind. But he simply said, "Cassandra, I have a few questions." He might have been reading from a briefing sheet from Doug because his accuracy was nearly one hundred percent. We went through a list of factors with me correcting and expanding as we did. "Most importantly," he said, "when I go public, we will need to share the results of your testing of radioactivity and magnetic energy with the press. You need to be ready to do that."

"Of course," I said.

Now, from my kitchen, I watched him, performance ready, on CNN with others about to broadcast him worldwide. Doug was behind him on the podium along with Heffly and Richmond. The brother, Helenus to my Cassandra, I mused.

I hadn't heard Pete come in and stand quietly behind to watch with me. When I turned slightly toward the stove, there he was. His skin gleaming with sweat and his hair was standing up in waves around his face, which was reddened from his run. He was not breathing hard so he must have been there for a bit.

"This is all your stuff," Pete said.

"I helped get him ready for this."

"Don't you feel used?" he asked.

"No," I said.

As I said that, I heard Bobby Moore say, "Cassandra Taylor is a scientist who lives in Hillston. She put these pieces together for us. You'll want to speak to her. For tonight, we're announcing this as a public safety message. This is to establish a townwide ban on the Essen accumulators and to warn citizens who might be using them to stop. We identified some of the users, but it is likely we haven't identified all of them."

I looked at Pete. "See?"

He nodded. "Okay."

"Finally," I said. "Some of what I believed in has actually been proven true." I was twirling my ring without realizing it. I glanced down at it; the red jewel underneath the lyre insignia glowed in the slanting rays of the evening sun streaming across my kitchen. It was as though the universe was celebrating this triumph with me. There was a tiny glow growing from inside my heart too. I felt calm. I felt joyful and grateful and a little bit smug at my accomplishment. "It feels pretty good," I said to Pete.

"I only hope you're right and this doesn't come back to haunt you," he said.

I wanted him to congratulate me. I wanted him to say we should celebrate. I wanted to feel that we shared this triumph together the way we had my discoveries at Sheffield, the way we had when Lila was born, when Mia and Allie came to us together.

"This will all fade away in a week or so," he said.

The moment was gone. The opportunity was gone. He'd missed it. I knew he was aware of it. He was withholding what he knew I desperately wanted from him. Either that or he was not paying attention, not really. His thoughts were elsewhere and I knew where they most likely were. His gaze had lifted to mine very quickly and had moved sideways to the cluster of foodstuffs on the counter. Pasta in a box. Marinara in a jar. Salad in a bag.

"Is that our dinner?"

I nodded. "While you're here, would you check the burner on the stove?" I lifted the Post-it note I'd attached to the refrigerator a week ago and handed it to him. "I have to boil water for pasta."

He put the note on the table. "Do I have time for a shower first?"

"Not really," I said.

"I'll order take-out," he said. "Don't cook."

"That will get us through tonight," I said. "Not tomorrow or the next day or the next…"

"You've been coping with it 'til now," he said. "It can wait a bit longer."

"I can't wait anymore," I said. "Can you please do it now? I need to get dinner on the table."

He pursed his lips. His brow furrowed then smoothed. He walked out of the kitchen and I heard water running through the pipes in the wall to the shower overhead.

I filled my largest pot with water from the tap and placed it on the burner. I turned the knob to the right to where the word ignite" was etched in white letters on the black plastic. I heard the tick tick tick of the electronic starter. I remembered the days when gas stoves had a pilot light that stayed lit under the surface of the cooktop and we didn't hear that tick tick tick. We only heard the swoosh as the gas met the pilot and caught. With the tick tick tick, we still hear the swoosh as the fire starts, but now it wasn't happening. Gas filled my nostrils and I turned it to off. I waited until I no longer smelled gas and turned it again to ignite. If I turned the knob too far, the word "high" was visible. Then "medium." Then "low." Then "simmer." It was all so clearly marked. It all should be so very easy, unlike the kerosene stove in Bahni's corrugated hut in Rahendra Najar. There, the liquid fuel required careful attention, a match struck and held just close enough to be able to pull the hand away quickly. Undivided attention was required and disaster was just a split second away. This modern stove required no instructions at all. But still, it was not functioning properly. I could use the back burner. But I persisted. Turn it on. Wait. Turn it off. Wait. Again. And again. Eventually, I knew, it would work but if I wasn't careful I'd get that burst again, the one that had singed the hairs on my arm a few weeks ago. While I waited for the scent of gas to dissipate once again, I examined my forearm. It was still bare. I rubbed across a soft prickly texture where new follicles of tiny hairs were sprouting.

I turned the knob again and held it. Then, I let go. I lifted the pot full of water from the grate and placed it on the counter. Maybe it just needed more oxygen. Maybe the pot was curtailing the flow of air.

Maybe I could no longer smell the natural gas that filled up my kitchen or maybe it was lighter than air and floated up toward the ceiling. Later, after the explosion I would remember to look it up, but just as I turned my attention back to the burner, it lit. A ball of flame appeared before my eyes, blue plasma and flicks of yellow. I felt the force of heat hit my face and chest and arms. Somehow, my hair, tied in a ponytail and tight against my head in a plastic clip, hadn't caught fire. Nothing had caught fire. The flame resumed the appropriate shape, a neat little circle of blue dancing under the grate. It was as though nothing had happened. My fear was the only thing that endured.

Thank goodness the girls were out. Imagine if they'd been sitting here doing homework...tomorrow night, the next night, the night after that...while Pete was again on the road, because I knew when he had walked out of the kitchen, he had no intention of fixing anything, let alone the errant burner on our expensive stove. I was sore. I felt a burning sensation on my skin, but, when I looked, there was no evidence of a burn. It was over. I was still here. I hadn't succumbed.

I moved the pot of water back to the burner where flame now glowed silent and purposeful. I used the microwave to heat the marinara and poured it over the cooked and drained pasta. I waited for my girls to arrive, for Pete to join us at the table, and I listened to the dinner conversation. Pete engaged the twins by asking them about their teachers and some banal aspect of riding the school bus to which they responded in their usual charming, thoughtful ways. On the surface, this seemed to be a scene of happy domestic life as though nothing in the world was wrong. Only in my heart and in my determined mind were things so very twisted and dark and deceitful. I knew then and there. Pete would pin a break up of this family all on me. He was pretending and he would continue to pretend. I would not. The battle for an emotional truth would be mine no matter what he tried to paint over the surface with his behavior. Mia and Allie were too young to process what was likely to come and that realization stung my soul. Lila was perceptive, but this wouldn't be her battle, it would be mine alone. I needed to prepare myself for the fight.

"…things we can't imagine, to make a woman stay in a burning house; there must be something there. You don't stay for nothing." - Ray Bradbury

CHAPTER 36

Pete attended Grace's graduation party for Catherine, although I believed his motive was the same as it was on the evening of our talk in the park and his continued presence in the house.

I had forgotten to get a card for Catherine. I didn't feel right asking Pete to run out to the drug store to help with that, but he did it. By the time we were all in the car, the girls in their dresses, Mia complaining that her shoes were too tight, and Lila whispering that if she took her shoes off at the party Lila would too, his presence by my side did nothing but rattle me. It was his calm. His smile. His perfect appearance in his khaki slacks and blue blazer. His perfect behavior in the role of husband and father. My hair refused to cooperate, my dress wrinkled when I sat down, my makeup looked too heavy over the bags under my eyes. I forgot lipstick and I knew I should have shopped for something new to wear. I had hurried the girls through showers, ironed dresses after long discussions about appropriate dress for a party not being their usual sneakers and denim shorts.

I had spent the last few days responding to phone calls, to requests for interviews, to explaining and explaining the background so that the news media could get it all straight. My own hair was unruly even clipped back in a ponytail. My spreadsheet with my Geiger counter and magnetometer readings had been displayed as a sidebar to articles in our local paper, in the *New York Times*, and on countless broadcasts from CNN, MSNBC, ABC, CBS. I was to be a guest on All Things Considered on NPR on Tuesday morning. Still, the public only got a snippet of the facts, enough to quell fear. It had only been a few days. No new burnings had occurred. No power failures either. Maybe the eleven-year cycle in CMEs was ending. Maybe all the potential victims were in the hospital in quarantine.

Grace had done seating arrangements and our table was just to the left of Grace and Charles, Lou and Jack, and Catherine. We were five and we could fit at their table as family, I noted, but a couple I didn't recognize and their three children sat where we might have. Then, I remembered the bracelet I'd chosen from the jewelry I'd snatched back at the garage sale. I'd wanted to give it to Catherine. It was at home in a box tucked into the drawer near my bed.

The room was lovely. Cardboard graduation cap centerpieces full of flowers decorated each table. Balloons floated above on curly paper ribbons. White tablecloths with blue and silver glitter sprinkled around which Mia and Allie began to immediately re-arrange into pictures and shapes. The bar was crowded, so Pete went to the end of the line to get us something while I poured lemonade for the girls from the pitcher on the table. I couldn't help but notice eyes on me when I stood and surveyed the room looking for Grace and Lou and any of Grace's friends I might have met before. I had not anticipated the attention I suddenly felt shifting toward me as more and more guests introduced themselves and thanked me. I found myself answering questions, listening to accounts of fear from women who didn't leave their houses for two weeks. I had to weather a few comments along the lines of how they never knew Grace had a sister who was a scientist. Where did I do my research? Who did I work for? Where did I teach? Where was my degree from? How long had I been overseas and how long had I been back in Hillston…and on and on. It was all flattering, but it was not what I had expected. When their questions were answered, they sauntered off and left me standing alone again. In the midst of this Pete handed me a glass of red wine. I didn't see him again until the buffet table was set and Charles announced that lunch was now being served. I hadn't spoken to Grace yet. I let her be hostess, greeting her friends, speaking to the red-haired banquet manager.

Catherine joined us and Grace pulled up a chair next to Lila. Grace turned her attention to the twins, pointedly asking them questions. How's school? What grade are you in now? Lila and Catherine broke off their quiet conversation to listen. Then, Lila broke in, "Aunt Grace, I still have to do your picture. Let's do it today. Let's do it here. It's so pretty here." Lila pulled out her camera. "Let's do one with you and Catherine near the rose bushes." She gestured toward the veranda. "It will only take a minute."

Grace said, "Oh, there's too much going on."

Catherine stood up. "Yes, let's do it. Lila, great idea. Then, show me how to work the camera and I'll do one of you and all your family. I'll get my dad too."

Gathering all of us outdoors in the sunshine was a bit like herding cats. As Catherine went to find Charles, Lila searched for Lou and Jack who were off in a far corner in a circle of people I didn't know. Pete and I stood and dropped our napkins on our chairs. I wanted to run to the ladies' room to check myself. I knew I needed lipstick and entertained myself with the impossible idea of finding an iron for my very wrinkled linen dress. That wasn't happening. So Pete and Mia and Allie were the first ones to stand hand in hand by the rosebush waiting for Lila, waiting for me, waiting for everyone to escape from the social ties that bound them to the guests. Pete and I and our girls went first. Lila composed the shot, adjusted her aperture, squinted at us over the top of the camera, decided she needed the flash due to the shadows of a tree and finally handed the camera to Catherine. "Now, make sure you have us centered. Make sure our whole bodies are in the shot. I don't want us looking like tiny heads at the bottom with the rose bush taking up the whole picture."

"Got it," Catherine said.

Lila had arranged us, Pete next to me, Ally and Mia just in front of us, and a blank spot for Lila to take next to me where she now positioned herself. Catherine took a photo. Lila set up a second and took her place on the far side of Pete this time. Then she insisted on doing another with just natural light, no flash, and turned us so the shadows were not darkening us. Lou and Jack joined us and as this went on I knew we were going to have to get some other guest to take the large family group photo with all of us in it. Lila didn't have her tripod. While Lila took the camera from Catherine and lined her up with her mother and father, I went through the door to the ballroom and, to my utter amazement, there stood Heffly with Doug and a photographer from the Jersey Star.

"Why are you here?" I said in amazement.

"We're here to find Grace Taylor," Heffly said. "She needs to be quarantined."

"You mean Grace Byrne," I said. Oh gees, Charles' last name is Byrne. I hadn't made that connection through this entire time. Grace's married name was Byrne. Catherine's last name was Byrne. "She's not in the women's group," I said. As I said it, I knew that wasn't the correct response. She was on the blog. She might also be on the list Krump had provided. "But I do know she's used the therapy."

"She's the only one left," said Heffly. "I understand she's your sister."

I nodded. "And this is her daughter's graduation party. Your timing couldn't be worse."

I looked to Doug for help. He shrugged.

"We're in the middle of taking family photos," I said. "At least let us finish. Do you really have to take her right now?"

"Sorry, Cassie," said Heffly. "It's for her own protection."

"She's not using the accumulator," I said. "Not anymore."

I followed them to the veranda. I felt awful. How did they know we were here? Grace was going to pin this on me and she'd likely be right. Ruining her daughter's graduation party. It would be on me forever.

"You want a picture?" the photographer said to Lila. "Get in it. Give me the camera." I smiled at him gratefully. "Thank you. I was just looking for someone to do this for us."

We were all now gathered. Lila had everyone lined up including a spot for me in between Grace and Lou. The husbands were behind us, the kids in front, their arms around each other's shoulders. Lila did her usual explaining and peering through her lens and waving her arms around to be sure the photographer knew what she wanted. He nodded several times and gestured her toward her spot. I took mine. I felt Pete's hand reach for mine and hold it. He was behaving exactly like I might have wished him to behave, but it felt completely false and dishonest. I stiffened. I tried to paste a smile on for the picture, but that felt false too. The photographer took several shots and Lila finally lifted her hand and stopped him but not before he used his own digital camera and snapped a few.

As we fell out of formation, I pushed Pete's hand off mine and stepped away from him. Heffly moved in on Grace. He spoke quietly to her and while he did she gave me a look with narrowed eyes. I went to them and said, "Grace, I told them the timing on this couldn't be worse."

"How did they know we'd be here?" she asked. "Did you tell them?"

I knew I had in the context of my long explanation of Essen that day in Heffly's office. Never did I expect them to remember the tiny detail of this party, but apparently someone had. "I didn't mean to...I had no idea they'd come here and..."

"They want to take me away in the middle of my daughter's graduation party," she said. "This is all you. Did you plan this?"

"No, I ..."

"And you didn't plan the invasion of my meeting here either," she said.

"No. I didn't. It hit me that you were in danger so I..."

"You never stop. You always punish me. Every chance you get. You're always looking for your chance to get back at me," she said. "That's why I can't be around you."

"Get back at you?" I asked.

"Oh don't act like you don't know," she said. "You're so passive aggressive. I can't believe you're acting so innocent."

"This has nothing to do with the past," I said. "You're in danger and you need to go with them."

"You've got the whole town believing your nonsense. And who gets to suffer for it? Me."

"Essen therapy and energy are dangers," Heffly said. "We've confirmed it. It's not just your sister who understands this. Please, come with us and don't make it difficult."

"Did you stop?" I asked. "When I asked you to stop, did you stop?"

She didn't want to answer. I asked her again. I waited out her silence. Heffly did too.

"Yes, I stopped," she said. "Okay?" She beseeched Heffly. "Please, I don't have any of the Essen energy in me. Cassandra saved my life that day. She told me water makes it go away." She called, "Charles, come over here?"

Charles obeyed her. "What's going on?" he asked.

Heffly took over. "Your wife here says she hasn't been practicing her Essen therapy for at least," he looked at me, "a few days, maybe a week, is that true?"

Charles paused. "Why?" he asked. His face reddened until he looked like his tie was choking him.

"Just answer the question," Heffly said.

I saw a long line of potential truths line up behind each other in the silence. I also saw the potential for lies and the consequences of them.

Charles said, "My wife stopped using that accumulator after her sister told her to." He looked right at me when he said it. "I took an axe to it on Wednesday night. It's in the trash for bulky waste day."

Heffly shrugged. "Okay," he said. "She stays."

Grace turned her back and stepped through the door to rejoin her guests.

Pete had been watching this from behind me. Doug had too. I believe the photographer had taken quite a few pictures of that exchange, but only one appeared in the Jersey Star the next morning along with Doug's article about how I had saved my sister's life. I knew that it would be up to Grace if she and I ever spoke of this again. We never did. The invitations to family gatherings didn't increase either. Not from Grace, but Lou made an effort to see me more often. She confided in me that Grace conceded that her distrust of me was because she had been on the alert for vengefulness since her nastiness in our teen years, especially the diary incident.

Pete thought that I had finally broken through and gotten her to understand me. When he said this, after he read Doug's piece in the paper the next morning, I looked at him and said, "Now if I could only get through to you."

I handed him a Post-it note with the phone number Dr. Gimpel had given me. She said she couldn't do couples therapy because she was my personal therapist.

"You make the call," I said.

"Really?" he asked.

"If you want this marriage to work," I said, "you'll do it."

He sipped his coffee, read his newspaper. When he rose from the table and left the kitchen a half hour later, the slip of paper with the phone number fluttered to the floor. I picked it up. I watched his receding back. I tore the thing into pieces and tossed it in the trash. That was my last attempt.

EPILOGUE

It was late Indian summer and the girls and I were off on an "excellent adventure." We'd done a few this past summer-- to the beach, to the Catskills for kayaking. Our bags were packed and lined up in the hallway. Mia and Allie slurped sweet milk from the bottom of their cereal bowls, a snack before bed, and Lila sat polishing her new wide-angle lens with tissue. I sipped a cup of tea and perused the newspapers. Our cab to the airport was due in the wee hours of the morning and I wanted the girls in bed by eight. This four-day weekend was an extra holiday for all the schools in New Jersey so the teachers could attend the annual convention in Atlantic City. We would extend it by a few days.

I was a curator now. It didn't matter when I took time off. And, because I was heading to the Grand Canyon, I'd been asked by our director to review the loaner collection at the Museum of Northern Arizona in Flagstaff for a proposed new exhibit here in Newark.

Derrick Barrow had invited us west. This trip was primarily so Lila and Brandon could see each other. According to Derrick, Brandon needed this. Their social media relationship was maintained long distance and was the most constant of Brandon's friendships now after their move. Derrick told me, "Kids who haven't lost don't understand loss. Lila seems to get it or, at least, she remembers Cindy. That helps. It's harder for him than I expected."

I stood and turned the knob to re-light the burner under the tea-kettle. There it was. A short staccato of ticks and a comforting whoosh as the gas lit and formed a tight blue circle of flame. We were finished with explosions...of flame of any kind and the past few months had been tranquil.

311

Pete found, or I should say, the realtor I contacted found him an apartment in a three-family house down toward Lou's end of Hillston. On the day he left, I changed the locks. Bruce had stopped in. These were not the best of circumstances under which to finally meet the husband he'd always questioned existed. But meet they did, passing each other on the front porch steps, Pete carrying his desktop computer and Bruce carrying one simple screwdriver. It might have been lost on Pete, but the simplicity with which Bruce fixed the stove and the sense of how easy things can be if the right person is on the job was not lost on me.

Pete blamed the entirety of my request that he move out on the affair I must be having with Doug, who Pete referred to as "that reporter." It hurt. But I was determined to remain strong by reminding myself of the truth. I didn't argue with him. I was just glad he was gone.

Doug was good for me. He was good to me. I owed him a debt of gratitude. He truly was the Helenus to my Cassandra, my brother who insisted that my words be heard even if it meant they were carried to the public by someone else. He'd recognized that he needed to do that for me. Once he had, my world changed in ways I never imagined possible.

The girls became accustomed to seeing him. But, even with Pete gone, with a separation agreement in place, it was way too early for anything else between us. I told him so. "I didn't say no," I said one evening on the porch after the girls were in bed. The fireflies were plentiful and we had shut off the overhead light to keep away the moths and mosquitoes. "I said not yet."

I'd imagined our friendship evolving slowly. But, as much as I expected it, I knew it was just as likely to not evolve into a relationship. It would be too easy for me to extricate myself from Pete only to fall right into a new relationship.

I was the new curator of geo-archaeology at the Newark Museum. I was mom to my three girls. I'd do a regular cycle of programs on NPR about geoscience in our local area. I'd figure out a way to earn my interrupted PhD and get used to people calling me Dr. Taylor.

On the plane, I twirled my own ring, pressed my thumb into the insignia, and reminded myself I should be in a state of repose, relaxed, attentive to my daughters on their first trip west…my first trip west. We would see the natural wonders of America's playground. We would visit with our old friends. The flight tracker software on the tiny screen in front of me indicated we were over the great plains. I let the girls have the window seats, so my view of the land below was not so great, but I imagined the herds of buffalo that had roamed this geography for centuries, supporting life for the Cheyenne and other Plains peoples.

We planned to visit the ancient pueblos at Wupatki National Reserve outside of Flagstaff. I also wanted to visit the wind carved landscape at Antelope Canyon in addition to the Grand Canyon and the red rocks of Sedona. Pete had bought Lila that wide angle lens and these were exactly the right places for her to use it. He was learning how to be a father and that was good.

I thought about the raw landscape of the painted desert and the open barren geography of our destination. We would see rock and pine forests and mountains. Time and distance burned away the free-floating anxiety I'd carried around for the last fifteen years. Funny how you don't fully notice it until it's gone. I imagined myself the mythical firebird just hatched anew from a pile of ashes and completing a cycle. I wanted space, this spirit of newness, and the sense of endless possibilities, here and in all that awaited me back home.

Acknowledgments

The phenomenon central to this story took much research, an examination of arcane knowledge accumulated by my zigzagging through life and imagination. This writing journey was a long one and there are many people I need to thank. My friend, Margo Krasne, recognized the potential of this idea when I first uttered it out loud at a reading and was the first to declare it finished many years later. Her friendship was there at every phase in between. My editor/writing coach, Gay Walley, helped with multiple reads and enlightened me with her sharp sense of story and narrative.

My thesis advisor at the Rutgers University MFA program, Tayari Jones, understood the territory of my mind and encouraged me to stay there and go deep rather than venture into unknown territories that would trip me up. Love your characters, she said, even if they don't deserve it. Endless thanks to Working Title Seven, David Popiel, David Holmberg, Karin Abarbanel, Marne Benson, and Priscilla Mainardi who mercilessly critiqued my work in progress and allowed me to do the same to theirs for the last two decades. They trusted my mix of realism and science fiction despite my own self-doubt at times...Let's do another group reading at Watchung Booksellers!

Taylor Fluehr and Angelica Casillas at Apprentice House Press at Loyola University showed utter devotion to this project through the most difficult of circumstances due to the COVID-19 pandemic and Kevin Atticks kept things going with his flawless leadership and inspiration during the campus shutdown. Eternal gratitude!

To Julie Maloney, leader of Women Reading Aloud, for her life-changing writing retreats and all the writers of Alonissos and the people of the island who welcome us every year, thank you.

Thanks to Warren, who, with the most amazing faith and encouragement, for some reason, loves me and believes in everything I do.

Then, there are the moms, the community that inspired a shared recognition of that feeling we all have about everything and the support we give each other. The moms who inspired me are: Cindy, Diana, Alice, Mary, Luce, Tracy, Judy, Susan, Emily, Lena, Ann, Lisa PL, Shirley, Karen, Lisa M and Jude. Joann Corrao Spera, you created a parallel universe to mine in your own town. We will be soul mates forever. There are more, but enough already! I love you all.

And above all, my three daughters, Melissa, Maura and Shannon, who have all of my love and for whom I do everything. You inspired the children in this story and inspire me everyday in real life. Carry on for all of us my darlings.

About the Author

Nancy Burke is the author of *From the Abuelas' Window* and *If I Could Paint the Moon Black*. Her short fiction has been published in several literary journals and her short plays performed at festivals. As of this writing her short story *At the Pool* is a finalist for the J.F. Powers Prize for Short Fiction. She earned her MFA in Creative Writing at Rutgers University, Newark in fiction with a concentration in dramatic writing. She is mother to three daughters and lives in Montclair, NJ, the community that inspired the setting for this book.

Apprentice
House Press
Loyola University Maryland

Apprentice House is the country's only campus-based, student-staffed book publishing company. Directed by professors and industry professionals, it is a nonprofit activity of the Communication Department at Loyola University Maryland.

Using state-of-the-art technology and an experiential learning model of education, Apprentice House publishes books in untraditional ways. This dual responsibility as publishers and educators creates an unprecedented collaborative environment among faculty and students, while teaching tomorrow's editors, designers, and marketers.

Outside of class, progress on book projects is carried forth by the AH Book Publishing Club, a co-curricular campus organization supported by Loyola University Maryland's Office of Student Activities.

Eclectic and provocative, Apprentice House titles intend to entertain as well as spark dialogue on a variety of topics. Financial contributions to sustain the press's work are welcomed. Contributions are tax deductible to the fullest extent allowed by the IRS.

To learn more about Apprentice House books or to obtain submission guidelines, please visit www.apprenticehouse.com.

Apprentice House
Communication Department
Loyola University Maryland
4501 N. Charles Street
Baltimore, MD 21210
Ph: 410-617-5265
info@apprenticehouse.com
www.apprenticehouse.com

CPSIA information can be obtained
at www.ICGtesting.com
Printed in the USA
FSHW021946200420
69301FS